BY DREAMS ENCHANTED

A Cheyenne princess of mixed blood, Jennifer "Morning Rose" Elkheart eagerly accompanies her senator grandfather on his goodwill tour abroad—dazzling London's high society with her vivacious charm and beauty. But the bewitching hellion's heart is troubled in this foreign land. For visions have foretold the coming of a fearless adventurer who will boldly sweep into her life—yet it is the jaded, infuriating, though strangely alluring aristocrat Thorne Blakesford who sets her senses afire.

BY LOVE ENTHRALLED

There is more to this handsome, enigmatic duke, however, than meets the eye—for Thorne is a man of many secrets. And in a faraway place of mystery and intrigue, Jennifer will learn the shocking truth about her dreams and the remarkable stranger who inspires them—and discover the danger and rapture that await her in equal measure in Thorne's tender, loving embrace.

Avon Romantic Treasures by
Kathleen Harrington

DREAM CATCHER
PROMISE ME

*If You've Enjoyed This Book,
Be Sure to Read These Other*
AVON ROMANTIC TREASURES

BEAST *by Judith Ivory*
EVERYTHING AND THE MOON *by Julia Quinn*
HIS FORBIDDEN TOUCH *by Shelly Thacker*
LYON'S GIFT *by Tanya Anne Crosby*
WANTED ACROSS TIME *by Eugenia Riley*

Coming Soon

FALLING IN LOVE AGAIN *by Cathy Maxwell*

KATHLEEN HARRINGTON

FLY WITH THE EAGLE

An Avon Romantic Treasure

AVON BOOKS ◆ NEW YORK

AVON BOOKS
A division of
The Hearst Corporation
1350 Avenue of the Americas
New York, New York 10019

Copyright © 1997 by Kathleen Harrington
Published by arrangement with the author
Visit our website at **http://AvonBooks.com**
Library of Congress Catalog Card Number: 96-95493
ISBN: 0-380-77836-X

First Avon Books Printing: July 1997

AVON TRADEMARK REG. U.S. PAT. OFF. AND IN OTHER COUNTRIES, MARCA
REGISTRADA, HECHO EN U.S.A.

Printed in the U.S.A.

WCD   10 9 8 7 6 5 4 3 2 1

With love to

Louise Persinger Cummings,

my cousin and friend,
remembering
the birthday parties,
the paper dolls,
the playhouse and make-believe,
the roller skating,
the high school prom,
the double dates,
the weddings,
the births of our sons,
the baby-sitting (thank you),
and all the
shared heartaches and joys
of a lifetime.

They told her how, upon St. Agnes' Eve,
Young virgins might have visions of delight,
And soft adorings from their loves receive
Upon the honeyed middle of the night,
If ceremonies due they did aright;
As, supperless to bed they must retire,
And couch supine their beauties, lily white;
Nor look behind, nor sideways, but require
Of Heaven with upward eyes for all that they desire.

. . . And still she slept an azure-lidded sleep,
In blanched linen, smooth, and lavendered,
While he from forth the closet brought a heap
Of candied apple, quince, and plum, and gourd;
With jellies soother than the creamy curd,
And lucent syrops, tinct with cinnamon;
Manna and dates, in argosy transferred
From Fez; and spiced dainties, every one,
From silken Samarcand to cedared Lebanon.

These delicates he heaped with glowing hand
On golden dishes and in baskets bright
Of wreathed silver: sumptuous they stand
In the retired quiet of the night,
Filling the chilly room with perfume light.—
"And now, my love, my seraph fair, awake!
Thou art my heaven, and I thine eremite:
Open thine eyes, for meek St. Agnes' sake,
Or I shall drowse beside thee, so my soul doth ache."

John Keats
"The Eve of St. Agnes"

Prologue

September 1886

"**J**ust think, *namhan*," Jennifer exclaimed, "tomorrow we will be in England!" She spoke to Julie in their native language, addressing her with the Cheyenne term for older sister. It was a long-standing joke between them. She'd been born a whole three minutes after her twin.

Juliette Star Elkheart smiled serenely. "I am well aware that we will reach Liverpool in the morning," she said. "Now, slow down and behave the way Madame Benét taught us. There is no need to go racing around the ship's deck like a war pony galloping at the front of a battle charge."

Unable to contain her excitement, Jennifer executed a little hop-skip on the promenade's weather-worn oak planking. "Yes, but after all the discussing and planning, I can hardly believe we are almost there." She slowed her pace, however, and linked her arm with her sister's. "What do you suppose the English nobility will really be like? Can they be as frivolous and idle as we have been led to believe?"

Juliette pursed her lips in mild reproach. "They will be annoyed and crabby, *nisima*, if you do not learn to curb your tongue."

Unrepentant, Jennifer pinched her twin's forearm playfully. "You are worrying over nothing," she insisted as

1

she looked around to be certain they were alone. "No one is close enough to hear us. And aside from Grandpapa and Uncle Benjamin, we are the only two people on board who understand a single word of Cheyenne. Even they know only one or two simple phrases."

"Whether or not the other passengers can understand what we are saying, you should practice self-restraint just to get into the habit," Juliette chided. She shook her head reprovingly, but her dark brown eyes glowed with amusement. "Remember, Jennie, in Great Britain we will be among strangers who hold different beliefs and follow unusual, sometimes incomprehensible, customs. You, especially, must be careful not to offend them. Grandpapa's status as an envoy of the United States government means that people in London will be watching you very closely. As Senator Robinson's granddaughter and hostess, you cannot simply blurt out whatever is on your mind. You must try to be more circumspect."

"I know, I know," Jennifer replied with an absent toss of her head. "I will be very careful." From the corner of her eye, she spotted one of the ship's officers standing on the deck above them. Without a moment's hesitation, she waved a cheery hello. The handsome, dark-haired man braced his hands on the railing, leaned forward, and smiled warmly in return.

Juliette followed her sister's gaze and awarded the gentleman a polite nod of recognition. As they continued their walk, she spoke in her usual composed manner, but the use of Jennifer's Cheyenne name betrayed her seriousness. "Promise me you will be careful, Morning Rose."

"I promise," Jennifer replied soothingly.

She knew what was worrying her twin. In only a few days, Juliette would be in Edinburgh with their uncle, Dr. Benjamin Robinson, and she would be in London with their grandfather. For the first time in their eighteen years, the sisters would be apart—not just for weeks, but for months. Neither was certain how she would adjust to the other's absence.

"You can always change your mind and go with me

and Grandpapa to London," Jennifer declared. "Then you would not have to worry about my reckless behavior." She came to an abrupt halt and gazed imploringly into Juliette's deep brown eyes.

Looking at her sister was like looking into a mirror. Today, they wore matching outfits to please their grandfather. The sea breeze ruffled the blue feathers on their perky straw hats and swirled the hems of their traveling dresses about their ankles.

"You know I must go to Edinburgh with Uncle Benjamin," Juliette countered. "My vision draws me there just as surely as your vision will take you eventually to Constantinople with Grandpapa."

"Yes, but your vision is of some old, forgotten battle," Jennifer quickly pointed out, "while mine is about the man I will someday marry."

Juliette frowned at the inference that her quest was not nearly as important as Jennifer's. The Elkheart twins had inherited the legacy of second sight from what their mother, who'd been raised in the Kentucky hills, called the spindle-side of the family. From their Cheyenne father, the girls had received the ability to interpret visions, both their own and those of others.

Juliette had brought with her the pink-and-lavender tartan of the McDougall clan, which she'd seen in her vision. The plaid had once belonged to her great-great-grandfather, who'd come from Scotland to the Cumberland Mountains before the Revolutionary War. Their mother had brought it west with her when she left Kentucky.

"Only my stubborn sister would insist that a stranger she saw in a dream is absolutely, positively the man she is meant by fate to marry," Juliette stated with a hint of impatience. "You know very well that we do not always understand everything we have seen in a vision. While you are in London, you might fall madly in love with some dashing nobleman and spend the rest of your life there."

Laughter bubbled up inside Jennifer at the preposterous suggestion. "You cannot be serious, *namhan*! Even if the Great Powers had not sent a vision to lead me, I would never, ever fall in love with an Englishman."

Juliette raised her brows. "Never is a long time."

At her sister's open skepticism, Jennifer continued defensively. "Remember the pictures of the British lords and ladies in our school books? All the men looked like pompous bores in their ridiculous white wigs and fancy satin clothes."

"People have not worn powdered wigs for a hundred years, silly," Juliette teased. "Not even the pompous English nobility."

"Well, Madame Benét said British aristocrats are filled with their own self-importance. She said they have neither the wit nor the style of the most common Parisian."

"Since our schoolmistress was born in Paris, she may have drawn her conclusions from a rather prejudiced point of view."

Unconvinced, Jennifer shrugged. "You only have to look at their pictures in the history books to know they lack a sense of humor."

"I do not remember your paying any particular attention to our history lessons, *nisima*. You were too busy gazing out the window, waiting for the moment when we would be released from the embassy schoolroom."

"One scholar in the family is enough," Jennifer said with an impudent grin. A sudden gust threatened her hat, and she caught the brim with one hand as she gestured expansively with the other. "I want to experience life, not just read about it! Anyway, Madame Benét seemed to think that learning the steps of the quadrille and how to curtsey properly to a duchess was far more important than studying ancient civilizations. You must admit, we spent a lot more time practicing diplomatic protocol than we did poring over our textbooks."

"After the dancing is over, *nisima*, you will be expected to carry on an intelligent conversation." Juliette's eyes twinkled as she squeezed her sister's hand. "Just how do you expect to do that, if you have nothing to talk to a gentleman about but riding, hunting, and fishing?"

"What else would a gentleman want to talk about, anyway?" Jennifer protested with a giggle. At her sister's look of reproval, she confessed sheepishly, "Honestly, *namhan*, I wish I were wise and prudent like you. You are truly my better half."

Juliette clucked her tongue. "That is absurd. You are perfect the way you are."

"Except for the fact that I am too talkative and too quick to jump to conclusions and too friendly with strangers and too—"

"Hush!" Juliette implored with a laugh. She slipped her arm about Jennifer's waist and gave her a quick, reassuring hug. "You are just like our mother, *nisima*, warm and outgoing and totally without deceit."

Her sister's words of praise brought a glow of happiness to Jennifer. "It is true that no matter how hard I try," she cheerfully admitted, "I cannot conceal my emotions. When I am sad, I cry buckets of tears. And when I am happy, I want to skip and sing and shout out loud. Right now, Evening Star, I feel like dancing for joy." She caught Juliette's hands and twirled them both around in a circle. It was a game they'd played as children.

"Be careful!" Juliette warned, dragging her to a halt. "You will get us both dizzy! We will land on the deck in front of everyone, with our skirts up over our heads and splinters in our you-know-what." But she laughed right along with Jennifer as they continued their walk around the Cunard liner's promenade.

Jennifer loved being outdoors. She loved the feel of the fresh wind that buffeted their dresses and tugged at their hats. Wisps of their dark, reddish-brown hair came loose from their braided chignons and blew into their faces, tangling in their lashes and tickling their cheeks.

She knew Juliette's pose of serenity hid the excitement they both felt at that moment. Though no one around them could possibly tell, her sister was as thrilled as she that they'd be in England tomorrow. The striking poise of a warrior-woman was a gift Juliette had inherited from their father, Strong Elk Heart. Their younger brother, Black Hawk Flying, had that same fathomless calm. But as their Kentucky-born mother, Little Red Fawn, would often say, no sense in chasing Havsevstomanehe, the evil-maker, around the choke cherry bush. Morning Rose was as rambunctious and impulsive as Evening Star was tranquil and serene.

As they made their way past a row of deck chairs, Jennifer spotted a familiar pair waving to them from the stern railing. "Look!" she said. "I think Lady Idina and her brother would like us to join them."

Juliette met her sister's gaze and smiled knowingly. Sometimes the twins shared the same vision. Both girls had known immediately that Lady Idina would become one of their most loyal and trusted friends. In their mutual dream, they'd even addressed the attractive, strawberry blonde as *nahan*, which meant aunt, although she was no more than six years older than they. High regard, indeed, to show a white woman of any age.

Juliette had been plagued by seasickness and confined to their cabin for much of the crossing. While her twin dozed, Jennifer shared long, heart-to-heart conversations on the first-class deck with the English woman, whom she quickly grew to love. She told Idina about their visions and how they could sometimes see things that would happen in the future. Rather than scoff in disbelief, her new friend expressed a keen interest in the twins' ability to interpret dreams.

Lady Idina had suffered an injury during childhood that had left her lame. Lord Basil Nettlefold-Clive, earl of Combermere, had hovered over his sister protectively, until Idina finally told him that if she needed any assistance she was certain she could depend on her new friend from America. He'd grinned and left them to their girlish confidences.

But Jennifer understood his concern. She'd seen the way some white people acted toward Lady Idina, treating her as though she were invisible. Such coldhearted indifference was not the Cheyenne way.

"It was very gracious of Lord Combermere to invite you to visit their home in Warwickshire," Juliette said, interrupting Jennifer's reverie.

"It certainly was," she agreed with a chuckle. "Especially after I shocked his sister with my frank opinions. When I told Lady Idina that I thought all white women should engage in daily strenuous exercise, burn their wretched corsets, ride astride, and campaign for female emancipation, I thought her pretty green eyes would pop right out of her head."

Juliette chuckled softly at her sister's brash remarks. "I can imagine her reaction."

Madame Benét had cautioned the girls that such outrageous beliefs were not to be mentioned to proper English ladies—or to English lords, either, for that matter.

"Actually, Dina is very broad-minded," Jennifer said with sincere admiration. "She agreed with most of my suggestions. But when it came to discussing courtship and marriage, we were miles apart. I tried to explain how our father had courted our mother, but she did not have the least notion what I was talking about. She never heard of a warrior counting coup on his enemies or presenting stolen horses to the parents of the young woman he wishes to marry. The only thing she seemed to grasp was that our father is one of the four head chiefs of the Cheyenne people. Dina claimed that made us both Indian princesses."

"Do you suppose we will be treated like visiting royalty?"

Jennifer giggled at the thought. "When it comes to living among the *veho*, anything is possible!"

The sisters met each other's gaze and burst into laughter. It was an undeniable fact that white people held the strangest beliefs and practiced the most incomprehensible customs.

The Hotel Sacher
Tegetthoff Strasse, Vienna

At the soft tap, Thorne Blakesford opened the door and stepped back to allow the man to enter. With a quick look up and down the hallway to make certain it was empty, he silently closed the door.

"Did you bring the map?"

Colonel von Hotzendorf tapped the spot over his inside coat pocket with one finger. "I have it here," he answered coolly.

Thorne surveyed the blond officer through narrowed eyes. The highest ranking official in the Cartographical Department of the Austro-Hungarian War Office was a tall, robust man. That morning, he wore an ill-fitting frock coat and wrinkled trousers, obviously borrowed from a much smaller civilian friend. Beneath the brim of his gray homburg, his forehead was beaded with sweat, though the weather was mild. It was the only hint of nervousness about the fellow.

Thorne was genuinely impressed. Traitors usually showed more fear. If the two of them were caught, they'd both be hanged—but only after a prolonged and uncomfortable interrogation.

"Do you have the money?" von Hotzendorf asked. His thin lip curled contemptuously beneath his heavy mustache.

Thorne jerked his head in the affirmative, then held out an open palm. "I'll see the goods first, Colonel."

The Austrian withdrew the document and handed it over.

Unfolding the creased paper, Thorne scanned it quickly. It was exactly what it had been purported to be. A military map of Turkey, down to the last battery emplacement. He glanced up to find von Hotzendorf watching him with cold-blooded hatred. If the officer was part of the Austrian military's wide-flung espionage system, Thorne knew he was as good as dead.

But he could read the avariciousness in the man's pale-blue eyes, smell his aura of greed as clearly as the expensive cologne he wore. Thorne's ability to see through a man's facade of respectability to the rotten inner core hadn't failed him yet.

He'd discovered that the bluff sportsman had suffered a disastrously bad run of luck at the turf. Added to that, a taste for beautiful young women and vintage French champagne had brought the scion of a noble but impoverished house to the point where he was willing to betray his comrades, his emperor, and his fatherland.

"Feel free to count it," Thorne said as he withdrew an envelope from his pocket and handed it to the officer.

"I will," von Hotzendorf snapped with unconcealed venom. He ruffled through the currency, making a point of counting it down to the last gulden.

Thorne recognized the display of impotent rage for what it was. He'd seen it before. A traitor often turned his self-contempt outward, blaming the man who'd offered a temptation impossible to resist. Without meeting his gaze, the Austrian turned and moved toward the door.

"Take the back stairs," Thorne suggested in an offhand manner. "And whatever you do, Colonel, don't deposit that money in a bank until I'm out of the country."

Von Hotzendorf stiffened and glanced back over his shoulder. "Burn in hell," he snarled.

But he closed the door quietly behind him.

In the silence that followed, Thorne poured a splash of brandy into a crystal snifter. He opened the French doors and stepped onto a private balcony.

On the sidewalk across the street, a slight, dapper silver-haired man sat at a cafe table drinking a cup of coffee and reading a newspaper. He glanced up briefly at Thorne, then resumed his reading.

It was exactly what Thorne had intended. By keeping the Russian at the front of the building watching him, von Hotzendorf would be able to slip out the back, unnoticed.

Count Vladimir Gortschakoff had been shadowing Thorne for nearly a month. He'd followed him from Belgrade, maybe all the way from Istanbul. Thorne waited long enough to be sure the Austrian had made it safely away, then stepped back inside his hotel room.

A feeling of utter contempt swept over him. Von Hotzendorf's willingness to betray his code of honor as a gentleman and an officer disgusted Thorne far more than he'd expected. Hell, the colonel's treachery should have come as no surprise. The fellow had merely proven, once again, a lesson Thorne had learned from his own father. Beneath every person's mask of integrity dwelt the cunning deceiver.

Thorne glanced restlessly around the luxurious suite, where his trunks stood locked and waiting, and took a fortifying swallow of brandy. His past eight years with British Secret Intelligence had deepened his already bitter cynicism. Nationalist rivalries were sweeping across Central Europe, bringing in their wake agitators, terrorists, and assassins. The capital of the Austro-Hungarian empire was a viper's nest of spies, counterspies, and agents provocateurs.

Damn, he was sick of Vienna.

The only thing he'd enjoyed on this last assignment was the lively brunet who'd shared his nights in the high feather bed that stood in the corner, its eiderdown still rumpled from their latest tumble.

Hermine Klimt was at the Burgtheatre now, hoping to snare a juicier role in the operetta opening next month. She'd made no effort to be more than a fortnight's amusement, and her earthy insouciance had been a refreshing contrast to the cloying intrigues of the Hapsburg Court. He intended to reward the opera dancer generously for her warmhearted companionship. A diamond necklace and matching bracelet would ease the pain of her readjustment to life without him.

Picking up paper and pen, Thorne hastily scribbled his farewell.

Liebchen,

I shall think of you fondly whenever I recall my stay in Vienna. I hope these trinkets will be a lasting memento of our brief, but pleasurable, idyll together.

E

Thorne gathered up his gloves, walking stick, and hat, satisfied that he'd done nothing to dispel the appearance of jaded world-weariness he'd brought to near perfection.

At that moment, Grigsby opened the door. "Your carriage is waiting, Your Grace."

Thornton Fitzhugh Jean-Pierre Blakesford, eighth duke of Eagleston, smiled at his valet in satisfaction.

He was on his way home to England, at last.

Chapter 1

❦❦❦

"The Hapsburgs may have been royal bores, Your Grace," Lord Doddridge commiserated, "but the information you gathered confirms our suspicions about the encroachment of Russian influence in the Balkans. The time you spent dallying in the most exclusive court in Europe was time well spent, indeed."

The duke of Eagleston paced back and forth across the carpet, barely attending. He glanced out the window at St. James's Park below, then back to the Foreign Office's permanent undersecretary. Lord Doddridge was in charge of the government's underfunded and understaffed secret service.

"Don't send me on another tedious assignment like the last one," he said. "I've had my fill of steering nearsighted archduchesses around a crowded dance floor. I'm beginning to find this game of cloak and dagger rather ridiculous."

"Don't make light of your accomplishments," Doddridge admonished. "The Austrian military map of Turkey you brought back is better than anything they have over at the War Office." He picked up a single sheet of paper and rose to his feet. "You're just tired."

Thorne rocked back on his heels, his hands jammed in his trouser pockets. "You're right there. I'm looking forward to spending some time in the country. It's been months since I had a rod and reel in my hands."

"Good," said Doddridge. "A few weeks of fishing will

12

make a new man of you. While you're in Warwickshire, you can have a go at breaking the new Russian code." He came around the desk and handed Thorne the paper. "It's a copy of a dispatch we borrowed from their ambassador's diplomatic pouch yesterday."

Thorne dropped into a nearby chair and scanned the page. Nothing intrigued him like the challenge of cryptography. The more difficult the secret writing, the better. "Looks like a substitution cipher," he mused, "but it can't be anything that simple. I'll give it a try."

"Fine, fine. And when you return to London, I have something very special for you."

"It's always something special," Thorne stated with his usual irony.

Doddridge ignored the remark. "Have you heard of an organization called Imro?"

"No."

"The letters stand for the International Macedonian Revolutionary Organization. We've been picking up mention of it in Russian dispatches coming from Constantinople, Belgrade, and Sofia. We think the Ochrana may be involved in shipping arms to the Macedonian Bulgars living in the western provinces of Turkey."

At the mention of the Ochrana, Thorne leaned forward, his attention caught. "The czar's secret police are smuggling arms to revolutionaries?"

"It's only a guess. But it's our best one, so far."

Thorne was well aware of the unrest spreading across the Ottoman Empire. People in vassal states, which had borne the Sultan's yoke for centuries, were forming revolutionary groups. The ancient region of Macedonia extended into what was now the Turkish province of Thrace. With its mixed population of Greeks, Bulgars, and Turks, it was especially fertile soil for a resurgence of ancestral pride and patriotism. The official British policy, however, was to maintain the status quo throughout the entire area in order to block Russian influence and the Romanov dream of imperialist expansion.

Thorne didn't try to conceal his skepticism about his own government's foreign policy. "I question the assumption that the Ottoman Empire has to be preserved in order to keep the czar from reaching his goal of a seaport on the Mediterranean. We should be sending the Macedonians arms ourselves, instead of continuing to prop up that bloody despot in Constantinople."

"I don't make government policy," Doddridge retorted impatiently. "I follow the foreign secretary's orders."

"Which are?"

"To send you to Turkey to see if our hunch is correct. I want you to find out if Imro is being aided by the Russians."

"I was in Constantinople only a month ago," Thorne reminded him. "There are some affairs at Eagleston Court that need my attention."

Doddridge's scowling features softened. "How is your mother, Lady Charlotte?" he asked with compassion.

"The dowager duchess remains the same," Thorne answered, careful to hide his inner sorrow. "I've given up on the doctors. There doesn't seem to be anything they can do for her."

"Has she ever spoken of your father since his death?"

"No," Thorne admitted. He shifted uncomfortably in his chair. If there was one topic he preferred to avoid, it was the late duke. But the concern in the undersecretary's gaze was sincere.

Colonel Lord Russell Doddridge had been his commander in the Life Guards when Thorne was only nineteen. The retired cavalry officer was the closest he'd ever come to having a real father. Eight years ago, the previous duke of Eagleston had died of a heart attack in a Parisian brothel. The excitement of taking the virginity of a twelve-year-old girl had proven too much for the bloody lecher. Henry Maxwell Blakesford had been a cold, distant man, who'd spoken to his son less than a dozen times in twenty-one years.

"I tried to broach the subject with the dowager duchess several times," Thorne explained in quiet frustration. "Each time, she refused to speak of him. If I persisted, she'd lock herself in her room without food or water and retreat further into her melancholy silence. I've no inkling how much she understands about the circumstances surrounding his death." He tried to force a smile. It felt more like a sick grimace. "It's not easy talking to your own mother about your father's twisted sexual appetites."

"I can understand how that might be a bit uncomfortable."

Doddridge gazed somberly at the man seated in front of him. After his father had died so scandalously, Eagleston had learned to conceal his shame and anger from prying eyes. His years with the secret service had only made him more cynical, more suspicious of others. The tragedy of his father's perverted life had cast a shadow over everything.

But Eagleston's avoidance of weakness or tenderness in himself and others made him an invaluable field operative. For despite the outer trappings of a cultured, somewhat bored, British nobleman, he had the ability to kill without compunction. And he was a born survivor.

"I think I'm being shadowed by a Russian agent," Thorne said in an obvious attempt to change the subject. "I must be getting clumsy."

"Do you know who he is?"

"Count Vladimir Gortschakoff. If he shows up in London in the next few days, we can be fairly certain he's working for the Ochrana."

"Until we know for certain, be careful."

Thorne smiled and shrugged. "Trout fishing is hardly a dangerous occupation. And I won't be much of a threat to anyone, if I retire from the service. "

"Lord Salisbury has personally requested that you take this assignment in Turkey," Doddridge informed him. "You have a patriotic duty to fulfill. You can't refuse the prime minister."

"The hell I can't. In the last three years, I've spent more time outside of England than I have at home. Get someone else."

"I would, if I could."

Thorne jerked to his feet, anxious to leave, and Doddridge lifted his hand in desperate entreaty. "Give it some thought, Your Grace. That's all I ask. Enjoy your holiday at home, but while you're there, give it some thought. We need a man who speaks Russian and Turkish fluently."

"I'm not the only man who does."

"We also need someone who can move in the highest diplomatic circles. With your title and wealth, you have the entrée everywhere. You'd be going to Turkey ostensibly to search for Greek and Roman artifacts to add to your collection. Your usual cover is perfect for the task at hand."

"No."

"I'll talk to you more about it when you get back from the country," Doddridge persisted. "Right now, I have another assignment for you. One that can't be put off. It's been arranged for tonight."

Already on his way to the door, Thorne turned and waited in noncommittal silence, unable to hide his impatience but too fond of the gentleman standing before him just to walk out.

Immediately recognizing the younger man's hesitation, Doddridge pressed his advantage. "The Court of St. James is giving a ball tonight in honor of Senator Garrett Robinson, the United States Special Envoy. The czarevitch will be there, as well as a host of other foreign dignitaries. An invitation is waiting for you at your town house. At precisely eleven o'clock, you are to be in the Green Drawing Room. A member of the German legation will appear on the quarter hour and slip you a very important document."

Thorne frowned. "Send another man."

Doddridge shook his head. "Herr Stieber won't be expecting another man. He'll be expecting you. We'd jeopardize the entire rendezvous if we made a change at this late hour. And while you're at the ball, try to pick up any information you can from the Russian staff."

"I've already made plans for the evening," Thorne hedged. "I'd hoped to meet a friend at White's for a night of drinking and gambling."

"You can drink and gamble after the ball."

"Not seriously enough. I'm scheduled to be at the British Museum early tomorrow afternoon to dedicate my latest contribution to their Greek exhibit."

Doddridge's good-humored smile split his graying brown beard in a flash of white. "Aside from patriotism, I can offer another inducement. The American representative's lovely granddaughter has taken London by storm in the two short weeks they've been here. Instead of having a nearsighted archduchess trod on your toes this evening, you can twirl a lithesome beauty around in your arms."

Thorne snorted in disgust. "And have her hanging on my sleeve for the rest of the evening? No, thank you, sir."

"You've grown very conceited," Doddridge said with an amused chuckle, "even for a wealthy, unmarried duke."

"Conceit has nothing to do with it," Thorne denied. "Greed is every Yankee's driving force, sprinkled liberally amongst their women with an incurable penchant for title hunting. Have you ever met an American female who wasn't awestruck to the point of spouting gibberish at the mere sight of a British peer?"

"I have it from the best of sources, the young lady doesn't gibber, Your Grace. Her Majesty was duly impressed by the debutante's elegant curtsey when she was presented at Buckingham Palace. I suspect you'll be the one who's awestruck."

"Hardly," Thorne said, affecting a shudder. "Several of my chums from Oxford saddled themselves with ambitious Americans. The heiresses seem to feel their fathers' fortunes purchased their entrée into upperclass society without any display of wit, grace, or talent of their own. Believe me, sir, no marriage settlement could possibly offset a lifetime spent in the company of a woman sprung from the merchant class."

Doddridge's smile grew wider. "Well, if the mere thought of an unwed female having your highly eligible person in her sights is too alarming, you have my permission not to dance with the pretty little Yankee at all."

It was Thorne's turn to grin. "As long as I attend the

bloody affair," he clarified, "and meet with Herr Stieber at precisely eleven fifteen as scheduled."

"And in the meantime, nose out any information from the Russians you can," Doddridge added with quiet seriousness. "Do it for an old friend."

The duke of Eagleston purposely arrived late at St. James's Palace. He'd attended enough state functions to know how tiresome the evening would be. He hadn't been able to refuse the undersecretary's personal plea, but the demands of friendship went only so far.

By the time he passed beneath the great Tudor arch, the Ambassadors Court was nearly empty, save for the rows of liveried footmen in their powdered wigs and satin breeches. The ballroom, however, was thronged with ambassadors, ministers, and envoys from countries around the world, as well as British admirals, generals, governors, peers of the realm, and their wives.

As he entered the crowded room, Thorne smiled in genuine pleasure. The earl of Combermere and his sister stood near the doorway. Basil had lost his lovely wife three years before, when Lady Catherine died in childbirth with her infant stillborn. The heartbroken widower came up from the country only three or four times a year. His younger sister, even more rarely.

Since her debut six years ago, Lady Idina had remained at Nettlefold Manor, making only a few excursions to London during the Season. Thorne set aside the task of ferreting out diplomatic secrets and immediately joined his friends.

"Hello, Dina," he said as he took her hand. "What a pleasant surprise to find you here."

Her cheerful smile deepened the dimples in her round cheeks. "I can say the same about you, Your Grace! We thought you were still in Vienna."

"I just arrived in London this morning," Thorne explained, shaking Combermere's hand.

"Tell us all about it," she insisted gaily. "Was Franz Joseph's court as grand as everyone says? And did you meet many gorgeous archduchesses?"

"The Hapsburg Court is even more pretentious than it's reputed to be," he replied. "And the city is practically crawling with archduchesses. Whether they are gorgeous or not is a matter of opinion."

As Basil offered Idina the support of his arm, he winked at Thorne knowingly. "Egad, don't tell me the Burgtheatre's corps de ballet isn't as lovely as it's reputed to be?"

"I'm pleased to report that it is," Thorne stated. The two men's gazes met in perfect understanding.

Hearing Lady Idina's weary sigh as she leaned on her brother's arm, Thorne smiled compassionately. She'd been injured in a fall from her horse when she was only seven. Her right hip had been permanently damaged, leaving her with an impaired stride and frequent bouts of pain. He knew better than to bring up the topic of her disablement. She was too proud to allow anyone to offer her sympathy, not even a man she looked upon as an older brother.

Thorne dropped his usual bored tone and met her gaze with sincere concern. "How are you, Dina?"

"Oh, I'm fine," she answered brightly.

Basil patted her hand with quiet affection. "Dina and I returned from a trip to New York only two weeks ago," he said. "We had a very pleasant holiday."

At the mention of their voyage, Dina beamed at Thorne. "Yes, in fact, I want to introduce you to a young lady we met on the crossing. She's here at the ball tonight with her grandfather. Senator Robinson is the United States envoy who's being honored this evening." She looked out at the couples swirling around the ballroom in search of her new American friend. "I think Miss Elkheart's dancing with Euan at the moment."

"Spare me," Thorne drawled. "I have no interest in meeting a Yankee."

"Bosh!" Idina scolded as she rapped his arm with her fan. "Don't be so opinionated. You haven't even seen the young lady."

"I don't have to see her," he countered. "I've met Lady Pembroke. And a more carping, shrewish female I've yet to lay eyes on. Her New England twang grates down a man's spine like fingernails scraping across a chalk slate. What induced Randolph to become shackled to that termagant is beyond me."

"I don't think the poor chap had much choice," Basil said with a sympathetic chuckle for their hapless friend. "It's been whispered that Pembroke was forced to marry the heiress because his father gambled his inheritance away."

"I'd prefer life imprisonment," Thorne stated. He gazed absently across the room, where he spied his prey. Czarevitch Nicholas of Russia, resplendent in the snowy white uniform of his Imperial Guards, stood chatting with the duke of Connaught and the marquess of Salisbury.

When Count Vladimir Gortschakoff came to stand quietly beside the Romanov heir to the throne, Thorne's suspicions grew even stronger. The count was very likely an agent of the Ochrana, a professional killer, employed by the czar's secret police to do their dirty work. Gortschakoff must have been in Vienna for the same reason Thorne had been—to unearth any information in that hotbed of intrigue which might be of use to his government. Whether he'd actually followed Thorne to England or come for another reason was, as yet, a mystery.

But the solution would have to wait. For with single-minded persistence, Idina refused to concede the argument. "Not every woman from America is crass and vulgar, Your Grace. Don't judge them all by one unfortunate example."

Thorne folded his arms, unimpressed with her logic, and awarded her a smug smile. "How many other rich colonials have come to London certain their wealth could buy a titled husband for their homely, spinster daughter? I can name a dozen without even trying." He looked to Basil for support.

Combermere's green eyes shone with wry humor. "Miss Elkheart is rather out of the ordinary," he commented. "I certainly wouldn't call her a homely spinster."

"Oh, there she is!" Idina exclaimed. "Over there, waltzing with Euan."

Thorne glanced at the throng of couples on the dance floor. A slim, auburn-haired girl whirled past them in the arms of one of his cronies from Oxford. She was talking earnestly, as though whatever the two were discussing was of the utmost importance.

Thorne felt a twinge of irritation. The last thing he wanted to see was yet another friend in the clutches of a scheming Yankee. The Honorable Euan Bensen had barely passed his examinations at the university. He couldn't possibly be discussing anything so clever as to warrant that much enthusiastic conversation. Either the young woman was as frivolous as Euan or she'd already set her sights on the title he'd inherit one day. Neither possibility recommended her as a future bride. When the waltz drew to a close, the couple headed in their direction, still chattering away.

"Let me introduce you to Miss Elkheart," Dina pleaded. "You'll see for yourself that she is most definitely not a carping, ambitious female."

Thorne brought Idina's gloved fingers to his lips to soften his refusal. "Later, perhaps," he replied in an offhand manner. He turned and strolled away in the opposite direction, making good his escape only seconds before it was too late.

From the look of disappointment on Lady Idina's face, Jennifer suspected that her friend had just been cut by the tall, golden-haired gentleman walking across the room with his broad back to them.

She knew boorish people sometimes treated the gentlehearted lady unkindly because of her awkward gait. On board the *Etruria*, Idina had confided that she never danced in public because of the unpredictable reaction of strangers. Perhaps the man had asked her for a waltz and hadn't realized why she'd refused him.

"Is everything all right?" Jennifer asked. She searched Idina's soft features for a clue as to what had happened. When her British friend seemed at a lost for words,

Jennifer glanced at Lord Combermere. He was watching the dance floor as though fascinated by the sight of a princess from Bavaria, crowned with a diamond tiara, waltzing by in the arms of an Indian maharaja with a ruby the size of a walnut stuck in his turban.

"I had the distinct impression a few moments ago that something was wrong," Jennifer stated, refusing to let the subject drop until she had an honest answer from one of them.

"Why, everything's perfect!" Lady Idina exclaimed. But her plump cheeks grew even rosier, confirming Jennifer's earlier assumption.

She leaned closer and whispered in Lady Idina's ear. "Did that man say something to hurt your feelings? Because if he did, your brother should be told."

"No, no, dear," Dina assured her with an overbright smile. "You're quite mistaken."

Jennifer realized that if someone *had* hurt her feelings, the sweet-tempered woman would never admit it. Unfortunately, there wasn't time to question her further. Jennifer's next partner was approaching. "If that rude man asks *me* to dance," Jennifer whispered, "I shall refuse him, point-blank, and that will teach him a lesson."

Lady Idina's jade-green eyes lit up at the brash remark. "I should say!" she agreed with a mischievous smile. "That *would* teach him a lesson."

Which was all the encouragement Jennifer needed.

As Lord Albert Wheeler, Viscount Lyttleton, led her onto the floor, she smiled at him warmly. Jennifer had met the gangly redhead when she first arrived in London. He was one of Combermere's closest friends. But in all the parties and balls she'd attended, this was the first time he'd asked her to dance. She suspected he was simply too shy.

"At last, I have the pleasure of waltzing with you, sir," she told the tall gentleman, attempting to put him at ease. "I was afraid you would never ask me, and I would have to go back home without once having danced with you. I should have been broken-hearted and cried all the way across the Atlantic."

Lyttleton seemed ready to bolt for the door, in spite of her effusive flatteries. "I just hope I don't step on your toes, Miss Elkheart," he warned, a look of near-panic on his freckled face.

Jennifer glanced down at his huge feet. "I will do my absolute best to stay out from under the soles of your shoes," she promised. Peeking up at him from beneath her lashes, she flashed him an encouraging smile. "There is no need to be alarmed, sir. Everyone assures me I am very light on my feet."

The music started, and he gathered her into his long, thin arms. "You'd better be," he said with a bashful grin, "because ready or not, here we go."

"Do not worry," she told him on their first awkward turn. "If we knock anyone over, I will pretend it was all their fault." To her relief, he stopped counting out loud long enough to chortle at her jest.

As they threaded their way through the other dancers, the viscount slowly began to relax. Jennifer chattered without pause, hoping her words would distract him until he got over his initial self-consciousness. Once they were in motion, the fluid steps of the waltz would become much easier.

"I'm feeling very proud of myself tonight, Miss Elkheart," Lyttleton said as they started their second turn round the floor. "I never thought I'd get up enough courage to waltz with someone as lovely as you."

"I was thinking much the same thing!" Jennifer told him. "You look very handsome tonight, and I am feeling quite proud of myself, too."

"Why is that?"

"Back in America, my sister and I attended a school at the French embassy. Our teacher spent hours and hours instructing us in the precise details of social etiquette. At the time, the countless rules seemed so confusing, I thought I would never remember them all. But since my arrival in London, I have steered my way safely through the intricate maze of a court presentation."

"Bully for you!"

"That is not all," she confided. "I have attended balls

at the German, Italian, and Portuguese embassies with my grandfather, as well as the dedication of a hospital and the opening of a new park. So far, I have managed not to embarrass Grandpapa once in the past two weeks!''

"Miss Elkheart," the viscount declared, "I applaud your brilliant success. Or I would applaud," he added as an afterthought, "if I could clap my hands and move my feet at the same time."

Jennifer laughed gaily, intent on keeping his mind off those same big feet. From the corner of her eye, however, she caught sight of the rude stranger who'd upset Lady Idina. Her glorious feelings of accomplishment faded like a rainbow on a summer day.

The man stood talking with several military officers, but he was watching her. A frown of disapproval drew his brows together in one brooding line. He had golden-brown hair and a thick mustache. The straight, strong nose made his angular features appear even sharper. The *veho* ribbon and silver star, which Lady Idina called the Order of the Garter, decorated his chest.

Although his air of restless boredom was unmistakable, his dark blue eyes were piercing, as though nothing ever escaped their notice.

He reminded her of an eagle.

A great golden eagle. Proud. Distant. Forbidding.

Jennifer's first instinct was to ignore Madame Benét's strictures on proper behavior and glower back at him, making no attempt to hide her scorn. Anyone who'd treat Lady Idina shabbily was a despicable, lowdown snake, and that was the end of it.

But after a moment's hesitation, she awarded the irascible fellow her most flirtatious smile. She wanted him to learn what it felt like to be snubbed in front of a crowd of people. To Jennifer's disappointment, the man looked right past her, continuing his desultory conversation without a flicker of interest.

Hesc! She could have sworn he'd been staring at her. She must have been mistaken.

"When our waltz is finished, your lordship, will you

take me to stand by the windows?'' Jennifer asked. ''The room is not so crowded near those soldiers over there.''

''I'll be happy to,'' Lyttleton agreed.

She debated asking if he knew the disdainful stranger, then decided against it. It was highly unlikely the viscount would be on a congenial basis with someone cruel enough to hurt Lady Idina's feelings. All of Lord Combermere's circle of friends were pleasant, courteous gentlemen.

Jennifer smiled to herself. Once they were introduced, she'd do her best to entice the mean-spirited *veho* into asking for a dance.

And then she'd refuse him.

He deserved it.

Thorne had joined the officers of the Russian imperial staff, who were delighted to talk with someone fluent in their own language. Little snippets of information, valueless in themselves, could later be pieced together into a meaningful whole. It was amazing how careless a homesick general could be when he found a sympathetic ear, even when the listener was only partially attending. For try as he might, Thorne was unable to keep his attention from wandering back to the vivacious little Yankee.

In mounting vexation, he watched Viscount Lyttleton gaze down at his partner with moonstruck eyes. Like Euan Bensen, Bertie was an eldest son. The red-haired giant would someday inherit the title of marquess of Egremont. For their own good, neither bachelor should be left on their own in the ballroom that evening. Not with a sloe-eyed beauty like Miss Elkheart on the prowl.

The girl wore a fashionable dress of white satin that swirled enticingly about her ankles. Unlike the gowns worn by every other American heiress he'd seen, hers was neither garish nor vulgar. She didn't wear great strings of pearls or heavy chains of diamonds, either. Only a black velvet band encircled her neck. The effect was amazingly seductive, as though its sole purpose was to tempt a man into placing a kiss in the hollow beneath that single, alluring ribbon.

From that come-hither smile she'd sent his way, Thorne was positive she wanted to be introduced. She must have learned by now that the duke of Eagleston was an eligible bachelor with a splendid manor house in Warwickshire. The kind that Americans drooled over.

His suppositions were confirmed the moment the waltz ended. She made her way toward him with the clearly besotted Lyttleton in tow. Before the pair could reach his side, Thorne left the Russians and casually wandered over to a group of acquaintances from the Italian embassy. Unless the girl spoke Italian, she'd be left out in the cold.

He couldn't resist glancing back over his shoulder. The look of consternation on Miss Elkheart's lovely face when she reached her goal—only to find her quarry had bolted—was worth giving up an evening of drinking and gambling at White's. After that, he made a point of leading her around the ballroom by her acquisitive, title-hunting nose. As soon as she was almost close enough for an introduction, he'd meander off to another spot and another cluster of diplomats, speaking in yet another language.

From his haven of safety beside the Spanish Ambassador, he watched the frustrated young lady perform the stately, complicated figures of the quadrille with Anthony Trevor-Roper, talking all the while. It seemed the little chatterbox was never silent.

But Thorne could understand why Queen Victoria had been impressed. The girl moved with an easy grace that was as natural as it was enchanting. He was forced to admit, for an American she was a remarkably fine dancer.

It became apparent as the evening progressed that all the other bachelors thought so, too. Whenever Thorne glanced out to the dance floor, he saw Miss Elkheart in the arms of a different partner. Every officer in the Household Cavalry who wasn't on duty seemed to be there that evening. Strong, handsome, charming to a man, the Life Guards practically formed a queue around the ballroom, waiting their turn to waltz with her.

But no matter whom she was dancing with, every time she caught Thorne's eye, the Yankee smiled enticingly. Bloody hell. She did everything but beckon him over.

Combermere had been right.

Miss Elkheart was definitely out of the ordinary.

She was the most outrageous flirt Thorne had ever seen.

And the most intriguing.

Although the sport of baiting her was far more interesting, Thorne knew he had to keep his clandestine appointment with the clerk from the German embassy. At ten minutes to eleven, he slipped quickly and quietly out of the crowded ballroom, making certain no one noticed his exit.

Candles in the sconces on the walls threw a dim, quavering light along the silent corridor as he passed the Grand Salon, filled with people seeking a respite from the dancing. Farther up the hallway, the much smaller Green Drawing Room stood empty, just as he'd hoped.

Dropping into a comfortable wing chair, Thorne rested his head on its high back, propped his feet up on a soft ottoman, and settled down to wait for Herr Stieber.

For the past two weeks, Jennifer had enjoyed the heady sensation of being the center of male attention. Since arriving in London, she'd flirted and listened and questioned and laughed. Her natural curiosity in everyone she met had won over the most stuffy, arrogant aristocrats.

Yet in spite of her resolve to meet the golden-haired stranger, he had avoided her all evening. He'd moved so casually around the room, stopping to speak with people he knew in that bored, distant manner of his, that she thought, at first, his actions were unintentional. Then she'd caught him watching her again. A ghost of a smile flitted across his lips before he turned away, and she realized he was deliberately leading her on a merry chase. That made her all the more determined to entice him into asking for a dance. Which she would, of course, refuse.

But when she realized the elusive gentleman had suddenly disappeared from the ballroom, Jennifer was forced to admit her plan to teach him a lesson had been foolish from the start.

Aside from the cat-and-mouse game she'd been playing, the task of being a diplomat's granddaughter had proven exhausting. Her cheeks ached from smiling so much. Her new slippers pinched her toes. And the crowded ballroom had grown ever more stifling. Jennifer decided the only way she was going to have a moment's peace was to find a quiet spot all to herself.

She found Lord Combermere chatting with Viscount Lyttleton and Anthony Trevor-Roper near the room's main doors. Basil smiled in his open, affable manner as she approached. "Well, Miss Elkheart, have you worn out your dancing shoes?"

"I am afraid so," Jennifer admitted. "Do you know where Lady Idina is? I was hoping the two of us could sneak away for a few minutes."

"My sister is in the Grand Salon, visiting with some friends," Basil told her. "It's just down the hallway. I'll be happy to take you there, if you'd like to join her."

Simultaneously, Lyttleton and Trevor-Roper stepped forward. "Please allow me—" Anthony offered.

"I'd be honored to escort you," Lyttleton said.

"No, thank you, gentlemen," she answered with a wave of her hand. "I do not want to interrupt your conversation, and I certainly do not need all three of you to lead me down the hall. I can find my own way."

She had no trouble locating the Grand Salon. Its high double doors were swung wide, revealing a large gold-and-white room filled with people. From the open doorway, she spied Lady Idina, who sat on a sofa surrounded by a flock of gossiping dowagers. Jennifer knew if she joined them, there'd be no getting away for the greater part of an hour. She immediately stepped back into the corridor before she was seen.

Searching in vain for a servant to ask where she might rest, she made her way down the long passage. A door on the left stood slightly ajar, and she paused in deliberation. The palace did, after all, belong to the Queen of England, even if the congenial, gray-haired lady didn't live there.

Peeking cautiously into the chamber, Jennifer didn't see a soul. She stepped inside, closed the door behind her, and breathed a sigh of relief. The noisy press of the *veho* world sometimes threatened to smother her. Moments of solitude like this had become rare since coming to London.

She looked around in pleasant surprise. For a room in an ancient stone building, the small salon was charming. Its varied hues of green and brown reminded her of a forest. Two high-backed chairs had been pulled close to the fireplace, where a large mirror hung over the mantel. Jennifer made a beeline straight for the mirror.

The only sound in the peaceful refuge was the soft rustle of her satin skirt as she crossed the Turkish carpet. The grandfather clock in the corner began chiming the hour when she leaned toward the looking glass and inspected her braided chignon, then checked to be sure both diamond earrings were fastened securely.

All at once, something in the glass caught her attention, and Jennifer realized with a start that she wasn't alone. In the mirror's reflection, a man sat behind her, perfectly still.

He'd been so quiet, she'd walked right past him.

With a gasp of surprise, Jennifer whirled and stared in amazement. The tawny-haired stranger, with whom she'd play cat-and-mouse all evening, was sprawled in one of the chairs, his long legs propped on a hassock in front of him.

His earlier air of weariness hadn't been a pose.

He was sound asleep.

Jennifer gently cleared her throat.

He didn't budge.

She knew she should leave at once. It was one of the *veho* taboos that a young female should never be alone in a room with a male. And somehow, a sleeping male seemed even more forbidden.

But Jennifer didn't leave.

Her Cheyenne sense of justice and fair play wouldn't let her.

Instead, she moved closer, bending down so she could study him. Here was the man who'd been unkind to Lady Idina. At least, Jennifer *thought* he'd been unkind. One thing was certain. He'd led her on a wild-goose chase all over the crowded ballroom.

The lazy gentleman was sleeping as peacefully as a baby. His eaglelike features were relaxed, his hands resting lightly on the arms of the chair. He didn't seem half so forbidding in repose. Or so aloof.

Jennifer smiled. He might have been unattainable earlier that evening, but the irksome fellow was completely at her mercy now. What should her retribution be?

She glanced around the room, searching for an appropriate means of punishment. On the sofa nearby lay a white ostrich plume that had fallen from some matron's boa. Jennifer tiptoed across the thick rug, snatched up the feather, and glided silently back to the chair. Barely able to keep from giggling at the fitting torment she was about to inflict, she bent down to tickle his nose.

In that instant, his lids flew open, and he caught her wrists in his strong hands. "Oh, no, you don't," he growled softly.

He'd been awake all the time!

Jennifer tried to jump back, but the trickster held her in an implacable grasp without seeming to exert himself. As the plume fell from her fingers, she sank slowly to her knees beside him, her elbows coming to rest on his muscled thigh.

"*Hesc!*" she whispered, giving the Cheyenne exclamation for astonishment. She was so rattled, she couldn't think of a single word in English.

"I beg your pardon?"

Her heart thudded wildly as she met the most intense gaze she'd ever encountered. Gone was every trace of languor, every hint of boredom. The clever shape-shifter had been playing possum with the intention of luring her closer. And like an inquisitive little mouse, she'd stepped right into his trap.

"Let me go," she insisted.

Thorne looked into a pair of dark eyes sparkling with surprise. They were slightly almond-shaped, heavily lashed, and framed by high, arched brows.

He could feel the quiver of alarm that ricocheted through her. In an instant, that excitement seemed to leap like an electrical charge from her slender, vibrant form to his much larger body, leaving him nearly breathless and more alive than he'd ever felt before.

He loosened his hold on her fragile wrists. Up close, she was even smaller and more delicate than he'd thought. He didn't want to bruise her, but he had no intention of setting her free. Not just yet, anyway.

"You've been chasing me around the ballroom all evening," he said in a deceptively calm tone. "Now that you've got me all to yourself, Miss Elkheart, tell me what you want."

"I did not chase you!" she denied. But an impish smile curved the corners of her full mouth. She spoke in a sensuous contralto, the kind of husky, bedroom voice that affected a man's respiration. "You were imagining things," she added with an impudent shrug of her shoulders. "Now, let me go."

Thorne found her playfulness captivating. He could well understand the surrender of the entire Household Cavalry, down to the last man. Any other girl would have been screaming the roof off by now, but the high-spirited Yankee didn't betray a hint of fear. He sensed, instead, that she was actually having fun. Something deep inside him, some long forgotten desire, responded to her vivacity. "Only if you promise me the next dance," he bargained in a silken tone.

"Why should I want to dance with you?" she asked, her throaty words tinged with amusement. Her face seemed to glow from within, like a candle in the window on a snowy night. Her laughing eyes were a deep nut-brown, the deepest brown he'd ever seen without actually being black.

He'd been wrong about the Yankee twang. She spoke with a barely discernible French accent, yet there was something more. A hint of an unfamiliar language. One he was certain he'd never heard spoken

"Admit it, Miss Elkheart," he coaxed. "You've been dying to dance with me all evening. You just couldn't finagle a proper introduction."

"That is not true!" she declared with a haughty lift of her chin. "I never had any intention of dancing with you."

"Now why do I find that so hard to believe?"

"I did want to meet you," she readily conceded, then wrinkled her nose and added mischievously, "so I could have the pleasure of turning you down."

"You enjoy refusing a gentleman's request for a dance?" he asked with a scowl. "Rather a strange pastime for a genteel young woman, isn't it?"

She drew back in shock, as though he'd accused her of torturing helpless creatures. "I have never done it before," she stated in an aggrieved tone, "nor would I ever do it again."

"To what do I owe the honor of being singled out for such drastic treatment?" he demanded.

Her smooth forehead furrowed into a frown as she met his gaze. "You upset a friend of mine."

"Who?" he questioned in disbelief. "I don't recall saying a harsh word to anyone the entire evening."

"The lady shall remain nameless."

Thorne pulled the dark-eyed girl closer, inhaling the scent of wildflowers that drifted from her hair. "Because there is no lady," he said gruffly. "The whole story is sheer fabrication. Now promise me that dance, and I'll let you go."

Her smile was brilliant. Too late, he realized he'd given her what she wanted all along. The opportunity to refuse him. "No, thank you, sir."

Thorne grinned at her audacity. No female had ever treated him with such impertinence. No young, unmarried female, at any rate. "Do you know who I am, Miss Elkheart?"

She lifted her brows and gave him a lofty look. "Why should I? As you pointed out, we were never introduced. And therefore, I could not possibly accept your invitation to dance."

Thorne let his gaze drift downward. The firm mounds of her breasts rose and fell in a tantalizing rhythm. Against the white satin bodice of her low-cut gown, her smooth skin seemed to have a golden glow. His body was reacting to her nearness in a very predictable male way. "You owe me something for spoiling my nap," he said in a velvety tone.

She stiffened with sudden wariness, and he dragged his gaze up to meet her dark eyes. "I did not spoil your nap, sir, because you were never sleeping. And if you do not release me at once, I *will* owe you something. Something you will live to regret."

"Just what are you going to do?" he taunted, expecting the typical feminine threat. "Scream for help and bring everyone running? Now, what would people say when I told them about your naughty little prank with the feather?"

"Only a cad would repeat such a childish tale," she scoffed.

"If you scream, Miss Elkheart," he lied softly and convincingly, "I'll have it printed in the morning papers. You can count on it."

The stubborn Yankee stared into his eyes for a long, silent moment, measuring her will against his. Then she lowered her lids and inclined her head toward him, for all the world like a queen bestowing a favor on the lowly subject groveling at her feet. "I had no intention of screaming like a frightened idiot. However, you may have the next dance," she acceded magnanimously.

"I'll have your promise on that."

Those impossibly long lashes flew up to reveal eyes flashing with indignation. She didn't like having her word questioned, that was obvious. "I promise," she snapped. "Now, let me go."

The moment he released her, she sprang to her feet.

But when he rose to tower over her, she didn't race to the door as he'd expected.

"Consider yourself warned, white man," she said in a pleasant, conversational tone. "If you ever touch me again without my permission, you are liable to lose a hand." She crossed the room with the same elegant grace he'd admired on the dance floor, then stopped and turned to look back at him. "So just who are you?" she asked with a scornful lift of one shoulder.

"Eagleston," he said, prepared for her gasp of shock when she recognized the vaunted name and the incredible wealth it implied.

Clearly, she'd never heard of him, for without another word, she opened the door and departed.

Thorne stood staring in mystification at the open doorway.

Lose a hand?

Bloody hell.

What a strange thing for an innocent young lady to say.

But he made no attempt to follow her. Herr Stieber could come through that same doorway at any moment.

Chapter 2

After concluding his meeting with the German spy, Thorne spotted Miss Elkheart hovering at the edge of the ballroom, a look of uncertainty on her lovely features. She clearly hadn't made up her mind just how she was going to tell her next partner that he'd been superseded by a man threatening blackmail. And Lord Combermere was fast approaching from the far side of the floor to claim his dance.

Thorne lengthened his stride. He was just in time to seize her hand and whisk her into the swirl of dancers before Basil could reach her. He shot his closest friend a victorious smile, and Basil grinned back with his usual good humor.

"You should be ashamed of yourself," the little Yankee told Thorne as she placed her hand on his shoulder. "This waltz was promised to another man hours ago." Although her tone was reproachful, her eyes gleamed with impudence.

"Too bad for him," he replied without an iota of guilt. "I just stole it."

She indicated Combermere with a graceful tilt of her head. "Yes, but do you know whom you stole it from?" The amusement in her gaze told Thorne he'd made a terrible mistake, and she, for one, was hoping to see him pay for it in spades.

"I'm sure you're going to tell me."

"That is the earl of Combermere," she informed him

smugly. "Lord Basil Nettlefold-Clive is influential with the prime minister and knows Queen Victoria. I only hope, for your sake, you have not angered him with your bad manners."

"I'm shaking in my shoes," Thorne drawled. "Do you think I'll receive a call from his seconds in the morning?"

Miss Elkheart's smile faded. She gazed at him for a long, thoughtful moment, her pensive expression revealing her confusion. "He does not have a second," she said with unexpected somberness.

Thorne felt as though he'd missed a turn somewhere in the conversation. "I'm not sure I understand."

"Although his first wife died in childbirth three years ago," she explained in a confidential tone, "Lord Basil has not married again. So if you assumed the earl has a second wife, you were mistaken."

"I didn't mean he'd send his wife to berate me," Thorne clarified as he guided his lithesome partner around the hefty duchess of Portland, who was clinging to a dashing, mustachioed hussar as if her life depended on it. "I meant that Combermere might try to call me out for stealing this dance from him."

Her brows lifted in mild astonishment. "To fight with you?"

Thorne nodded abstractedly. His gaze drifted over her in beguilement. Her deep chestnut hair was pulled into a loosely braided chignon. Wisps floated around her ears and at her nape. The braid, woven with tiny white flowers and twisted into a large figure eight at the crown of her head, seemed too thick and heavy to be supported by her slender neck. He found himself imagining those brilliant tresses loose and drifting about her bare shoulders.

"Would you go outside with Lord Combermere tonight, if he called you out there?" she asked, a glow of pure elation sparkling in her eyes.

"Don't look so hopeful," Thorne said dryly. "In the first place, the earl wouldn't call me outside tonight. It wouldn't be correct. His representatives would come to my home in the morning and present his challenge.

They'd set the time for our meeting and ask if I preferred rapiers or pistols."

Her smile was positively gleeful. "They would?"

"I'm sorry to disappoint you, Miss Elkheart," he said, "but I've been speaking in jest." He drew her closer to avoid the czarevitch and Louisa, duchess of Devonshire, who were romping madly around the room, narrowly missing other couples in their terpsichorean abandon. "Dueling is no longer allowed in Great Britain," Thorne explained, breathing in the perfume of blossoms that drifted from Miss Elkheart's hair. "Stealthy meetings at dawn to protect one's honor or the honor of a loved one are against the law. Any man caught participating in a duel is subject to legal prosecution."

"The earl of Combermere is a very important peer, and I am certain he would never disobey the law," she said righteously. But her words were tinged with disappointment, as though she'd been looking forward to watching Thorne get beat to a bloody pulp.

At the mention of a peer, he tried to look suitably impressed. "Do you know many important people?" he asked.

"Yes, I do," she answered without a trace of guile, "but not because I am anyone of importance, myself. My grandfather is the United States Special Envoy being honored tonight. I merely bask in his reflected glory."

"You're being far too modest, Miss Elkheart," Thorne said. "You have a glory all your own."

Jennifer met the Englishman's gaze, expecting to find a glitter of mockery in his *veho* blue eyes. But the expression on his keen-edged features was anything but derisive. "Thank you, Mr. Eagleston," she replied in a choked voice.

Held in his strong arms, she felt totally immersed in pleasant sensations, as though she were walking in a soft summer rain, her face lifted to the sky. She wanted to close her eyes and simply enjoy the extraordinary feeling his nearness brought her.

Hesc! Her first impression of the man must have been wrong. He hadn't been scowling at her in disapproval.

Perhaps he hadn't been unkind to Lady Idina, either.

Jennifer missed her sister's calming influence. Julie would say her overactive imagination had been playing tricks on her or that she'd jumped to the wrong conclusion once again. Then she remembered the way he'd threatened to print the tale of her silly prank in the newspapers and admitted to herself she wasn't sure what to think. Except that he still reminded her of a great, predatory golden eagle.

As they swept around the room, Jennifer gave herself up to the enjoyment of the waltz and allowed the attractive man to guide her with supple strength. He weaved his way through the blurred rainbow of colors with the magical skill of a shaman.

When the music ended, Mr. Eagleston placed her hand on his sleeve and guided her off the floor. "I believe that was the last dance of the evening," he said in his aloof, indolent manner. "Would you like me to take you to your grandfather?"

Jennifer looked around, unable to find Grandpapa or Lord Combermere and his circle of friends. People were milling about the ballroom, saying their farewells or enjoying their last chance to gossip and plan for the coming day.

"Yes, but I am not sure where to find him," she admitted gaily. "I have not seen Grandpapa for several hours now. He probably went into hiding before some other lady could ask him to waltz. These court functions can become very tiring, especially for a man in his sixties."

Thorne fought the urge to run his fingertip along one high, wide cheekbone. Her whole being seemed to shimmer with vitality and an inner joy. "Lord Salisbury and several gentlemen from the American legation were in the Tapestry Room when I passed by. I'll be happy to take you there," he offered.

Miss Elkheart nodded, and they went in search of Senator Robinson. The corridor was packed with people. Thorne drew her close to prevent her from being crushed. She was a little thing, only coming up to his shoulder, but he sensed an intrepidness about her he'd never seen in a woman.

"Have you met my grandfather, Mr. Eagleston?"

"No, I haven't. Unfortunately, I arrived too late to be formally presented."

"I was wondering why I had not met you sooner," she confided blithely. "Grandpapa and I were introduced to *everyone* in the reception line." With a secretive smile, she leaned toward him and added softly, "I thought perhaps you sneaked into the palace without an invitation. I decided not to report you to the authorities unless you seemed dangerous."

Thorne bent his head and spoke in her ear. "I assure you, Miss Elkheart, I came in through the front gate, and I am absolutely harmless."

She laughed, a husky gurgle of amusement. Thorne felt as though he'd just been sprinkled with fairy dust and some of it had caught in his lungs. She was definitely affecting his breathing.

He opened the door to the Tapestry Room and ushered her inside, but the group of distinguished gentlemen who'd been conversing before the great Tudor fireplace were no longer there. "I'm afraid we've missed him," he said. "We'll try the Grand Salon."

Her interest, however, was immediately caught by the magnificent tapestries on the walls, and she walked to the center of the room. "How pretty," she said in admiration as she turned in a half-circle to study the priceless hangings. "Are they very old?"

Thorne quietly closed the door and moved to stand beside her. "About two hundred years," he estimated. "They were woven for Charles II."

She tilted her head and looked at Thorne, her dark eyes revealing a light-hearted bemusement. "My sister told me that Englishmen no longer wear white wigs and fancy silk clothes. She will be surprised to learn that British servants still dress that way. I must admit, though, I am a little disappointed."

"That our servants wear livery?"

She giggled infectiously. "No, that your noblemen do

not! I hoped to dance with a man in a curly wig while I was in London. I wanted to see his long pigtail swinging out behind him as we waltzed."

"I'm afraid you're doomed to remain disappointed, Miss Elkheart," he said laconically. "I've no intention of wearing a powdered hairpiece just to satisfy your misguided expectations."

At the sound of her rich, throaty laughter spilling into the quiet room, Thorne's body reacted with jarring male urgency. His breathing grew restricted. His pulse raced. Bloody hell. He'd never responded to any woman with such overwhelming and immediate carnal need in his life. What was it about the bright-eyed little Yankee that affected him so?

Fortunately, she was oblivious to the effect she had on him. Her direct, open gaze mirrored her innocence. "I would like to see you in a hairpiece," she announced with glee. "And while you were dancing, watch it fly off your head and sail across the room."

"To land on . . . ?" he prompted.

"That chubby, bearded man in the white uniform with all the gold braid."

"Miss Elkheart," he protested with a shocked air, "do you know who that man is?"

"Yes," she said, making a futile attempt to stop giggling. "Well, no, not exactly," she conceded. "I met him in the reception line, but I did not quite catch his name. It is Nicholas something or other."

"My dear girl," Thorne reproved, "you've been speaking with casual irreverence about the heir to the Romanov dynasty. What would your grandfather say?"

She pressed her hand to her breast and gaped at Thorne in delighted dismay. "Grandpapa would skin me alive!" she declared, her face aglow with unholy mirth. "You cannot imagine how many tedious lectures I have endured on the subject of diplomatic protocol." She took his hand and tugged insistently. "Come with me, Mr. Eagleston, and I will introduce you to him. But you must promise not to say a word about powdered wigs or ostrich feathers."

He grinned at her total lack of repentance. "Before we go, Miss Elkheart, tell me your first name."

"I am called Jennifer by the white people," she replied. Her eyes twinkled mischievously. "I was named after my grandmother on the spindle-side."

He cocked his head, intrigued by the quaint expression. "And what are you called by others?"

She responded with a radiant smile, and Thorne felt that he'd somehow won a prize of great value.

"My real name is Vonahenene, or Morning Rose in English. But *nihoe*—my father—calls me Mohehya, which means magpie in my people's tongue."

"I can't imagine why he'd call you that," Thorne teased.

"Only because you do not know me very well," she retorted pertly. She used her ivory fan, which had been dangling from her wrist on its golden cord, to great advantage, fluttering it outrageously before she continued. "To my people, the magpie is a symbol of the sky above and, thus, anything heavenly."

"I stand corrected," he said with a grin.

"You were right in the first place," she confessed with artless candor. An impish smile danced about her lips. Leaning toward him in a conspiratorial manner, she snapped the fan shut and wrinkled her nose disarmingly. "It is because I am always talking."

Thorne slipped his arm around her waist and pulled Miss Jennifer Morning Rose Elkheart, otherwise known as Magpie, closer. The urge to kiss her was nearly overpowering. "Are you always so happy?" he murmured, his gaze fastened on her mouth. Her lips were soft and moist and unbelievably enticing.

At the suggestive timbre of his voice, she sobered at once. "Not always," she replied. "Sometimes I am very unhappy."

Her expressive eyes grew wary. She leaned back against his arm, searching his face as though suddenly suspicious of his motives for escorting her into the empty room. Thorne castigated himself for being a blundering dolt. He was growing clumsy, if he'd signaled his thoughts so blatantly.

He knew he should take the young lady to her grandfather and beat a hasty retreat. What could be more perilous for an eligible bachelor than to be found in a deserted room kissing a foreign diplomat's unmarried granddaughter? But instead of following the cold advice offered by his intellect, Thorne bent toward her, his silken words meant to cajole and ensnare. "What makes you unhappy, Jennifer?"

Jennifer stared into the Englishman's seductive eyes and frowned in deliberation. She had no intention of tempting fate. Her mother had told her time and again that Havsevstomanehe—the evil-maker—sweetens the way to ruin with honeyed words.

"For one thing, I hate mustaches," she stated baldly. "I do not know why white men always wear them. They look so stiff and wiry."

"I'll shave it off."

"Would you?" she asked in astonishment. "For me?"

He shook his head, grinning with supreme male confidence. "You'll get used to it."

"No, I do not think I shall."

In spite of her attempt to match his bravura, her words sounded a trifle breathless. Jennifer was aware that her voice was an octave lower than most females'. All too frequently, men assumed she was trying to "throw out lures," as her Aunt Lucinda put it.

Jennifer's contralto seemed to have that very effect on the golden-haired Englishman. He bent his head, as though intending to kiss her without permission, and spoke in a velvety tone. "I'd be more than happy to prove it isn't nearly as wiry and stiff as it looks."

"I do not think that is a good idea."

"I think it's a very fine idea," he countered. His lips curved in a tantalizing smile. He leaned closer, and she could feel his cool breath fanning her face. "That way you could base your dislike of mustaches on verifiable fact, instead of false assumption. Assuming, of course, that you've never felt a gentleman's mustache brush across your lips before."

"Of course, I have never felt that!" She glared at him, annoyed that he'd even question it. His look of smug acceptance rankled, spurring her to add, "My people consider hairy faces very unattractive."

The sudden glint in his eyes told her she'd just given the wrong answer. This was one man who'd go to any length to prove his point. His deep voice rumbled coaxingly. "Do you find me so very unattractive, Miss Elkheart?"

She raised her voice for added emphasis. "We should find my grandfather now. He will be looking for me."

"We'll go in a minute," he reassured her.

He ran his fingers lightly up her arm, and Jennifer realized that if he persisted in his imprudent behavior she would have to force him to stop. She never went anywhere without her knife. Its slim leather sheath was strapped to her thigh, hidden beneath her petticoat. Earlier in the green salon, he'd held her wrists imprisoned in his grasp, but she could reach the weapon now, if she needed to. She bent her head and stared down at the hand resting boldly on her bare arm.

The man was either obtuse or even more audacious than she suspected. He ignored her obvious hint and continued smoothly. "Why do you speak of white men as though they're alien creatures? It sounds very peculiar coming from a little Yankee like you."

She was appalled at his preposterous supposition. "*Haxc!*" she cried "I am not a Yankee!"

His brow knitted in puzzlement. "I thought your grandfather was Senator Robinson?"

"He is, but that does not make me an American." She smiled proudly as she touched the tip of her finger to her chest. "*Nazestae.* I am Cheyenne." At the Englishman's blank stare, she cheerfully explained. "Grandpapa is my mother's father. He is a *veho*—a white man—just like you, but I love him as much as if he were Cheyenne."

"I see," Thorne said, though none of it made any sense. If her grandfather was a representative of the United

States government, then, obviously, she was an American citizen, whether or not some of her forebears were native to that country. Mixed heritage among their people was hardly unknown.

Miss Elkheart smiled encouragingly. "You know who I am, Mr. Eagleston, but you have not told me anything about yourself."

"I'm a British citizen," he replied, skirting the issue of his name and rank. He wanted to postpone the moment when she learned that he was a duke. Thorne knew from past experience how quickly she would change from a refreshingly spontaneous young woman to a simpering featherbrain the moment she realized his vaulted station in life and what an excellent matrimonial catch he'd be in the eyes of the world.

"I had guessed as much," she replied with a chuckle. "But I thought you might be the second son of a baron or earl."

"I'm not."

It wasn't a lie. He was simply allowing her to draw the wrong conclusion.

To his surprise, she beamed at him in approval. "I am glad you are not a lord," she said earnestly, "and I will not have to remember the correct form of address each time we meet. It becomes very tedious. To tell you the truth, I have never met so many people so excessively proud of their own names."

"You find the English excessively proud?" he asked, not unduly displeased. They *were* a proud lot. Bloody hell, they had a right to be. They'd extended their empire across the face of the globe.

"The ordinary populace are rather pleasant," she confided. "But I have noticed a tendency among your aristocrats to be filled with their own self-importance, regardless of the fact that they seem to do nothing all day but eat, drink, and make idle conversation. I have never seen so many people spend so much time doing so little of a worthwhile nature. Lord Combermere and his sister are the exceptions, of course. They have shown me nothing but kindness, and their lives are filled with meaningful endeavors."

"Miss Elkheart," he protested mildly, "you must give my countrymen the benefit of the doubt. Not every British nobleman is quite so useless as you portray."

She patted the silver star that blazed on his chest in a soothing manner. "I did not mean to accuse you of sloth, drunkenness, or gluttony. In truth, I have been admiring your regalia. My grandfather explained that this particular decoration is bestowed only by your queen and is the highest honor an Englishman can be awarded. Was it given to you for bravery in battle?"

Even before he replied, Thorne knew the light of admiration glowing in her eyes was about to fade. "No, I was given the Order of the Garter in appreciation for the extensive collection of Greek and Roman antiquities I donated to the British Museum."

"*Ahahe!*"

Hardly even a word, but it contained an untold wealth of disappointment.

For the first time in his life, Thorne was seriously tempted to boast about the risks he'd taken for his country. Blast it, he had a half dozen scars to prove his courage, and he was quite willing to strip off his coat and shirt and display them to her, if it'd wipe the look of disenchantment off that beautiful face.

But his wounds had been earned in the secretive business of espionage, not on the battlefield. He'd never spoken of his injuries to anyone, not even his closest friends. Who else but an empty-headed little Yankee would think the only thing that counted was a man's valor under fire?

"Let's go find your grandfather," he said in disgust.

Jennifer allowed the tall gentleman to lead her through the maze of people around the dance floor. *Haxc!* She had no idea why the Englishman was suddenly so angry.

A few moments ago, she'd thought he was going to try to steal a kiss. Now he looked mad enough to wrestle her to the ground and stomp on her. She'd mistakenly thought the adornment was a badge of honor for counting coup. It seemed an honest error. Why else would everyone value it so highly?

The man's unpredictable behavior only proved what she'd known since she could barely walk. White men were alien creatures. She was sure her grandfather and uncle were the only ones she could ever love.

Then she remembered the dream that haunted her. There would be someone in her life she'd love beyond all measure. Someone not Cheyenne. Someone whose shadowy outline she'd seen through the mists of sleep. Yet, regardless of who the man standing beneath the arch in the blue-tiled courtyard turned out to be, one thing was certain.

He wouldn't be a snooty, indolent, prickly-skinned Englishman.

They found her grandfather talking with Lord Salisbury, the British prime minister, and Count Vladimir Gortschakoff. She'd met the Russian nobleman in the reception line earlier that evening. He was a nattily dressed man in his midfifties, with a full head of silvery hair, a pencil-thin mustache, and a pointed goatee.

Grandpapa smiled at Jennifer with doting affection as they approached. "I see you've made a new friend," he said. "I watched the two of you dancing earlier." Her grandfather turned to the stranger, his hazel eyes scrutinizing the newcomer. "I don't believe we've been introduced, sir."

"Grandpapa," Jennifer began, "this is Mr. Eagleston—"

The marquess of Salisbury took a quick step forward and hastily intervened. "Senator Robinson, may I present His Grace, the duke of Eagleston?"

A duke! One of the highest ranking members of their idle, self-indulgent aristocracy! Jennifer glared at the mischief-maker who'd purposely misled her. She would never have spoken so candidly had she realized who he was. He'd known that, too.

Tapping her fan against her palm in unconcealed vexation, she watched the two men shake hands with stiff formality.

Eagleston wasn't in Grandpapa's good graces, either. She'd never seen *namsem* behave quite so coldly. But, of course, the British lord outdid him in frigid arrogance.

"Usually my granddaughter doesn't dance with a gentleman who hasn't been properly introduced," her grandfather said in a tone of reproach that even a swell-headed duke couldn't mistake. "But she is very young, and her outgoing nature is easily taken advantage of."

Eagleston stiffened perceptibly, his jaw clenching. It was clear he wasn't used to being dressed down by any man, and he didn't like it one bit.

"Miss Elkheart didn't realize I held a title," he explained. The words seemed to be torn from his throat. "I apologize for any unseemliness."

Lord Salisbury gave his long black beard a thoughtful tug. "We saw the two of you waltzing earlier, Your Grace. Senator Robinson was merely concerned that his granddaughter was dancing with a man he'd never met."

The prime minister's gaze seemed to convey an unspoken warning. Jennifer knew that Lord Salisbury held the highly respected rank of head chief over all the British Empire. She wondered if he realized that the tall, golden-haired man had purposely deceived her. There was so much about these strange people she didn't understand.

"The fault was mine," she said, forcing a smile. "I should have been listening more closely when we were first introduced."

That was a boldfaced lie. She felt like Wihio, the wily trickster her mother had told her about. If there was one thing Little Red Fawn had tried to impress upon her twin girls, it was always to tell the truth.

But she couldn't take the chance that Eagleston would make good on his threat to tell everyone about her flirtatious behavior in retaliation for embarrassing him in front of the prime minister. She hadn't the least idea what punishment might fall on both their heads should the full truth be known.

"No doubt, it was all a simple mistake," Count Gort-schakoff offered smoothly.

Thorne met the Russian's shrewd gaze. The man had eyes like a damn chameleon, changing from a washed-out blue to pale green. He inclined his head in the briefest of acknowledgments. "Your stay in Vienna was pleasant, I take it?" Thorne asked.

The sly nobleman smiled and brushed the tips of his nails across his closely-trimmed goatee. "And yours, Eagleston?"

There was little doubt the bastard had followed him to England. What he was after here in London was the question. Until he found out, Thorne intended to watch his back.

"If you'll excuse me," he said with unruffled aplomb, "I'll say good night to some friends."

"I think that might be a very good idea," Lord Salisbury agreed.

With a slight nod to Jennifer and her grandfather, he turned on his heel and left.

Thorne threaded his way through the bevy of departing guests until he found Combermere and Lady Idina waiting for their carriages. "I'm planning on some trout fishing in a few days," he told Basil. "I was hoping you'd join me."

"I got your note this afternoon," Combermere replied cheerfully. "But I can't spend more than an afternoon at Eagleston Court. Neither can you, for that matter."

Thorne scarcely heard his friend's comment. From the corner of his eye, he saw Miss Elkheart and Senator Robinson walking toward them.

"I'm having a house party at Nettlefold, Your Grace," Lady Idina explained, her voice raised slightly to regain Thorne's wandering attention. "Everyone is coming. You're invited, too. Didn't you read my invitation?"

Thorne scowled. "I'm going fishing."

Brother and sister exchanged grins. "Then you'll go alone," Idina said unequivocally. "All my other friends are coming to my party."

Thorne stared at her in consternation, aware that was exactly what would happen. Dina was a superb hostess. Her house parties were known for their dash and style. There would be riding or driving through the park, hunting and shooting for the more adventurous, as well as lawn games and musicales for the guests' enjoyment. No one was ever bored at Nettlefold Manor.

"I've made other plans," he stated baldly.

"Miss Elkheart will be staying with us," Lady Idina added with a dimpled smile. "We'll all be sorry to miss you." She turned and beckoned for the auburn-haired Yankee to join them. "Here she is now."

"I'll attend your confounded house party, Dina," Thorne said gruffly as they watched the young lady approach. Miss Elkheart's distinguished grandfather waited nearby, conversing with the duke of Connaught

Idina caught Jennifer's hand and drew her close. "We'll be looking forward to welcoming you to Nettlefold Manor in a few days," she told her. "The duke of Eagleston has graciously agreed to join us, as well." She paused and glanced at Thorne. "His Grace is our nearest neighbor in Warwickshire, my dear. I'd hoped to introduce you earlier, but he wasn't able to meet you at the time."

Jennifer looked into the peer's frosty blue eyes and realized what had actually happened that evening. No wonder Dina had been so embarrassed and flustered by her questions. It hadn't been the kindhearted lady he'd snubbed. Idina had wanted to introduce Eagleston to Jennifer, and he'd refused.

"We have already met," Jennifer stated, making no attempt to hide her newfound insight. "I am sure everyone will be thrilled that the duke can attend. However, my grandfather may need me to stay in London with him. I may not be able to join you as I had planned."

"Surely, Senator Robinson wants you to enjoy yourself while you're in England," Eagleston said smoothly. His eyes flashed her an unspoken challenge. "Lady Idina's gatherings are too special to be missed."

"Yes, say you'll come, Miss Elkheart," Basil urged with

an engaging smile. "I know my sister would be terribly disappointed if you didn't, and so would I."

"Very well," Jennifer agreed, unwilling to upset her unsuspecting friends. She didn't want to tell them that their nearest neighbor was a cunning, devious mischief-maker.

At that moment, the earl of Combermere's town carriage arrived, and brother and sister bid them a quick farewell.

Finding herself alone with the imperious British lord, Jennifer started to edge slowly and cautiously toward Grandpapa. The Englishman watched her like some great, brooding eagle about to swoop down on its hapless prey. He'd tossed a black cloak over his broad shoulders, one side flung back to display a gold satin lining. With his high silk hat, he appeared even larger than before, looming over her.

Jennifer and her sister had grown a full two inches past their mother's diminutive five feet, but at the moment, Jennifer felt uncomfortably small. She lifted her chin to let the duke know she wasn't the least bit afraid of him, all the while trying to sidle away.

"Miss Elkheart," he said, before she could make good her escape, "I wonder if I might call on you tomorrow at tea time."

At the unexpected request, she gave the Cheyenne exclamation of dismay. *"Ahahe!"* she cried. "You cannot come to my house tomorrow, Eagle's Son. I am attending a dedication ceremony with Grandpapa in the afternoon and giving a dinner party in the evening. I will be far too busy to receive visitors."

"Eagleston," he corrected with a quirk of a smile. The expectant look in his eyes told her that he'd never be so gauche as to invite himself to dinner, but he'd like to be asked.

"You cannot come to my party," she blurted out, then cringed at her own inexcusable rudeness. She hurried to explain. "You do not have the right name."

"You don't know my name," the duke pointed out with irksome logic. He tugged on his white gloves as he stepped closer. "You know my title, but you don't know my name."

"What is it?" she asked. She held her breath, dreading his answer. Could he possibly have a similar surname? One ending in the word *bottom*, which she'd found so common among the English, but which sounded so ludicrous to her ears? The Cheyenne people bestowed appellations that reflected the personal traits or physical characteristics of their owners. She was always trying to make sense out of the meaningless *veho* names, sometimes to her great amusement.

"Thornton Blakesford," he said. "My friends call me Thorne."

Thorn. That fit him perfectly! He'd been a thorn in her side since the moment they'd met.

Jennifer smiled in vindication. "It is just as I thought, Thornton Blakesford. You have the wrong name." At his ferocious scowl, she waved her hand back and forth in a placating manner. "Oh, it is a very fine name to be sure. But it is the wrong one for my dinner party."

"Evidently, I need a military rank to qualify for an invitation," Thorne growled. Her look of wide-eyed ingenuousness didn't fool him. He was well aware of the young lady's predilection for uniforms. "Perhaps, if I held the title of captain or colonel and displayed a chest full of medals, I'd be welcomed."

She gaped at him, pretending stupefaction. "Sir?"

He was furious with himself for having been taken in by her air of innocence when they were alone together. Every person wore a mask. He knew that. And he'd still fallen for her pretense of artless candor.

"Come, come, Miss Elkheart," he goaded. "I saw you dancing with every officer in the Life Guards. You made it clear where your preferences lie."

The young lady had the temerity to bat her lashes like a fickle coquette. "There are no warriors invited to my party, Your Graciousness," she replied, drawling the last word with the impudence of a sassy schoolgirl.

"Your Grace," he bit out tersely, then realized too late that she'd been baiting him. He locked his jaw, determined not to give her the satisfaction of seeing him ruffled. How could one insignificant green girl succeed in riling him so easily?

Miss Elkheart arched her brows at his brusque tone. Her dark eyes twinkled with naughtiness as she lifted the hood of her green velvet cape over her magnificent hair. "Now, if you will excuse me, I shall join my grandfather," she said, adding sotto voce as she turned away, "Your Grrr-ace."

Thorne stared after her, his temper soaring. He'd be damned if he'd let the little Yankee poke fun at him or his title. The idea that a female—any female—would refuse his courteous request to call on her was something he'd never imagined. That an avaricious, title-hunting American heiress would find him so unattractive left his male pride smarting. Bloody hell. The unmannerly minx needed to be taught a lesson in British civility.

He'd attend her dinner party—with or without an invitation—and he'd make her eat those insolent words for dessert, if he had to spoon them down her throat one by one.

Chapter 3

"**W**e are honored to have His Grace, the duke of Eagleston, with us this afternoon to dedicate these wonderful artifacts from ancient Greece," Mr. Hugh Bottomsby told the gathering. "And privileged to have two other distinguished guests at the museum today, as well. Senator Robinson, the United States Special Envoy, and his lovely granddaughter, Miss Elkheart, are gracing us with their presence." He looked over at Jennifer and Grandpapa and smiled broadly. "Please extend a warm welcome to our American friends."

As the assembly clapped politely, Jennifer looked about the small, crowded room filled with Greek sculpture. At one end was a large reclining figure of a bearded god playing a lyre; at the other, a magnificent young athlete stood on a marble pedestal, poised to hurl a discus.

The museum curator picked up a plaque from a nearby table. Eagleston, standing beside the diminutive, balding man, scarcely glanced at the bronze tablet inscribed with his name. Arms folded in a pose of elegant nonchalance, the duke watched Jennifer with hooded eyes.

She stared right back at him, refusing to be intimidated.

"Your Grace," said Mr. Bottomsby, "please accept this small memento of our gratitude. The artifacts you've donated to our exhibition are priceless. It is through the generous support of philanthropists like yourself and the late Lord Elgin that the British Museum has acquired one of the world's foremost collections of Greek antiquities."

Eagleston took the award with a brief nod of acceptance. "Thank you, Mr. Bottomsby," he replied and immediately handed it to the handsome, brown-haired man standing next to him. "You're to be commended for your fine stewardship of the Greek and Roman exhibitions."

Beaming with pride, Hugh Bottomsby concluded the ceremony by thanking everyone who'd attended. As the other visitors drifted away, he walked over to Jennifer and her grandfather. "If you'll join me, Senator," he said, "I'll escort you and Miss Elkheart on a tour of our newest acquisitions."

Jennifer soon discovered that Mr. Bottomsby's private party included the duke of Eagleston and the duke's personal secretary, John Woodman. The group had barely entered the next exhibit room before Eagleston maneuvered himself beside her, while directing his employee to join her grandfather and the curator with a barely discernible nod.

She made a point of ignoring the presumptuous lord as she stopped to admire a charming sculpture. It was of a girl, with her head held high and a tambour upraised, leading a boy playing pipes, while a third figure looked down at a sleek panther walking beside him.

"Their procession is in honor of Dionysus," the duke said languidly, dispelling the hope that he'd catch up with the other gentlemen and leave her to explore the museum's treasures in peace.

But her curiosity outpaced her resolve to ignore him. "Why is the panther with them?"

"To the ancient Greeks, the god Dionysus represented the forces of life and nature in animals and the fruits of the growing plants."

"That must be why they look so happy," she said, enchanted. The lively trio seemed to radiate joy.

Eagleston smiled at her frank delight. "Dionysus was also regarded as the god of wine, so his followers may have tippled a little on their way to his temple."

Jennifer knew the Englishman had purposely tossed out those tidbits of information to beguile her. She knew he was going to do it again, in his offhand way, keeping her beside him like a greedy goose.

She moved to a glass case, where several large, two-handled vases were displayed. "I suppose you know all about the pottery here, too," she challenged with a lift of her chin.

His lips twitched, but he continued in his lackadaisical fashion. "These urns are superb examples of Greek art. Early artists painted the figures in black against the red pottery clay. Their designs are bold, even striking, but you'll notice the lack of realistic detail."

Her interest caught, Jennifer bent down and peered closer at one of the vases. Two warrior figures with spears and shields were bending over a fallen opponent. Belatedly, she wished she'd paid more attention when Julie had tried to interest her in the myths of ancient civilizations.

"What are they fighting over?" she asked.

"Probably a woman."

She straightened and met his heavy-lidded blue gaze, expecting to find him amusing himself at her expense. He seemed quite serious. "What makes you say that?" she demanded.

"The Greeks fought the Trojans over a lady who'd been stolen from their king," he said mildly. "The siege of Troy lasted for ten years, but the lovely Helen was eventually restored to her husband."

Fascinated, Jennifer cocked her head and sent him a quizzical look. "Such a very romantic tale, Your Grace! Did you make it up just to amuse me?"

He raised a sardonic eyebrow. "Do you find it so difficult to believe that a war would be waged over a woman? I assure you, it's true. Men have been battling each other for the fairest prize of all down through the centuries."

"Have you ever fought for a lady?"

"On one occasion only, Miss Elkheart," he replied with a rueful half-grin. "I was twelve at the time and suffering from a painful bout of puppy love."

"Did you win?"

"The lady or the fight?"

"Either."

"I suffered a black eye and a bloody nose," he admitted. "But given that my opponent was five years older and twice my size, I managed to make a pretty good showing." He took Jennifer's elbow and guided her to the next case.

"And the lady?"

"Like all females," he said drolly, "she proved fickle in the end. She ran off with the head gardener."

"At *twelve*?" Jennifer asked in horror.

Eagleston reached out and brushed back a wisp that had come loose from her chignon. The tip of his finger grazed her cheekbone, sending tingles of sparkling energy shimmering through her. His words were filled with an amused self-derision. "Did I forget to mention the young lady was twenty at the time and the daughter of our coachman? I'm afraid mine was a case of unrequited love."

Shaking her head in disbelief, Jennifer laughed. She pointed to the next set of vases. "Tell me about these," she urged. "Is there a story that goes with them, too?"

Thorne glanced at the display, then back to the auburn-haired girl beside him. Her nut-brown eyes shone with a liveliness seldom seen in his jaded, aristocratic world. "The first one shows a youth leaving home, possibly going to war," he explained. "The second is a battle scene, complete with chariots and horses."

She crouched and brought her nose closer to the glass. "Who are the warriors on this vase?"

"Athenians and Spartans." He looked down at the silk rosettes on her jaunty hat. She was like a fresh morning breeze wafting through that room of dusty relics. He was seeing them all again, as though for the first time. "Unless I'm mistaken, Miss Elkheart, you have a great deal of admiration for valor on the battlefield."

She rose, a brilliant smile lighting her features. "My father is a great warrior," she boasted with immeasurable pride. "*Nihoe* saved our entire band of people from destruction." She tipped the brim of her black velvet hat toward Thorne expectantly. "Were you ever a soldier?"

"I served in the Life Guards," he replied, "but for a brief time only."

"Why a short time?"

"I found military regimen rather fatiguing," he stated, "and I disliked the design of the uniforms even worse." The practiced lie threatened to stick in his throat, but he managed to continue placidly. "It was impossible to get a decent fit, no matter how expensive the tailoring."

Miss Elkheart stared at him, appalled. Her gaze swept over the meticulous cut of his coat and trousers, the gold-headed walking stick, and the expensive felt hat he held in his hand.

"*Haxc!*" she said tartly. "My mother would say you are as fine as frog's hair today." She turned and sailed toward the open door, her firm back taut with disapproval.

His mood grown thunderous, he stalked after the aggravating little Yankee and quickly caught up with her. They marched side by side in tense silence across the next room's polished oak floor.

Leaving the Household Cavalry had been one of the hardest things Thorne had ever done. Though he'd served for only two years, his regiment had become the family he'd never known. When his former commander, Colonel Lord Doddridge, was put in charge of the British secret service, he'd implored Thorne to resign his commission and work for his country as an undercover agent. Thorne had reluctantly agreed, knowing his friends would never understand why he'd left the Guards so precipitously. And knowing he would never be able to tell them. Now, with the uncanny wile of a black-hearted sorceress, Miss Elkheart had touched a raw wound he'd thought long since healed.

Jennifer peeked at the English lord from the corner of her eye, stunned by his incredible vanity. Who would suspect a man with a granite chin like his was nothing more than a popinjay?

"I'm afraid I've shocked you, Miss Elkheart," he said in half-hearted apology.

She was too disgusted to mince words with him. "My father would gladly give his life to protect his family or any helpless ones entrusted to his care. And the last thing on his mind would be the fashionable cut of his clothes."

"I'm duly chastened," Eagleston said gravely.

"You should be," she muttered, "but I doubt that you are."

The strained pair joined the others standing in front of a great frieze with hundreds of figures of horses and riders carved in marble. She read the bronze plaque listing the duke of Eagleston as the donor.

"You gave this to the museum?" she blurted out in surprise.

He folded his arms and answered with irritating complacency, "I brought it back from Athens a year ago."

Mr. Bottomsby was practically quivering with excitement. "The original frieze was over five hundred feet long," he told Jennifer. "It ran around the top of a building, and much of it depicted a throng of people on their way to pay homage to Athena, patron deity of the great temple."

"What temple is that?" she asked the curator.

"The Parthenon, Miss Elkheart," the British lord drawled.

"It must be very exciting to find such marvelous treasures, Your Grace," she commented politely for her grandfather's sake. "Do you visit many foreign places searching for artifacts?"

Meeting the young lady's critical gaze, Thorne lifted his brows in a show of disinterest. "I go, Miss Elkheart, to relieve the tedium of everyday life."

Senator Robinson chuckled indulgently. "My granddaughter doesn't know the meaning of boredom, Your Grace. Jennifer finds each and every day a new adventure."

"Speaking of new adventures, Miss Elkheart," Hugh Bottomsby said with patent enthusiasm, "I'm looking forward to attending your dinner party this evening."

Thorne's gaze snapped from the gray-haired American diplomat to the short, baldheaded scholar of antiquities.

Bloody hell. She'd invited the curator to her party, but the duke of Eagleston couldn't attend!

As everyone drifted toward the next room, Thorne spoke to the unpredictable female in a low, gruff tone. "I'm curious to know, Miss Elkheart, if you've invited my personal secretary to your home this evening, as well."

She looked at Thorne, her brown, almond eyes twinkling with merriment. *"Hesc!"* she said softly, a winsome smile curving her lips. "Though I should like to invite Mr. Woodman, I cannot. He has the wrong name, just like you."

Thorne heard her surreptitious giggle, as she slipped her hand through her grandfather's crooked elbow and sauntered away. He clenched his teeth to bite back his caustic retort.

The fault-finding, judgmental little Yankee could giggle all she wanted. Come this evening, he'd be the one laughing. And he'd have the last laugh, dammit.

It wasn't difficult for the duke of Eagleston to discover that the special envoy from the United States had leased a Georgian mansion on Park Lane for his stay in London. He presented the butler with his card and was immediately ushered in.

He'd expected his appearance to be questioned. The houseman, however, took his hat, gloves, and cane with an air of pained resignation. "I'll show you the way, sir," he said.

Thorne was escorted into the formal salon, where people milled about in a festive mood. It was an odd assortment of guests. Elderly matrons sparkling with jewels rubbed elbows with young men in tweed suits, their frayed cuffs denoting their occupations in the city as clerks and bankers. Schoolboys barely out of Eaton, middle-aged solicitors, a magistrate he recognized, a friend's former mistress, even an actress currently performing at Drury Lane were laughing and chattering together as if they were all bosom friends. What these people had in common to support such lively conversations defied all reason. It appeared the American concept of democracy had been transplanted, lock, stock, and barrel, to London.

Growing more and more bewildered, Thorne searched the crowded room for Miss Elkheart and spied her, at last, standing near one of the windows with several of her guests.

She was the picture of radiance. Laughter sparkled in her dark eyes. Her rose-colored gown heightened her vivid coloring, the fitted waist and perky bustle with its poofed draperies showing off her sweet little figure to perfection.

Not that he was impressed. The only reason he'd come tonight was because she'd told him he couldn't. Thorne had been born with an inherent aversion to the word *no*.

As though suddenly conscious of his presence, she looked over to find him watching her. Visibly startled, she blinked in disbelief. When he didn't disappear like some treacherous desert mirage, a flush spread across her high cheekbones. She looked as if a great bull elephant had just wandered into her blue salon.

Jennifer forced a smile to her dry lips as the duke of Eagleston cut a path straight for her. People stepped aside in deference at his approach, their lively conversations fading to murmurs of grudging admiration. There was something about the dratted fellow that exuded wealth and class. His evening clothes had the fine cut and flawless fit that only piles of money can buy.

"Welcome, Your Grace," Jennifer said, extending her hand when he halted imperiously in front of her. "How fortunate you were able to come, after all. I was afraid you would have a more important engagement."

"I knew how disappointed you'd be, Miss Elkheart, if I didn't attend your fete," he answered glibly. "So I made my apologies elsewhere." His bold eyes dared her to have him ejected in front of a roomful of people.

Throwing the duke of Eagleston out of her house was the last thing Jennifer intended to try, much as she'd like to do exactly that. She swallowed the lump in her throat, certain he was not going to be amused this evening. He was vain enough and stuffy enough to believe she was making fun of them all, rather than playing a good-natured joke.

If Eagleston stalked from the room enraged, the story would be all over London by morning. By afternoon, the United States minister would be making a call at the Foreign Office with his profound apologies. Worst of all, Grandpapa would be terribly disappointed in her. *Namsem* might even send her home, destroying all hope of ever finding the man in her vision.

"I am delighted you came," she lied, summoning all she'd learned of feminine stratagems from Madame Benét.

"The pleasure is mine," he said with a smirk. He glanced expectantly around the room.

"My grandfather is not home this evening," she explained, the smile still frozen on her face. "He is attending a dinner at the German Embassy."

"I was looking for your knight in shining armor, come to slay the dragon."

She laughed at his mocking insouciance. "The dragon being yourself?" she quizzed. "I can save my guests from any ogre who might threaten to disrupt my party. And in *my* world, warriors dress in paint and feathers." She paused to inspect his elegant attire, then added meaningfully, "And precious little else."

"Your people sound as barbarous as the Scots."

"I *am* part Scot on my mother's side," she told him gleefully.

"I should have guessed," he retorted, his gaze moving to her reddish-brown hair. A smile spread across his sardonic face. "Do you want me to bare my chest for the edification of your invited company, Miss Elkheart?"

"And ruin your finely tailored ensemble? I should say not! Let me introduce you to some of them, instead." She gestured to the couple beside her, who'd been listening to the scandalous interchange in mute fascination. "You probably know Lord and Lady Bottomside already."

It was all Jennifer could do to keep from chewing her lower lip in despair. Every guest there, except for Eagleston, had the word *bottom* in his or her name. What had seemed like a harmless bit of fun a few moments ago had taken on the aspect of outrageous effrontery the moment the British peer walked through the door. She wondered how long it would take him to figure it out. *Then* he would stalk from the room in a rage.

She breathed a sigh of relief as Eagleston gave them a polite nod of recognition. "And of course, you know Mr. Bottomsby," she said, drawing closer to the slightly built curator, who shook the duke's hand with a welcoming smile.

Nearly sick with apprehension, she slipped her arm through Eagleston's and led him to the next group. "Allow me to present Mrs. Broadbottom," she said, indicating a voluptuous woman displaying ropes of jet beads on her ample bosom. Jennifer closed her eyes, held her breath, and waited for his acid retort.

"Mrs. Broadbottom," she heard Eagleston say with suave cordiality, "I don't believe I've ever had the pleasure."

Jennifer's lids flew open. For the space of a second, a ghost of a smile seemed to skip about his mouth. Then he was his usual vain, blasé, dukish self.

Tittering jovially, the gray-haired matron wagged her painted silk fan under his nose. "Why, I should think not, Your Grace!" she gurgled. "My husband is director of the Hospital for the Diseases of Women in Soho."

Clearly surprised, Eagleston met Jennifer's worried gaze. "You don't say?"

"I do, indeed!" Evangeline Broadbottom declared. "Miss Elkheart visited our facility along with her grandfather. The Lord Mayor himself accompanied them."

Jennifer searched the duke's sharply chiseled features. His astonishment seemed to be centered on the fact that she'd visited a charity hospital. Thankfully, he was missing the larger picture. The feeling of being caught in a childish prank began to ease. If she hurried him out the door, he might never realize what she'd done.

"I think you have met enough strangers for tonight, Your Grace," she stated, attempting to lead him away from the curious circle of onlookers. "I am certain you have far more interesting places to go. We would not want you to disappoint any friends who are eagerly awaiting your arrival."

"My entire evening is at your disposal, Miss Elkheart," he replied. "I would like to meet each and every one of your guests."

Jennifer clutched his arm in mounting panic. He'd come to a complete halt in the middle of the room, and no amount of discreet tugging could budge him. The aura of fastidious aristocrat belied his surprising strength. She had the uncomfortable sensation that she was experiencing only a tiny fraction of his physical power.

"Ahahe!" she exclaimed, an undertone of panic shading her cry of woe. "I would not want to bore you with all my new friends."

The duke placed his strong hand over hers and squeezed it reassuringly. His voice was cool, subdued, implacable. "Please believe me, Miss Elkheart, when I say that my being bored in your presence would be an absolute impossibility."

Jennifer nearly jumped out of her skin at the provocative words. She looked at him in dread, searching for some hidden irony in the courteous statement. But there wasn't a hint of awareness on his patrician face. She released a pent-up breath and relaxed a tiny fraction.

Clearly, the Maiyun—those mysterious powers who controlled the affairs of men—were watching over her, for the duke of Eagleston was a whole lot dumber than he looked. Hundreds of years of inbreeding on this tiny island was the only possible explanation for his total lack of discernment. By the Great Powers above, he hadn't caught on to a thing!

"Very well, Your Grace." She led him to the next cluster of guests. "This is Mr. Stanley Figbottom, who was kind enough to sell me two lovely bonnets last week. He and his wife have the finest millinery shop on Bond Street. Mrs. Figbottom is on the far side of the room right now, visiting with Dame Vesta Rothbottom, the famous actress." She paused to take a quick breath, then hurried on. "I saw her in *Othello* the other night. Have you seen her performance?"

"I've had the pleasure of seeing Dame Rothbottom on several occasions. She's very talented, indeed."

Jennifer couldn't get over her amazement. Although all the other visitors had grasped her joke within minutes of their arrival and reacted with resounding good humor, Eagleston seemed unaware of anything the least bizarre. She had to bite the inside of her cheek to keep from howling.

What a dunce!

By this time, however, her nerves were rubbed raw. Her voice quavered as she forced herself to continue the introductions. "Mr. Throckbottom is the clerk who waited on me at the Bank of England, and Mr. Uriah Springbottom took my grandfather and me on a tour of Kensington Gardens. He is the head gardener there."

With smooth urbanity, the duke shook hands and made an appropriate remark to each. He followed her around the room, greeting everyone with consummate politeness.

Trying not to look hopeful that he'd change his mind, she turned to Eagleston when dinner was announced. "Are you sure you want to stay for the meal, Your Grace? I am afraid you will find my simple party somewhat flat compared to what you are used to."

"Quite the contrary, Miss Elkheart," he said with a diabolical grin. "I can't remember when I've been so entertained."

Jennifer wondered if her smile looked as sickly as she felt. "How marvelous."

As they walked into the dining room together, Eagleston bent his head and spoke softly in her ear. "What are you serving for dinner tonight, Jennie? Hind quarter of mutton? Rump roast of beef? Or a ham butt?"

Her eyes flew to meet his. Their intelligent blue depths sparkled with hilarity.

He knew!

He'd known all along.

And he'd purposely tormented her.

"Yes, you wretched man," she whispered behind her outspread fan. "And I hope you choke on all three!" She tried to look indignant, but it was impossible. Giggles of ecstatic relief bubbled up inside her. Now Grandpapa wouldn't send her home in shame, after all.

The table gleamed with polished silver. Painted Chinese lanterns on the snowy cloth spread a jeweled glow over the baskets of autumn blossoms trailing lushly down the center. The pungent fragrance of crab apples, coreopsis, cleome, and wild rose hips mingled with the tangy scent of juniper candles.

Jennifer listened with pride to the cries of admiration from the ladies. She'd worked hard to make the evening special. She wanted her guests to know that she valued their friendship and their wonderful sense of humor.

The moment everyone was seated, Jennifer clinked her spoon against her crystal goblet. "Ladies and gentlemen," she announced, "we have all enjoyed a hearty laugh over your mutual names, but I think the duke of Eagleston is feeling somewhat left out. So just for this evening, I propose a new title." She lifted her glass and raised it high, meeting his arrested gaze with a saucy grin. "Tonight, Your Grace, I declare you the duke of Ironbottom."

The entire company froze in shock. Gasps of dismay could be heard up and down the table, as all eyes turned to the arrogant peer. Everyone waited, breathless, for him to rise imperiously to his feet and stomp out of the room.

Instead, Eagleston tipped back his head and gave a shout of laughter. "Only if we can call you Miss Bottomly," he rejoined. He lifted his wineglass, a devastating smile softening his sharp features. "And as you will learn, my dear girl, I always insist on having the last word."

Chapter 4

❦

"You're just in time for the archery competition," Lady Idina told Thorne as he strode across Nettlefold Manor's drawing room. "And it's about time you put in your appearance, too," she scolded. "For shame! My other guests have been here for two whole days. Several young ladies were on the verge of tears last night when you hadn't arrived by dinnertime." She took his arm and led him through French doors that opened onto the redbrick terrace.

"Which young ladies?" he queried, then mentally flailed himself for revealing such an immediate interest. Weepy-eyed women were not his style, and Idina knew it.

She grinned at him, aware of his slip. "You know very well that Miss Trevor-Roper is pining her heart out for you," she said. "And Lady Avice has tried to keep up a brave front for the last two days, but we all know who she's looking for each time she glances at the doorway. When Bertie arrived at teatime yesterday, their sighs of disappointment nearly unsettled him. For one terrible moment, I thought our gentle giant was going to turn right around and leave." She pursed her lips in rebuke at Thorne's unrepentant chuckle. "How would you like to walk into a room and have all the young ladies groan in dissatisfaction?"

"You've had a tendency to exaggerate since you were five years old," Thorne said.

"Oh, well, not *all* the young ladies," she admitted, clearly enjoying her role as tormentor. "But you wouldn't want to monopolize every available female at my house party this weekend, would you? You have to leave at least one heiress for the other gentlemen to squabble over."

He shook his head at her obvious tactics. They both knew exactly which heiress she meant. "Dina, you're a hopeless romantic."

Leaning on his arm for support, Lady Idina accompanied him down the wide green lawn that sloped from the terrace to a meandering brook. A pavilion had been erected on a flat stretch of grass along the stream bank. Dining tables and chairs stood in the shade of the gaily striped tenting, where servants scurried about laying china, silver, and crystal on the lacy cloths. Later, after the contest was over, there would be an elaborate banquet.

Beneath the branches of a giant oak, a group of musicians played brisk martial airs. Flags, bunting, and banners added a festive touch, creating the atmosphere of a medieval joust.

"As Lady Paramount of the tournament," she told him, "I've assigned you to help our newcomer from America. Miss Elkheart has agreed to take part in the competition, but I think she's a little confused over the rules of procedure and scoring. Will you give her some guidance?"

"Only if you insist," he said.

"Surely you don't blame Jennifer for the gossip in the society pages?"

He met his neighbor's perceptive green eyes. "I just want to make it clear that the insinuations in the *Gazette* and the *Sun* are rank bilge."

After Miss Elkheart's dinner party, the story of her practical joke had been repeated with roaring hilarity all over London. Reports in the papers carried the titillating news that the duke of Eagleston had been the sole guest in attendance without the required surname, and that he'd good-naturedly gone along with her spirited raillery. The inference that the highly eligible bachelor had been bowled over by the United States envoy's lovely granddaughter couldn't have been missed by a single reader.

The morning he'd seen the gossip columns, Thorne had decided to maintain an attitude of polite disinterest toward the troublesome Yankee. His plan was to visit the earl of Combermere's estate for several days, dividing his attention equally among all the unmarried ladies, thereby scotching the notion that he felt any partiality for Miss Elkheart. After that, he would make damn sure he never came within arm's length of that capricious magpie again.

How he'd gotten himself into such a predicament in the first place was a source of relentless self-recrimination. The plain truth was his temper had gotten the best of him. What other explanation could there be for his unprecedented lapse in sanity?

But refusing Lady Idina's request to assist Jennifer now would be tantamount to admitting to everyone at the house party that he was disturbed by the idiotic gossip in the press. He had no choice but to go along with his hostess's proposal.

"Here you are," Idina called brightly, as she led Thorne up to the dark-haired young woman.

"Miss Elkheart," he acknowledged with cool reserve, "how do you do?"

Jennifer's stricken brown eyes told him she hadn't been pleased with the newspaper articles, either. Her grandfather had probably given her the tongue-lashing she deserved for her hoydenish prank. "Your Grace," she replied with equal restraint, although a rosy flush suffused her cheeks. "It is a pleasure to see you again."

"Eagleston is going to help you during the tournament," Lady Idina told her, inferring by her joyous tone that the whole idea had been his. "Should you have any questions, don't hesitate to ask him." She glanced from one to the other, her dimples flashing. "Now, if you'll both excuse me, I must see to the drawing of lots." With a cheerful flutter of her fingers, she left them.

Jennifer met the nobleman's frigid gaze. "I do not want

to be a bother," she said, knowing why he was so angry. At her grandfather's home three nights ago, this same unbending man had been an incomparably charming dinner companion. He'd held her guests in the palm of his hand as he told them one story after another with a droll wit that had them practically falling off their chairs with laughter.

She'd had her vision-dream again, the night he'd come to her grandfather's house uninvited. It was as if the Great Powers were warning her that the duke of Eagleston was not the one. She mustn't be misled by the Englishman's charms. No matter that those charms were many and exceedingly appealing.

He made no attempt to reassure her now. Instead, he was studying the longbow in her hand with a doubtful frown. "You may have chosen a bow that's too heavy for you, Miss Elkheart."

"No, the bow is fine," she insisted. "I can handle it easily."

To prove her point, she placed the lower tip against her instep, bent the supple lemonwood, and slipped the string's loop into the grooves of the bow's upper tip.

At that moment, Miss Trevor-Roper hurried up, her round, slightly protuberant eyes aglow. "Eagleston," she trilled, "you're here at last!"

Jennifer cocked her head and surveyed the large female in wonder. The Englishwoman spoke in a shrill soprano, her words quivering with adoration. Though not as tall as the duke, Muriel Trevor-Roper soared a good eight inches above Jennifer and probably outweighed her by a solid fifty pounds.

"I was hoping you would come stand beside me and watch my technique," Muriel continued in a coaxing whine. She gazed at the duke beseechingly. "You could give me some suggestions on how to improve my style."

"I'll be happy to watch you, later," he said in his suave, unhurried manner. "At the moment, I've promised Lady Idina to help Miss Elkheart."

The statuesque woman turned to stare at Jennifer. Muriel's hair, brows, and lashes were white-blond, giving her long face a peculiarly colorless appearance. "By all means, Thorne," she said with a disparaging sniff. "We can't have our quaint little visitor from America feeling like an outsider, can we?"

"Do not stay on my account, Your Grace," Jennifer said brightly. "I would not want to monopolize your time, especially if Miss Trevor-Roper needs your assistance."

"I'm sure Muriel will do fine without my suggestions," Eagleston replied. "She's held the title of Champion Lady Archer of the Toxophilite Society for the last two years."

Muriel laid a broad, mannish hand on her breast and simpered coquettishly. "Oh, dear, Your Grace, now you're embarrassing me!" She turned with obvious reluctance and walked away.

"Toxophilite," Jennifer repeated, rolling the strange word around on her tongue. The English language was always full of surprises. "What does that mean?"

"It means someone who enjoys the challenge of archery," Eagleston said. "There are private clubs that people who share an enthusiasm for the sport can join. It's a very popular pastime here in England."

"The *veho* notion of having fun never ceases to amaze me," Jennifer stated with a happy laugh.

"Why is that, Miss Elkheart?" he asked, his sardonic voice mellow.

"*Hesc!* The idea of standing nearly motionless and shooting arrow after arrow at a stationary target as a means of recreation seems ludicrous to me."

"Do you really know how to shoot a bow and arrow?"

"Yes," she answered, "my father taught me. But I have never been in a tournament before. I do not know your rules."

She looked out across the open field. There were two rows of targets, one at each end. Circles of various colors had been painted on strong cloth and fastened to solid backings of straw. These butts—as the British called them—were mounted on wooden tripods.

Eagleston regarded her with patronizing benevolence. "Don't worry if you don't do well, Miss Elkheart. It's only a friendly rivalry. There are no championship titles in jeopardy today, although there will be some stiff wagering on the final scores."

"I have already made a bet with Lord Basil," she confided.

"Not a large one, I hope."

She met his complaisant blue gaze and wished she'd been more adventuresome. "No," she admitted grudgingly. "While I am confident of my own ability, I wasn't certain how skilled the other archers might be."

Thorne eyed the longbow she'd chosen. "You're certain you know how to use that?" At the exasperated jerk of her head, he cautioned, "Just be sure not to point an arrow at anyone."

She wrinkled her nose and smiled at him in puckish delight. "Unless, of course, I intend to shoot somebody."

"Remind me not to step in front of you."

A footman handed Thorne his tackle, which he'd brought with him from Eagleston Court. Together, they walked to the nearer row of targets.

Everyone was in a convivial mood. The ladies were stunning in fashionable white gowns trimmed in green, de rigueur for an archery tournament. With little feathered hats perched jauntily on their heads, they wore their hair neatly braided or twisted into a tight chignon to prevent a stray lock or long curl from getting caught in a bowstring. Most of the gentlemen wore the traditional Lincoln green frock coats with gold insignias and white trousers.

Thorne nodded and waved to his friends as he crossed the lawn with his charge. Lady Avice, Viscount Lyttleton's seventeen-year-old sister, blushed and ducked her head when the duke returned her smile of greeting. Painfully shy, the girl always grew tongue-tied around him. He invariably tried to ease her discomfiture with a kind word.

Lyttleton was checking his sister's leather armguard to be sure it was properly fastened. Their heads, both a bright, carroty red, were bent close together. Aware of Avice's sudden tension, Bertie looked up and, seeing Thorne and Jennifer, straightened to his full, imposing height of six foot six. "If you need any help with your equipment, Miss Elkheart," he said, "I'll be happy to assist you."

"The duke of Eagleston has already been assigned that duty," Jennifer answered with a gay smile. "But thank you for offering."

"I'm the one who should be helping you," Euan Bensen protested as he hurried up, bow in hand. His intent gaze swept over Miss Elkheart's lithe form and came to rest on her lips, which were parted slightly, revealing even white teeth. "I'm a member of the Sherwood Bowmen. Eagleston doesn't even belong to an archery society anymore. He's too busy traveling to foreign places. He hasn't won a championship since he left the Life Guards."

Thorne watched in annoyance as Jennifer beamed at the ebony-haired braggart. Although Bensen was the heir to a barony, he possessed the burly physique of a prizefighter. He and Thorne had been rivals since Eaton. Although the two had been on the same soccer and cricket teams at Oxford, they'd vied against each other for four years in amassing total points. Their rivalry had even extended once to the petticoat line, when they'd set their sights on the same curvaceous opera dancer. That heartless jade had spurned them both for a fling with the Prince of Wales.

"Have you held a title, too?" Jennifer asked, exactly as Bensen had hoped she would.

"As a matter of fact, yes," Euan replied with a satisfied smirk. "Last year I won the Grand National Archery Championship."

"Congratulations!" she exclaimed. "You must be very skilled with the bow." Her wholehearted admiration was unmistakable. Apparently, prowess in archery rated right up there beside medals for valor with the provincial Yankee miss.

Euan preened like an imbecilic peacock. "I shot my very best that afternoon," he demurred, his words ringing with false modesty. "But I'll be happy to give you some guidance on your form, if you'd like."

Thorne felt a spark of irrational fury. "As Miss Elkheart pointed out a moment ago," he said with glacial politeness, "Lady Idina has assigned that task to me." He glared at Bensen, continuing ominously, "You'd better move out of the line of fire before someone accidentally shoots you in the backside."

Euan had the effrontery to glower back. "Such an *accident* would provoke immediate retaliation," he warned. His black eyes flashed an undiluted male challenge at Thorne. "Enjoy the contest," he said with smug arrogance, "and may the best man win."

Thorne stared at Bensen's retreating back. He'd show the overweening jackass who was the better man.

"How does the scoring work?" Jennifer asked, her question barely penetrating Thorne's overwhelming and illogical reaction to Euan's baiting. "Do I try to put a certain number of arrows in each of the colored bands on the target?"

Thorne tore his gaze away from Bensen to find her watching him with wide, curious eyes. "No. The goal is to put every arrow directly into the center of the target."

"Into the same spot each time?" She gaped at him, incredulous. "That sounds like a very simple game to me."

He smiled at her naiveté. "It does, doesn't it?" he agreed. "I suppose it would be more varied the other way, but today's winner will be the one who shoots the most arrows into the gold circle."

Running the tip of one finger over the smooth, varnished wood of her bow, she shook her head. "White men do the strangest things for fun," she muttered, half to herself.

"Humor us on this one," he urged, unable to keep from grinning at her absurd overconfidence. "Put every arrow you can, smack into the center of the target."

"Very well." She nodded in breezy anticipation. "What else do I need to know?"

"We'll start sixty yards away, then move to fifty. Ordinarily, men shoot from a greater distance." He smiled with forbearance at her frown of concentration. "But the gentlemen won't take unfair advantage of the fairer sex this afternoon. Otherwise, at the Hunt Ball that Lady Idina is planning none of the women would dance with the men and they would have to dance with each other."

Jennifer burst into laughter, the sound as infectious and carefree as a child's. "I should like to see you waltzing with Euan Bensen," she said. Her dark eyes sparkled with merriment, and Thorne felt his heart trip and stumble. She had the happiest way about her. Her brilliant smile sent a shaft of warmth straight through him, like a beam of sunshine breaking through the clouds on a rainy day.

"Perhaps you'd care to make a small wager with me," he suggested, ignoring a twinge of conscience.

"If you lose, you'll dance with Euan?"

"No, I can't bet on Bensen's willingness to make a fool of himself. But we could wager on something involving just the two of us."

She spoke with astonishing self-assurance. "The highest score between us wins?"

"Exactly. What would you like to win—aside from seeing me trip around the dance floor with Euan Bensen in my arms?"

"Mm." She tapped one finger against her pursed lips. "Lady Idina told me you have an exceptional stable of Thoroughbreds at Eagleston Court. I would like to choose one of your hunters to ride in Lord Combermere's fox hunt."

"Agreed."

"And you?" she asked. "What would you like to wager for?"

"A walk together when the tournament is over. Nettlefold has a lovely woods on the other side of the stream. I'd like to explore it with you."

"Agreed."

"Just the two of us," he clarified. "No one else."

She foolishly stuck out her gloved hand. "We will shake on it."

As he took her slender fingers in his, he had the guilty feeling he was filching candy from a youngster. But it wasn't candy he intended to steal on the stroll that afternoon—his guilty feelings be damned.

It was time for the contest to start. There were eight archers in all. The order of succession had been determined by the drawing of lots earlier. Thorne would shoot fifth, Jennifer last. He knew he could best her easily. Every person in the competition would probably surpass her score. He was also determined to defeat Euan Bensen.

Combermere, Anthony Trevor-Roper, Lady Avice, and Bensen all shot before Thorne. Of the first four participants, Euan took the lead, putting one in the gold, one in the red, and one in the blue. A polite murmur of encouragement ran through the onlookers after each person completed his shots.

Thorne's turn was next. With his left shoulder facing the target, his feet spread far enough apart to ensure a relaxed, well-balanced stance, he carefully nocked his arrow.

There wasn't the faintest whisper of a breeze. In a smooth movement, he relaxed his hand and allowed the bowstring to slip off his gloved fingers. The arrow flew in a graceful arch to the center of the gold. He put the next two shafts in the red. A ripple of applause rewarded his fine performance. Thorne looked over and met Euan's envious gaze.

"Well done," Combermere called to his friend.

"Thank you, Basil," Thorne replied with satisfaction.

Muriel Trevor-Roper and Viscount Lyttleton followed, neither improving on the previous scores. Then it was Jennifer's turn.

Thorne watched indulgently as she took her place in front of the nearer target. She loosed all three arrows in rapid-fire succession, not even taking time to aim fully and carefully, but snap-shooting in the premature fashion of a beginner.

Zip. Zip. Zip.

He wasn't surprised at her hurried approach. He'd tried to warn her that she was overbowed. No one with her slight frame could hope to control such a heavy draw weight.

Keeping his eyes fastened on her trim little figure, he didn't even bother to look downfield at her target. Thoughts of the coming stroll in the woods brought a smile of anticipation. He intended to taste those provocative lips, to discover if they were really as soft and sweet as they promised to be.

One kiss.

That was all.

Just to satisfy his curiosity.

The burst of unexpected applause jarred Thorne from his daydream. He swung his disbelieving gaze to her target.

All three arrows were buried in the center of the gold!

Jennifer smiled to herself at the comical look on the duke's face. He was flabbergasted. But it was just as she'd expected. Nothing could be easier than shooting at an immovable target from a fixed position on even ground.

After the clapping and shouts of praise died down, the archers advanced together to the targets at the opposite end of the green.

"I thought you'd never taken part in a tournament before," Eagleston chided, as he strode beside her across the closely cut grass.

"I never have," she replied. She took a happy little skip, hurrying to keep up with his long stride. "But my sister and I hunted with a bow and arrow since we were young."

"You must have had a very fine teacher," the duke grumbled. "But I still intend to win my bet."

She shrugged complacently. "We shall see."

Thorne longed to see the light of admiration in Miss Elkheart's exotic brown eyes. He wanted her to look at him the way she'd looked at Euan when she'd learned about his championship title. The way she'd looked at Thorne before he'd told her the Garter hadn't been awarded for bravery in battle.

Certain she'd never repeat her incredible success, on his next turn Thorne carefully placed his arrows in the target. Two in the gold and one in the blue, again besting Bensen's shooting by a single hit.

When it was time for Jennifer to shoot, she loosed her feathered shafts in the same lightning-bolt fashion as she'd done before.

"Six gold," the scorekeeper called.

"Hooray!" Lady Idina cried from her chair on the sideline. She tossed her dainty plumed hat into the air, while the audience broke into spontaneous applause.

"What phenomenal shooting!" Combermere shouted from his place on the field. The earl grinned and raised his bow in salute to her skill.

Jennifer whirled about and gave her host a quick, happy curtsey. "It was easy!" she cried with a gurgle of laughter.

By this time, even the kitchen servants had stopped their duties and come to watch. The upstairs and downstairs maids, along with the tweenies, scullery girls, and cooks, joined the footmen, stableboys, gardeners, coachmen, and grooms on the green lawn. They stood behind the seated aristocrats, barely able to suppress their excited hurrahs. The thought that an untitled miss from the brash, democratic country across the sea could outshoot this gathering of la-di-da lords and ladies tickled their fancies.

Of her rival archers, only the earl of Combermere, Viscount Lyttleton, and Lady Avice, his sweet little sister, were smiling at Jennifer in warmhearted reassurance. She was taken aback by the other contestants' disgruntled expressions.

Ahahe! she thought woefully. Had she known they'd be such poor sports about losing, she'd never have agreed to play their silly game.

Once more, they all marched to the opposite end of the clearing and took their places. This time Eagleston didn't say a word. Jennifer watched in growing curiosity as the first four took their turns. No one matched her accuracy.

When Eagleston took his position, she smiled at him in sincere encouragement. Of all the other archers, he had the best form. *Nihoe* would have been impressed with the Englishman's smooth, relaxed movements, his superb coordination, and his instinctive aim. This time, he buried three arrowheads in the gold, then turned to meet her gaze, his deep blue eyes glinting with satisfaction.

She clapped enthusiastically. "Excellent shooting for a *veho!*" she called to him. He grinned with diabolical charm, as if daring her to repeat her previous successes.

She did.

At the completion of three rounds, Jennifer still retained a flawless lead.

Chapter 5

Miss Elkheart won the archery tournament with a near-perfect score, placing seventy arrows in the gold and two in the red. Thorne came in second. Euan followed closely on his heels to take third place. Jennifer accepted the winner's prize—a gold lapel pin crafted in the shape of an arrow—with the easy grace of a born winner.

Whistling and cheering in delight, the entire Nettlefold staff, from the highest ranking land steward to the lowliest lamp boy, gave her a standing ovation. Her fellow contestants, with the exception of Miss Trevor-Roper, displayed the good sportsmanship so revered by the British ruling class. To everyone's disapproval, Muriel stormed off the field in a blind rage.

"I'll give you that tour of the Eagleston stables anytime you're ready, Miss Elkheart," Thorne said.

"Thank you, Your Grace," she answered, her expressive eyes warm and generous. In an impulsive gesture, she reached out and took his hand, gently squeezing his fingers.

"No thanks are necessary," he protested with a rueful shake of his head. "I always pay my debts, Miss Elkheart. I'm just grateful you didn't insist on wagering for a diamond brooch or half of my yearly rents."

She chuckled as she released his hand. "I am certain you were not the only person who expected me to place dead last. And I would much rather take that walk in the woods you spoke of earlier, Your Grace, than extort a piece of jewelry or a large draft of money from an unsuspecting white man. Does your invitation still stand?"

"Of course," he said, quickly hiding his surprise.

She looked over at the pink-and-white pavilion, where the housemaids and footmen were scurrying about. "We would have to go right away," she pointed out, "before the banquet table is ready and everyone is invited to sit down." She glanced at her hostess and added, "If that is all right with you, Lady Idina."

"Go, go!" Dina insisted with an imperious wave of her hand. "The staff won't be bringing the food out from the kitchen for another quarter hour or so. Go and enjoy your stroll. Eagleston knows our oak grove as well as his own. He can point out all the bucolic sights." She turned to the duke with a knowing lift of her brows. "Be back in fifteen minutes sharp," she instructed, "or I'll send out a search party."

Euan Bensen, who was standing at Lady Idina's elbow, immediately tried to wedge his way in between Thorne and Miss Elkheart. "If you're going for a walk, I'd like to come along," he said with a triumphant grin. "We can invite Viscount Lyttleton and his sister, as well. I'm sure Lady Avice would enjoy an invigorating tromp through the glen."

Jennifer scarcely glanced at the handsome fellow. "Perhaps another time, Mr. Bensen. Right now, I have something of a private nature to discuss with His Grace." She tempered her refusal with a dazzling smile.

Euan's square jaw dropped. If there was one thing the ladies adored about him even more than his bulging muscles and massive shoulders, it was his irresistible charm. He couldn't have been more astounded had Jennifer just administered a swift kick to his behind.

Lady Idina took Euan's arm and patted his sleeve in consolation. "I can't have all the available gentlemen traipsing off willy-nilly and leaving me here alone. As Lady Paramount of the tournament, I'm choosing you to be my assistant for the rest of the evening."

Euan turned to Lord Basil, expecting their host to offer his sister the help she needed.

The stocky, sandy-haired earl shrugged. "Dina knows I'm no good at that kind of folderol. I'd set a bishop next to butcher, if it were left up to me."

Thorne drew Jennifer's hand through the crook of his elbow as he favored his rival with a victorious grin. "Sorry, old man," he said, "but someone has to help Lady Idina with the last minute touches, while I perform the duty of entertaining our visitor from America."

Jennifer laughed, the sound as joyful as sleigh bells on a Christmas morning. "Should I be deflated to learn that entertaining me is considered a duty, Your Grace?"

Combermere clapped Thorne soundly on the shoulder. "You have exactly fifteen minutes to talk yourself out of this one, my friend."

"Then we'd better be off," Thorne agreed.

The two walked side by side over a quaint wooden bridge that spanned Nettlefield's rushing stream. They were soon in the midst of a grove of giant trees, the brick manor house and its cultivated lawns hidden from view. The ground was littered with tiny acorns that crunched beneath the soles of their shoes. Jennifer tipped her head back and looked up at the branches rising fifty feet or more above them.

"This stand of oaks is part of the ancient forest that once covered much of England," Eagleston told her. "Only isolated pockets of the primeval oakwood still remain."

"What happened to the rest of the forest?"

"Our navy always favored English oak for shipbuilding." He pointed to a nearby tree. "Those large horizontal branches gave the shipwrights the strong brackets and angle-pieces that held a British man-of-war together beneath the pounding of cannon balls and smashing waves."

Jennifer had spent nearly three weeks in London, and the fresh outdoors smelled like very heaven. Butterflies danced on the pale yellow blossoms of woodbine that trailed along the dirt path they followed. Thick green leaves fluttered in the broken canopy above their heads, allowing patches of the late afternoon sky to show through.

She drew in a deep breath and exhaled in delight. *"Nakoe!"* she said. "It is beautiful here!"

"What does that word—"

"Shh! Listen," she whispered.

The duke paused and glanced over his shoulder, but seeing no one, he looked at her questioningly.

Before he could say another thing, she placed a finger to her lips. *Listen!* she mouthed silently.

Bumblebees hummed in the air, gathering nectar from the yellow-and-white daisies and the lavender mallow that bordered the pathway. Hidden in the dense foliage beyond, grasshoppers chirped their rasping songs.

Then they heard the faint rustle in the undergrowth that had first attracted her attention. They turned their heads to spy a squat, ugly toad hop out from under a hollow log. The creature sat perfectly still, watching the pair of trespassers with bulging, inquisitive eyes before hopping away.

Following the direction of its escape beneath a leafy bramble, Jennifer recognized the bough's glistening ripe blackberries. "We should have brought a pail," she said joyously. "We could have taken some back for the cook."

Thorne watched with interest as she approached the prickly bush. A startled blackbird rose with a noisy flutter from a fruit-laden branch. It gave an angry chatter of alarm as it flew away.

Plucking a berry, Jennifer placed the luscious fruit in her mouth and sighed with pleasure.

He shook his head, indicating that she'd just made a terrible mistake. "There's an old English tradition that says it's unlucky to eat blackberries after Michaelmas Day," he warned.

Her hand froze in midair above a clump of the tempting fruit. She blinked at him, her eyes filled with dubious wonder. "Why?"

"Satan is supposed to have fallen from heaven into a

patch of blackberry bushes on that particular day."

She snatched her hand away from the bush and looked around in amazement. "You mean the evil-maker my mother told me about actually came here to your tiny island?"

He bit the inside of his lip and nodded solemnly. "When the devil landed, his horny hide was pierced by the bramble's sharp thorns. He became so angry that every year, on the anniversary of his fall, he comes back, spits on the fruit, and curses it."

"Nehe!" she cried in disgust, making a terrible face.

Thorne's bark of laughter rang out. "Don't worry, Mohehya," he teased. "It won't be Michaelmas for three more days. You can eat all you want this afternoon. Go ahead and stuff yourself."

Her face lit up at the endearment spoken in her people's tongue. "You remembered my special name."

"Languages come easily for me," he confessed with a lazy, disparaging shrug.

"My father is the same way." Her words were filled with admiration. "He speaks many languages with ease."

Thorne could tell that he'd just risen several notches in her estimation. Unaccountable pleasure surged through him. "What did that word you just used mean?"

"Nehe? It is a Cheyenne exclamation of dismay or disgust. The same as saying, 'Oh, drat!' or, 'Oh, no!' "

"Or, 'Oh, yuck?' "

She giggled. "That, too."

"And the word you used earlier?"

Her eyes twinkled joyfully. *"Nakoe* is a cry of surprise and astonishment. It means, 'Oh, my goodness, how wonderful!' "

"Tell me your real name again," he urged. "This time, I'll remember it."

"Vonahenene."

"Vonahenene," he repeated thoughtfully, committing the word to memory. "Morning Rose."

"But not the rose that Lady Idina cultivates in her garden," Jennifer quickly explained. "I am named for the wild rose that grows on the prairie." She lowered her thick lashes, then peeked up at him with a wistful smile. "You will make me yearn for my home and my family."

He moved to her side in three swift steps. "I don't want to make you homesick," he said, without pausing to think. "I hope you'll come to like it here in England." Where the bloody hell had that come from? The pretty little Yankee was starting to get under his skin. He'd better watch what he was saying, or she was liable to misunderstand his intentions.

She popped another blackberry into her mouth and rolled her eyes in consideration. "I like your countryside much better than I like your cities."

"I do, too," he agreed, his gaze fastened on her lower lip, stained with purple juice.

It took all his self-control not to reach out, catch the enticing drop on his fingertip, and place it on his own tongue. The rich berry juice wasn't all he wanted to taste.

"So your mother warned you to beware of the devil's cunning ways," he said, his words low and raspy.

"My great-grandmother, too," she replied in perfect innocence. "When my sister, Julie, and I were little girls, Porcupine Quills told us the story of Wihio, an evil spirit known for his stinginess and gluttony, who could take the shape of humans. Sometimes, the clever Wihio would dress up like a poor, hungry widow and try to steal dried elk tongue from the parfleches stored with food for the winter. *Niscem* warned us to beware. Not everyone we meet in life will be as honorable as he pretends to be."

Thorne searched her magnificent almond-shaped eyes. There wasn't a trace of suspicion in their soft brown depths. "Your great-grandmother was very wise," he admitted, reassured that Jennifer hadn't noticed the telltale hoarseness of his voice.

"So was my mother," she added with an angelic smile. "Little Red Fawn always told us not to stir up the underworld with a long-handled ladle."

"Advice which, I'm sure, has stood you in good stead."

"There have been times when I should have taken her advice more seriously than I did," she confessed. "My impulsiveness is the character flaw I am working hardest to correct.''

He could envision Jennifer as a child, listening, big-eyed, to her parents' lectures and promising next time to look before she leaped. But they hadn't succeeded in taming the reckless, madcap streak in her nature. He knew, intuitively, that she would bring that same playful spontaneity to her lovemaking. The thought nearly robbed him of his breath.

Thorne knew he was caught on the horns of an unresolvable dilemma. He wanted the half-wild little Yankee miss.

But he couldn't have her.

He dared not even consider it.

Miss Elkheart was, after all, the unmarried granddaughter of a distinguished American senator. Short of creating an international incident, Thorne sure as hell couldn't seduce her. And he damn well couldn't marry her. He couldn't think of any female less suited to be his duchess. Unless, of course, he suddenly found himself a penniless invalid, in which case, she could provide their daily sustenance by hunting game with her bow and arrow and picking wild berries in season.

As though reading his thoughts, she plucked another berry from the bough. This time, she held it to his mouth, offering to feed him the ripe fruit as if it were a perfectly natural thing to do. Her fingertips grazed his lips, and Thorne's heart thudded to a halt. He met her clear gaze, opened his mouth, and let her drop the berry inside.

To Thorne, the intimacy of her gesture was unbelievably, staggeringly erotic. It was all he could do to stand there, trying vainly to control his erratic pulse, while he waited to see if she'd repeat her actions. He had no idea what the gesture meant to Jennifer.

"Is that a custom among your father's people?" he asked, forcing himself to speak in his usual languid manner. "To feed one another?"

Her friendly gaze held no awareness of the drugging images that were befogging his overtaxed brain. "No," she confessed with a pert wrinkle of her nose, "I just wanted to sweeten you up." Her smile faded, and she looked at him with somber eyes. "I have something very important to say to you."

"Let's sit down on that fallen tree over there," he suggested, "and I'll be happy to listen."

He led her to the log, spread his handkerchief out so she wouldn't spoil her stunning green-and-white dress, and then sat down beside her. He waited for her to begin, the lengthening silence filled with the pleasant sounds of the forest.

Miss Elkheart folded her hands primly in her lap and stared down at her thumbnails, as though what she was about to say was going to be painful.

"I want to apologize for being the cause of those stories in the newspapers about us," she said contritely. "My grandfather explained that my reckless actions brought embarrassment down on you." She looked up from beneath her thick lashes to meet his gaze, her earnestness mirrored in her soft brown eyes. "I know you were angry with me when you first came today, and I do not blame you. It is just that sometimes I do not understand the manners of the white people." She offered him a remorseful smile. "And like all Cheyenne, I love to play jokes."

"You have nothing to apologize for, Miss Elkheart," he said, startled by her confession. Most women would have been quick to place the blame where it belonged—squarely on his shoulders. "It was my fault, not yours. I was far more angry at myself this afternoon than at you. I should never have come to your dinner party uninvited. And there's no excuse for my unmannerly behavior, for I knew exactly what I was doing."

She removed her forest-green hat, balanced it on her lap, and absently ran her fingertips across its long feather. "Why did you do it?"

"I've been asking myself that for the last two days," he admitted with a grimace.

She peered at him from the corner of her eye. "And what was your answer?" she queried saucily.

"I've the devil's own temper when I'm crossed, Miss

Elkheart, and you made the mistake of telling me 'no.' ''

She tipped her head back and laughed in merriment. Then she clutched her hat, jumped to her feet, and glided over to the blackberry bush. "I thought I was the only one who acted on impulse and landed herself in a patch of prickly pear," she said gaily. Her eyes sparkled as she plopped another berry into her mouth. "I have not been caught in such a naughty prank since I was a child."

"Did you get into mischief often?"

She nodded, clearly untroubled by the sins of the past, and pressed the tip of her finger to her lips to lick off the berry juice.

"Tell me about it," he encouraged. "What was the worse scrape you were in?"

Twirling the green hat on the tip of her moist finger, she looked up at the branches overhead in pensive reminiscence. "The summer my twin and I were thirteen—"

"You have a twin?" he interrupted.

She smiled at his astonishment. "Yes, my sister and I are identical twins."

The thought of another sloe-eyed beauty exactly like Jennifer Rose Elkheart boggled the imagination. "Where is she now?"

"Julie went to Edinburgh with our Uncle Benjamin, while I came to London with Grandpapa."

"Do you have any other brothers and sisters?"

"A brother. Black Hawk Flying is eight years younger. Now do you want to hear my story or not?"

He gestured with a languorous wave of his hand. "By all means, go on, Miss Elkheart. I'll try not to interrupt again."

"The summer my sister and I were thirteen," she repeated with an impatient sigh, "we were out riding. We were supposed to stay within the boundaries of our parents' ranch, but this time we disobeyed the rules. I was showing Julie my new trick of standing on my pony's back while at a gallop, when I took a tumble. I flew in a great somersault and landed on my backside." She demonstrated the vault by spinning her hat over her hand.

"Did you hurt yourself?"

"Only my pride. But two cowboys from a nearby ranch were mending fences, and they saw me fall. They were our neighbor's sons, only a few years older than my sister and I. The youngest one laughed out loud and hooted at me for being such a show-off. I was embarrassed and furious, so I called him a nasty name. When Julie and I got home, my mother could tell that something was wrong. My shirtsleeve was torn, and I had a bruise on my elbow. Rather than admit the truth, I told her that the boys had made fun of us for no reason and called us terrible names."

"What did your mother say to that?"

"She believed me," Jennifer answered sheepishly, "even though Julie stood there in silence the whole time, which should have alerted her. My mother has bright red hair and a *vehoka* temper to go with it. She was lifting down her old squirrel rifle from above the fireplace when my father walked in. He could tell she was not planning to hunt squirrels."

Captivated by the artless innocence of her tale, Thorne leaned forward and rested his elbows on his knees. "Did your father believe you?"

Jennifer rolled her eyes and slowly shook her head. "*Nihoe* can look right into your soul and read it like a book. He sat me on a kitchen chair, crouched down in front of me, and asked me to tell him the whole story from beginning to end. Naturally, I started to bawl like a baby because I knew he would quickly sense the truth. I admitted through sobs of humiliation that I was the one to call out a derogatory name."

Although her cheeks were flushed with guilt, Thorne was positive she hadn't used an obscenity. "What did you call the young cowboy, Mohehya?"

Jennifer lowered her lashes and stared down at the ground. "I called him a pimply-faced *veho*," she admitted, the words barely discernible.

"Shame on you!" he scolded, unable to smother a chuckle. "If you got a spanking, you deserved it."

"Cheyenne children are never spanked," she said solemnly, "but the disappointment in my father's eyes hurt far worse than any spanking ever did. And I had to write a letter of apology, which was a rather unpleasant task, believe me."

"Well, I hope you learned your lesson," Thorne teased with a grin. "Surely, you don't go around calling people bad names anymore."

She moved to stand directly in front of him, where he sat on the fallen log. Plopping her hands on her hips, she bent forward, till they were almost nose to nose. Her dark eyes twinkled with impishness. "I would never call *you* a pimply-faced *veho*, Your Grace," she promised, her words brimming with laughter. "All Cheyenne children are taught to be respectful to their elders."

Giving no warning, he caught her by the waist and pulled her between his knees. Her skirt brushed against his legs, and the muscles of his thighs tautened in pleasurable anticipation. "I'm no graybeard, yet," he growled.

Jennifer looked down on Eagleston's upturned face and searched his smoldering eyes in fascination.

Hesc! He'd shifted shapes again!

His lazy, indolent mood had disappeared without a trace. This virile, aggressive man, who held her so easily imprisoned in his grasp, exuded an air of strength, courage, and an unwavering intensity of purpose. Something deep within her responded, like a prairie blossom opening its petals to the morning sun.

"I think we should go back to the manor now," she stated, breathless. "Lady Idina and Lord Basil will be wondering where we are. Perhaps they are worried."

"They're not worried," he assured her. "They know you are perfectly safe with me."

His long fingers easily spanned her waist. He moved his thumbs across her ribs in a deliberate, exploring manner. Unlike the foolish white women, Jennifer never wore a corset. That, however, was supposed to be a secret.

It wasn't anymore.

The light of discovery glittering in his shrewd eyes told her he didn't mind one bit.

Unhampered by the presence of boning and lace,

Thorne felt her trim figure stiffen with umbrage at his shocking familiarity. The childhood years on her father's ranch had left her as lithe and supple as a willow. It took all his strength of will not to slide his hands upward to capture her small, uptilted breasts. His gaze locked with hers. He searched the brown eyes for some trace of guile, some glint of deception. No one could be so pure and untainted.

She glowered at him, daring him to say a word about the lack of stays. "We were supposed to return in fifteen minutes," she insisted. "I am going back now."

"You can't return alone," he coaxed. "You might get lost in the woods and have to spend the night outdoors with the toads and crickets."

"I am not afraid of the little forest creatures," she scoffed. "It is the two-legged rodents who are dangerous."

"I've never been called a rat before," he complained with a laugh. "At least, not to my face."

Jennifer tried to wriggle free, found it impossible, and decided she'd have to pull her knife. Just how she was going to get to it with his hands clamped securely around her waist, she wasn't sure.

But his sense of fair play must have surfaced, for he released his hold and rose to stand beside her. "Very well," he agreed with obvious reluctance. "We'll go. But first, there's something I've been longing to do all afternoon."

"What?" she asked warily.

He slid his arm around her and drew her close, till her body rested against his muscled frame. Jennifer felt the formidable strength she'd only suspected until that moment. He cupped her chin in his hand and gently lifted her face to his.

"This," he whispered as he bent his head and brushed his lips lightly across hers.

He'd been right.

His mustache wasn't stiff and wiry.

Jennifer had never been kissed by a beau before. Eager for her first experience, she closed her eyes, puckered her lips, and waited for the harmless buss she expected.

To her astonishment, Eagleston's mouth parted slightly. He nibbled her upper lip, the edge of his teeth tracing a line of greedy exploration from one corner of her mouth to the other. Then he traversed her lower lip, drawing the delicate tissue between his own lips as though he was sipping a delicious and intoxicating nectar.

Hesc! What kind of a kiss was this?

Her eyelids popped open. She shoved ineptly at his chest, as a shimmering sensation of pleasure rushed through her.

"I've been yearning to discover if your lips taste as sweet as they look," he murmured against her mouth. The delectable scent of blackberries mingled on their breaths.

At the sound of his husky voice, a slow, languid heat flared up in Jennifer's abdomen and spread through her lower limbs. The combination of dreamy lethargy and breathtaking excitement proved so enthralling, she slid her arms around his neck and proceeded to taste his mouth, exactly as he'd demonstrated a moment ago.

As she greedily drew his lower lip between hers, he pulled her even tighter, till their bodies were pressed together. Then he tilted his head and covered her mouth with his, his tongue slipping boldly between her parted lips.

Jennifer could feel his heart pounding. Or was it hers? She met his questing tongue with her own, and each soft, warm stroke they shared sent liquid lightning through her veins. A mysterious energy seemed to fuel her, making every muscle tighten with an unfamiliar tension. Yet she was certain that if he released her, she'd fall to the ground in a heap. So she clung even tighter.

With a groan deep in his chest, he slid his hand down, cupped her bottom beneath her bustle, and lifted her up against him. His hard male bulge reminded her forcibly of a rutting stallion, and in that frantic instant, Jennifer realized that she had aroused his reproductive instincts.

Instincts that should never be called forth, except in the most restricted and controlled situations.

She hadn't been raised on a horse ranch without learning something.

Eagleston must have felt her sudden panic. He broke the kiss and let her slide slowly to the ground. His sharp, aristocratic features were harsh, his eyes shuttered and unreadable. He appeared to be struggling to regain control of his emotions.

Jennifer stepped back, her incredulous gaze locked with his. She'd never felt so . . . so confused. She touched her bruised lips with the tips of her shaky fingers. *"Nakoe!"* she murmured on a long, drawn-out sigh.

A corner of his mouth twitched sardonically. "My thoughts, exactly, Miss Elkheart," he said. He took her elbow and guided her down the path that led to the manor. "We'd better rejoin the others before Lady Idina sends out that search party."

Chapter 6

Lady Idina paid no attention to protocol when it came to seating her guests. Thorne wasn't surprised at the lack of formality. At Nettlefold house parties, Dina tended to do pretty much as she pleased. If people took offense and made a fuss, they weren't invited back.

So when he found the untitled American miss had been given precedence at the table over a duke, a viscount, the heir-apparent of a barony, and the daughter of a marquess, Thorne didn't blink an eye.

What did amaze him, however, was that not even Muriel Trevor-Roper raised her brows in question. Everyone seemed to accept the fact that Miss Elkheart would be awarded the place of honor next to Lord Combermere. Perhaps because she'd bested the Britons in archery, they made a point of waiting politely behind their chairs until she'd been seated, as though she were visiting royalty. Now that he thought about it, they'd been treating the victorious Yankee like a little princess all afternoon.

Nevertheless, Thorne was pleased to find himself sitting beside her at the dinner table. Jennifer's conversation—as unpredictable and convoluted as it might prove to be—was never boring. To his further satisfaction, Euan had been placed next to Lady Idina at the far end of the table.

"Did you enjoy your ramble?" Lord Basil asked Jennifer when everyone had found their places and were comfortably settled.

She gave him a cheerful nod. "His Grace tried to scare me by saying I might get lost," she replied in a scoffing tone. "But I am more at home outdoors than I am in your great stone buildings. I almost got lost at St. James's Palace the night of the court ball. I wandered into a small room and found the duke..." She stopped short and looked down at the fragile china setting in front of her.

Basil met Thorne's gaze, his perceptive eyes twinkling at the heightened color on the young woman's cheeks.

Thorne essayed the slightest shake of his head. He had the distinct feeling that both Basil and Dina were watching his growing attraction to the American with avid, if not to say *delighted,* fascination. He would have to quash that misunderstanding immediately. There'd be no wedding bells pealing at Eagleston Court in the near future.

"You're a born toxophilite, Miss Elkheart," Euan complimented with a toadeating smirk. "That's the first time I've been bested by a lady. I hope it's the last."

Jennifer looked up from the soft-shell crabs on her plate and met his gaze with a bright smile. "I was only five years old when my father made my first bow and set of arrows. He took me and my sister hunting, showing us how to creep quietly up on small game at first. As we grew older, we hunted deer and elk with him, using stronger bows."

Muriel's high-pitched voice was strident with incredulity. "You've shot wild game with a bow?"

"My father is an excellent hunter," Jennifer proudly informed her mesmerized audience. "When I was a child, *nihoe* killed several grizzlies with a rifle. But he said it was a much greater thrill to bring down a black bear with one well-placed arrow."

Up and down the table, everyone paused in their meal to study her with wondering expressions.

"Have you ever killed a bear while bow hunting?" questioned Avice in an awed voice.

"No," Jennifer admitted, "though I begged my father to let me try. He insisted it was too dangerous. My largest trophy was an imperial stag with seven points."

Viscount Lyttleton gave a low whistle of appreciation.

"That *is* impressive." As everyone's gaze turned his way, he flushed to the roots of his orange-red hair.

"Luckily, we'll have a chance to redeem ourselves in your eyes after our poor showing in archery," Basil told his American guest. "My sister has a hockey game planned."

Jennifer's brown eyes sparkled inquisitively. "A hockey game?"

Thorne leaned closer to Jennifer and spoke in a sardonic tone. "Lady Idina's idea of a successful house party is to have as much bruising competition as possible without starting an all-out war. Today's tournament was only the beginning. If we're still speaking to one another after field hockey, there will be parlor games guaranteed to alienate an only child from his mother."

"Wrong!" Dina contradicted with a burst of laughter. "There'll be a cribbage match with prizes for the players who tote up the highest scores."

"Naturally, if you'd rather just watch the hockey game, Miss Elkheart," Lord Basil said kindly, "you needn't feel obliged to participate."

"I will join in everything you do," Jennifer replied without a moment's hesitation. "I want to learn as much as possible about your customs."

"I'll just bet you do," Muriel commented with a snide curl of her lip. She affected an air of disdainful superiority and looked away, as though the trivial conversation was beneath her.

Anthony glared at his sister, then turned to smile ingratiatingly at Jennifer. "What Muriel means, Miss Elkheart, is that we all hope you'll enjoy learning about our country."

"British people have a great love of sports," Bensen said in an attempt to smooth things over, "and they always strive to win. We wouldn't want to shock you with our aggressiveness. We can be rather brutal on the playing field."

Lady Idina forked a bite of crab into her mouth and looked around the table, her jade-green eyes bright with mirth. "To my knowledge, Euan, the only thing that's

shocked Miss Elkheart, so far, is the barbaric English custom of buying husbands for our young virgins."

"Of *what*?" Muriel demanded. She set her wineglass
down with a plop. The dark red liquid splashed on the
snowy cloth. A lackey hurried to mop up the stain, and
she glared at the man as though the spilled wine was his
fault.

Jennifer lowered her lashes, then peeped up, afraid
she'd offended them. "I *was* shocked when I learned of
your custom," she admitted. "But I do not wish to judge
what has been a common practice in your country for
hundreds of years." She ventured a placating smile.
"Naturally, if the strange tradition has worked well for
so long . . ." She paused, too polite to go on.

"What is she talking about?" Lady Avice asked. She
looked from one person to another, her wide eyes filled
with confusion, then ducked her carroty head in a belated
attack of shyness.

"Our marriage settlements," Lady Idina clarified.
"Miss Elkheart and I were shipmates on board the *Etruria*. During our voyage across the Atlantic, we had ample
time to explore the differences in our cultures. Jennie
couldn't conceal her repugnance, when she first learned
that the father of an English bride must pay a veritable
king's ransom to a titled lord before there can be any
wedding feast. She was nearly as appalled as if she'd
learned we were all cannibals."

"But we understood your grandfather to be quite
wealthy, Miss Elkheart," Euan blurted out. "Surely,
there's no reason not to expect that you'll one day be an
heiress."

Thorne knew the reason for Euan Benson's distress.
His parents, Lord and Lady Guilford, would never allow
their eldest son to wed a penniless nobody from America.
The strapping heir-apparent was expected to make an
ample contribution to the family fortune through his
marriage. Euan had a raft of younger brothers and sisters
depending on him.

Jennifer's brow wrinkled in puzzlement at the ill-mannered remark. "What has my grandfather's wealth to do with anything?"

"It could prove to be quite important, my dear," Lady Idina said, "if you wanted to marry an English nobleman. Not to mince words, Euan is wondering if you could afford the blunt it would take to entice a fine gentleman like himself to the altar."

Benson had the grace to flush with embarrassment.

"Idina," Thorne scolded gently. "You make us sound incredibly crass."

Dina lifted her brows in feigned bemusement. "How else would you explain our custom of the dowry, Your Grace?"

"You need not worry about whether my family is rich or poor, Mr. Benson," Jennifer assured him with a husky laugh. "I am never going to marry an Englishman. And I would be humiliated if my father or grandfather tried to purchase a *veho* husband for me." At their dismayed expressions, she sobered at once and shrugged in apology. "It is not the way things are done among my people," she added lamely.

Thorne felt a surge of anger at her breezy amusement. What made her so bloody certain she'd never want to marry an Englishman? It sure as hell wasn't a very flattering remark to make in front of the English lord who'd just kissed her.

Damnation. He'd been told on more than one occasion that his kisses could set a woman on fire. Although she was patently unsuited to be his duchess, the thought of Jennifer kissing any other man chafed like an over-starched collar.

Only Muriel had the gall to ask the question on everyone's mind. "How is it done among your people, Miss Elkheart?"

"Yes, tell them, Jennie," their hostess prompted. "I'm sure everyone here would like to know." The lilt in Idina's voice told Thorne she already knew the answer and could hardly wait to see their reaction.

Jennifer laid her fork down and calmly met their rapt gazes. "It is the Cheyenne custom for a man to court a young girl with soft words of love. When he feels certain that she will accept his proposal of marriage, he sends a trusted friend to her parents. He offers as many horses and furs as he can afford to give, as a sign of his great esteem for their daughter."

"That sounds like a very civilized approach to me," Lord Basil stated in bluff approval.

She rewarded his sagacity with a radiant smile and proudly lifted her head. "When my father asked for my mother's hand, he gave her grandmother a herd of seventy ponies, fifteen trained for war and fifteen for the buffalo hunt. He also presented Porcupine Quills with a stack of pelts, a Henry repeating rifle, and his sacred war shield."

Silence descended the entire length of the table as the British lords and ladies pondered this startling revelation.

"So, it is only the bridegroom's wealth that really matters," Lady Avice clarified softly.

"Oh, far from it," Lady Idina said. "Before a young man can even be considered a fit candidate to court a maiden, he must prove himself to her family by counting coup."

"What's that?" Euan asked. The idea of having to prove himself a fit candidate for courtship was clearly preposterous to him. Since he'd turned sixteen, the unmarried ladies had been throwing themselves at his feet.

One by one, Dina looked at her guests, her dimples peeking out mischievously. "Why, it simply means the young man has killed an enemy in battle. Preferably in hand-to-hand combat, of course, but a shot between the eyes with a high-powered rifle will do in a pinch. And if the suitor has the scars to prove his bravery, so much the better."

"Surely not!" Muriel gasped, clutching her serviette to her magnificent bosom in horror.

No one paid the least attention to her overblown theatrics. All eyes turned to stare at Miss Elkheart, who was serenely cutting her roast beef.

"How else will the parents know that a warrior is able

to protect and provide for their daughter?" Jennifer asked.

"How, indeed?" Lord Combermere concurred. He grinned at Thorne.

"If Jennie should ever wish to marry an Englishman, he more than likely wouldn't be an eldest son," Lady Idina pointed out with a blithe wave of her hand. "The lucky chap would probably be a second born—someone who traditionally enters the military." She looked about the table, her gaze coming to rest on the duke of Eagleston. "Who among the gentlemen here would qualify as a would-be suitor?"

"Well, as far as that goes," Basil said thoughtfully, his eyes also alighting on Thorne, "Eagleston served in the Life Guards, even though he is an only son."

"My father didn't care if I joined the French Foreign Legion and never returned," Thorne remarked dryly. "But I never fought in so much as a skirmish, so I clearly wouldn't qualify."

"You can't mean to say, Miss Elkheart," Euan protested, "that you'd never marry a man who hadn't killed an enemy on the battlefield."

Jennifer looked from one startled face to another, unable to comprehend their disbelief. "Yes, that is precisely what I mean, sir."

"Well, by Jove!" Trevor-Roper said beneath his breath. The exquisite dandy slouched back in his chair and twirled the stem of his wineglass between his thin fingers. "Looks like I'll have to buy a commission in the Seventh Lancers and pray for war."

"Anthony!" his sister scolded peevishly. "What a terrible thing to say."

"I don't suppose it'd count if we shot someone in a duel?" Lyttleton asked hopefully.

"Duels have been outlawed for years," Lady Avice told her brother. "Have you ever killed someone in a duel, Bertie?"

"No, but I could always try," he answered sheepishly. "Trouble is, I don't really have an enemy."

"You'd be more likely to end up getting yourself

killed," Thorne admonished. "We'll just have to satisfy Miss Elkheart's bloodthirsty cravings on the hockey field."

"But no one's ever been killed in one of our hockey games," Avice complained, frowning in disappointment. It was apparent the green girl thought Jennifer would make a wonderful sister-in-law.

Thorne folded his arms in disgust at their patent idiocy. "Maybe we'll get lucky, and someone will break his foolish neck."

"Well, whatever happens, the game won't take place till tomorrow afternoon," Muriel said, anxious to change the topic. "What activities do you have planned for the morning, Lady Idina?"

"Nothing in particular," she told them. "Everyone is on their own. You can go riding or driving in the park. Or sleep till noon, if you're so inclined."

"Then would you care to go riding with me, Miss Elkheart?" Euan asked, taking immediate advantage of the situation.

"Thank you," she replied, "but I cannot. Tomorrow morning I am going to visit the duke of Eagleston's stables and choose a mount for the coming fox hunt. I won the privilege in a wager this afternoon."

"How very clever of you!" Avice cried, clapping her hands in admiration. "The duke has bred some of the finest hunters in England. Were you certain you'd win the tournament?"

"Not at all," Jennifer protested. "I had no notion of what to expect."

Basil met Thorne's narrowed, contentious gaze and grinned. "That wasn't very clever of you, old chap," he goaded, undeterred, "to chance one of your best hunters on an unknown rider."

"I merely hoped to be generous to our foreign visitor." Thorne spoke in his most bored, affected drawl. "We wouldn't want our little Yankee visitor to go home thinking we were uncivilized barbarians—marriage settlements and dowries not withstanding."

*　　*　　*

The next morning, Lady Idina drove Jennifer over to Eagleston Court in a low-sprung basket phaeton pulled by a dainty Welsh pony.

"I am so happy I finally got a letter from Julie," Jennifer told her friend as they clattered over an ancient stone bridge.

When the post had arrived earlier, she'd sat down on the manor's wide steps and read it through twice while she waited for Dina to be ready to leave.

"Is Julie enjoying her stay in Scotland?" Idina called above the rackety crunch of the wheels.

"Yes," Jennifer replied. She clutched her bonnet, the long ribbons flying out behind her in the early autumn breeze. "She wrote all about Edinburgh and its great castle. Uncle Benjamin rented a quaint little house covered with ivy, where they can see the castle looming on the rocky cliff above the town. They would like me to come for a visit with Grandpapa, but there is not enough time before we leave."

When their stay in England came to an end, Jennie and her grandfather would travel on to Constantinople. As his country's special envoy, Senator Garett Robinson was scheduled to visit Turkey, where he would present the diplomatic petitions of the American president to the sultan.

"The house in Edinburgh sounds quite lovely," Lady Idina said, negotiating a sharp turn in the road. "But you sound a bit worried, Jennie. Is there something wrong?"

"Not that I can tell," she answered with a frown. "But I wish Julie had written less about the medieval city and its surrounding countryside and told me more about the vision quest that took her to Scotland in the first place." She pulled Julie's letter from her handbag and stared down at it thoughtfully. "Did Julie write you, too? I know you received something in the post."

Idina shook her head. "Your uncle wrote to thank me for my kindness to you and your sister during our ocean crossing, which is pure foolishness on his part, for I never do anything that it doesn't please me to do."

"It was thoughtful of Uncle Benjamin to write," Jennifer said as she returned the letter to her bag. "Perhaps he will invite you and Lord Basil to visit Edinburgh."

Idina cast a brief speculative glance at Jennifer. "Dr. Robinson's interest is strictly professional," she said. "Did you know that he asked permission to examine me on board ship? He hoped to suggest some type of surgery to correct my impaired gait."

"Yes, he told me. My uncle likes you very much."

"There's no doubt in my mind," Lady Idina continued with studied disinterest, "that the kind doctor was motivated by the most altruistic of reasons."

"I also know you refused his request," Jennifer chided. "And while his examination would have been strictly professional, I suspect my uncle was motivated by something more than a physician's desire to heal."

Lady Idina touched Jennifer's sleeve. "That's what I admire most about you, my dear. You and your sister are so incredibly honest. From the moment we met, you both accepted my infirmity without batting an eyelash. No sad, pitying looks. No embarrassed questions. No worrying about being seen with a cripple, lest people think you were not quite fashionable. You never even asked me how the accident happened or if the injury could be fixed. You simply accepted me as I was and offered your friendship. Do you realize how unique and special that is for someone like me?"

"*Hesc!*" Jennifer cried. "Julie and I do not judge people by their outward appearance. Our father taught us to look for the person within and not be fooled by fancy costumes. *Nihoe* said no amount of battle regalia can hide a coward's heart. And our mother warned us many times that no one can make a soft deerskin parfleche out of an old bull buffalo's hide."

"Or a silk purse out of a sow's ear, either," Lady Idina said with a laugh. "Oh, Jennie! I can hardly wait for you to meet the dowager duchess of Eagleston. You will bring a breath of fresh air into that poor woman's life."

"What is wrong with the duke's mother?"

"Nothing that a little happiness wouldn't set right."

They left the dense grove of trees and broke into a

clearing. Idina drew back on the reins and brought the pony to a halt. "Now, there's a sight that never fails to dazzle me," she said, "no matter how many times I see it."

Ahead, the country seat of the duke of Eagleston rose up against the wooded hillside, four stories of golden stone bathed in the morning sunlight and surrounded by acres of lawn, gardens, and parklands. Its rambling wings and galleries were partially hidden by a screen of ancient oaks and lime trees.

"*Hesc!*" Jennifer exclaimed in amazement, unable to believe her eyes, for she'd immediately recognized the palatial dwelling.

"It is impressive, isn't it? Most of the time, only Lady Charlotte and the servants are there. Thorne comes down from London to visit his mother every so often, but he rarely stays long. He's always jaunting off to foreign places. Restless, I guess." Lady Idina signaled the little pony, and off they went up the long, graveled driveway, Jennifer clutching her hat.

"No wonder she is so unhappy," Jennifer said, "living alone in that enormous building."

"It's more than a building," Idina replied. "It's a historical site of great importance, and a museum, too, of sorts. Eagleston Court houses a collection of treasures accumulated over the course of four centuries. Thorne's ancestors acquired rare books, manuscripts, and paintings with a diligence seldom equaled by their contemporaries. There are sculptures, murals, and tapestries created by the most skilled artisans in the world."

"But it is not a home," Jennifer insisted solemnly.

Lady Idina searched her eyes in puzzlement. "Why do you say that, dear?"

"Because I have seen this place before."

"You've been to Eagleston Court? When?"

"Many times in my dreams. I have seen a white-haired lady, dressed in widow's black, weeping, alone and broken-hearted."

Idina tightened her fingers around the reins, and the little pony tossed its head in complaint. "My land, Jennie!

You've seen Lady Charlotte in one of your visions?"

"I did not know her name," Jennifer said with a perplexed frown, "but if the duchess lives in this house, then it is her I have seen. The grieving lady's tears have touched my soul."

"Welcome to Eagleston Court, Miss Elkheart," the dowager duchess said with a gracious smile. She took Jennifer's hand in both her own. "Come and sit down, my dear. Tell me all about yourself. I so rarely get visitors, and I have never met a young lady from America."

Jennifer squeezed the thin fingers with gentle compassion. "I have wanted to tell you for a long time that you must not be downhearted anymore, Your Grace." She heard Idina's startled intake of breath, but persevered in her self-appointed mission. The older woman's anguish, coming to her in dreams, had troubled Jennifer for the past ten months. "You have wasted too many tears already," she said, "on a matter that is best forgotten."

Lady Charlotte made no attempt to pull away. Rather, she clutched Jennifer's hand as though afraid to let go. Her voice was thin and reedy. "What do you know about my heartache, *ma belle?*"

At the touching endearment, Jennifer grinned. "*Voyons,*" she said, immediately switching to the easier language, "how nice to hear someone speak French! I learned it long before I studied English."

"*Hélas!*" the duchess exclaimed, following her lead. "English is such a barbaric tongue, *n'est-ce pas?*"

"I thought I was the only one who believed that!"

Her sad eyes brightening at her visitor's happy laughter, Lady Charlotte slipped her arm about Jennifer's waist and drew her to the sofa, where they sat down together. "I get so lonely for someone to gossip with in my own language," she confided in French, "but this morning, we must converse in English for Dina's sake. Like all genteel young ladies on this island, she's had a few cursory lessons from a French governess. I love Idina as though she were my own daughter, but the truth is, females in Great

Britain are shockingly uneducated by Continental standards."

"I understand enough to know when you're talking about me," Idina said with a dimpled smile, unperturbed by the criticism. She sat down in a small settee across from them.

Lady Charlotte patted Jennifer's hand, her narrow, patrician features solemn as she returned to English. "Now, tell me, *ma mie*, why did you say that my tears were wasted?"

"Because your dead husband was a *veho*, Your Grace," Jennifer told her with quiet candor. "And like every white man, he broke his promises. It was to be expected."

The duchess stared at Jennifer in astonishment. "You mean because he was an Englishman?" Her accent grew more pronounced in her agitation. "My father arranged my marriage to the British peer," she explained in a rush. Unshed tears pooled in her violet eyes. "I was only fifteen, but I looked and acted much younger. I never once thought of refusing to obey *mon pére*, though I secretly cried my heart out at the thought of leaving my home and everyone I loved. Henry Blakesford was twenty years older than I and far more worldly. He . . . he wasn't kind to a frightened, innocent girl, not even at the start." She paused and stared blankly into space. "To others he appeared cultured and urbane. I am convinced Papa had no inkling of his true nature."

On the striped silk love seat, Lady Idina sat motionless. Jennifer knew by her stricken silence that she'd never before heard these searingly painful confidences.

"You must not continue to be disheartened," Jennifer told the duchess, her voice steady and grave. "None of your husband's faults were your doing, and the world understands that you are entirely blameless."

"Do . . . do you know what his faults were?" Lady Charlotte asked in a voice so low the tortured words were barely audible.

"No, I do not," Jennifer freely admitted, "and I do not have to know. For through the mists of sleep, I have seen you walking beside the white-tailed deer, the powerful symbol of true love between a man and a woman. The Maiyun, the mysterious spirits who watch over mankind, know that you share no part of his guilt." She looked at the middle-aged duchess, whose hair had turned white prematurely, and offered a comforting smile. "Set your sadness aside, Your Grace. It is time to return to life."

The duke of Eagleston sat at one of the carved octagonal tables, deep in thought. He was poring over the letter, deciphered nearly a week ago, which Lord Doddridge had "borrowed" from the Russian Ambassador's diplomatic pouch. What proved to be a simple substitution cipher had revealed a text containing such mundane information, it seemed hardly worth the effort of employing a secret code.

"This is the library," Lady Charlotte said, swinging open the tall double doors. She ushered two ladies, attired in ravishing day dresses straight from Paris, into the cavernous room filled with thousands of books.

At the trio's unexpected entrance, Thorne casually slipped the paper beneath a heavy Russian dictionary and rose to his feet.

"There you are, *mon cher*," his mother called. "I thought you were still out riding, or I would have sent someone to fetch you. Come and meet the lovely guest Dina has brought over from Nettlefold. We've been having the nicest chat."

"I've met Miss Elkheart," the duke said with a welcoming smile as the three women joined him. "In point of fact, the young lady has come to collect a bet."

His mother beamed, a rare smile lighting up her long, thin face. "Did you know that Jennifer is part French on her paternal side? Her great-grandfather's name was Antoine Tréfouret. The Tréfourets were originally from Bassompierre in the Loire Valley." She turned to Jennifer and confided, no doubt for the second, if not the third time, "My father was the marquis de Bassompierre. I may have even known the descendants of your great-grandfather's cousins when I was a little girl."

Stunned, Thorne studied his usually morose parent. He

hadn't seen his mother so animated since before the death of his father eight years ago. Charlotte Marie Blakesford, née Le Fresne, had been locked in the throes of melancholy for so long, Thorne had almost forgotten the natural gaiety and charm that once brightened his childhood. What could have wrought this sudden, miraculous transformation?

"I didn't know that about Miss Elkheart," he confessed, his mind whirling in confusion.

"Oh, la, la, she speaks perfect French!"

"Does she, indeed?"

"My father always spoke French to my sister and me when we were little," Jennifer expounded with a puckish grin. "My mother and everyone else around us spoke in Cheyenne."

The sympathy in Lady Charlotte's voice was as touching as it was sincere. "So you never spoke English as a child, either, *ma mie*?"

Thorne's frail mother still pronounced her adopted language with a heavy accent, making it difficult for outsiders to understand her, especially when she was excited. It was one of the reasons she'd never felt truly at home in England.

"Only a little," Jennifer said. "Sometimes the Mounted Police would ride over from Fort Walsh to ask my father to be their guide. Constable McLean would try to converse with us girls in pidgin English mixed with sign talk. When my mother got angry, she chattered away in a kind of English all her own. Mountain talk, she called it. My sister and I didn't really study the language until we were sent away to school at fourteen."

With a beguiling smile, Lady Charlotte touched Jennifer's thick, braided chignon. "*Ma petite*, you have the most beautiful hair. It must be absolutely gorgeous when it's down." The dowager duchess appealed to her son in her old lilting, lighthearted way. "Don't you think so, *mon cher*?"

"Yes," he answered with a choked voice, amazed and overjoyed at the incredible change in his mother.

"I've helped Jennie brush her hair out in the evenings,"

Lady Idina offered, her serene expression revealing no clue to his mother's remarkable metamorphosis. "It comes all the way down to her hips. I doubt it's ever been cut."

To Thorne's astonishment, his mother smiled joyously as she stroked her fingertips across Jennifer's smooth cheek. "You'll make a beautiful bride one day, *mon ange.*"

He expected Jennifer to pull away in embarrassment. Instead, she reached up, clasped the older woman's hand, and pressed a kiss to the thin fingers. "Thank you, *nisem,*" she said with a gentle smile, as though some secret bond had been established between them.

Holding the American girl's hand in both of her own, Lady Charlotte turned to her son. "Jennifer saw me in a vision long before she ever left her homeland. *Vraiment,* the child recognized me the moment we met." The duchess touched the beaded ornament hanging round her neck and continued with a beatific smile. "She gave me this medicine bundle with the feather of a sandhill crane to protect me. Suddenly things that have been weighing on my mind, for far too long, have no power to disturb me."

Thorne looked in shock at the amulet fashioned in the shape of a turtle. "Mother," he adjured, "surely you don't believe in—"

At Idina's sudden, startled look of warning, he halted and stared at the three women, speechless.

Visions?

Dreams?

Medicine bundles?

Sheer lunacy.

Yet after eight years of trying and failing, of ponderous physicians and well-dressed quacks, of silver-tongued clergy and paid lady's companions of every age and description—hired in the hope that if his mother wouldn't talk to him, she'd confide in someone—he had ceased his futile attempts to lift her lingering malaise. And now, now in the space of a single conversation, the gay, darling *maman* of his childhood had been restored to him.

Thorne wouldn't destroy his mother's newfound happiness, no matter what piece of insanity had brought it about. Magic charms, incantations, witchery, omens, or soothsaying, it made not one bloody jot of difference to him. For whatever the means had been, he wouldn't chance breaking this enchanted spell and sending his mother back into her private world of despair. Not if his very soul depended upon it.

Later, when it was safe, he'd get the answer from little Miss Chatterbox herself.

The duchess misinterpreted his silence. "Were you busy, dear? I'm sorry if we interrupted your work."

He glanced down at the stack of books piled on the table, making certain the letter in Russian was completely hidden. "You didn't disturb me at all. I was merely looking a word up in the dictionary."

"Did it have anything to do with the gamble you lost?" his mother asked.

"No, I foolishly wagered that I would best Miss Elkheart in Lady Idina's archery contest yesterday. I was thoroughly and soundly defeated. The clever Yankee is here to choose a hunter from our stables to ride in the Nettlefold fox hunt."

"Can you choose any hunter you wish?" Lady Charlotte asked the young woman in genuine surprise.

"No," said Thorne.

"Yes," Jennifer replied in the same instant. "The wager was for me to choose any horse in your stables."

"Any horse that's safe for you to ride," he corrected.

"You never said that."

"It was implied."

"*Hesc!* You would renege on a wager in front of your own mother? I would not have believed such lowness of you."

"Did you make such a caveat, Your Grace?" Lady Idina inquired sweetly.

"Whether or not I said it out loud is immaterial. I refuse to put Miss Elkheart up on a mount that would be dangerous for her."

"You needn't worry about that," Dina assured him.

"I've seen Jennie ride. She's an expert horsewoman."

"*Eh, bien,* that settles it," Lady Charlotte announced serenely. "Let's go out to the stables and watch *la petite* pick out a mount of her own choosing."

Chapter 7

"**H**e is the one!" Jennifer exclaimed the moment the stableboy led the stallion into the paddock. "I shall ride that beautiful creature in the fox hunt." She executed a little hop-skip of happiness as she clapped her hands in anticipation. "I can hardly wait!"

Lady Idina immediately agreed. "Oh, Jennie, he's marvelous!"

"Gillard should never have brought the black out," Eagleston said smoothly. "Barleymow is an unacceptable choice. Make another." He smiled with indulgence at the two excited ladies, then turned his cool blue gaze on the towheaded lad who had the bad luck to be holding the animal's bridle. The hapless Gillard touched his fingers to his cap and cringed.

Her straw bonnet hanging down her back by the length of its burgundy ribbons, Jennifer stepped closer to the railing. She shaded her eyes with one hand and stared in delight at the hunter.

"*Nakoe!*" she whispered in breathless admiration. "Barleymow is magnificent!"

With a well-shaped head on a muscular neck and spirited eyes that flashed a warning, the horse whinnied and pranced about in a spectacular display of beauty and grace. A blaze of white covered his forehead. Two long white stockings stretched up his hind legs from the fetlocks nearly to his hocks.

"The men will bring out another choice," Eagleston in-

111

formed her in a honeyed drawl. "There are plenty of mounts to show you."

"I do not need to look at any more horses," she replied gaily. "We have seen ten already, and it would not make any difference if you showed me thirty more. I have made up my mind. Barleymow is the one I shall ride in Lord Combermere's hunt."

Eagleston paid no attention. With a languid wave of his hand, he gestured another groom to come forward. The burly fellow stood in the open stable door, holding the reins of a gentle chestnut mare. At the duke's signal, he dutifully paraded the sturdy, short-legged animal back and forth in front of them.

"You couldn't go wrong with Ladybug," Eagleston counseled like a doting uncle. Resting his hand on the paddock fence, he braced one booted foot on its lower rail. "She's well-mannered, trained to wait patiently at a gate, takes her turn without a nip or a kick, and never refuses a jump. She has all the qualities of a good, safe hunter."

From the corner of her eye, Jennifer scrutinized the broad-shouldered man beside her. The perfect fit of his dark blue hunting jacket only hinted at the solid arms and chest hidden underneath. But the tight riding breeches boldly displayed his corded thighs, and the shiny black boots, reaching almost to his knees, showed off his well-muscled calves.

She was reminded of the splendid Greek athlete holding the discus at the British Museum. Beneath the static suppleness, the still grace, the poised, unmoving elegance, lay the promise of a swift, controlled explosion of male strength and dexterity. The potential of all that unleashed energy made her as nervous and fidgety as a prairie dog scampering past a nest of rattlers.

In an outward display of composure, Jennifer propped her elbows on the fence's top railing beside him. "Ladybug is a fine mount," she politely agreed, "but I am going to ride the black stallion."

"Barleymow's too much horse for you," Eagleston said, his words edged with the faintest ruffle of annoyance. "He'll jump you right out of the saddle." His reproachful gaze drifted down her small frame and up again, as though it were her fault she hadn't grown any taller.

Cupping one hand to her mouth, Lady Charlotte leaned closer and whispered in Jennifer's ear. "I don't think the black stallion has ever carried a woman, *ma fille*."

The sharp-eared duke cocked his head and grinned. "Mother's right, Miss Elkheart. I should have thought of that in the first place. Barleymow's never been trained to a sidesaddle. He'd refuse to carry you out of the paddock."

"No problem there," Lady Idina offered succinctly. "Jennifer always rides astride."

"She . . . what?" The duke stared at his lovely neighbor as if she'd announced that a woman had just been elected to their Parliament. Then he swung his shocked gaze to Jennifer.

She shrugged and smiled victoriously. "I have ridden astride since I was a toddler and my father took me up before him on his great war horse. I do not remember ever seeing a white woman's saddle until I visited my grandfather's home in Lexington when I was fourteen years old."

At that unhappy piece of information, Eagleston glanced over to the head groom waiting patiently at the stable door. "That will be all, Worsley," he called to the elfin, bowlegged man. "You may put the rest of the cattle back in their stalls."

The duke turned back to the three ladies standing beside him at the paddock fence with a peaceful, utterly charming smile. "Mother, why don't you take Lady Idina back to the house and enjoy a little visit over some tea, while Miss Elkheart and I discuss this matter privately?"

"That's a wonderful idea, *mon cher*," the dowager duchess agreed. Her violet eyes alight with pleasure, she slipped her hand through the crook of Idina's arm. "It's been far too long since I've enjoyed a cozy gossip."

Flashing Jennifer a look of encouragement, Lady Idina

had the audacity to give her a thumbs-up sign. "We'll see you both inside shortly."

Jennifer watched the two women walk away, arm in arm, under the shade of Lady Charlotte's lavender parasol. Taking a deep, fortifying breath, she cast a speculative glance at Eagleston. He was studying her beneath hooded lids.

"What would you like to discuss, Your Grace," she asked breezily, "now that we are alone? If you think you can dissuade me from my decision, you are sadly mistaken. My mother always said I had the born stubbornness of a Kentucky mule when it came to getting my own way."

"Let's go have a better look at Barleymow," he suggested, a hint of deviltry in his smile. "Once you meet the brute up close, you may realize he's no fit mount for a lady."

"Very well," said Jennifer with a confident toss of her head. "I will be happy to take a closer look at Barleymow. I do want to make his acquaintance before I ride him."

As they entered the cool, dimly lit building, Thorne gave an imperceptible nod of dismissal to the three grooms hovering just inside the stable door. His well-trained servants immediately disappeared, heading toward the carriage house.

Jennifer's hand rested lightly on his sleeve. Thorne felt the faintest tremor of uncertainty in her fingers. He suspected it wasn't fear of the stallion that had brought on her sudden bout of wariness.

She paused for a moment in the shaft of bright sunshine flowing through the open doorway. Her lustrous hair, fastened at the crown of her head in a braided chignon, reflected the rays of light in a bewitching display guaranteed to stop a man in his tracks. Deep reddish highlights in the dark brown mass gleamed and shimmered like moving waves of satin. Miss Jennifer Rose Elkheart was a beauty, all right. He couldn't take his eyes off her.

Thorne shoved one hand in the pocket of his riding coat and assumed a pose of nonchalance. He was determined not to reveal what an entrancing picture she made with her bonnet swinging on its ribbons. The young lady from America was entirely too strong-willed for her own good. Her mother was right. Any gentleman foolish enough to wed Jennifer would spend a lifetime trying to slip a halter on her without getting kicked black and blue in the process.

He led the obstinate little Yankee up to Barleymow's stall, making a satisfying thump with the toe of his boot against the lower board as he approached. He hoped she didn't realize the blunder was purposeful.

At the sudden noise, the temperamental stallion neighed and shook his long mane, the bridle reins slapping restlessly in the close confines of the enclosure.

"As you can see," Thorne said equably, "the nasty beast is not very well-mannered. Watch out he doesn't try to bite you."

She shook her head and tsk-tsked in reproach. "Maybe you should wear spectacles, Eagleston."

"I can see where I'm going without eyeglasses," he informed her. "Just be careful around the stallion. He's high-strung and restless on the best of days. This morning he's dangerous."

She cast him a look of pure disgust. "Any spirited horse will try to take a chomp out of you, if you startle him, Your Grrr-aciousness. And if you intend to lumber around the stable like a grizzly stuck in a buffalo wallow, it might be better if you waited outside."

Thorne ignored the mangling of his title, along with the unflattering description. He smiled and spoke in a dulcet tone. "Not a chance, Miss Elkheart."

"Please yourself."

"I always do."

To his disappointment, Jennifer chose not to respond to that leading remark. Instead, she placed her foot on the gate's lowest slat and, without an apparent qualm, stepped up.

"Hello, big fellow," she said, stripping off her gloves and stuffing them into her handbag. She reached out and patted the splash of white on Barleymow's forehead. "I shall call you Moxtavevoe. That means Black Cloud in Cheyenne. Would you like a treat?"

She'd come prepared. She withdrew a carrot from her bag, leaned out over the gate's top board, and offered it to the formidable stallion. Her full silk skirt, capriciously gathered over her little bum in an enormous rose pouf, presented a target a half-blind abbot would find hard to ignore.

Thorne was no monk.

His vision wasn't failing him, either, in spite of her clever insinuations.

He lifted his cupped hand in automatic response to that inviting derrière, then thought better. He wasn't exactly in her good graces at the moment. First, he'd convince the headstrong Yankee she should ride Ladybug in the hunt tomorrow, then he'd follow his natural inclinations.

Barleymow whickered in curiosity at the unfamiliar sound of Jennifer's deep contralto. He nuzzled her hand, learning her scent, then helped himself to the carrot.

She leaned closer and ran her palm over the finely chiseled head. "Such bold eyes tell me you are very smart," she confided. "Smarter than most of the people who ride you, I think." She glanced briefly at Thorne, an elfish smile playing about her lips, then back to the big animal. Her words were soft and beguiling. "Are you smarter than me, Moxtavevoe? Will you please take me riding in the fox hunt and not try to toss me off at the first jump we make?"

The stallion nodded his head vigorously, throwing it up and down as though he actually understood what she was saying.

Thorne watched, incredulous.

He'd never seen Barleymow, whose disposition bordered on the diabolical, behave like a tame house pet. Although the stablemen never complained in front of him, Thorne knew they hated to take their turn exercising the black when its owner was away.

The sight of the diminutive woman in the chic Parisian gown calmly feeding the spirited stallion had a strange affect on Thorne's respiration. He felt as though he'd just had the wind knocked out of him and couldn't quite catch his breath. He made a strangled sound deep in his throat, but she seemed not to hear.

Giving Barleymow a quick, reassuring pat, she stepped down from the gate. "I will be back in a moment," Jennifer told the horse with a blithe smile. She ducked into an empty stall without so much as a glance at Thorne and reappeared in only minutes holding a length of white material edged with ruffled lace.

Her petticoat.

Before he could guess her intention, she opened the slatted gate and entered the stallion's crib.

"Now, Moxtavevoe," she said beguilingly, "you and I will become friends in the old Cheyenne way."

Holding the swath of fine cotton lawn in her hand, she ran it over the large animal's glistening ebony coat, gently stroking the tapered neck and massive shoulders, then sliding the soft material across its powerful withers and flank. All the while, she crooned to the beast in a low, husky, singsong chant.

Thorne stared in disbelief as the slender girl gentled the mighty stallion, moving the undergarment bunched in her hand down the long forehead and over the velvety muzzle. With every movement she made, with every strange yet soothing word she spoke, Barleymow grew more and more docile.

Something deep within Thorne responded to that entrancing scene in the tranquillity of the dim stable. He gripped the gate's top rail with a white-knuckled hand as a sudden and unexpected primal urge clutched his loins. He would have jerked spasmodically had it not been for the years of practiced subterfuge, resulting in an unflagging self-control. It was as though Jennifer were rubbing the smooth cloth, permeated with her captivating female scent, over Thorne—gentling him, seducing him, breaking him to her touch.

Barleymow nickered playfully and nudged her shoulder whenever she paused. Like a loving mother with her child, she laughed and chided the stallion for his naughty behavior in her people's soft-spoken language.

Thorne bit his lip to stifle a groan.

She was as carefree and joyous as a butterfly.

He was insane with lust.

His suffocated breath seared his lungs. His heart hammered painfully. Hard and hot, more taut with sexual excitement than he'd ever been in his life, he moved quietly up behind the heedless girl. Without a word, he dragged the petticoat out of her hand and tossed it across the gate's top rail.

Jennifer whirled and blinked at him in surprise, as though she'd actually forgotten his presence. A humbling thought. Thorne's male pride rebelled at the possibility.

"Come here, you stubborn little Yankee," he said gruffly. He caught her hand and drew her into the empty cubicle nearby, which had been filled with fresh, clean straw that morning.

Jennifer looked up at the tall English lord with a doubtful frown. Those heavy-lidded blue eyes watching her now showed no sign of his previous vexation. Rather, they beckoned her with a promise of some sweet, unknown, unimaginable pleasure.

Hesc! Eagleston couldn't have changed his mind so quickly about her riding the black. She suspected the proud aristocrat rarely changed his mind about anything.

"Why do you persist in calling me Yankee?" she demanded in an attempt to regain her equilibrium. She tugged her hand free of his grasp and stepped back, bumping up against the wall behind her. "I think you do it just to provoke me."

His lips quirked, a spark of laughter lighting his eyes. The message in his shuttered gaze sent the blood rushing to her extremities, leaving her brain numb and her lungs constricted. He placed his hands on her shoulders and moved closer, till his riding boot brushed against the toe of her dusty kid shoe. "Now why would I want to do that, Miss Elkheart?"

"Perhaps because I irritate you?"

"No *perhaps* about it," he agreed in his faintly amused, self-indulgent manner. "You're the most exasperating, unpredictable female I've ever had the misfortune to lose a wager to."

He firmly, inexorably, edged her backward, not stopping until her flounced skirt was smashed flat against the stall's rough boards behind her. Eagleston's shrewd *veho* eyes were positively wicked with delight, telling her he knew exactly what she was feeling in her posterior region.

Jennifer splayed a hand against his chest in a futile attempt to force him to keep his distance. She half-expected the resilient padding on her rump to spring back into shape and bounce her right into his waiting arms.

A tingling excitement spread through her, heightening her awareness of her own small figure standing so close to his muscular frame. They shouldn't be alone together like this, and he knew it.

Jennifer shrugged to show her lack of concern. "Is that why you wanted to discuss the matter in private? So you can talk me out of my chance to ride Barleymow?"

His slow, lazy grin released a flood of shimmering anticipation deep within her, which she immediately tried to contain. If he attempted to kiss her, she'd have to tell him no. He was, after all, not the man waiting in her future. The Maiyun had sent the dream again to tell her to beware of this golden-haired *veho*. She would never be so foolish as to fly in the face of their warning.

Still, what was the harm in a kiss?

The duke seemed strangely unaware of her dilemma. He untied the satin bow at the base of her throat, releasing the ribbons of her bonnet. "You refuse to listen to reason," he stated philosophically. "What's the use in trying to discuss your choice of a mount for the hunt, Miss Elkheart, when you seem to be immune to any appeal to logic?"

She watched in dismay as he calmly tossed her hat on the large mound behind him, the dark burgundy ribbons a vivid contrast against the bright yellow straw. The certainty that he'd removed ladies' headpieces many times before—in just that elegant, casual manner—left her rattled and short of breath.

"I am a great believer of logic and reason," she asserted. But her deep voice cracked, revealing her conflicting emotions. It was a conflict she didn't want him even vaguely aware of.

As she stared into his half-lidded eyes, she fought the impression of being ensnared in a paralyzing web of seduction. A practiced seduction, with no quarter given to innocent lambs. His confident gaze drifted over her upturned face and came to rest on her mouth, making it all but impossible to think rationally.

He bent down, till his lips were only inches away. "You believe in superstitions and dreams like a foolish child," he scolded gently.

She jerked her head away, smarting beneath the arrogant skepticism. "You do not believe in visions?" she challenged.

"No." He caught her chin and turned her face to his. "I believe in what I can hold in my hands, in what I can see with my own eyes."

Incensed by the cool irony in his cultured British voice, Jennifer tried to wriggle free. "Let me go," she insisted. "I want to rejoin the others."

"Don't, Vonahenene," he whispered, her Cheyenne name on his lips as soft and enticing as a bearskin rug on a lodge floor. "Don't push me away, Morning Rose."

Thorne drew the infuriated girl into his arms. He could feel the calming effect of her language on her stiff form. God, if only he knew her people's words of seduction . . . he'd be so gentle . . . so tender.

As though reading his thoughts, she stopped trying to break away and relaxed against him. "Eagle's Son," she breathed on a sigh.

For a long, hesitant moment, she rested her forehead on his chest. Then rising up on her toes, she slid her arms around his neck and lifted her face for his kiss.

As their lips met, her tongue brushed the tip of his in an unabashed greeting, her willingness giving rise to the hope that she'd longed for this moment as much as he.

He gently drew her warm, moist tongue into his mouth, reveling in the sweet, sweet taste of her, prolonging the intimate penetration till they were both breathless and gasping for air.

Thorne broke the kiss to follow the delicate line of her jaw with his open mouth, then trailed soft kisses down her throat, as he inhaled the floral scent of her golden skin. His frustration earlier that morning had aroused the need to dominate, to bend her to his stronger will, to force her to admit she'd been wrong, that she couldn't ride the stallion in the hunt, but that she bloody well could ride Thorne here and now.

The graphic picture his thoughts conjured up sent a sharp thrill of desire spiraling through him. The image of her incredible softness pressed up against his hard, naked body, her slender arms clinging to him as he sheathed his aching manhood deep within her, left Thorne verging on the loss of control.

Jennifer's fingers tightened at the nape of his neck in shy invitation. He could hear her breath coming in quick, shallow drafts. With a muffled groan, he swept her up in his arms, placed her gently on the mound of loose straw, and lay down beside her.

God above, she was so unbelievably appealing, so vital and filled with life. Some long-forgotten dream, buried deep in his childhood, responded to that inner radiance. He was like a ship-wrecked wanderer, who'd just flung open a treasure chest of priceless jewels. The need to touch her was more than any man could resist.

Why even try?

Propping himself on one elbow, he leaned over her. "Jennifer . . . Mohehya," he murmured.

He cupped her high, firm breast in his palm. His swollen sex pushed against the crotch of his snug riding breeches in frantic anticipation. She watched him with dark almond eyes that grew luminous and dreamy beneath his caress.

Thorne unfastened the tiny pearl buttons that held the front of her dress closed and slipped his hand inside. Beneath her sheer white camisole, her soft nipple rose up

in welcome as he flicked the tiny bud with his thumb. A
startled intake of air told him she'd never experienced a
man's touch like this before. He smiled in heady male
satisfaction.

"That's good," he said huskily. He sensed her confusion and brushed his lips across hers in tender reassurance. "I want to make it so good for you, Jennie."

A voice inside Thorne's head warned him that this was
insane, but his entire body throbbed with an erotic need
that refused to be ignored. He gently pushed the silk bodice of her gown aside to expose one round, smooth globe.
At the sight of the delicate coral tip, faintly visible beneath the gossamer lingerie, his heated blood raged
through his veins.

Covering her breast with his open mouth, he laved the
tautened peak through the fragile undergarment with
quick, rough strokes of his tongue. His heart kicked
against his ribs as she arched her back in a natural, uninhibited response.

"Ah, Eagle's Son," she whispered, "your touch sets me
burning like a wildfire on the prairie."

His spirit soared at her guileless confession. Thorne
closed his eyes in relief, as he smoothed his cheek back
and forth against the satiny mounds that rose above the
ruched lace.

That's what he'd wanted to hear since their walk in the
oak grove the previous afternoon. He couldn't bear to
think their kiss had left her unmoved, when it'd been
such a shattering experience for him.

She threaded her fingers through his hair, cupped the
back of his head in her palm, and guided him to her other
breast, at the same time lifting herself for his lips. He
suckled her through the thin batiste, and she whimpered,
a tiny, feminine sound of delight in the back of her throat
that blasted every iota of his commonsense straight into
oblivion.

"Sweet, sweet, Mohehya," he rasped. "My beautiful,
little magpie."

The deep straw cushioned her bustle, raising her pelvis
slightly, as though resting on a pillow. His hand moved

over her corsetless figure, memorizing the delicate curve of her waist and hip. He reached down and pulled the hem of her gown upward in slow, heart-stopping increments. The memory of her pristine ivory petticoat draped over the stall gate brought a smile to his lips. That was one less tangle of material to overcome on the way to his goal. His practiced fingers glided smoothly over the white silk stocking that covered her shapely calf, then brushed against the frilled edging of her drawers.

He would only touch her.

That was all.

Just this once.

He had to feel her respond to his caress. To hear her cry out in fulfillment as he tenderly stroked her delicate folds.

"I won't harm you, Vonahenene," he promised. "I only want you to enjoy the incredible pleasure I can give."

Thorne slid his hand up her loose-fitting drawers. He knew exactly where to find the tapes that held the two pieces of the undergarment together. The accustomed task of disrobing a female didn't calm the pulsating ache in his groin, but the preposterous feeling that he was about to careen out of control ebbed, if only a little. For the first time since he'd met the unpredictable little Yankee, he was on familiar ground.

"I'm going to untie your ribbons," he said. The urgency in his low voice made his words sound much harsher than he'd intended. God, he didn't want to frighten her. He nuzzled the silken skin behind her ear and ran his tongue around the delicate shell. "Don't be frightened," he soothed.

"I am not frightened, Eagle's Son."

At that moment, his fingertips brushed against something fastened over the cotton material of her drawers, something that felt amazingly like the hard leather sheath of a knife. Thorne paused, searching for some rational explanation.

"That is only my knife," she said softly.

A knife?

Hidden beneath her skirt?

He tried to slide his hand further up her thigh. His fingers became entangled in a thin cord. Familiar ground had just turned into an uncharted maze laid over a bed of quicksand.

"What the deuce?" he muttered.

"And that is my *nihpihist*," she explained.

"Your *nihpihist*?"

"A chastity rope."

"You wear a chastity belt?"

"All Cheyenne maidens wear one. It is our custom."

"What do you do with the knife?" he asked hopefully. "Use it to cut the rope?"

Laughter bubbled up inside her, joyous and unrestrained. She was clearly tickled by his ignorance. "No, we use the knife to cut off the fingers of any white man foolish enough to violate the *nihpihist*."

Jesus.

Lying comfortably in the loose straw, Jennifer looked up into the nobleman's astonished blue eyes. "Do not worry," she told him reassuringly. "I did not warn you to stop. Therefore, you are safe from harm . . . at least for the moment." She smoothed her palm across the velvet lapel of his riding jacket, not at all eager to call a halt to this fascinating new experience. "Of course," she added with reluctance, "I must insist that you stop now."

Propped up on one elbow, Eagleston bent over her. Instead of withdrawing his hand from beneath her skirt, he drew a small circle on the inside of her thigh in a slow, enticing movement. His voice was coaxing and deep. "Must I, Mohehya?"

"I am afraid so," she answered on a long, drawn-out exhalation of air. The feel of his hand on her leg, the sound of her pet name on his lips were doing strange things to her sense of propriety.

She'd been drilled in the strict rules of *veho* courtship at the French embassy school in Washington, D. C. More importantly, her mother had taught her the proper way to behave. A Cheyenne girl did not give herself to a man before marriage.

"I must not let my impulsive nature run away with

me," she added with renewed conviction. "Besides, we came into the stable to discuss the matter of our wager and whether you intend to honor your promise."

He scowled at her choice of words. "I don't think it's a matter of honor," he quibbled. "It wouldn't be very honorable if you tumbled off Barleymow tomorrow and broke your pretty neck." He gave her a teasing smile as he continued to caress her. "You'd be a martyr, while everyone would blame me for letting you ride the brute in the first place. I'd have to flee the country before your grandfather had me hung, drawn, and quartered."

With a laugh, she reached up and brushed the pad of her thumb across the edge of his mustache. He immediately opened his mouth, drew her thumb inside, and stroked it with his tongue. "If I should break my neck," she said, "I would have only myself to blame, for you have warned me not to ride the stallion. But Barleymow will not toss me off."

The duke nipped her thumb with his sharp teeth, and she jerked it free. "How do you know?" he queried.

"Because he told me so."

He grinned down at her. "Barleymow said he wouldn't throw you?"

She nodded serenely. *"Hehe."*

"I take it that means *yes*."

She plucked a piece of straw off his sleeve and flicked it away. "For a blue-eyed *veho*, you are sometimes surprisingly intelligent."

"How do you know that's what Barleymow was saying?" Eagleston scoffed. "Maybe he was telling you the opposite. Maybe you misunderstood him."

"I understood him perfectly," she said with a giggle. "The mighty stallion spoke in Cheyenne."

Eagleston's grin widened. He clasped her leg just above the knee and squeezed playfully. "So, Barleymow spoke to you in Cheyenne, did he? Imagine that. How very peculiar to find a horse here in Warwickshire that speaks your people's language."

She lifted her brows at his blatant disbelief. "It is not the least bit peculiar, Your Grace. All horses can speak

Cheyenne. They are born with the knowledge. Did you not see him talking to me?"

Thorne didn't bother to answer that ridiculous question. Instead, he bent down and kissed her delectable mouth, lingering over the sweet task of persuasion. No woman had ever successfully resisted his determined attempt to have his own way. And in the choice of a hunter for Jennifer Elkheart to ride, he was resolved to make the decision—even if they had to stay there in the straw for the rest of the day, till she finally gave in.

"Talk to me in Cheyenne," he urged. "Teach me some love words, little magpie."

Jennifer shook her head, her eyes aglow with a mischievous charm. "You are dangerous enough as it is, Englishman. I'd be as foolish as the hummingbird who befriended the eagle to give you any words of seduction." But she slipped her arms around his neck and laced her fingers in his hair. She lowered her long, curving lashes and gazed at his mouth. Her contented tone betrayed the assumption that she was going to get her own way. "Since you know, now, that I will not get hurt, will you agree to let me ride Barleymow tomorrow?"

"No."

The drooping lids flew open. He could see in her startled gaze the unhappy realization that he hadn't budged an inch from his intention of talking her out of their wager. "Then you are a man without honor," she declared, "and I will have nothing more to do with you." She braced her palms against his chest. "Now, let me up."

Thorne recognized the streak of obstinacy that tautened her mouth into a tight, thin line. How in blue blazes did she get to be so headstrong? She must have given her parents more than a few sleepless nights when she was growing up. He knew, now, why they lectured her on the virtue of prudence.

"Jennie, be reasonable," he coaxed. "You can choose any other mount in my stables, but I can't let you ride a horse I believe is dangerous. I wouldn't have any honor at all, if I did. Try to understand, little girl. It's a matter of your safety."

"I understand that you are not honoring your promise." She shoved against his shoulders impatiently. "Now, please, let me up at once."

Knowing that if he attempted to persuade her further, she'd try to fight him, Thorne moved back to sit beside her in the straw.

She sat up, twitching the folds of her skirt down over her trim ankles in quick, angry movements. The bodice of her dress gaped open, revealing the entrancing cleavage that dipped below the lacy camisole. She followed his distracted gaze and hurriedly refastened her buttons with an injured air.

Jennifer rose to her feet and brushed the straw off her gown. Sniffing contemptuously, she stuck her aggrieved chin in the air. "It is just as my mother said," she announced, apropos of nothing. "As certain as the wild goose walks without moccasins, a white man can never be trusted."

Mystified, he looked up at her from his place in the straw. "Your mother said that?"

She dusted her hands together as though wiping away the past few minutes from her memory forever. "Many times, Englishman. Little Red Fawn is a very wise woman."

While he was wondering how to politely refute that piece of sheer nonsense, she turned on her heel.

"Wait!" he called, clambering to his feet. "I want to know what you said to my mother."

But by that time, she'd already stalked out of the stable.

Chapter 8

On their ride to Nettlefold Manor in the landau, Thorne realized just how profoundly his mother's demeanor had changed. Lady Charlotte chatted and laughed with the charm and wit that had once seemed inborn in her.

Her sudden decision to accompany her son to Nettlefold that afternoon had thrown the servants into a flurry of excitement. The stablemen had removed the canvas dust cover from her favorite carriage, cranked down its folding top, greased the axle, oiled the springs, and waxed the dark green leather interior. The housekeeper had packed a basket of delicacies from the pantry for the Nettlefold cook, and the head gardener had gathered an enormous bouquet of yellow roses for Lady Idina's drawing room. The entire staff, indoors and out, beamed with approval at the marvelous change in their beloved mistress.

Immediately after the former duke's death, Thorne had believed his mother's vacant sadness was the usual shock every widow suffered at the sudden, unforeseen loss of her spouse. But when the melancholy deepened with the passing years, he'd grown increasingly more baffled.

Henry Maxwell Blakesford had been a selfish, critical, abrasive man, whose key ambition was to one day be prime minister. He rose to the Cabinet post of chancellor of the exchequer, but his arrogant belligerence ended in his political isolation from his colleagues in Parliament.

He had no personal friends. The late duke of Eagleston was scarcely someone whose death would be the source of unremitting sorrow. His son sure as hell had never mourned him.

Finally, Thorne had insisted that his mother be examined by a London physician who specialized in disorders of the mind. After a lengthy and thorough examination, the eminent doctor had stated that the dowager duchess was as sane as anyone. He'd prescribed an herbal tea to relieve her chronic insomnia and left his bill.

The sudden change in Lady Charlotte now was incomprehensible. How could their Yankee visitor, in less than a quarter hour, remedy a despondency that no one else had managed to dispel in eight years?

Thorne hesitated broaching the subject with his mother. But she seemed so cheerful, so like her old, sparkling self, that he decided it would be safe to probe into her conversation with Jennifer.

"What did Miss Elkheart tell you, Mother, aside from the fact that she'd seen you in a vision?"

Lady Charlotte smiled enigmatically. "The young lady knew without being told that I'd become a recluse. She pointed out the grievous error in my thinking. A burden that had weighed on my mind was lifted as though by a miracle." The duchess's violet eyes glowed with an inner serenity that touched Thorne's heart. "Maybe she's not an American heiress after all, *mon cher*," his mother added with a gay laugh. "Maybe she's really an angel sent from heaven to ease my suffering."

After his conversation in the stable with the young lady in question, Thorne had no doubt she was all too human. However, he refrained from shattering his mother's pleasant fantasy. "Exactly what did Miss Elkheart point out?"

"That I had no reason to be ashamed. Jennifer told me that all Englishmen are born incapable of keeping their promises. She said the rest of the world knows this for an absolute fact. Therefore, no one could possibly hold me in contempt because of Henry's deceit."

Thorne gazed at his mother, wondering just how aware

she was of his father's baser qualities. All these years, he'd been certain she knew nothing of her husband's penchant for sexual perversions. She'd given no hint, by word or gesture, that she suspected the true nature of the late duke's perfidious behavior.

"I'm sorry," he said. "I thought, all this time . . ." He paused, not wanting to put into words anything she might not already know. "I'm not sure what I thought."

Lady Charlotte patted his sleeve. "I know, *mon cher.* Even now, I cannot bring myself to talk of your father. Maybe someday, but not yet . . . not today."

Thorne covered her gloved hand with his and squeezed her fingers in consolation. "The last thing I want to do, Mother, is cause you more pain." Relief washed over him. He had no desire to confront his own bitterness or the acrid, lingering guilt that had been his father's legacy.

Blinking back tears of joy, she dabbed at the corners of her eyes with a handkerchief. "To think a slip of a girl would speak so frankly, yet so compassionately, to a woman she'd just met. Only a vision could explain her understanding of a sorrow buried deep in the past."

Thorne made no comment. The obvious answer was that Idina had told Jennifer about his mother's affliction on their way to Eagleston Court.

Before Miss Elkheart had left that morning, Thorne had hoped to question her about what she'd said to the dowager duchess. But the stubborn Yankee had refused to speak to him after their disagreement in the stable. In fact, she'd refused even to look at him.

While the three ladies had lingered over tea and biscuits in his blue-and-gold drawing room, he'd paced back and forth across the rug, hoping the sexual energy that pounded through his veins wasn't half as apparent as it felt. The trio ignored him for the better part of half an hour, until his mother finally asked him to sit down and stay put for five minutes, before he made them all nervous wrecks.

Even when he'd helped his two visitors into their phaeton for the return to Nettlefold, Jennifer had resolutely ignored her host. Thorne attempted a mild jest about her riding the little Welsh pony in the fox hunt. She'd stared right through him as though he were invisible. Lady Idina, however, laughed out loud. Whether his neighbor was laughing at him or with him, Thorne wasn't sure.

Thorne and Lady Charlotte arrived at Nettlefold Manor that afternoon just as the hockey players were ready to take their positions on the field. The gaily striped pavilion was now being used as a spectator's gallery. He led his mother to a chair beside Lady Idina and waited for her to be comfortably settled in the shade of the awning.

"We've already chosen the teams," Idina told Thorne with a welcoming smile. "You're on the Renegades. Our guest from America will play with the Bulldogs. We've gone over the rules for her benefit."

Thorne turned to survey the gathering. "I suppose Miss Elkheart's never played this game before."

Lady Idina followed his gaze to the slim figure in the ivory blouse and lavender plaid skirt. "Her people have a stick-and-ball game somewhat similar to ours. From what Jennie described, it's probably closer to the shinny we played as children."

"Fewer rules and more whacks on the shin," he guessed with a chuckle.

"Exactly." The dimples in her cheeks deepened as Dina smiled in remembrance. "I think everyone plans to give Jennie a little assistance today. We're letting her play center forward in the hopes that she might score a goal. It'd be a nice memory to take back home with her."

If his friends played up to their usual level of competence, there wasn't much chance of that, but Thorne refrained from putting a damper on Idina's plans. He watched the little Yankee talking earnestly with her teammates and was struck with a brilliant idea. There just might be a way he could keep her from riding Barleymow in the hunt and still maintain his honor in her eyes. For some unexplainable reason, he wanted—no, *had* to have—her respect, if not her wholehearted admiration. He couldn't let her go on thinking he was untrustworthy.

Jennifer turned a cold shoulder when Thorne stepped up close beside her. As her teammates moved off down the field, he kept his voice low, so no one else could overhear his astounding proposal. "How would you like to make another wager, Miss Elkheart?"

She peered at him from the corner of her eye, her words tart with suspicion. "What kind of wager?"

"I'm willing to bet my black stallion that your team loses the hockey game this afternoon." He casually tapped the toe of his boot with the curved end of his stick, as though whether she agreed or not was a matter of complete indifference to him.

Come on, little doll. Take the bait.

Jennifer turned to glare at him, a scowl puckering her smooth brow. "I have already won the right to ride Barleymow in the hunt tomorrow. Why would I want to risk losing it in a second wager?"

"You misunderstand me, Jennie," he explained in an apathetic tone. "I'm willing to bet my horse that your team can't win. If they do, Barleymow is yours to keep."

The thrill of owning such a magnificent creature shone in her dark brown eyes. She raised up on her toes in exhilaration and caught his arm, her words filled with wonderment and a burgeoning hope. "Barleymow would be mine?"

"Yours forever."

"And if my team loses?"

He shrugged, making the consequence seem too trivial for words. "If they lose, you ride another mount in the hunt."

Jennifer whirled to look at the players on her team, who were waiting for her midfield. He could almost hear her brain whizzing through the various possibilities. Besides herself, there were ten others, including the goalkeeper. Only Euan Bensen, Viscount Lyttleton, and his young sister, Lady Avice, were familiar to her.

Her eyes narrowed in contemplation as she turned her

head and studied the players on the farther side of the center line. Thorne's team included the earl of Combermere, Anthony Trevor-Roper, his sister, Muriel, plus seven newcomers. There was no way she could assess the performance of either team with any degree of certainty.

Jennifer clutched her stick in both hands and pursed her lips, pondering the wisdom of making such an unlikely wager. Thorne held his breath as the silence between them lengthened and his chances ebbed slowly away. But in the end, her desire to own such a marvelous animal won out against her better judgment.

"Very well, Your Grace," she said. She offered her hand to seal the bargain. "It is a bet. If my team loses, I will ride Ladybug in the fox hunt. But if we win, Moxtavevoe belongs to me."

He clasped her hand, maintaining an expression of cool disinterest. "It's a bet."

She cocked her head and grinned at him. "I can hardly wait to tell the beautiful creature he is mine. And I promise," she added with a lighthearted laugh, "that I will take very good care of him. I will sing him a lullaby every night."

Thorne steeled his heart against the look of joyous anticipation in her eyes. After years of practiced dissembling, it was just too easy taking advantage of her inexperience. He salved his conscience with the fact that the wager she was certain to lose was for her own good.

Yanks were supposed to be shrewd horse traders. He'd certainly gotten the best of this one. "Don't worry, Miss Elkheart," he replied, making no effort to hide his conviction that she didn't have a ghost of a chance to win. "Ladybug will give you a fine, safe ride."

"You just keep your word, Englishman," Jennifer advised before turning to walk away.

As she took her position on the field under a glorious autumn sky, Jennifer looked about in heady anticipation. One of her favorite games as a child was *ooxnistoz*. There were differences in the rules between the Cheyenne stick-and-ball game and British field hockey, of course, but the skill of dribbling a ball on the end of a curved stick as you raced across an open meadow was the same.

She gazed across the center line at the opposing team, scarcely able to keep from laughing out loud for the sheer enjoyment of it. Playing for the ownership of a spirited black stallion added zest to an already exciting afternoon.

Win or lose, this game was going to be fun.

"You're playing left wing," Anthony Trevor-Roper announced the moment Thorne joined his teammates.

"The hell I am," he shot back. "I play center half, and you damn well know it."

"Not today," Trevor-Roper replied as he brushed at the monogrammed pocket of his striped blazer. "I'm captain, and I'm going to play center half."

Thorne clenched his jaw and spoke through gritted teeth. "You don't know jack about playing center half."

"Idina appointed the captains before you arrived," Basil explained with his easygoing charm. "She named Bensen and Trevor-Roper, and they've already designated each player's position. You're left wing."

Thorne stared in disbelief. Center halfback was the most responsible position on the field, the pivot on which the rest of the team revolved. "What the devil—"

"Sorry, old man," Basil commiserated, "but it *is* my sister's house party. You know how Dina loves to upset the apple cart and then watch everyone scurry."

Thorne turned to glower at Idina, who fluttered her fingers at him and smiled waggishly. Damn! She'd done it on purpose! How could she have guessed he'd make that extravagant wager with Jennifer?

Commonsense told him that no one could have foreseen he'd be willing to risk his splendid Thoroughbred stallion on a hockey game. Such a wager defied all reason. And Thorne wasn't known to behave irrationally. Up until the moment he met Miss Jennifer Rose Elkheart.

He unleashed his frustration on Trevor-Roper, jabbing his finger against the man's narrow chest in a rapid tattoo. "All right, I'll play left wing. But if we lose this game today, they're going to serve your liver for supper."

"For God's sake, Eagleston," Anthony complained

with a puzzled frown, "it's only a friendly game. There are ladies playing, in case you haven't noticed. And I don't intend to make a swaggering ass of myself acting the part of the conquering male."

"I don't intend to swagger," Thorne said. "I intend to win."

"Trevor-Roper's captain, old chap," Basil commented in a calm tone. "This afternoon, he's calling the plays." The censure in Basil's green eyes warned Thorne that he was behaving out of character. Where was the usual sardonic, jaded forbearing?

"Hell," Thorne muttered and walked away.

"What the devil's got into Eagleston?" Anthony demanded. "I've never seen him like this before."

Basil grinned. "I guess he doesn't like to lose."

"For Christ's sake, we haven't even played the game yet!"

At the first bully-off, Jennifer seized immediate control of the white leather ball and dashed for the goal with everyone chasing after her, pell-mell. When she crossed the twenty-five-yard line, the opposing goalkeeper, wearing a pair of stout pads to protect his legs, came out of the goal cage to intercept her. A short, stocky man with an enormous walrus mustache, Victor Houlton sniggered confidently as she entered the striking circle.

One thing Jennifer could always count on.

A *veho* would underestimate her ability every time.

She came in close, glanced in a different direction than she intended to shoot, and made a quick scoop pass, lifting the ball slightly off the ground and flicking the shot right by him.

Her astonished teammates cheered in delight. Everything had happened so fast, the other side stared in appalled silence. Nothing was so demoralizing to a team than a goal scored against them in the opening minutes of the game.

"Hooray for Jennifer!" Idina called from her place beneath the pink-and-white pavilion.

Lady Charlotte blew a kiss, and Jennifer waved happily in return. *Nakoe!* She'd known all along this was going to be fun.

The Renegades gained control of the ball on the next bully. As team captain, Anthony Trevor-Roper had placed his sister, Muriel, in the center forward position opposite Jennifer. The tall blonde was strong, but far from fast. She should have been playing defense.

Trevor-Roper passed the ball to his sister the moment he had the opportunity. Euan Bensen easily tackled the ball from Muriel before she could reach the striking circle. The score remained 1 to 0 in favor of the Bulldogs.

The game continued without a pause as Bensen sent the ball to Lyttleton, who quickly moved it downfield. On the smooth grass, the ball traveled fast and true. The Bulldogs played a short passing game. They purposely kept to their left, on the side farthest from Eagleston and Combermere.

Trevor-Roper was responsible for marking Jennifer. Instead of shadowing her, however, he kept on the run between her and Lyttleton, the Bulldogs' inside forward. Evidently, Anthony thought the goal she'd made was blind luck and paid her no heed.

Euan, seeing Jennifer in the clear, sent her the ball. She hit a long diagonal pass between the Renegades' right half and right back to Lady Avice, her energetic left wing. Avice started sprinting almost simultaneously with the pass and gathered the ball before it crossed the sideline. The sprightly redhead returned the ball to Jennifer, who'd shaken off Trevor-Roper once again. When it came to Cheyenne hockey players, flaxen-haired Anthony was a slow study.

The only thing now that stood between her and another score was the Renegade's brawny fullback. From Jennifer's viewpoint, he looked large enough to block out the sun. But big men usually weren't all that fast.

She made a beeline for the goal.

This time their goalkeeper wasn't smiling. Houlton watched her with shrewd eyes, prepared for her trick of glancing in the wrong direction. Instead, she shot right where she was looking.

The goalkeeper cleared the ball easily, sending it

straight back to the middle of the circle, just as Jennifer hoped he would. She returned the shot to the far corner of the goal before he had time to recover.

The score was now 2 to 0.

The Bulldogs roared in triumph. Jennifer whirled around at the sound of their cheers, her arms spread wide, her stick clenched in one hand. Euan Bensen rushed up, grasped her by the waist, and lifted her off the ground.

"Miss Elkheart," he shouted as he twirled her in a circle, "you're fantastic!"

Laughing ecstatically, Jennifer braced one hand on his solid shoulder and clutched her hockey stick with the other. The lavender plaid tam on her head went flying. Her chignon, loosened by her wild ride, fell down her back in one long braid.

From his position at the far side of the field, Thorne stood beside Basil, watching stone-faced. "If he kisses her, I'll kill him," he said quietly.

A discerning smile spread across Basil's genial features. "You'd better keep your mind on the game," he advised.

By halftime, the score was 3 to 0 in favor of the Bulldogs. The players, panting and exhausted, stopped for a rest. The men stood on the sidelines and quaffed mugs of beer, while the ladies plopped down on the grass and sipped tall glasses of lemonade.

Thorne was well aware it was time for the Renegades to review their dismal strategy. When a match was going against a team, the captain was responsible for making a change of positions or devising a new and better plan. Trevor-Roper seemed disinclined to do either.

"If you're going to keep playing center half, you have to start rushing her," Thorne instructed his captain. "Don't hang back. Press her and make her fumble."

No one had to ask who Thorne was talking about. Their looks of mild censure reminded him that proper conduct on the field demanded grace in defeat, not loud-mouthed belligerence.

As the players returned to their positions on the field, Thorne purposely brushed against Euan Bensen. "Keep your clammy hands off Miss Elkheart," he warned in a low tone.

Bensen had the temerity to grin. "Or what?" he taunted. "Pistols at dawn?"

"Or I'll break your neck."

"Your sportsmanship is commendable," Bensen replied with a chuckle. His black eyes glinted with an arrogant challenge. "But we're going to whip your ass, Eagleston. And then, I'm going to give the pretty American heiress a victory kiss."

"You do and you're a dead man."

When the game resumed, Thorne knew he'd have to take matters into his own hands. A player was supposed to stay in his designated position and not tear around the field, getting in another teammate's way while leaving his own area unguarded. But if he was going to save his finest Thoroughbred and keep Jennifer Elkheart from possible injury in the bargain, he'd have to rewrite the strategy books.

At the bully, Thorne intercepted Jennifer's ·pass to Avice. Keeping the ball close to his stick, he dribbled downfield at breakneck speed. The second he was on the edge of the striking circle, he shot.

Goal.

After that, Thorne played a game of hit-and-rush, his sheer determination, power, and pace controlling the Renegade's passing combinations. Two more times he let fly from the edge of the striking circle, hard and true, and the game was tied at 3 to 3.

But time was running out.

With only seconds to go, the Bulldogs gained possession of the ball. Euan Bensen charged down the field with all the finesse of an enraged bull. He passed to Lyttleton on his inside right, who immediately sent the ball to Jennifer. Once again, they were keeping the game as far away from Thorne as possible.

Jennifer slipped by her opponents with the grace of a gazelle. Thorne saw the two Renegade fullbacks waiting for her and knew they'd never keep her from scoring. She was far too quick and nimble for them.

Knowing he had no choice if he wanted to win the game, Thorne charged across the field at full speed, certain that his physical size alone, coming at her like an approaching freight train, would rattle the diminutive girl and make her fumble. Not very sporting of him, considering the fact that he'd been the one to suggest the wager in the first place. He'd make it up to her this evening.

He fully expected Jennifer to pull back in alarm at his headlong approach, flustered into believing that he was going to smash into her, if she didn't leap out of the way.

She never faltered.

With her eye on the ball in front of her, she moved at top speed in a relentless race toward her target. In the last split second, Thorne realized she couldn't be intimidated. He veered aside. Hell, it was either that or crash into her.

By this time, Houlton should have expected her to do the unexpected. Instead, the dolt made the fatal mistake of coming out to meet her once again. Without a pause, she shot the instant she reached the edge of the circle. The ball whizzed right past the dumbstruck goalkeeper.

The game was over.

Thorne had lost Barleymow.

His dream of a stud that would be the envy of his peers had just been blown to Kingdom Come by a sloe-eyed girl who ran like the wind. He hoped to hell she could ride half as well as she played hockey.

Shaking his head ruefully, Thorne glanced over at the spectators watching from beneath the pavilion and paused in his tracks for the space of a heartbeat.

There, seated beside Lady Idina, was Count Vladimir Gortschakoff. The Russian nobleman met Thorne's guarded gaze, a faint smile hovering about his thin, bloodless lips. The shrewd appraisal in his cold eyes told Thorne he'd been watching with keen interest as the supposedly blasé, world-weary British lord played field hockey as if his life depended on it.

Hell and damnation.

Chapter 9

❝**I** do not think I shall ever become skillful with the white man's playing cards," Jennifer confessed to Eagleston. She studied those scattered face up in front of her. "When I go back to London, I am going to buy a set and practice every morning with anyone who knows how to play. Then the next time I am in a cribbage match, I will make a better showing."

Jennifer hadn't lasted long in the tourney, despite the fact that Lady Idina had paired her with the duke, who proved to be an excellent player. Not excellent enough, however, to make up for her disastrous shortcomings. After they'd gone down to a hasty defeat in their initial foursome, he'd suggested the two of them retreat to the library, where it wasn't so crowded and noisy, and he'd instruct her in some of the finer points of card play.

"Just remember in cribbage to count your combinations to fifteen first," Eagleston explained. "Next your runs within the same suit, then your pairs, and lastly, nob if you have it." He pointed to the cards spread across the library table. "Fifteen, two. Fifteen, four. Fifteen, six. And a pair is eight."

At their elbows sat an ivory and jade board intricately carved with Chinese dragons and rows of tiny holes. Eagleston pegged his points with one of the small ivory sticks that served as counters. Earlier, Jennifer had used a jade one to mark her place on the same board. It was easy to see she was falling farther and farther behind as they played.

"Cribbage combines skill with luck," the duke added with amusement. She hated to lose at anything, and he was beginning to sense her mounting frustration. "A player has to be ready to take advantage of any good fortune that comes his way in the deal."

"My sister and I never saw a cribbage set until we were adults," Jennifer stated in her own defense. "We enjoyed simple card games with my parents when we were young. While we lived with Grandpapa in Washington, D. C., *namsem* and a few of his close friends played poker, but only after Julie and I had gone to bed in the evening. It was not considered proper for young ladies to observe gentlemen gambling for money. When we visited Ashwood Hall, his home in Kentucky, card games of any kind were absolutely forbidden."

She watched the duke gather the cards from the tabletop and shuffle the deck with extraordinary ease. The cards seemed to respond to his nimble fingers as if by magic. Eagleston had strong yet graceful hands, a heavy signet ring their only adornment.

The memory of those agile fingers fondling her breasts brought a sudden heat to her face. She lifted her lashes to find him scrutinizing her. A faint smile turned up the corners of his mouth as their gazes met, and she knew her cheeks were stained with a blush of embarrassment.

"Forbidden by whom?" he asked languidly.

The English lord had the deepest, bluest eyes she'd ever seen. The color of the Canadian sky over the sunburned prairie on a summer day. Intense. Brilliant. Sparkling with heat and a hidden danger, as though way up high, just barely out of eyesight, a great golden eagle soared and drifted on the breeze as it searched for its prey.

He dealt the cards without once glancing down. "Was it your grandmother who forbid games of chance?"

It took her a moment to remember what she'd been saying. She shook her head absently, trying to concentrate on their conversation. "No, my grandmother died when my mother was born. Later, Grandpapa married a woman named Eliza Bruckenridge, but I never knew her, either. She was struck and killed by a trolley when they lived in the capital. That was after *namsem* had become a senator. Julie and I were less than a year old at the time."

"And you were living on the ranch in Canada with your family?"

"Yes." She rested her chin on one hand and gazed at the fire across the book-filled room. The burning wood crackled and popped with a cozy sound, reminding her of the enormous stone fireplace that covered the length of one wall in the log house her father had built. "I miss them," she said wistfully. "My father and mother and brother. And, of course, my sister, most of all. Julie and I have never been separated until now."

She paused and picked up the cards he'd placed face-down in front of her. "Games of chance are considered the work of the mischief-maker by Kentucky's genteel society," she added in clarification. "I never understood what Havsevstomanehe had to do with playing cards, but Grandpapa said Julie and I had to abide by the rules laid down by the crabby old ladies who sat on their front porches in Lexington and scowled at the passersby. When in Rome, we do as the Romans, *namsem* told us." She smiled happily as she rearranged the red and black cards in her hand. "Now I am in Britain, and I can do as the Britons."

"I take it your father's people don't subscribe to the idea that games of hazard are intrinsically evil?"

She laughed. *"Hesc!* All Cheyenne love to gamble. We like to win most of all."

"Especially Thoroughbred stallions," he replied with a wry grin.

"Especially that," she agreed. "We often bet for horses during races or contests of any kind. But this is the first time I have won such a marvelous prize in a game of *ooxnistoz.*"

He looked up from his cards, his intense gaze thoughtful. Jennifer knew he was committing the unfamiliar word to memory.

"I'm ready to make another wager, if you are," he offered with good-natured nonchalance. "We could make a little bet right now."

"I am not so foolish as to think I can best you in cribbage," she answered with a knowing lift of her chin.

"You did fine this evening," Eagleston said. "I thought you played amazingly well, considering you're only a beginner."

Jennifer chuckled softly as she placed her unwanted cards in his crib. "Is that why you offered to bet on which one of us would peg the most points in the first round of the tournament this evening?"

He grinned, unrepentant at his brazen ploy. "You can't blame me for trying, Miss Elkheart."

"And you cannot blame me for refusing to risk Moxtavevoe, now that I own him. Particularly on an amusement I have only just learned." She grew quiet, studying her cards, then laid down an eight of clubs.

He immediately followed with a seven of hearts. "Fifteen for two," he said idly. She frowned in concentration as she watched him peg the points. *Nehe!* She wouldn't lead off with an eight again.

The faint sounds of voices raised in excitement could be heard through the closed double doors. The cribbage match was still going on in the manor's large formal drawing room.

"What about a game you know well?" he suggested. "A pastime from your childhood which you could teach me. That way the advantage would be yours."

Jennifer tipped her head to one side and regarded him thoughtfully. "There is a game I could teach you." She wrinkled her nose in deliberation, then shook her head and played her next card. "But even so, I would never risk losing my beautiful stallion."

"We could wager for something else." His soft-spoken words were as sweetly enticing as the fragrance of choke cherry blossoms in springtime.

"Something else?"

"Certainly."

The Englishman had the most beguiling smile when he

chose to be charming. Small crinkle lines gathered at the corners of his eyes. Even white teeth flashed beneath the golden-brown mustache as he laid down another card.

Jennifer absently took her turn, her thoughts drifting further away from the game. She'd heard that some white men had pelts of fur growing on their chest. It might very well be true. They were a hairy race, with all those stubbly whiskers, thick, wiry beards, and huge muttonchop sideburns.

Cheyenne males, who had very little body hair, often went shirtless. Her own father wore nothing more than a breechclout and moccasins during the warm summer months. The Royal Mounted Police, however, always kept their uniforms buttoned up tight, even in the sweltering sunshine. It was a peculiarity she remembered from childhood.

In America, she'd never seen any grown male, even a field hand or a factory worker, without a shirt on. Businessmen wore vests, ties, and coats as well. She'd learned that the stifling layers of clothing were required by polite society.

Like the proscription of gambling by the Lexington matrons, the strange *veho* attitude toward masculine attire made no sense to Jennifer. Especially when one considered that their females sallied forth in evening gowns that exposed not only their bare arms and shoulders, but practically their entire bosom as well.

Jennifer failed to follow the convoluted logic that decreed the sight of a man's unclothed upper torso was indecent. How else could a warrior display the marks of his courage earned during the Medicine Lodge ceremony? Or the scars won in battle?

Realizing that the duke had been waiting patiently for her to take her turn, she tried to bring her mind back to the card play. But the thought of seeing Eagleston barechested created a fluttering sensation deep inside her. Suddenly, inexplicably, Jennifer was obsessed with the idea. She stacked the rest of her cards facedown on the tabletop.

"What would you like to wager for?" she asked, her

low voice sounding even huskier than usual.

He tossed his remaining cards down and answered without a moment's hesitation. "A kiss."

She frowned in reproach. "You have already kissed me," she reminded him. "Twice."

With an unabashed smile, he leaned back in his chair and folded his arms. "I'd like to do it again, Yankee. Indulge me."

"Mm." She tapped her finger on the stack of cards in front of her.

Eagleston tipped his head toward her in inquiry. "What would you like to win, Miss Elkheart?" he persisted in that smooth, honeyed way of his. "A diamond necklace to match those diamond earrings you're wearing? I'm a very wealthy man. I can afford to be generous."

She shook her head. "No, no. Nothing like that." She propped her elbows on the smooth, polished wood and cupped her cheeks in her palms as she gazed at him intently. Dare she suggest it?

Curiosity shone in his eyes. "What, then?"

Realizing his gaze had drifted downward to where the tops of her breasts peeked out above her low décolletage, Jennifer straightened in her chair and folded her hands primly in her lap. "I would like to see you without your shirt on."

His quick intake of breath told her she'd shocked him. For a fleeting second, his eyes widened in astonishment. Then from beneath hooded lids, he gazed at her across the library table.

Before he could utter a word, she blurted out an apology. "I should not have said that! I am sorry. I forget, sometimes, that the *veho* taboos are taken quite seriously by the British as well as the Americans." She offered him a weak smile. "When in Rome . . ." she began lamely and trailed off in mortification.

"It's a bet."

Apparently, he wasn't as shocked as she'd thought.

"You do not even know what the game is," she pointed out in all fairness. "It would not be right for me to take undue advantage of you." Her smile widened into a teasing grin. "The way I did on the hockey field this afternoon."

Thorne didn't care if the little Yankee wanted to play ducks and drakes down by the stream or hopscotch on the roof. The thought of removing his coat and shirt, while she watched with those innocent brown eyes of hers, set his heart pumping like a blacksmith's bellows at a forge. He made a conscious effort to control his labored breathing. He didn't want her to guess the incredible effect her words had on his rampaging desire.

He kept his tone light and whimsical. "I'm willing to learn whatever childhood diversion you wish to play, Mohehya."

Her gaze was filled with misgiving. "I did not shock you?"

"No, not at all."

Bloody hell.

Jennifer smiled in obvious relief. *"Nakoe!"* she breathed on a sigh. "First, I will show you the game. Then you can decide whether you really want to wager or not."

Thorne had every intention of playing, whatever the childish amusement turned out to be. It didn't matter if he won or lost, though this was one time he might definitely prefer losing.

He watched in fascination as she scooped the cribbage pegs up in her hands and rose from the chair. She was wearing a confection of white ruffles and black ribbons, with a single velvet band and cameo fastened around her throat. The full, tiered skirt was draped over a perky bustle, and the ruffled train swished back and forth tantalizingly as she walked over to the fireplace and sank to the rug. The frothy gown was cut low, revealing the shadowy valley of her cleavage in the wavering firelight. The desire to bury his face between her firm breasts and breathe in her heavenly scent hit him with the force of a well-thrown punch to the abdomen.

He was burning with need.

"It is better if we sit on the floor in front of the fire," she explained. "That is how I am used to playing it." She modestly tucked her black satin slippers under the hem of her skirt and motioned for him to sit down across from her.

Thorne jumped to his feet and hurried over before she had a chance to rethink her proposal. "I believe I'm going to like this game," he said with absolute conviction. He sank down on the thick Aubusson carpet and crossed his legs, the black worsted material of his trousers stretching tightly across his swollen member. He smiled as he casually draped his hand over his bulging crotch to hide the telltale evidence from view. "What's it called?"

"*Noosanistoz.*"

"Which means?"

"Translated exactly, it means 'They are hiding.' But it is often called the hand game by white men." Jennifer laid a neat row of four ivory and four jade pegs on the floor between them. She looked up, a bashful smile skipping across her adorable mouth. Her flushed cheeks betrayed her discomposure. "The one who collects all the counters is the winner," she added hesitantly.

He rubbed his hands together in playful anticipation, attempting to put her at ease. "What do I do to get a counter?"

"You watch."

"What do I watch?"

"The green peg."

He scanned the row in front of him. "Which green peg?"

"This one." She opened both fists. Cradled in each palm was a counter, one ivory, one jade. He hadn't even seen her hide them.

"All you need to do," she said with a soft, little chuckle, "is keep your eyes on the hand with the green peg. No matter what I do, do not lose sight of which hand is holding the green one."

He nodded to show he understood. "I'm ready."

Jennifer started slowly, singing in Cheyenne. The song quickly became far livelier than the soothing lullaby she'd crooned to Barleymow in the stable that morning. As the tempo of the chant increased, she moved her hands faster and faster in time to the music, making many quick, unexpected gestures to confuse him. She raised her hands high, brought them low to the floor, moved them from side to side, and back again. Finally, she hid both hands behind her back for the space of a second, then thrust her closed fists out in front of her.

"Which hand holds the green stick?" she asked. Her bright eyes, sparkling with gaiety, appeared almost black in the firelight.

Thorne didn't have the slightest inkling which small fist hid the jade peg. "That one," he guessed, pointing to her left hand.

She uncurled her fingers to reveal the ivory stick. "Too bad," she gloated with a happy laugh. She dropped the counter into her lap and picked up another from the row of six on the floor. "My point."

Without waiting for him to be ready, without even a warning that she was about to begin, she started to chant. Her hands flew to the ever-increasing beat of her song. Once more, he failed to choose correctly, and she picked up another marker.

Thorne had every intention of losing the game, but his sporting blood was aroused. He wanted to see if he could fool her as easily as she'd fooled him. The whole thing looked pretty simple. "When do I get my turn to hide the pegs?" he demanded.

She couldn't keep from giggling at his obvious frustration. "When you guess correctly, white man."

This time, he was ready for her to begin. He studied every move she made but still met defeat. Finally, on the fourth attempt, he succeeded.

"Very good!" she exclaimed. The surprise and esteem shining in her eyes revealed the fact that she'd never expected a clumsy British duke to win a single point.

He sure as hell wasn't about to admit it'd been pure luck. "My turn," he said, holding out his hand for the pegs.

Thorne started to move his closed fists about in a confusing manner, but it was far more difficult than he'd expected. He'd hardly begun when she waved her hand back and forth for him to stop.

"You have to sing a gambling song," she instructed with unconcealed impatience. "You cannot simply flap your arms in the air like a turkey gobbler looking for a mate."

He scowled, irked at the unflattering comment. She had an uncanny way of sticking a pin into his male pride and deflating it like a child's party balloon. "I don't know a gambling song," he grumbled.

A impish smile played about her lips. She lifted her shoulders as though to say, what could anyone expect from an Englishman? "Then another song will have to do, I suppose. I do not have the time to teach you the Cheyenne verses."

He searched his brain for something he could sing in her presence. Bawdy camp songs were about the extent of his repertoire. Then he remembered a foxhunting ditty from childhood. He belted out the words in his deep baritone, ending each chorus with a rousing, "Tally-ho! Tally-ho! Tally-ho!"

Jennifer never took her eyes from his, in spite of his quick-moving hands. She seemed to pay no attention to his clever gyrations, but smiled in delight as she swayed to the spirited melody. When he finally extended his fists for her choice, she instantly tapped the left one.

Incredulous, Thorne opened his hand. There was the jade peg in his palm. "How did you do that?"

Plucking another counter from the floor, she dropped it into her lap beside the others. Her confident smile lit up her exotic features. "The same way you make the *veho* playing cards come alive in your fingers, Your Graciousness. With a lot of practice."

One by one, Jennifer collected the rest of the counting sticks, until all eight were in her possession. After dropping the last one on the pile, she waited, her hands folded loosely on top of them, to see what Eagleston would do next. She wondered if he'd actually honor his pledge in this particular bargain.

Eagleston's words were warm with approval. "You

may not be very accomplished at cribbage, Miss Elk-heart," he said generously, "but you're a magician when it comes to playing *noosanistoz*." Without a quibble, he reached up to unfasten the sapphire stickpin that held his white silk neck scarf in place.

Suddenly, Jennifer wasn't at all sure she should have made such a daring proposal. "If you want to forget our wager, I am willing to pretend we never made it," she offered timidly. She lowered her lids and looked down at her folded hands, unaccountably shy at the thought of seeing him bare-chested. At his silence, she forced herself to raise her lashes and meet his frank, uninhibited gaze. "That is," she added, "if you feel ill at ease or . . . or in any way uncomfortable about keeping our agreement. After all, you have never played this game. Perhaps I was not being fair."

"No, no." His azure eyes glowed with a strange inner light as he awarded her a slow, sideways smile. "I always keep my word, little magpie. I can't have it bruited about that I welshed on a bet with a young lady. Where would my reputation be then?"

At the mention of his reputation, Jennifer belatedly remembered her own. She sat up straighter, tense with conflicting emotions. But no matter how scandalous her behavior was in the eyes of *veho* society, she wasn't about to stop the Englishman now. A stampede of wild mustangs galloping through the library couldn't have forced her to leave before she collected her prize.

Eagleston dropped the jeweled pin in his coat pocket. He untied his scarf, pulled it from around his neck, and tossed it on the rug beside him. "Next time, we'll have to choose a diversion from my youth," he said teasingly. "I can't afford to keep losing the shirt off my back."

Jennifer knew he was trying to lessen her tension. She realized with a twinge of conscience that her fingers were locked together so tightly her knuckles were white. Belatedly, her mother's warning rang in her ear. *Certain as Maheo made little apples green, impulsive little girls make the evil-maker smile.*

Unable to keep her gaze off the English lord's hands,

Jennifer ran the tip of her tongue over her dry lips and didn't venture a word.

Thorne shrugged out of his formal evening jacket and satin waistcoat, and the two articles of clothing joined the neck scarf on the floor in a heap. He kept his tone coolly impersonal as he loosened the gold cufflinks at his wrists. "This is a heck of a lot easier than losing my favorite Thoroughbred," he assured her.

From the wary expression in her dark eyes, he was afraid she was going to spring to her feet and bolt from the room. He'd catch her before she reached the door, of course. Once he had her in his arms, he'd use all his powers of persuasion to keep her there. And his talents of persuasion were many and varied.

He moved smoothly and quickly before she could change her mind, but not so fast as to startle her into action. He unfastened the front of his starched white shirt, then pulled its long tails from the waistband of his black trousers. In one unhurried movement, he slipped off the shirt and dropped it on the pile of clothing beside him.

Thorne had planned some clever quip about playing tic-tac-toe on his chest to make her laugh and forget her self-consciousness. But at the stunned look of awe on her face as she gazed at his bare skin, his breath caught in his throat.

Jennifer stared in wonder at the English duke. She had half-expected him to be as soft and weak as his pampered lifestyle suggested.

Instead, he was corded with muscle.

His shoulders, no longer hidden beneath the layers of apparel, were much broader than she'd envisioned. The massive upper arms bulged with strength. His chest was wide and deep, the pectorals firm and well delineated. The outline of each rib was clearly visible as his torso tapered to his slim waist. Above the band of his trousers, his abdomen was flat and ridged with sinew. The Englishman was hard, strong, and very, very male.

But that wasn't what made her stare in fascination.

She'd seen Cheyenne warriors as powerfully built. Her father, for one.

Eagleston had a mat of golden-brown hair across his chest so thick she could bury her fingertips in its depth. Growing in the shape of an inverted triangle, his chest hair ran from his collarbone down to his abdomen, where it narrowed to a thin line that disappeared beneath his trousers.

But that wasn't what made her stare, either.

It was the battle scars.

Four of them.

What had once been made with a blade were now jagged scars crisscrossing his upper torso, their tortured paths still visible despite the wiry covering of hair. One scar narrowly missed his left nipple. A short, puckered blemish gouged his right side as though a knife had been plunged between his ribs. Another old wound ran from his right shoulder down to his belly button, the impressions of the large stitches still visible in the tautened skin. The last mark stretched beneath his trousers to end somewhere over his left hipbone.

Jennifer knew the British army had fought wars in such far-flung places as Afghanistan, Egypt, and southern Africa in recent years. She was certain, somehow, that Eagleston's injuries had not been received in a single encounter. He'd risked death in combat not once, but several times.

Without conscious awareness, she reached out to touch him. She longed to run her fingertips across the length of each battle wound, to press her lips gently to the badges of honor that marked him as a courageous soldier. With a sudden realization of what she was doing and how scandalous it would seem to him, she stopped, hesitated, and started to pull back.

Thorne caught her hand and brought it to his chest. He pressed her open palm over his thundering heart, letting her feel the effect she had upon him, reveling in the knowledge that her fingers were trembling beneath his own.

"Jennifer," he whispered hoarsely. "My God, how I want you."

She slowly raised her eyes to his, and the unbounded admiration he saw in their velvety depths sent shock waves of longing through him.

"You have the marks of a true warrior, Eagle's Son," she said with hushed reverence. "The wounds of battle which proclaim a man's bravery to the world."

"No," Thorne said. "These are not battle scars, Jennie. I was never in combat." He hated himself as he repeated the well-rehearsed lie. "I was in a carriage accident while traveling in Italy a few years ago. The people who found me hauled my half-dead carcass to a nearby inn and patched me up as best they could, but no one thought I was going to survive. The village doctor didn't spend a lot of time sewing fancy stitches on what he believed was a dying Englishman."

She drew back slightly, the doubt in her husky voice explicit. "An accident? I do not think so."

"I was thrown onto the splintered shafts of the coach. It wasn't a pretty sight." He tried to grin with his usual detachment and failed miserably. The falsehood had always worked before because he'd wanted it to work. Most women knew nothing about wounds suffered in hand-to-hand fighting, which was exactly how he'd received them. "Surely you believe me, Mohehya," he coaxed. "I'd have no reason to lie."

"I believe you almost died," she answered. But the seed of doubt he'd planted slowly had its desired effect. He sensed her conviction wavering, till she was no longer certain how he'd been injured.

Thorne lifted her hand to his lips and tenderly kissed the inside of her palm. He closed his eyes, enthralled by the marvelous sensation of her cool fingers crossing his bare shoulder and down his upper arm. Her light, hesitant touch ignited a feverish heat deep in his belly. His muscles bunched in glorious male response as she timidly explored his naked upper body.

When he was with Jennie, all the rank greed, the vile corruption and treachery he'd exposed and used in others for his own means faded like a nightmare in the brilliant morning light. She was so sweet, so incredibly feminine, so achingly trustful. How could any man resist her?

Lifting her chin, he bent his head and brushed her lips with his own. "Vonahenene," he murmured. "Beautiful Morning Rose."

As Jennifer leaned forward to meet his kiss, the creak of the library door swinging open seemed to fill the quiet room. They pulled apart, simultaneously turning their faces to the source of the intrusion.

Lady Idina entered with a swish of taffeta petticoats. "Jennie, are you in here?" she called brightly. The instant she glimpsed them sitting on the rug, she shut the door behind her and leaned against it to prevent anyone else from wandering in uninvited.

Jennifer jerked her hand away from Thorne's shoulder and stared at her hostess with huge, solemn eyes. "We were playing *noosanistoz*," she explained, "and Eagleston lost. He is not very good at games."

"I can see that," Idina replied without so much as a blink of an eyelash. She smiled serenely, giving Jennifer the impression that she often found two of her guests, one bare from the waist up, playing games on her library floor.

The couple rose guiltily to their feet. The ivory and jade pegs in Jennifer's lap scattered across the rug. "*Ahahe!*" she cried softly, watching in dismay as several rolled under a nearby chair.

"Never mind, dearest," Idina consoled. "The maids will find them when they clean." She met Thorne's gaze, the dimples in her plump cheeks deepening irrepressibly. "The cribbage tournament is over, and Lady Charlotte is ready to leave for home now," she told him. "I've already called for your landau to be brought round."

"Thank you," he answered with stiff politeness. "Please have a servant inform my mother that I'll be there momentarily."

"Why don't you come with me, Jennie," Lady Idina suggested sweetly, "while His Grace puts his clothes back on. The duchess has invited all the ladies to Eagleston Court tomorrow morning. She wants to know if you'd like to do some fishing while you're there."

"I love to fish!" Jennifer exclaimed, her previous embarrassment apparently forgotten. "But I did not bring any fishing tackle on this trip."

"Don't worry, we have everything you'll need. Now be an angel and tell Lady Charlotte that her son will be there shortly," Idina told her. "I'll follow right behind you." The Englishwoman gave her guest a soothing pat on the cheek and gently shooed her out, closing the door behind her. Then she turned back to Thorne, who'd pulled on his shirt and was hurriedly fastening the buttons. A smile still hovering about her mouth, Lady Idina had the contented look of a chaperone smelling orange blossoms in the air.

"Dina," he cautioned, "this is not what you think."

"I think, my very dear friend, that you are incapable of doing anything dishonorable, especially when it comes to an innocent young girl. Therefore, I feel no need to ask your intentions toward my lovely American guest."

He grimaced uncomfortably.

"Nothing would please me more than to have Jennie for my nearest neighbor," she continued before he could say a word. "And not just for my own sake, but for yours." Her smiled faded, and she studied him with solemn green eyes. "When were you injured so terribly? And why was neither I nor Basil ever told?"

"It was a carriage mishap near Milan," he said. "Not worth the mentioning."

"And so you never did. Not even to your closest friends. Not even to your mother, I suppose." She waited for a moment, and when she realized he wasn't going to offer any further explanation, she stepped toward him. "Your bitterness is devouring you, Thorne, like some insatiable cannibal feasting on your heart. Where is the fun-loving boy I used to know?"

"You're making too much of this," he said sourly. "Nothing happened between Miss Elkheart and me, and nothing's going to happen."

Dina glanced at the doorway through which Jennifer had just scurried and then met his eyes once again. "My fine, foolish friend," she said softly, "I look at that ingenuous, open-hearted girl and ponder whether she isn't your last hope for happiness. For if you cannot find your lost sense of purpose and wonder in her pure, undefiled spirit, you will surely find it nowhere else in that broad, bustling world you roam like some restless, embittered, alienated ghost. Your father is dead, Thorne. Bury him. And then get on with your own life."

He folded his arms and spoke with acrid cynicism. "My father has nothing to do with my travels or my lack of deeper feelings for the ebullient Miss Elkheart. Jennifer would be totally unsuitable as the next duchess of Eagleston. And I'd appreciate it if you'd save your overblown, histrionic conjectures for someone who believes them."

Idina looked down at her clasped hands and sighed in defeat. "In that case, I think it's only fair to warn you that Jennifer has a far different attitude about courtship than we do. Don't misinterpret her naive, albeit impetuous, behavior to mean she's setting her cap for you or your title. She is simply indulging a girlish whim to learn more about the curious British nobility."

Thorne scowled as he snatched his silk neck scarf from the floor. The inference that Jennifer saw him as a mere oddity rankled. "What exactly do you mean?"

Idina shrugged. "I mean, Thorne, that your feelings toward Jennie are immaterial. She would never accept a proposal of marriage from you."

His sharp words rang with disbelief. "And why not?"

At his furious reaction, Idina's blue eyes twinkled mysteriously. "Because you are not the man of her dreams."

"How would you know that?" he scoffed.

"She told me so."

Thorne lit a fine, hand-rolled Havana, poured a splash of brandy into a crystal snifter, and dropped into a comfortable overstuffed chair. He stretched his legs out in front of him and propped his stockinged feet up on an ottoman. Scrubbing his face with one hand, he closed his eyes for an exhausted moment, then looked absently about him as he puffed on the aromatic cigar.

Aside from his shooting lodge in the north, the billiard room at Eagleston Court was his favorite retreat. Its oak-paneled walls were decorated with paintings of the favorite horses and hounds of previous dukes and duchesses, along with trophies from his own hunting and fishing expeditions. Tonight, however, the treasured mementos of years gone by seemed to stare down at him in silent, mutual condemnation.

Thornton Fitzhugh Jean-Pierre Blakesford, eighth duke of Eagleston, had behaved like an unprincipled ass. Not just once, but twice in the same day. What in God's name had he been thinking of? Or had he been thinking at all?

An honorable gentleman never, *ever* placed an unmarried young lady in a compromising position.

No matter how irresistible he found her.

No matter how willing she might be.

No matter what.

One of the pillars upon which the courtship rituals of the six hundred families who comprised London society depended was the precept that virginal misses were inviolable when it came to a dalliance of the fleeting kind. Period.

Unattached young ladies were expected to flirt and simper and bat their long lashes provocatively. But they never even learned the facts of life until their wedding night. The British laws of primogenitor depended upon a titled lord's complete assurance that his heir-presumptive was his own issue and not the by-blow of some other chap.

A feeling of self-disgust swept over Thorne. With the smoke of the imported cigar swirling above him, he leaned his head on the back of the chair and contemplated the full extent of his folly. Had anyone but Idina discovered him and Jennifer in the Nettlefold library that evening, playing patty-cake on the floor, there would have been no alternative but marriage. And marriage with Miss Elkheart would be a disaster.

He scowled down at the brandy swirling in his glass before taking another slow sip. How could a genteel young woman have proposed such a fantastic wager in the first place? Not that he didn't share the bulk of the blame. He was older, wiser, and far more experienced. As her esteemed grandfather would be quick to point out, Thorne was the responsible party.

But the headstrong American miss seemed to have no sense of proper etiquette. No comprehension of the importance of class distinction and the strict rules of deportment that guided the lives of the British nobility. She seemed to have no idea what a delicately nurtured female did and didn't do. And no commonsense, whatsoever, when it came to behaving with a modicum of propriety and decorum while in the company of an eligible bachelor.

Strangely enough, her hoydenish behavior didn't seem to bother anyone else. Everyone treated her like a princess. They rose whenever she entered a room and remained on their feet until she was seated. Not a soul, from the oldest to the youngest, retired for the evening until she'd left the salon. Miss Elkheart had them all wrapped around her little finger.

But her brash Yankee attitude set his teeth on edge. Christ, she still addressed him as *Your Graciousness*. Thorne had the uncomfortable feeling she was laughing at the lot of them—him most of all.

What kind of a duchess would she make with her wild, uninhibited, romping ways? Hell, the energetic little witch was half-savage with her belief in shape-shifters and mischief-makers and amulets.

And visions.

Thorne rose and stalked over to the cabinet where his liquor was stored. Clenching the cigar between his teeth, he poured another healthy splash of brandy, cradled the snifter in his hands, and gazed at himself in the mirror above the row of cut-glass decanters.

So the duke of Eagleston wasn't the man of her dreams. By God, he didn't give a bloody damn.

With a detached, critical eye, Thorne studied his prominent nose, his ordinary light brown hair, and the thick mustache that she so disliked. Placing the burning Havana in a crystal ashtray, he ran his fingers across his upper lip.

Maybe he should shave it off.

He snorted in disgust at that piece of idiocy. Other women were more than willing to overlook the fact that he wasn't the handsomest man in England. There were a few qualities the unmarried ladies coveted more.

Thorne didn't merely hold the title to a dukedom. He'd inherited hundreds of thousands of acres in arable land farmed by well-fed tenants, pasture lands with grazing livestock, forests of oak, beech, and ash, as well as lakes and streams filled with trout. He owned three country estates with their full complements of indoor and outdoor staff, a hunting lodge in Yorkshire, a town house in Grosvenor Square, and enormous investments in railroads and shipbuilding.

He turned away from his reflection in the glass and wandered out onto the terrace, hoping the cool night air would dispel his restless discontent. He stood beneath the canopy of stars and sipped the rich amber liquid, deep in thought.

Since the age of puberty, the future duke of Eagleston had been considered one of the British empire's most eligible bachelors, in spite of his father's notorious shortcomings. But Thorne wasn't good enough to be the man in Jennifer Rose Elkheart's dreams. What he didn't have— or so the exasperating Yankee believed—were the scars that marked him as a courageous warrior.

At the thought of his adept portrayal of a jaded, world-weary dilettante, another concern intruded on Thorne's brooding contemplation. An uneasy feeling about the cipher he'd decoded for Lord Doddridge continued to nag him. The text of the innocuous letter taken from the Russian ambassador's mail pouch had fallen into place much too quickly and easily. Its contents hadn't been worth the effort of transcribing into secret writing in the first place. He was certain he'd broken the cipher correctly. He'd rechecked his work twice to be sure. Yet something felt wrong.

As if that wasn't enough, he now had Vladimir Gortschakoff to worry about. His appearance at St. James's Court, immediately following their mutual stay in Vienna, had been more than vaguely disconcerting. But the nobleman's intrusion that afternoon into the Nettlefold house party was downright alarming. When Thorne questioned Idina, she told him she'd invited the Russian on the night of the court ball in London, so his presence was easily explained. But Thorne couldn't shake the notion that Gortschakoff's appearances in Vienna, London, and now here in Warwickshire were all a little too coincidental.

He doubted that the Russian presented a danger on English soil. But if Gortschakoff discovered proof that the duke of Eagleston was working for the British secret service, Thorne's next visit to a foreign country might well be his last.

Thorne prided himself on the fact that he was a logical man. As always, he would solve his problems in a cool, rational, systematic manner.

First, he'd decode the cipher once again, starting from the beginning. If the message turned out the same for the fourth consecutive time, he'd set the matter aside and forget it.

Second, he'd keep a close eye on Vladimir Gortschakoff, while making certain that he, himself, did nothing to arouse suspicion.

And third, but not least, he would keep his bloody hands off Miss Jennifer Rose Elkheart.

Chapter 10

❦

"**J**ennie, you've caught another one!" Lady Idina exclaimed. "You're a fisherman's wonder, darling. Now don't let it get away!"

"I will not lose it," Jennifer said with a delighted laugh. "My great-grandfather taught me how to fish. Flying Hawk could tell where they were hidden by reading the surface of a river like a *veho* reads a map." She let the line play out just enough to be sure she'd snagged her prize securely, then landed the thrashing, silvery trout with smooth expertise. It was a beauty. The largest she'd caught that morning.

From her place on the picnic blanket behind them, Lady Charlotte called to her merrily. *"Trés bien, chérie. C'est incroyable!*

Jennifer turned to the white-haired dowager and executed the sweeping curtsey she'd practiced for the queen.

The ladies of the Nettlefold house party had arrived at Eagleston Court shortly after dawn with bouquets of pumpkin-colored trumpet lilies from the greenhouse, mixed with branches of hawthorn, bittersweet berries, and wild rose hips. After consuming quick cups of coffee and hot buttered scones, they waved a cheery good-bye to the duke. At Miss Trevor-Roper's starry-eyed entreaty, Eagleston promised to come and check on them later in the morning.

Then the two open carriages, piled high with chattering females, baskets of sandwiches, boxes of fruit and

161

nuts, tarts and cakes, jugs of apple juice, pails of ice, tackle boxes, and fishing poles were driven to the spot on the River Leigh known to have the best angling in all of Warwickshire.

On the grassy, undercut bank, Lady Avice hopped up and down beside Jennifer, her red curls bobbing. I—I have one, too!" she squealed. Jennifer laid her borrowed fly rod on the ground and hurried to help the novice.

"Be careful," she warned. "Do not let that wily fish trick you."

Without explanation, the seventeen-year-old suddenly stopped cranking her reel. She dropped the end of her bamboo pole in the water and frowned. "Oh, look, Jennie," she said sorrowfully. "That poor little fellow isn't going to make it"

Jennifer glanced to where Lady Avice was pointing and spotted a puppy struggling to keep its head above water. The small animal had been swept into the river's strong current and was being carried swiftly downstream. Avice was right. The puppy was tiring fast and would never reach shore on its own.

Without a moment's hesitation, Jennifer unfastened her bustled skirt and stepped out of its confining yards of navy serge.

"Jennie! What are you doing?" Idina cried.

"I am going to save that puppy," she answered, surprised at the needless question. She quickly unbuttoned and removed her blouse, then untied the tapes of her petticoat, letting the ruffled cotton drop to the grass.

"Wait!" Idina called as Jennifer headed for the river. "Jennie! Stop!"

But there wasn't a moment to waste in useless conversation. Pausing at the edge of the bank just long enough to kick off her sturdy Oxfords, Jennifer dove into the River Leigh.

It was cold, but not nearly as cold as the mountain-fed streams of Alberta, where she'd swam as a girl. As Jennifer cut through the water, she heard the women screaming at the top of their lungs on the shore behind her. Strange how the typical *vehoka* reaction to a crisis was an ear-splitting wail. But there was no need for anyone to jump in with her. She was a strong swimmer, and the puppy was small.

Beneath the autumn canopy of beeches and willows, the duke of Eagleston reined in his big gray horse just in time to hear his mother's guests start to squawk in concert, like a gaggle of geese being chased by a ferret. He scanned the riverbank, unable to make sense of their high-pitched caterwauling, till he caught sight of Idina.

"Help! Thorne! Help!" She pointed to the middle of the Leigh, her face drained of color, her voice shrill with panic. "Jennie's in the river! No one else can swim!"

He pressed his heels against Tacitus's flanks, and the gelding raced toward the edge of the bank where a flustered coachman and footman hovered on its brink. Thorne dismounted, running, before the horse came to a complete halt. He jerked off his high riding boots, tore off his jacket, and made a flat, shallow dive into the water. He could see Jennifer's dark head, moving rapidly downstream in the rushing current.

He expended neither time nor energy shouting to her. With long, powerful strokes, he sliced through the water, every movement fueled by the terrifying thought that he might not reach her in time.

Midway out in the river, Jennifer grasped the soggy, black-and-white spaniel by the thick scruff of its neck. At her touch, it whimpered pathetically. "Do not worry," she assured the exhausted dog, "I will save you." Propping its head against her bare shoulder so the shiny black nose was safely above the choppy surface, she turned shoreward.

To her amazement, she found the duke of Eagleston swimming up to her. The knowledge that he also wanted to rescue the unfortunate tyke pleased her immensely. She wasn't the only person willing to take a chilly bath that morning to save a weaker creature.

"I have him!" she called.

But the foolish man paid no heed. Just as Jennifer set out for land, her legs scissoring in strong, steady kicks,

Eagleston reached for her. Her foot struck him squarely in the groin.

With a low, guttural groan, he bent forward and slid under the water.

She caught him by his tangled hair and jerked his head above the frothy surface. His eyes were screwed tight, his jaw clenched in silent agony. "Stay calm," she instructed, a trifle breathless herself. "I will pull you to the bank."

It wasn't going to be easy holding the little pup with one hand and the large man's collar with the other, but she had no intention of letting either of them drown.

Suddenly, Eagleston clasped her waist in a grip of steel. "You holy terror," he said with a roar of laughter, as he surged above the lapping waves. "I'm supposed to be saving you!"

Treading water one-handed, she gaped at him in bewilderment. "But I do not need to be sa-saved," she spluttered, spitting out water as she spoke. "This poor little pooch was being swept away."

In its agitation, the spaniel tried to climb up her neck and sit in her hair.

"Give the dog to me," he said.

"No, I have him now. He is perfectly safe."

His long fingers encompassing her waist, the duke brought Jennifer closer, till her breasts brushed against his chest and her cold nose grazed the corner of his dripping mustache. His blue eyes shone with a wicked light. She realized, belatedly, that her unorthodox swimming costume had caught his full and complete attention. She tried to wriggle away.

"Watch your knees," he warned. With one arm around her waist he also tread water. "I can't take another blow like the last one and still hope to produce an heir."

"I did not mean to kick you," she apologized in a hoarse gasp. "That was an accident."

Eagleston's grin was practically diabolical. "Give me the dog, Jennifer Rose," he ordered. "I'm not going back empty-handed. If I can't rescue you, I'll at least rescue that damn mutt. I'll tow him to shore in my teeth, if I have to."

She laughed and swallowed a mouthful of water. Coughing and sputtering, she surrendered the puppy.

Together, they swam to the river's edge and clambered up the bank. Holding the frightened animal in the crook of his arm, Thorne took Jennifer's elbow to steady her.

Despite his chivalrous intentions, Thorne was unable to keep his gaze from her adorable figure. Her lacy camisole and drawers clung, nearly translucent, to her firm, lithe body. Against the white cotton, her golden skin shone lustrous and smooth as burnished satin. The tidy chignon had come loose and her hair fell down her back in one long, massive braid.

He forced himself to ignore the overwhelming urge to slip his arm around her waist and pull her up against him; to kiss her in front of everyone with an intimacy reserved for lovers, and let the devil take the hindmost.

Murmurs of admiration for their courage and prayers of thanksgiving swept through the group as he released the puppy, now struggling to be free. The women clustered around them, staring thunderstruck at the slender girl. It was clear what held them mesmerized. Strapped on Jennifer's shapely leg was a knife in a beaded leather sheath. A thin cord, fastened about her waist, was tied to each slim thigh.

"We need to get a blanket around you, dear," Idina said frantically, "before you catch an inflammation of the lungs." She waved to the Nettlefold coachman, who hurried toward the nearest landau.

"*Hesc!* I have swum in much colder water than this," Jennifer protested cheerfully. "Do not worry about me. I never get sick. I am as strong and healthy as a grizzly bear in the summertime."

But one member of the fishing party was not impressed with the rescue mission or the water-logged spaniel that raced around at their feet, stopping only long enough to shake its heavy coat and spray water all over the front of their skirts.

Muriel drew back in disgust from the excited, frolicsome puppy. Grimacing at the sight of her ruined dress, she turned on the soaked, dripping girl. "You little savage!" she sneered. "Only a pathetic cripple would befriend an uncivilized native like you and try to foist her on polite society."

Before anyone could express their outrage, Jennifer's knife was in her hand. In the bright morning sunshine, its razor-sharp blade glittered mere inches from the tip of Muriel's nose.

"Do not say another word, *vehoka*," Jennifer warned in her husky contralto. "If you speak cruelly of my friend again, I will slit your nostrils up to your eyes. It is the punishment reserved for evil-tongued women."

Thorne calmly grasped the small hand curled around the mother-of-pearl handle. "Put the knife away, Jennie," he said placidly. "No one is going to hurt Lady Idina's feelings while she's on Eagleston land. I'm sure Miss Trevor-Roper wishes to apologize for her unthinking comments."

Too late, Muriel realized that in her malicious attack on Jennifer she'd revealed her own secret, ugly prejudice against the one person everyone in their social circle loved and protected. She turned to stare at Thorne, and on her stricken, bone-white face was the certain knowledge that she'd ruined, irredeemably and forever, any chance she might have had to win his affection. The tall, flaxen-haired woman started blubbering hysterically. "Lady Idina, I'm sorry. Oh—oh, please—please forgive me. I'm so—so sorry."

Dina accepted the carriage blanket from her coachman's hands and wrapped the warm plaid wool around Jennifer's shoulders. Her plump cheeks stained with color, she met Muriel's watery, pale-lashed gaze. "Of course, I forgive you," she said, her voice gently reproving. "Why, everybody knows I am lame. It's hardly a secret. But whether my guest can forgive your coarse words is quite another matter."

Jennifer's brown eyes sparkled as she grinned at Muriel. "As long as your words are aimed at me, Miss Trevor-Roper, I do not care what you say. My father taught me that name-calling is the last resort of a small mind." With a roguish glance at Thorne, she returned her weapon to its sheath and pulled the blanket closer, then looked around for the little puppy.

The spaniel hadn't wasted any time, once he was on solid ground. He'd sniffed out the basket of chicken salad sandwiches and was chomping away with relish.

"*Non! Non!*" cried Lady Charlotte as she started toward the naughty puppy. "Shoo! Shoo!"

In his excitement, the puppy gamboled around the picnic blanket, turning over the containers of buns, nuts, and fruit, stepping into the plum cake, smashing the gooseberry tarts, and spilling the opened jars of apple juice. He paused, periodically, to shake his spotted fur and shower everything with river water.

"I'll catch him!" Lady Avice shouted. She flew across the grass, past the dowager duchess. In her attempt to grab the barking dog, the gangly redhead skidded on the loose walnuts, tripped over the rolling apples and pears, and fell, full-length, across the already-ruined cake.

Shouts of laughter and cries of encouragement rang out as everyone tried to catch the mischievous puppy. With a wisdom far greater than his tender age, the clever little fellow dashed beneath the blanket draped over Jennifer's shoulders and lay down, panting, on her wet, stockinged feet.

"We need to get you in front of a roaring fire," Eagleston told her. "Your teeth are starting to chatter."

Jennifer met his eyes and felt suddenly shy at the frank approval glowing in their summer-sky depths. "I think Homavovoasz is cold, too," she said prosaically. She picked up the black-and-white dog and wrapped her blanket-covered arms around it.

"Who?"

"Spotted Beaver," she explained with a smile of entreaty. She had no idea how the duke felt about adopting strays. "I have named him after the stout-hearted, flat-tailed animal that swims in our rivers back home."

"By all means," he replied, his cultured voice light and insouciant. "Let's get Spot bundled up before the hearth. We wouldn't want the little darling to catch pneumonia."

At his signal, a footman brought over a magnificent

gray gelding. Eagleston lifted Jennifer, still wrapped in the blanket and with the spaniel cradled in her arms, up on his horse, then mounted behind her. Gathering the reins, he surveyed the disaster that had been his mother's picnic.

"We'll have the kitchen staff prepare another lunch," he told Lady Charlotte with a consoling smile.

The dowager duchess nodded, not the least perturbed. "We can eat on the floor in the drawing room, *mon cher*," she said, "so *la petite* can stay warm and cozy by the fireside. It will be almost like dining alfresco."

"No, this is all my fault," Jennifer stated earnestly. She lifted her chin higher as the enthusiastic puppy started to shower her with grateful kisses and continued with gritty determination. "I will fix lunch for everyone, including the people who worked so hard to prepare the delicious food for today's outing. We will eat with the cook and her helpers in the kitchen."

"You'll fix the meal?" Lady Idina asked with a laugh. "What will you cook, dear?"

"The trout," she answered proudly, pointing to the two long stringers of fish held high by Idina's grinning coachman.

Avice's sherry-colored eyes grew round with wonder. "Do you know how to cook trout, Miss Elkheart?"

"*Hesc!*" Jennifer exclaimed. "Why would I go fishing, if I could not cook the fish? My great-grandmother taught me how when I was little more than a baby."

Eagleston brought her closer against his solid chest and chuckled. "I'm beginning to think there's nothing you can't do," he said, his deep voice resonant with a teasing admiration.

She glanced up at him over her shoulder. "Like all Cheyenne," she told him with a saucy grin, "I am too modest to answer that."

He bent his head and whispered in her ear. "If you don't stop wiggling your little behind, Miss Elkheart, I'll be sorely tempted to put your modesty to the test."

Before she could think of a suitable answer, he signaled his mount, and they took off at a gallop.

* * *

The great kitchen at Eagleston Court was wonderfully old-fashioned. Although a new gas stove and oven had been installed by the present dowager duchess at one end, at the other, the enormous redbrick fireplace, which had served the manor house for over three hundred years, was still used on occasion. Polished copper pots and kettles, along with bunches of dried herbs, onions, and garlic, hung from the massive oak rafters.

The duke had gone upstairs to change out of his wet riding clothes after turning his blanket-draped charge over to Lady Charlotte's personal maid, who clucked her tongue sympathetically and offered to draw a warm bath. Once in dry clothing, Jennifer had instructed the other ladies to wait in the salon until she called them to come and eat.

Dressed in one of Lady Charlotte's dove gray gowns, she flitted about the large cookroom, overseeing the luncheon preparations while trying not to step on her dragging hem. The gutted trout was seasoned with herbs, wrapped in broad spinach leaves, and set among the glowing coals on the hearth. She made cornbread, which she planned to serve with butter and honey, and put it in the oven to bake.

The head cook refused to sit down while a genteel lady commandeered her kitchen, so Jennifer let Mrs. Beeton contribute her share in the form of three mince pies for dessert. Meanwhile, Spotted Beaver romped around the floor, getting in everyone's way and barking for no reason at all.

Mrs. Beeton's daughter, Flora Peckham, and her two children had come from the nearby village for a visit, expecting the dowager duchess and her guests to be down by the river and her mother to be free for the rest of the morning. When Flora attempted to leave, Jennifer refused to allow it.

"You came to see your mother," she told the flustered, ruddy-faced woman. "I will not let your visit be spoiled on my account."

"Why, 'tisn't your fault, Miss Elkheart," Flora protested, holding her cherubic daughter propped on her ample hip and clasping her son's hand firmly in her own.

"It will be my fault if you leave earlier than you planned," Jennifer said. "I have caused enough trouble this morning. Please do not add that to my list of failures." She wiggled the baby's fingers playfully. "What is your name, little one?" she asked.

"Jo-Jo," the black-haired child replied.

"Her name's Joletta," Mrs. Beeton said proudly. She wiped her hands on her voluminous apron and smoothed her grandson's dark, wavy hair back from his forehead. "The children's pa is the farrier at Chiltenstone."

"Hello, Baby Jo-Jo," Jennifer said. She bent down and smiled at the boy. "And what is your name, young sir?"

He awarded her with a broad, gap-toothed grin. "Johnny, ma'm. I'm eight now."

"How would you like to look after my puppy, Johnny Mam, while I shell some peas?"

The boy immediately scooped the spaniel up in his arms. "I'd be happy to!"

One by one, the entire party of females drifted into the cook's domain to watch the unexpected display of culinary skills in fascination. Jennifer immediately put them to work, claiming that, if they were going to be underfoot, they wouldn't be allowed to stay.

When Thorne peeked into the kitchen he hadn't set foot in since the summer before he went off to Eaton, he found his mother had been given the place of honor in a cozy chair by the fire. Her violet eyes shining with joy, Lady Charlotte held a toddler in her lap. The twosome was happily playing patty-cake.

The Ladies Idina and Avice, white bibbed aprons over their dresses and smears of flour on their cheeks, were rolling out pastry on a marble-topped counter under the direction of Cook Beeton. Muriel and Jennifer sat together on a wooden bench, busily shelling green peas into a crockery bowl perched on Jennie's lap.

From the flushed, happy expression on Miss Trevor-Roper's face when she looked over at him, Thorne realized that Jennifer had made a special point of including the chastened woman in the activities. The intrepid Yankee's example of forgiving and forgetting was clear and unequivocal. He told himself not to be so easily impressed, without first questioning the underlying motives. No one was that magnanimous without a reason.

Eagleston Court's entire kitchen staff, with the exception of the head cook, was seated at the large trestle table, drinking mugs of beer and chattering gaily. There were eleven in all, including an assistant cook and a baker, stillroom maids, vegetable maids, dairy maids, and scullery maids. The minute he'd appeared in the open doorway, the servants jumped to their feet and bobbed up and down in a flutter of nervous curtseys. They peeked at each other from beneath lowered lashes, too abashed to say a word to the employer they'd rarely even caught sight of. One maid grew so flustered, she covered her face with her apron and started to cry.

"Don't mind me," Thorne told them with a resigned wave of his hand. "Sit down and enjoy the fun." He met Jennifer's dark brown eyes and continued sardonically. "Now we know why the Yanks played 'The World Turned Upside Down' when Cornwallis surrendered to General Washington at Yorktown."

Miss Elkheart grinned, not the least disconcerted as she invited him into his own kitchen. "Come in, Your Grace. Meet Johnny Mam and Baby Jo-Jo. They are Mrs. Beeton's grandchildren." She gestured with a pea pod toward a woman, who sat knitting on a low stool nearby. "This is their mama, Flora Peckham. Her husband is the farrier in Chiltenstone."

Thorne tipped his head politely at the introduction. The rotund female gasped, tried to stand, sank back down in befuddlement at being introduced to a real, live duke, and uttered a strangled, "How do, Y'r Grace."

Johnny Peckham was rolling around in front of the hearth with Spot in his arms. The black-and-white puppy recognized his erstwhile savior and bounded across the room, barking excitedly.

Thorne dropped to his haunches and stroked the frisky

pup's neck. Its silken fur had dried, feathering luxuri-
antly on the ears, brisket, abdomen, and backs of the legs.
He recognized the quality blood lines of the English
springer spaniels raised by his neighbor, Squire Ramsey,
at Compton Croft. The strong, well proportioned body,
the square muzzle, the long ears, the thick, wavy coat
proclaimed the ancestry of swift, hardy retrievers bred
for hunting.

Jennifer came over and sank to her knees beside them.
"Do you think we can find Spotted Beaver's owner?" she
asked. The concern on her striking features conveyed the
fact that she was prepared to relinquish the dog to its
rightful master—but she wasn't looking forward to it.

"I'll make some inquiries," Thorne said, casually rubbing behind the floppy ears. "If no one in the neighbor-
hood claims him, the little fellow is yours."

He avoided meeting Lady Idina's alert green eyes. She
had to have guessed that he planned on sending a bank
draft to cover the cost of the mislaid puppy. To anyone
living within fifteen miles of Compton Croft, the pooch's
pedigree was too obvious to miss.

The meal was as delicious as Jennifer had promised.
While the servants ate in their usual places at the long
trestle table, the ladies plopped down on two blankets
spread before the fire.

Thorne sat crossed-legged beside his mother's chair,
balancing his plate on his lap and trying hard not to show
his incredulity when the uninhibited Yankee served four
bottles of his finest Chateau Lafitte to the members of his
kitchen staff. Surely a good sherry, or even a vintage port,
would have sufficed. When he met his mother's gaze, her
eyes twinkled knowingly. Lady Charlotte lifted her
brows, as though daring him to protest this unprecedented expression of social democracy at Eagleston
Court.

Baby Jo-Jo left her mother's arms to crawl across the
blanket to Jennifer, who immediately pulled the child
onto her lap. To the clapping toddler's delight, Jennie
nimbly played cat's cradle with a piece of bright yellow

yarn from Mrs. Peckham's knitting satchel.

Spot tried to stick his nose into the middle of the string design looped over her fingers, and she spoke to him softly in Cheyenne. The frisky puppy flopped down on his stomach, laid his head on his paws, and watched her with gentle brown eyes. It seemed horses weren't the only animals that understood her people's language.

The ease with which Jennifer entertained the baby made it plain she enjoyed being around children. When Johnny came closer to watch, she drew him into the animated tomfoolery and taught him a fingerplay called Johnny-jump-up. She seemed scarcely more than a child herself with her lively antics.

The disarming sight of the vivid, dark-eyed woman playing so freely and spontaneously with the two youngsters caught Thorne unprepared. His protective cloak of cynicism hung in tatters around his suddenly vulnerable heart. He looked away, furious at himself and at the raw ache of yearning that stabbed like a hot brand straight through his chest. Bloody hell, what was the matter with him, anyway, sitting on his damn kitchen floor in the presence of his hired help?

Lady Idina's question cut through his sour preoccupation. "Is that fingerplay a Cheyenne amusement, Jennie?"

"No," Jennifer told her gaily, "my mother taught me that one. It is a rhyme from the Cumberland Mountains." She glanced at Avice and smiled with sincere affection. "*Nakohe* is a redhead, just like you," she explained. "My father's people have a great fondness for red hair. To the Cheyenne, red is the symbol of fire ... of heat ... of the warm summertime ... and of the center of life, which is the heart. You would be very much admired by our people."

Lady Avice blushed to the roots of her carroty curls. "Thank you," she said shyly.

A whimsical smile played on Jennifer's lips as she turned her brilliant gaze on Thorne. "But golden-brown hair like the duke's is considered the most beautiful of all."

"What does my son's color signify, *ma mie*?" the dowager duchess inquired sweetly.

Thorne glared at Jennifer in silent warning. At the last question, the servants at the table behind him had stopped chattering among themselves and were listening for the talkative magpie's reply with avid interest.

Jennifer rested her chin lightly on top of Baby Jo-Jo's curly head and sent him a look of pure devilment. "Golden-brown is the symbol of ripeness ... of beauty ... of the sun setting in the western sky." She paused just long enough to glance around the room and be certain she had everyone's attention. "His Grace is the living symbol of perfection."

"I could have told you that," he said with a phlegmatic lift of his shoulders, and their captivated audience dissolved into snickers of muffled laughter. No servant would dare laugh out loud.

"Do all Cheyenne women know how to cook?" queried Lady Avice.

"Yes," Jennifer replied. "Unlike the white people, the Cheyenne have no servants. Everyone, man, woman, and child, is expected to contribute to the common good in some way with the labor of his own hands."

"Are there other differences, Miss Elkheart?" Flora asked, intrigued with such a novel approach to the social order.

Jennifer tipped her head, considering. "For one thing, Cheyenne women have always been able to own property. Their lodge belongs to them, as well as all their household furnishings, and their ponies and trappings. My great-grandmother, Porcupine Quills, was one of the richest people in our band."

A thoughtful hush followed Jennifer's blithe statement. Only after a decade of acrid debate had a long overdue reform of the married women's property law been passed by Parliament.

Lady Idina's soft laugh intruded on their sober reflections. "Jennie was horrified to learn that, until just thirty years ago, everything a wedded female in England held dear, right down to her handbag and the coins inside it, belonged to her husband. Even *she* belonged to her husband."

The only male present folded his arms, his straight brows meeting in a scowl of irritation. "That's quibbling a legal point," the duke of Eagleston said gruffly. "In the courts of common law, a husband and wife were considered one person."

"And that person was the husband," Idina offered concisely.

"What else can your women do besides own property?" Mrs. Beeton asked, rolling the stem of her wineglass between her thick fingers.

"They make their own decisions," Jennifer promptly replied. "Women have always been important members of our bands, and they discuss matters freely with their husbands. Every Cheyenne, male or female, learns from childhood to be independent. So we grow up rather impatient of control or restraint of any kind."

"Isn't a wife subject to her husband's authority?" Avice questioned in astonishment.

"Only if she chooses to be. And if the man is abusive, she can divorce him without any social stigma. My mother threw her first husband away."

Gasps of amazement rippled through the room full of females.

"Threw him away?" squeaked one of the scullery maids, her eyes enormous.

Jennifer nodded serenely. "Yes, at a throw-away dance. Of course, she'd left the pony soldier on their wedding night, so it was never a real marriage in the first place."

The duke's broad shoulders were rigid with censure. His rich baritone grated in the absolute stillness that ensued. "Don't you listen to any authority higher than yourself, Miss Elkheart?"

She met his caustic blue gaze, not retreating an inch. "From an early age, we are taught self-effacement in the presence of our elders, Your Graciousness." She paused and smiled at Lady Charlotte, who immediately blew her a kiss. "But our self-control comes from within. We strive to be brave in the face of danger, kind and generous to those less fortunate, and strong-hearted in times of adversity."

"Admirable qualities," he rejoined with a curl of his lip. "Your people must be the epitome of selfless courage."

She grinned as though oblivious to the biting sarcasm of his lethal tongue. "Being Cheyenne, myself, I am too well-mannered to agree."

"How was the musicale, Mother?"

Lady Charlotte closed the door behind her and walked across the billiard room's plush Turkistan carpet. "Delightful, *mon cher*," she said, signaling him not to get up with a wave of her hand. "You should have gone with me to Nettlefold. All your friends inquired about you. *Vraiment*, this morning's courageous rescue from the River Leigh was the only topic of conversation. Jennifer is being pursued by every eligible bachelor in Warwickshire." She paused before adding meaningfully, "Save one."

Her son addressed the dying embers in the fireplace, unwilling to meet her perceptive gaze. "Beneath that veneer of Western civilization, Miss Elkheart is as untamed and unpredictable as the wildcats that roam her homeland."

"*Eh, bien*, that is as good an excuse as any, I suppose, for not throwing your hat in the ring."

"I have no intention of pursuing the indomitable little Yankee."

Charlotte stood beside the hassock on which his feet were propped and studied him with maternal care. Why was it that he failed to see what his loved ones perceived so clearly? Thorne and Jennifer were made for each other. The dazzling girl's joyful spirit was the one, luminous ray which could pierce, at last, the dark depths of her son's shuttered soul.

He moved his feet to the floor, and she sat down on the low stool in front of him. "How long have you been sitting here like this?" she asked in a placid tone.

He shrugged and reluctantly tore his gaze from the

smoldering hearth to meet hers. "Awhile."

Charlotte had seen the bleak longing in Thorne's eyes that morning as he'd watched Jennifer and the children. She'd half-expected to find him blind drunk when she returned this evening. He wasn't. He was stone-cold sober. The calm detachment on his sharp features frightened her more than his dogged cynicism. She wouldn't let him throw his happiness away, not even if it meant the anguish of baring her own battered and bruised soul.

"I think it's time for us to talk," she said, folding her hands in her lap. "Eight years of silence is long enough for any pilgrim's sojourn through the fires of purgatory."

He sat perfectly still, his hands resting loosely on the arms of his chair. "Are you sure . . ." he began, and she touched her fingertips to his lips to forestall him.

"Yes." She slipped her hand into his and gazed down at the long, elegant fingers. *"Bon Dieu*, where to begin? I shall simply start by saying that you are the single, brilliant light in my life, *mon fils.* The star of happiness on every Christmas tree, the unflawed jewel in my treasure box of tarnished, broken dreams."

He snorted derisively, and she looked up to meet his ironic gaze. "Don't ever think for a moment that I regret having you, Thorne. No matter what your father was like."

His handsome face contorted in disgust. His low voice reverberated with self-loathing. "In spite of the fact that I am his exact image?"

She gazed at him lovingly. The gold highlights in his hair glowed in the lamplight. The azure eyes, the aristocratic nose, the stubborn chin had been inherited from his Blakesford forebears. "Only the outside wrappings were bequeathed by your father," she said. "For my dear one, you are nothing, nothing like him where it counts." She placed her hand over her son's heart. "Here, inside you."

"What is it you wish to tell me?" he asked in quiet resignation, and she could hear the unspoken dread in his words.

She rose and went to the fireplace, where she stared

down at the glowing ashes. As she began, her voice sounded faint and faraway to her own ears. "I was only seventeen when I found Henry Blakesford in our drawing room with the estate steward's daughter under very suspicious circumstances. Of course, he vehemently denied that anything was wrong. In my shock, I barely noticed the incriminating evidence, the rumpled cushions, the wrinkled dress, the girl's solemn, frightened expression before she bolted from the room." Charlotte turned and faced her son, gathering her courage as she went on. "You were less than a year old at the time. I couldn't go home to my parents and leave you here at Eagleston Court. For one thing, I knew they'd never believe my conjectures. And the thought of losing my baby boy was unbearable."

Thorne make a strangled sound deep in his throat, and Charlotte forced herself to continue. "Your father got down on his knees before me. He swore that nothing had happened. That nothing like that would ever happen as long as he lived. He was so convincing—God help me—I believed him. Knowing a divorce was unthinkable, that in the eyes of the law, not only did you belong to him, but that he was my legal representative and moral guardian, as well, I accepted his professions of innocence and his promises, sworn on a Bible, that I would never have reason to doubt him."

"My father was a very persuasive man," Thorne said with quiet somberness.

Charlotte walked back to the hassock and sank down in front of her son. She bit her lip, refusing to succumb to the tears until her story was told. Her hands clenched into fists, she met his compassionate eyes. "The steward's daughter was . . . only ten years old. In my inexperience and naiveté, I couldn't comprehend . . . could scarcely imagine . . . such depravity. To my relief, your father immediately left for London, and in the years that followed, he rarely returned to Eagleston Court, and then only to prevent the gossip which might have harmed his political career. We never . . ." She swallowed the painful sobs that choked her throat. "We never had marital relations from the day you were born, *mon enfant*. As far as Henry was concerned, I had produced the necessary heir and had served my purpose."

Thorne clasped his mother's trembling hands. His heart ached for the torment she had suffered alone and in silence. His misguided attempt to protect her had kept him from speaking out. If only he'd known that she had discovered his father's ugly secret years ago.

She bent her head and kissed Thorne's hand, and her tears of remorse splashed on his fingers. "It was only at Henry's death—and the dreadful circumstances surrounding it—that I finally allowed myself to face the truth. The nightmares came then, like grisly specters in my darkened bedroom, asking what I could have done to prevent such unspeakable corruption."

Thorne lovingly kissed his mother's soft, white hair. "You cannot blame yourself for my father's perversions," he said gently, repeating the words he'd said of himself time and time again. "I listened to Henry Blakesford on a similar occasion, when I suspected him of the vilest debauchery and accepted his tearful protestations of innocence. You and I were fooled by a cunning, experienced liar, who'd spent an entire adulthood concealing his despicable acts."

She lifted her head and looked at him with unutterable sadness. "After the shocked whispers and hushed innuendoes at his death, I presumed that you knew about him, *mon cher*, though I couldn't bring myself to speak of it. In the years since, I have watched in despair as your bitter alienation from everyone around you has deepened. Don't let your father continue to destroy your faith in your fellow man, even from his grave."

Thorne cupped his mother's tearstained face in his hands and placed a gentle kiss on her forehead. "Henry Blakesford has no hold on me now, Maman," he declared, knowing in his heart that it was a lie. He prayed that his mother would attain the peace of mind she truly deserved.

He knew in truth that he would never forgive himself for his father's deeds. Nor would he ever trust anyone completely again.

Chapter 11

The fountain splashing in the inner courtyard was the only sound to disturb the still night. Morning Rose waited, trembling with fear, wavering between a fading hope and gut-racking, unbearable despair. She was seated on a velvet-cushioned divan beneath a lacy gold canopy. As she looked about the open pavilion, she tried to conquer the terror that threatened to suffocate her.

Exquisite blue-and-white tiles covered the walls, the octagon floor, and the portico that surrounded the pavilion on all sides. In the center of the room, a glowing brazier provided enough heat to ward off the evening chill. On a low table beside the blue divan, a gold tea set, trimmed with rubies and lapis lazuli, had been left for her convenience.

Along the portico's eastern wall, a series of graceful arches supported by blue marble pillars framed the darkened outlines of minarets against the star-studded sky on the seaward side. Below, terraced gardens led to other pavilions, other courtyards.

In the midst of this sublime display of wealth and beauty, Morning Rose waited for her beloved, the hope of his safe return fading with each passing moment. She bowed her head and prayed to Maxemaheo, the Creator of Life, to save her courageous warrior. And if the All-Father could not rescue her loved one from his enemies, to take him swiftly to that place of bliss in the world above the clouds.

The hushed sound of a footfall brought Morning Rose to her feet. She raced across the tiled floor, only to halt at the portico's *edge. Her heart pounded in dread. Was it him? Or a messenger bringing news of his torture and death?*

A tall man stood beneath an archway on the far side of the reflecting pool, partially illuminated by a moonbeam. He wore a flowing, hooded cloak, dusty and travel worn. Most of his face remained in shadow. She couldn't see his eyes, but the heavy black beard and mustache were clearly recognizable. Even through her tears, Morning Rose could see him smiling at her foolish worries.

He was here!

He was alive!

The man she loved more than life itself.

The man she would love for all time, though the stars faded from the sky, and the moon gave up its light.

Sobbing with joy, Morning Rose rushed to him. "Zehemehotaz," she cried, her deep voice choked with emotion. "Thou, my beloved one."

He opened his arms and drew her into his sheltering embrace. "Namehota, Vonahenene," he whispered. "I love you, Morning Rose."

Closing her eyes, she lifted her face for his kiss, and the familiar tickle of his beard and mustache against her skin seemed like very heaven . . .

Jennifer's eyes flew open. The vision had come again. More clear and vivid than she could ever remember. The Maiyun were warning her that she risked jeopardizing her future happiness. Her reckless behavior with the seductive English lord would cost her more than just her reputation among the whites or the approval of her Cheyenne family. It would cost her a love that comes once in a lifetime.

Trembling and disoriented, she started to push the comforter aside. Spotted Beaver bounded up from beneath the covers, barking excitedly. Jennifer snuggled him close, pressing her cheek against his thick, silky fur. His docked tail wagged in pure elation.

"Are you always this happy in the morning?" she asked, and he showered her with puppy kisses in reply.

They were in the lovely yellow-and-white bedroom

Lady Idina had provided for her stay at Nettlefold Manor. When someone tapped softly on her door, the spaniel leaped down and raced across the room, barking a euphoric welcome.

"Come in," Jennifer called. She rose and stood next to the bed, expecting an upstairs maid to enter with a pot of hot chocolate.

Her hostess, attired in a quilted apricot robe, stepped inside. "I couldn't wait to meet you downstairs at breakfast," Idina admitted with an excited smile as she closed the door behind her. "Are you ready for your first Nettlefold foxhunt?" She bent and patted the frisky spaniel before crossing the room with her halting gait, then took a closer look at her guest. "Why, Jennie," she said with concern, "you look upset about something."

"I am, in a way," Jennifer answered. "I have been communing with the spirits in my sleep." She reached up and lifted a small hoop decorated with the black and white feathers of the magpie down from the pale yellow canopy above her pillow.

"Ghosts? But Nettlefold isn't haunted." Idina came to stand beside the bed, where her attention was immediately diverted by the object in Jennifer's hands. "What have you there, dearest?"

"A dreamcatcher," Jennifer explained. "My father gave it to me the day I left home to stay with Grandpapa for the first time. *Nihoe* made it especially for me. I was fourteen years old and terribly frightened." She offered the hoop to her friend to examine.

"What a lovely ornament!" Lady Idina exclaimed.

"It is more than ornamental," Jennifer said. "It possesses extraordinary powers. Anything *nihoe* makes—from love flutes to peace pipes—is magical. Although my father's real name is Strong Elk Heart, the Cheyenne people often call him Dream Catcher for his ability to interpret visions and to create such wonderful gifts as the treasure you hold in your hands."

Idina turned the dreamcatcher over, scrutinizing it with sincere interest. "How does it work?"

"Unhappy dreams are caught in the hoop's web, where

they stay until the morning light fades them away." Jennifer pointed to the tiny hole in the center of the fine netting of buffalo sinew. "Only dreams of happiness can slip through, bringing images of hope and encouragement to the fortunate dreamer."

Lady Idina's melodic voice was filled with admiration as she returned the hoop to its owner. "What a lovely idea."

Reverently, Jennifer touched the fragile shells caught in the circle of fine webbing, then brought the dreamcatcher to her face. Closing her eyes, she stroked the silken feathers against her cheek. Thoughts of her parents and brother on their ranch, nestled in a beautiful valley southwest of Medicine Hat, filled her with a heartsick yearning.

"This morning, Black Hawk Flying will be handling the yearlings and the colts and fillies born in the spring, brushing their coats and leading them with rawhide halters to get them used to gentle human hands. The two-year-olds are being slowly and carefully trained under my father's directions. No one understands horses better than a Cheyenne. And no Cheyenne warrior understands them better than *nihoe*."

Recognizing the depth of her homesickness, Lady Idina listened in quiet sympathy. She made no attempt to dismiss her guest's low spirits with cheery platitudes.

Jennifer laid the dreamcatcher on a stand near the bed. Moving to the window, she pulled back the yellow silk drapes and stared out at the vista of rolling green pastures bounded by hedges and low stone walls. The morning's first glimmerings of light were spreading across the verdant countryside. "Warwickshire is greener than our Canadian prairies," she stated solemnly. "More beautiful in its way. But this lovely place will never be my home."

"You had the dream again." Idina's hushed words betrayed her disappointment.

Jennifer's head drooped. She traced an invisible symbol of the evening star on the glass pane, wishing her sister were there to confide in. Julie always managed to put her overblown fears into perspective. "The Great Powers are telling their foolish Cheyenne daughter that her path leads far away from this small island." She paused, not wanting to mention the handsome English lord who seemed to intrude into her every conversation with Lady Idina.

"Must you follow their advice?"

"In the end, the decision is mine. If I listen to their prophecy, I will find a love that will last a lifetime and beyond." She looked back over her shoulder and met Idina's discerning gaze, leaving the unspoken alternative to her hostess's imagination. Jennifer could surrender to her temporary infatuation with the duke of Eagleston, but she'd spend the rest of her years regretting her hasty actions.

"How can you be so certain?" Lady Idina protested. She sank down on the tousled bedcovers, lifted Spotted Beaver onto her lap, and absently stroked the spaniel as she continued. "Your vision is filled with strange objects you can't possibly understand. Perhaps you've misinterpreted its true meaning."

Jennifer sighed. She left the window and sat down on a bench in front of the dressing table. Idly picking up an ornate hand mirror, she turned to face her friend. "No, dear lady, I have not been misled. I saw a painting of Constantinople in a museum once. There were terraced gardens and minarets and blue-tiled pavilions exactly like I've seen in my vision."

"But that still doesn't mean you've interpreted the dream correctly," Idina argued.

Jennifer stared at her father's gift lying on the nightstand, the black and white feathers brilliant in the morning light that streamed through the window. "I do not always understand my visions perfectly," she confessed. "Sometimes, what I think will happen in the future shifts or changes as events unfold. And sometimes, I mistake their symbolism." She looked up from the dreamcatcher and met her friend's gaze. "But I am certain that the man I will truly love is a warrior. A man like my father, who has proven his courage under fire and earned his badge of honor on the battlefield. A valiant man who can protect his wife and children from all evil-doers."

Idina responded with a gentle, teasing smile. "From what you've told me of Strong Elk Heart, he sounds a little bigger than life."

"Perhaps he is," Jennifer admitted with a grin. "But I will not fall in love with a lesser man."

"The duke of Eagleston was once in the army," Idina reminded her in an entreating tone. "He served in the Life Guards."

"Yes, and resigned his commission because he did not like the cut of their uniforms!"

"What makes you say that?"

"He told me so." Jennifer scowled down at her bare toes peeking out from beneath the hem of her voluminous nightdress. With stubborn resolve, she clutched the gilded mirror on her lap and tried to ignore the ache in her heart.

Lady Idina made no attempt to deny it. "Jennie, there's nothing wrong with falling in love with a man who's not a decorated war hero," she asserted emphatically. "Thorne knows more about early civilizations than most Oxford dons. He's absolutely brilliant in foreign languages. Why, I swear, the man's a genius when it comes to deciphering ancient writings."

"*Hesc!* I know that. I attended the dedication of his gifts to the British Museum. I have no doubt that His Grace is extremely intelligent," Jennifer said. "But like all your British lords, he spends his days in such meaningless endeavors. Of what purpose is a life devoted to attending soirees and dinner parties, where the most important topic of conversation is the latest fashion in hats? It is no wonder he is so bored that he falls asleep at a court ball."

"Oh, surely he wouldn't do that!"

Raising her lashes, she met her friend's amused gaze and smiled wryly. "I think he was merely pretending. But in any case, the duke of Eagleston lacks the qualities I am seeking in a husband. He doesn't even like children."

Lady Idina stared at her in shock. "What makes you think so?"

"Perhaps you did not notice, but when I was holding the baby on my lap and playing with Johnny, the duke found the sight of us so distasteful, he looked away in disgust. From his horrible scowl, we might have been a pack of wolves attacking a newborn fawn."

"I noticed him look away," Idina said quietly, "but I drew an entirely different conclusion."

"What was that?"

She shook her head in exasperation. "Jennie, I can tell you unequivocally that Thorne loves children. Why, he supports two orphanages, one in London and the other in Paris. Waifs who are picked up by peace officers for stealing or other crimes are taken to the Le Fresne Children's Home rather than placed in jail or sent back out on the streets to fend for themselves. The youngsters are given the best of care and are taught a trade or a profession according to their ability."

"He never spoke of it," Jennifer said dubiously.

"He wouldn't. It would sound like boasting." Putting the black-and-white puppy down, Idina rose and walked haltingly over to the bench. She placed her plump fingers under Jennifer's chin in an endearing gesture. "I've known Thorne since I was a toddler, Jennifer Rose Elkheart. You'll never meet a more honorable gentleman, no matter where you go."

Jennifer's husky voice quavered. "But the duke is not the man I am meant to love."

The room grew still. With the curious spaniel following at her heels, Lady Idina walked slowly to the door, then stopped, her hand on the latch. Her voice was soft and unaccusing as she looked back with a rueful smile. "Have you told Thorne that you'll be leaving soon?"

Jennifer sat up straight, unable to conceal her anxiety. In three more days, she'd leave England with her grandfather to continue their travels abroad.

"No," she admitted. She jumped to her feet, and Spotted Beaver tore across the rug to join her in happy expectation. "Please do not tell him, Dina. I beg you! From the things I have seen in my vision, I am certain it will be in Constantinople that I shall meet the man I am destined to marry."

Idina's eyebrows arched upward in doubt. "You think so?"

Jennifer clamped her lips tight, not wanting to reveal her own ambivalence. Surely, she could control her wayward emotions for three more days. Her intuition told her that if Eagleston knew she was leaving, he might press his advances all the stronger. And if he continued to practice his alluring *veho* wiles upon her, she wasn't at all positive she could resist.

Lady Idina tipped her curly blond head to one side and regarded Jennifer thoughtfully. "Very well," she said at last. "As you wish. But I think you are making a mistake."

"You will not change your mind?"

"No, Jennie. But I know Thorne rather well. If he decides that he wants you, he'll follow you all the way to Constantinople."

Jennifer caught her breath, aghast at the thought. "*Haxc!*" she cried softly. "Surely, he would not do such a thing!"

Lady Idina opened the door. "Oh, he's quite capable of it, my dear. And if you don't tell him the truth now, he'll arrive there in a most unhappy frame of mind. I've seen the duke of Eagleston in a fit of temper. It was enough to make a grown man shake in his boots."

With that parting shot, she left her guest to her worries.

Jennifer gulped in dismay. If Eagleston followed her to Constantinople, he might meet the man of her dreams. He might even tell the man of her impetuous kisses and wanton behavior.

Ahahe! The irascible *veho* could ruin everything!

Mounted on their sleek horses, the Nettlefold guests gathered on the curving gravel driveway in front of the manor house. The ladies, up on sidesaddles, were elegant in full skirts, the wispy veils of their hats billowing in the gentle breeze. It would have been hard to find a prettier sight in all England.

Thorne held the reins of his two magnificent hunters. In spite of the crackling tension that always prevailed just before a hunt, Tacitus waited with well-behaved patience. Barleymow, anxious to be off, was up to his customary tricks, stamping and sidling nervously.

Thorne still hadn't resigned himself to putting Jennie up on the powerful stallion. He could picture her being thrown at a jump and seriously injured, and the image tormented him more than he could have imagined possible. Her safety was the only reason he'd come that morning.

"Behave yourself today," he warned the black. "If you toss Miss Elkheart on her pretty head, I'm going to rent you out for a plow horse."

The stallion shook his bridle reins and whinnied in derision, as though he knew he belonged to that harmless bit of femininity who'd sung to him in the stable.

"Here I am, Your Grace," Jennifer called in her husky contralto. "Ready at last."

Thorne turned to greet her with a welcoming smile and froze in his tracks, momentarily speechless.

She flashed him a carefree grin as she scampered down the wide front steps and hurried over to where he stood waiting. "I had to explain to Spotted Beaver why he could not go along today," she expounded. She stopped short and frowned reproachfully. "It is not polite to stare."

"When Lady Idina told me you rode astride," he said with a slow, admiring grin, "I assumed you wore a divided skirt. I never dreamed you'd show up dressed like a boy. Though why the thought never occurred to me is a mystery now. Any young lady who'd strip to her undies and jump in a river after a drowning pup would scarcely hesitate to prance around in men's breeches."

She glanced down at her outrageous outfit, then back at him. "I do not prance in these," she boldly announced. "I ride in them. And I ride very well, if I must say so myself. I hope I have not shocked you, Your Grace." She grinned with impish delight, making it evident she didn't care if she had.

He shook his head in mock reproach. "Shocked isn't exactly the word I had in mind," he said laconically. "I believe *bowled over* would come closer."

"That is two words," she was quick to point out, "not one. I think I like the sound of *entranced* even better. Although, *enraptured* has a nice ring to it, too."

Before he could answer, Lady Idina moved up beside them, mounted on her short-legged bay mare. "How lovely you look, Jennie," she called cheerily. She turned to meet Thorne's gaze. "I explained to the other guests earlier, Your Grace, that Miss Elkheart is attired to ride the way she's ridden since she was a child. She'll be taking fences and ditches at a smashing clip. It'll be safer for her and everyone around her."

Thorne lifted his hands in surrender. "Do you hear me complaining?"

Jennifer stroked the black's long, arched neck as she checked his halter and bit. Running her hand soothingly across his gleaming coat, she examined the girth, adjusted the stirrup straps, then carefully investigated every inch of the lightweight jumping saddle. With a final, encouraging pat on the stallion's flank, she looked over at Thorne.

"Why is Moxtavevoe wearing a red ribbon on his tail?" she demanded, sounding like an indignant mother whose precious little darling has been unjustly criticized.

"Because the last time Barleymow rode in the Combermere hunt, he committed the unforgivable crime of kicking a hound."

"Black Cloud will not kick today," she stated with supreme confidence as she tugged on her riding gloves.

Thorne chuckled skeptically. "I suppose you told him not to?"

"For a *veho*," she said, her dark eyes twinkling in mischievous delight, "Your Graciousness learns very quickly." The faintest hint of a smile turned up the corners of her kissable lips. The effect was devastating.

"Come on, Miss Elkheart," he drawled as he presented her the reins. "I'll give you a leg up."

He cupped his hand for her booted foot and tossed her lightly into the saddle. The longer cut of her ebony riding coat concealed the outline of her compact rump, but her slim thighs and calves were exposed to view, covered only by the form-fitting breeches. His gaze drifted down her lithe frame. She seemed even smaller and finer-boned in the daring male costume. And, ironically, even more feminine. Of its own accord, Thorne's male anatomy reacted in feverish appreciation.

Bloody hell. He should have taken the train for London that morning as he'd wanted—just as he'd purposely stayed away from Nettlefold Manor last evening. In the solitude of his comfortable retreat, he'd slammed the door shut on his erratic emotions, though it had taken every ounce of fortitude he possessed. Some inner instinct told him that the glowing innocence in Jennifer Rose Elkheart's brown almond eyes was the one great threat to his sanity. And apparently, an arm's length between them was not enough distance. He needed to be on the other side of the world. After the hunt was over, and he knew she was safe from harm, he'd return to London. He'd tell Lord Doddridge that he was ready to leave for Istanbul at once.

"When you start into a jump," he warned her, "be prepared for an unexpectedly long takeoff. Let him have his head. Barleymow dislikes any kind of interference with his mouth. He'll go through the fence instead of over it, just to teach you a lesson. And it'll be a lesson you won't soon forget."

She nodded, her beautiful eyes serious. "I will remember."

At the direction of the Master of Foxhounds, the Huntsman gave the signal. Staff and hounds moved off down the road, with the earl of Combermere in scarlet and carrying the horn, in the lead.

The weather had cooperated fully. The morning air was brisk and invigorating. Patches of clouds were interspersed with brilliant sunshine. It wouldn't be long before the first frost came and the leaves turned to scarlet and gold.

Once mounted, Thorne fell in next to the audacious Yankee. Euan Bensen drew up on her other side, his ready smile as ingratiating as ever.

"Have you ever ridden in a foxhunt, Miss Elkheart?" the dark-haired charmer asked.

"Yes, I hunted frequently in Virginia with my sister and grandfather when we lived in the American capital."

Thorne took the opportunity their conversation afforded to study Jennifer. She was adorable in the boyish riding outfit. Her dark chestnut hair was pulled neatly back into a braided chignon, with a small top hat perched forward on her head at a dashing angle. His fingers fairly itched to remove the jaunty hat and pull out the combs holding the heavy mass in place. Only last night, he'd dreamed of burying his face in those perfumed tresses, of feeling her long, silken locks slide over his bare chest. Hell and damnation, he had to stop torturing himself like this.

Ahead of them rode Viscount Lyttleton, Muriel Trevor-Roper, and Victor Houlton, the Renegade's defeated goalkeeper. In another group of equestrians, which included many former hockey players, Count Gortschakoff sat astride one of the Nettlefold hunters. Bringing up the rear, Anthony Trevor-Roper, Lady Avice, and Lady Idina rode side by side, talking quietly.

The cavalcade hacked to Nettlefold Wood, an extensive stand of trees consisting mostly of birches and elms. Everyone brought their horses to a halt and waited quietly as the Combermere hounds swarmed into the covert, their noses to the ground, their tails feathering in excitement.

At the sudden increase of tension, Barleymow started to dance restively. Jennifer leaned forward and spoke to him in a quiet tone. The stallion's ears twitched in immediate response.

"Uncanny, isn't it?" Lady Idina said softly. She'd guided her mount up beside Thorne, who sat watching, enthralled, as the temperamental brute stood stock-still at his mistress's whispered command.

He nodded. "Uncanny, indeed."

"What did you tell him, Jennie?" Idina asked fondly.

Jennifer's eyes glowed with pride. "I told Moxtavevoe that if he behaved himself like a true Cheyenne war pony today, I would sing him a strong-heart song tonight. One that my grandmother taught me. And Porcupine Quills knew the prettiest songs of all. I also promised him that he would never have to wear the detested red ribbon again."

"Oh, doesn't he like wearing the ribbon?" Lady Avice inquired with total sincerity, as she drew her roan hunter to a halt beside the black.

"Hesc!" Jennifer cried, as though surprised that anyone would have to ask such a foolish question. "He absolutely hates it."

"I thought the stallion's name was Barleymow," Euan said in puzzlement.

The little Yankee wrinkled her nose in commiseration for the poor, mistreated animal. "He hated that, too. It is no wonder he has been so unhappy in Eagleston's stable."

"How do you know he's been unhappy, Miss Elkheart?" Avice asked, her eyes huge with amazement. "He looks in good spirits to me."

"Miss Elkheart talks to horses," Thorne offered languidly, "and they talk to her in return. Of course, they converse in Cheyenne, so you won't be able to understand a word of it."

"Christ," Euan muttered beneath his breath. He jerked on his reins, and his hunter executed a miniature *passage*.

Thorne grinned at the handsome beau's slip of the tongue in front of the ladies, followed up by his horse's display of bad manners. And to think he'd actually considered skipping Combermere's hunt. Hell, he wouldn't have missed this morning for the world.

"Does your new puppy speak Cheyenne, too?" questioned Avice.

"Certainly," Jennifer replied with a happy smile. "My

people are especially attached to horses and dogs. But we love children most of all." She turned her brilliant, dark-eyed gaze on Thorne. "Do you like children, Your Grace?"

Her question caught him by surprise. "Well enough, I suppose," he drawled, adding in a sardonic tone, "as long as they're not mine."

He'd meant it for a jest. She glared at him as though he'd said he liked them served for dinner.

Before anyone could make another comment, one of the hounds gave tongue. The rest immediately cast about in fevered excitement for the fresh scent. One by one, they all took up the cry.

Within minutes, the entire pack of bitches burst out of the woods, the scarlet-clad Huntsman after them. He rose in his stirrups, lifted his velvet cap, and pointed as the fox made for open country.

"Tallyho!" he cried.

The hunting horn sounded a short, staccato, double note, and they were away!

By the time the riders crossed the first meadow, the fearless Yankee had stolen the lead from the rest of the field. Thorne stayed right beside Jennifer, prepared to come to her rescue the moment Barleymow took the bit in his teeth.

Together, Thorne and Jennifer sailed across the first obstacle, a solid stonewall. She was so light, Barleymow jumped her clean out of the saddle. But she knew how to keep her hands down, her weight forward, and her feet in the stirrups, so she wouldn't get left behind.

Damn, she rode like a centaur.

No, like Artemis, goddess of the hunt.

They landed in perfect unison, and the horses stretched out, neck and neck, in full gallop, flying after the hounds flying after the fox. Behind them, the rest of the field followed as best they could, trying in vain to catch up.

Thorne smiled to himself at the thrill of it. There was no more marvelous sport in the world. To ride a magnificent hunter, chasing after the hounds at breakneck speed across the changing English landscape, the sporting blood racing in his veins, and a beautiful, spirited woman, who rode like no one he'd ever seen before, at his side.

Chapter 12

Without a single rider coming a cropper despite the deep going, the entire field crossed a stream at the bottom of a wide valley. Jennifer and Eagleston held the lead as they thundered across a turnpike and flew by the thatch-roofed village of Watersham. There, a thick hedge ran alongside a rushing brook. The riders took hedge and water together with the gallantry of a party of charging Cheyenne warriors astride their painted war ponies. Even Lady Idina's gentle mare and Lady Avice's small, sturdy roan soared over with the rest of the field.

The grassy pasture widened again, and the hunters spread out across it. On the far side of the meadow lay six acres of privet and blackthorn. The fox made for the thick covert and disappeared under the hounds' very noses. The riders who'd stayed the course came up, their exhausted horses steaming.

Euan Bensen's black eyes glowed with admiration as he leaned forward and patted his soaked horse's neck. "That was a splendid display of riding, Miss Elkheart!" he exclaimed. "I don't remember when I've ever seen a young woman throw her heart over the hurdles the way you did today."

"Yes, I agree," Count Gortschakoff said. "I have never seen such magnificent riding. My countrymen would be most impressed." The dapper, middle-aged aristocrat stood beside his heaving mare, his gaze riveted, not on Jennifer but on the British duke.

She glanced at Eagleston, who, strangely enough, looked vexed at the Russian's fulsome praise. At that very moment, a large bumblebee landed on Tacitus's velvety nose.

Before she could utter a word of warning, the gray gelding reared and bolted, catching his rider unprepared. The others, who'd all dismounted and now stood beside their spent horses, watched in alarm as Tacitus charged wildly across the hilly grassland.

Jennifer jammed her heels against her tired steed's flanks, and the game stallion burst into action. She leaned forward and spoke to Black Cloud in Cheyenne, urging him to even greater speed. But Tacitus was galloping out of pain and terror, while the black was merely accommodating his mistress's freakish desire for yet another race.

Thorne made no great effort to bring his frightened horse under control, knowing Tacitus's frenzied behavior would quickly burn itself out. He gave the gray gelding its head as it charged across the hilly grassland and out of sight of the other riders. Before he could gradually bring his mount to a halt, he heard hoofbeats pounding from behind.

The next thing he knew, Jennifer drew alongside, reached out, and snatched unsuccessfully at Tacitus's bridle. "Whoa!" she commanded the gray. "Take it easy, boy. Take it easy. Everything is okay."

Thorne reined his horse to an immediate halt. Bloody, living hell! The insignificant slip of a girl he'd been prepared to rescue all morning had just tried to rescue him.

She brought her own mount to a stop and trotted back to Thorne. Her dark eyes were huge, her face drained of color. He realized in disgust that she'd been truly frightened for him. Once again, she'd assumed he was nothing more than a useless, self-indulgent aristocrat. He clenched his jaw to stifle a roar of frustration. Dammit to hell and back. It was no wonder she thought he wasn't the man of her dreams.

He dismounted and grabbed Barleymow's reins. "Get

down, Jennifer," he ordered curtly, making no secret of his aggravation.

"There is no need to be angry at me," she gasped, nearly breathless. "I was trying to assist you."

"I said, *get down.*"

She eyed the crop he clutched in his fist. "Why?"

"Because I told you to," he replied in a silky, ominous tone. "Now, are you going to dismount, Miss Elkheart, or do I have to drag you out of that saddle?"

She looked about her in speculation, estimating how far she'd get before he caught up with her.

"Don't try it," he warned her softly. "Don't even think it."

Wisdom overtook valor, and she slid slowly down from her horse. She folded her arms and stared sullenly at Thorne's chest, the small brim of her top hat hiding her eyes. "I was only trying to help," she muttered, half to herself.

Thorne lifted the silk hat with its frothy puff of black netting from her head and tossed it on the grass. He smiled at her huff of indignation. "Come here, you little savage," he ordered thickly. "I owe you something."

She glanced up in surprise. *"Hesc!* I do not need a reward for coming to your aid. It was merely the Cheyenne thing to do." She retreated a step and found herself pinned against Barleymow's heaving side.

"But I insist, Mohehya," he said, his implacable words sheathed in velvet. "It isn't everyday that a knight is rescued by his lady fair. What kind of a gentleman would I be if I didn't give you a token of my gratitude? After all, you just saved my life."

She looked at him warily. "Were you frightened?"

"Out of my wits," he answered with a grin. His annoyance dissolved at the sight of those enormous brown eyes, fringed with their unbelievably long black lashes, staring up at him in mute consternation. Her lips parted, as though she were about to question his veracity. She wisely thought better of it.

"For once, little magpie, I've rendered you speechless," he said. "And here I didn't think that was possible." He stepped closer, till her stubborn chin was mere inches from the second button on his hunting jacket. "Now about that reward . . ."

Thorne drew her into his arms before she had a chance to protest. He crushed her to him, covering her lips with his in a kiss filled with a raw, throbbing hunger he'd never known before. The hard ache of desire reverberated through every fiber of his being.

How could she think him some prinking fop when every time he was near her, he grew as swollen and turgid as a stud around a mare in heat? He wanted to rip off her clothes and take her there in the soft grass, to bury himself deep, deep in her adorable, feminine body, pounding and thrusting until she screamed his name in ecstasy.

"Vonahenene," he murmured against her soft mouth, his words brittle with need, "tell me you want this as much as I do."

She slid her arms around his neck and pressed her slim, lithe form against him. "I want this," she confessed in a throaty whisper. Their tongues met, touching and tasting with greedy abandon.

Thorne cupped her buttocks, encased in the tight breeches, and lifted her up. Pressing her against his thickened manhood, he continued the kiss. The incredible feel of her curved bottom in his hands, unencumbered by layers of petticoat, bustle, and gown, sent a lightning stab of heat through his groin. Blood surged into his heart as he held her against him.

He closed his eyes, savoring an unbelievable and exquisite torture as she wrapped her slender legs around him. A low, male warning of sexual intent rumbled deep in his chest.

God, she felt so damn good.

Jennifer broke the kiss with a soft, feminine sigh of pleasure. She tugged off her gloves and dropped them on the grass. Her pulse beating erratically, she framed Eagleston's face in her hands. She ran the pads of her thumbs across his thick mustache, reveling in the utterly masculine feel of it. The memory of the golden-brown pelt of hair on his scarred chest seemed to ignite a fire deep inside her.

"You were right, Eagle's Son," she admitted on a deep exhalation of air.

"About what?" he asked, searching her eyes.

"You said I would get used to your hairy face."

He nuzzled the curve of her neck where it met her white silk stock, letting her feel the wiry brush of his mustache across her sensitive skin, then nipped her with his sharp teeth. She heard his muffled laugh. "You'll get used to my whole hairy body," he promised.

A shiver of anticipation started at the top of Jennifer's head and rippled all the way down to her toes. Every resolution she'd made that morning faded like a mist in the summer sun. Thoughts of visions and prophecies, no matter how vibrant and clear, couldn't withstand the driving, instinctual need to touch him again, the way she'd touched him as they sat on the library floor. She longed to run her fingers across his bare skin, to feel the reflexive tensing of his muscles beneath her caress, to trace with her lips the scars that so resembled a warrior's battle wounds.

"I want you, Jennie," he said hoarsely. His tongue dipped into the sensitive hollow of her ear, like a honeybee plunging to the center of a prairie crocus. She trembled beneath the lingering, sensuous touch. His breathy tone was low and urgent. "Teach me how to say 'I want you' in your language."

"Nihoatovaz," she whispered.

"Nihoatovaz, Vonahenene," he murmured. "Nihoatovaz."

The Cheyenne love words spoken so seductively in her ear sent a thrill of excitement coursing through Jennifer's veins, a wild, nearly frantic excitement she'd never experienced before. She pressed closer, shamelessly rubbing her swollen breasts against his broad, solid chest. She could feel her nipples tighten as the aching pleasure spread in undulating waves through her abdomen and thighs.

A soft whimper of yearning deep in her throat told him what she couldn't say out loud. She wanted him. She wanted him in the way that a woman desires her life's mate.

Their lips met in a kiss of unrestrained passion. Jennifer's people placed no shame on lovemaking the way the white people did. The physical union of male and female was considered as natural as breathing, eating, or sleeping.

But Cheyenne girls kept their virginity until marriage.

It took all of her willpower to break the kiss, once again. She leaned back, her hands resting on his shoulders. Their gazes met, and Jennifer read the naked desire in his hooded eyes. She drew a deep, ragged breath. "We . . . we must stop."

"Yes," he agreed in a clipped, cold voice. He immediately set her on her feet and pushed her between him and the black stallion. "We have company."

Jennifer peeked around Eagleston's shoulder. On the top of a knoll sat a rider on his still hunter, watching them. "It is the Russian count," she said in surprise. She peered through narrowed eyes, trying to see if the man really held a pistol, or if it was only the sun glinting off the handle of his riding crop.

"Count Vladimir Ilich Gortschakoff," the duke said softly, the words sounding like a curse, as the Russian turned his mount and galloped away.

She looked up at Eagleston. "You do not like the gentleman."

"Correct," Thorne said. "I do not like the man." He cupped his hands for her foot and tossed her up on Moxtavevoe's back, then retrieved her hat and gloves and gave them to her.

"I do not like him, either," she confided as she drew on her gloves. At his questioning glance, she held her left hand in a horizontal position and slid her right hand under it, giving the Plains Indian sign for death, then glided her fingers in a sinuous movement toward him. "He has the eyes of a dead rattlesnake."

Thorne grinned at her apt description. "For once, little magpie, you and I are in complete agreement."

He suspected that if Jennifer had not been there, Gortschakoff would have taken his best shot. Her presence had probably saved Thorne's life, for while one death could be explained as an unfortunate accident, two could not. Especially if one of the slain was the granddaughter of an American diplomat.

Thorne knew, without being told, that Jennifer would take Barleymow for an early morning ride the next day. In the faint, gray glimmerings of dawn, he waited for her on a rise above the road that led from Nettlefold Manor. When she saw him, she waved and turned in his direction.

"What are you doing up so early?" she called merrily as she approached at a canter. "I thought all British aristocrats slept until noon."

"Not if they want to catch energetic little Yankees at play." He surveyed her scandalous riding outfit. "I see you're back to wearing men's breeches again. Quite a change from the enchanting pink satin you wore last evening."

"I did not think you even noticed what I was wearing," she said in mock reproach. "You left Dina's festive gathering very early."

"I'm not much for parlor games," he informed her. "Besides, I knew I'd have to rise with the roosters to keep up with you."

She laughed and then looked around in pleasure. "Which way shall we go?"

"Come with me," he said with an inviting smile. "I'll show you a bit of our English past." He urged Tacitus into a gallop, and she followed without a moment's hesitation.

They rode together in the fresh morning air, crossing streams and hedges in an easy camaraderie. There was something about Jennie's natural and unguarded curiosity that made Thorne feel as though he were seeing everything around him for the first time. Even the lands he'd roamed as a boy appeared new and marvelously appealing.

He led her to the highest point of the surrounding

countryside. Dunson Hill, crowned by the picturesque ruins of Dunleigh Castle, commanded a magnificent view of the central plains of Warwickshire. The two dismounted and, leading Tacitus and Barleymow, they walked up the grassy rise to the massive stone ruins. At the crest of the hill, they turned and looked out on the thatched roofs and church spires of the hamlets below. The River Leigh cut through the pastoral landscape like a silver ribbon.

He pointed to a village of half-timbered Tudor houses to the east. "There's Chiltenstone," he said and added with a teasing grin, "the home of Mr. and Mrs. Peckham and their brood. Over there is Watersham, where we rode yesterday in the hunt." He put his gloved hand on her shoulder and turned her slightly. "That woodland on the hills across the river is one of the last remnants of the great forest of Arden. At one time it covered most of this district."

"It is lovely," she said with quiet politeness. Her somber tone surprised him, and he studied her intently. She stood motionless, a slight frown etched on her exotic features, her hands clasped in front of her as she gazed, transfixed, at the scene below. Such faint praise from the effusive Miss Chatterbox left him searching for an explanation.

"You're not afraid to be here alone with me, are you?" Thorne asked with genuine concern. "Surely you know by now that I'd never harm you, Jennie."

She met his worried gaze with a faraway look, and it seemed to take her a minute to comprehend his question. "No, I am not afraid," she said at last. "Although I always carry my weapon with me, I am certain I will not have to use it against you." She pulled her corduroy jacket open to reveal the knife sheath strapped to her trousered thigh and smiled absently. He had the feeling she was only half attending to their conversation.

"In that case, let's go explore the castle," he suggested and felt a sense of relief as she immediately acquiesced with a brief nod.

They walked their horses through the main gateway,

which still stood after seven hundred years, crossed the enormous courtyard to the back wall of the crumbling Norman ruins, and passed through a gap in the stones. Thorne tied the animals in a sheltering grove of oaks where they could graze.

Most of the medieval inner bailey was a hollow shell, its broken walls rising up against the blue autumn sky. But one sturdy square tower remained intact. He guided her up the stone stairway, its corners thick with moss, and they walked to a tall arched window that opened to the morning sun.

His beautiful, grave companion stood at its edge and gazed down on the peaceful vista. "There was once a great battle fought here," she said softly. Her face seemed to reflect an inner pain. "Many men died ... horrible deaths."

"So Idina and Basil brought you here already," he said in disappointment.

No one had mentioned the Nettlefold house party making an excursion to the famous site. For some reason he couldn't explain, Thorne had wanted this morning to be memorable for her. It was the same convoluted reason that had kept him at Eagleston Court, instead of returning to London as he'd planned.

"No, I have never been here before," she told him, her tone distant and preoccupied. "Nor has anyone told me about this place." She pointed to a high knoll below the fortress walls. "There was a cavalry charge led by a determined warrior, who defeated his foes that day. He followed his victory with a ferocious massacre of the wounded. The survivors fled, taking sanctuary in this castle."

"How do you know that?" he inquired with amused captivation. "I didn't realize you were a student of English history."

Jennifer pressed her hands to her flushed cheeks. She always felt warm and somewhat drained after experiencing what her mother called the second sight. "I am no scholar, Your Grace, as my sister would be quick tell you." She took a fortifying breath before going on. The power of the vision had left her shaken and with a feeling close to bereavement. "I could see it happening before my eyes as clearly as you see the valley floor below us now."

Eagleston turned his head to look down at the sylvan scene, then back to her with a disbelieving scowl. "What are you saying, Jennie? What could you see that I don't?"

"I saw the clash of two great armies. I heard the shouts of men on foot and horse as they met in the valley. The hills shook with the thunder of cannon that day." She looked at the lichen-covered walls around them. "The people who lived in this stone fort thought it could withstand the cannonballs. But the mighty walls fell beneath their onslaught, and the residents were murdered."

The duke leaned his shoulder against the rough stone, clearly mystified. He folded his arms, studying her for a moment. "You must have read it in a book," he said, his blue eyes filled with confusion. A smile of disbelief played about his generous mouth. "If Basil or Dina didn't tell you, there is no other way you could have known."

She tipped her head and met his doubting gaze with a gentle smile of admonishment. "The Cheyenne people believe what happens in one place is always there . . . always happening. Time is an illusion, Your Grace. We can experience the past, if we have the courage to behold it with our inner eye. But though I saw the fighting, that does not mean I understood the reason behind the conflict. Tell me about it."

"What's the point," he demanded almost crossly, "when you're already familiar with the story?"

"Humor me," she answered with a soft laugh. "Pretend that I know nothing of the circumstances surrounding the hostilities."

He left the wall and moved to stand beside her at the window. "As I'm sure you already know," he stated, his deep voice terse with irony, "the captain who led that cavalry charge was Oliver Cromwell. It was one of the first engagements of the Civil War, otherwise known as the Puritan Revolution."

"I have heard of the Puritans," she said brightly. "We

studied them at Thanksgiving time. Or was it the Pilgrims?"

He raised his brows skeptically at her lighthearted remark, but continued. "Yes, well, Cromwell fought in the army of the Parliamentarians led by the earl of Essex. The other force, made up of the Royalists loyal to Charles I, were soundly defeated. As you said, Dunleigh Castle fell and its occupants were put to the sword, with no quarter given."

"What were they fighting over?"

He gazed out across the sweeping panorama. "Oh, many things. Constitutional rights, for one. Religion, for another."

"It is a continual source of bafflement to me," she admitted, "that white men are always so willing to slaughter one another in their religious fanaticism. My people see the earth and its inhabitants as sacred. We believe that Maxemaheo, the All-Father Above, looks over us all. Our brother and sister animals, the plants and the trees, even the rocks and rivers are living creatures and must be protected from harm. We would never kill another human being because of his spiritual beliefs."

He started to reply, but Jennifer raised her hand. "Listen," she said. "Someone is coming."

The sound of approaching horses carried upward on the morning breeze. This time it was no vision. Eagleston quickly caught her elbow and pulled her away from the open window. He put his finger to his lips, and she waited silently beside him, pressed flat against the rough wall.

Then, as the visitors dismounted in front of the tower, she heard their voices. Two men were speaking in an alien tongue. Jennifer raised up on tiptoe and whispered in the Eagle's ear. "It is the Russian count."

Eagleston jerked his head in agreement. He motioned for her to follow him, and they stealthily descended the moss-covered steps. For some unknown reason, he wanted to listen without detection to the Russians' conversation. Delighted to be a part of the conspiracy, regardless of the motive, she moved as soundlessly as she could in his wake.

They reached the side of the wall opposite the new-comers, whose exchange could now be heard distinctly. The two men were arguing with each other. At one point, Count Gortschakoff shouted what must have been an expletive. She looked at Eagleston for some clue to what was being said, but his sharply-chiseled face remained impassive.

When Thorne had learned enough, he touched Jennifer lightly on the shoulder and pointed toward the oak grove where their horses stood tied. Her dark eyes shone with the excitement of their mutual adventure. She had no notion that if they were discovered, he'd be forced to use the derringer hidden in his boot—a contingency that would require an explanation he wasn't prepared to give.

He would have stayed at the ruins longer, if she hadn't been with him. The thrill of mortal danger was one of the reasons he enjoyed working for the secret service. Only when his life was at risk did he feel truly alive.

Today was different. The chance brush with discovery had taken a chilling turn with Jennifer beside him. Thorne was quite willing to sacrifice his life for his country. Jennie's life was another matter.

They crept along the inner courtyard wall, slipped through the break in the stones, and raced across the high grass. Mounting their horses, they moved deeper into the stand of trees. When they were far enough from Dunleigh Castle not to be heard, they urged their steeds to a gallop.

Thorne and Jennifer rode across miles of open pastureland, then turned onto a road that led to the ancient bridge that spanned the River Leigh near Eagleston Court. There they stopped and dismounted.

"What was that all about?" Jennifer asked with a happy gurgle of laughter. She was nearly bouncing up and down in her excitement. "Why did we hide from those two men?"

"I didn't want them to find us alone together," Thorne

explained. "They might have leaped to the wrong conclusion."

She gaped at him with a mixture of deflation and incredulity. "You mean all that creeping around was just to protect my reputation?"

"What about *my* reputation?" he responded dryly. "You didn't think I was afraid of them, did you? I knew you had your knife to defend us."

"Do not worry," she said with an infectious giggle. Her eyes sparkled with puckish delight. "You are safe with me, white man."

Enchanted by her playful vivacity, he clasped her elbows and drew her nearer. He was determined, at whatever the cost to his pride, not to let her suspect the truth. "I was prepared to hide behind your skirts," he told her with a languorous grin, "till I remembered you weren't wearing any. That's when I decided we'd better take to our heels without saying good-bye."

She tipped her head back and burst into gales of laughter. The throaty, seductive sound sent his heart slamming back and forth inside his rib cage. Capturing the nape of her neck in his hand, he bent and grazed the smooth column with his open mouth. The feel of her silken skin beneath his lips, coupled with the scent of wildflowers in her hair, snapped the fragile bonds that held his willpower in check.

"Jennie," he murmured against the beating pulse of her throat. He slipped his arm around her waist and drew her nearer.

Jennifer stiffened warily at the ardor in his voice. She was not going to let this happen again. The man was an indolent, hedonistic peacock, who didn't even like children. If she needed proof that he wasn't the courageous warrior of her dreams, their recent encounter with the Russians made it irrefutable. She pushed sharply against his shoulders, and he released her at once, his gaze questioning.

She immediately stepped away from him. "I like you very much, Your Grace," she said in breathless confusion. "But . . . but only as a friend."

He didn't say a word, just stood watching her with inscrutable eyes as she hurried to stand by the bridge's stone wall.

Ahahe! There was so much about him that she *did* like. His ready wit, his unflappable insouciance, his keen mind. Add those charming gifts to his undeniable good looks, and it was no wonder that every time they were together, she forgot the more admirable qualities she desired in a husband. She glanced back at him and stammered awkwardly, "I—I hope we—we can be friends."

His reply was low and filled with tenderness. "If that's what you want, Mohehya."

"I do."

Her mind spinning in turmoil, Jennifer rested her elbows on the wall and gazed blindly down at the rushing water. She bit her lip and fought back the unexpected tears that blurred her vision, then forced herself to concentrate on her surroundings.

They weren't far from the place where she'd rescued Spotted Beaver. She could see the stand of beeches and oaks from where she stood. When she peeked again at Eagleston, he was staring out across the water. She suspected he was thinking about their swim—and the way she'd looked in her wet camisole and drawers.

He came over and stood beside her. "Basil and I used to dive from this bridge when we were boys," he said pleasantly as though nothing disconcerting had happened. "The current would carry us downstream to our favorite fishing hole, where we'd already stored our tackle and poles."

Jennifer squeezed her eyes shut and released a pent-up sigh of thanksgiving. She'd been afraid he was angry at her, and that possibility had brought with it a bleak, desperate feeling of abandonment. "It must be very deep at this spot," she said, praying he wouldn't notice the telltale quiver in her voice.

"Deep enough for two foolhardy youngsters," he replied with a chuckle.

Her emotions bobbing up and down like heads of wild clover in the warm prairie wind, she uttered a nervous titter of laughter. "After our adventure at the ruins, I am feeling a little foolhardy, myself."

"Would you care for a morning swim?" he inquired, the invitation as cool and enticing as the river below. "We could ride to the site of my mother's picnic, where we swam the other day."

Jennifer peered at him from beneath lowered lashes, then down at the rushing water. At that moment, she wanted to do something rash and tempestuous and completely unexpected.

Thorne could sense Jennie's hesitation. The thought of frolicking with her in the River Leigh—this time without an audience of screaming, agitated females—spurred him on. Moving closer, he spoke softly in her ear. "Come on, little Miss Magpie," he cajoled, "I dare you."

Jennifer's nut-brown eyes lit up at the challenge. "All right, I will swim with you. But only if we dive from the bridge."

"What?" He looked down at the swiftly moving water, then grinned. "I haven't jumped off this damn bridge since I was twelve years old."

"Hesc! If you do not want to swim . . ." she began, mistaking his meaning.

"The hell I don't."

Without another word, they sat down on the stone wall and pulled off their high riding boots and stockings, then removed their jackets and laid them on top of their boots. Jennifer took off her hat and set it carefully on her jacket. Clad in breeches and shirts, they rose to their feet and stood poised, side by side, on the wide ledge.

Thorne looked at the dauntless girl. "Are you sure you know what you're doing, Yank?"

She smiled, her eyes brilliant with anticipation. "Yes! You just tell me when, veho."

"All right. Ready, set, dive!"

They flew off the bridge as one, making perfect twin dives.

Jennifer savored the glorious, heart-stopping exhilaration of flying through space, of plunging into the water and going down, down, down beneath the bubbling foam. As she tucked and headed back to the top, she saw Eagleston gliding smoothly upward beside her.

They breached the surface together, and she whooped the wild, ululating Kentucky yell her mother had taught her. His answering shout of laughter rang to the treetops, joyous and clear. It was one of the few times she'd heard him truly laugh with the genuine spontaneity and honest enjoyment of a carefree boy. Then they were caught by the strong current and carried downstream to the fishing hole of his youth.

Clambering up the bank, they threw themselves on the grass.

"Where did you learn to dive like that?" he asked between gulps of air. Before she could answer, he waved his hand. "No, don't tell me. I know. Your father."

Jennifer's heart pounded and her lungs burned. She took deep drafts of air, waiting for her respiration and pulse to return to normal. "During our childhood," she gasped, "my sister and I swam throughout the summertime, diving into our mountain rivers from high rocks and ledges." Her chignon had come loose, and she sat up and squeezed the water out of the long, thick braid as she continued. "Once, we found an underwater hole in a bank, and I talked Julie into exploring it. When we entered the tunnel, we could feel the fur of a large, strong animal pushing past us in the opposite direction. We saw a light ahead and surfaced inside the dam of a family of beavers."

Eagleston rolled to his side and propped his head on one hand, listening in fascination. "What did you do then?"

"We were afraid the beaver would come back. So we broke through the top of the dam and ran home, all excited, to tell our parents." She rolled her eyes at the memory. "My father gave us the scolding of our young lives for taking such chances. I tried to explain that none of it had been Julie's idea, but they seemed to expect her to keep a rein on my more outlandish and dangerous schemes."

"Jennifer Rose," Thorne stated with a slow, wondering

shake of his head, "you are without a doubt, the most incredible female I've ever met."

She wrinkled her nose at him, suddenly self-conscious. "I am not sure that is a compliment."

"Believe me, it is."

Thorne rose and walked to the river's edge. Placing two fingers in his mouth, he gave a piercing whistle. Not long after that, Tacitus and Barleymow came galloping toward them. He removed a blanket from behind the gelding's saddle and tossed it to Jennifer. "You'd better get that around you before you catch cold."

Instead of wrapping it about her shoulders, she spread the blue-striped wool on the grass, then looked at him with guileless eyes. "It is warm here in the sunshine," she announced with an expression of untrammeled innocence. "We can lie on the blanket and both dry off before going back. That way you will not catch cold, either."

The thought of lying beside Jennifer in that swath of golden sunlight on that soft, tempting blanket more than matched the phenomenal sensation of diving from the bridge. He started to speak, cleared his throat, and began again, finding it difficult to achieve his usual air of restless boredom. "That ... ah ... that sounds like an excellent suggestion, Miss Elkheart."

Chapter 13

With his elbow crooked and his head propped on his hand, Thorne took the opportunity to study Jennifer in silence. She lay on her back, her face to the sun, her eyes closed. His gaze lingered on her striking features, the high cheekbones, the lustrous ebony fans that feathered her cheeks, the delicately arched brows, the burnished satin skin. The wet linen shirt clung enticingly to her high, firm breasts. Her soaked breeches were molded to her slender legs. He watched the steady rise and fall of her chest and wondered if she'd dozed off to sleep.

The blood pounded in his veins and the air scorched his constricted lungs as Thorne feasted on the sight of her. From the very core of his being, he hungered for Jennie. It was more than sexual need, though, God knew, there was that. It seemed the harder he tried to fight his physical attraction to her, the stronger it became.

Scarce wonder he was roasting in the fires of carnal torment. In repose, she was the living image of a man's most secret dreams.

Awake, she was something else again.

He smiled at the memory of her standing on the bridge beside him, fearless and invincible. No other woman he'd ever known would have made that dive with him. Hell, he probably wouldn't have made it himself without her impudent challenge. And no other genteel young lady would be lying here beside him now, for that matter.

212

Miss Jennifer Rose Elkheart seemed to follow a moral code of her own. He wondered just how much she knew of the evils and perversions of mankind.

He plucked a blade of grass and traced the delicate line of her mouth. She giggled deep in her throat, but didn't open her lids.

"Tell me something, Jennifer," he said lightly, and her lashes fluttered at the sound of his voice.

"What?" she asked, her eyelids still closed.

"Exactly what did you see in your vision of my mother?"

Her eyes flew open, and she rolled to her side to face him. Her joy was unmistakable. "You believe in my visions!"

"I didn't say that," he cautioned. "I'm just curious to learn what you think you saw."

Her smooth brow puckered at his skepticism. "I saw a white-haired *vehoka* weeping," she said, a tinge of peevishness in her reply. "The lady was crying because her husband had broken his promises. But I did not know who the lady was," she clarified, "until I met your mother."

"Did you know what my father's broken promises were?"

"From the depth of the lady's grief, I assumed that he'd been unfaithful to his marriage vows," Jennifer answered without hesitation. "What else would leave a woman so completely filled with despair?" She met Thorne's gaze, and he recognized the unqualified sincerity in her soft brown eyes. He was certain she knew nothing about the more sordid parts of life. And therefore, nothing of his father's twisted sexual appetites.

Relief surged through him, bringing with it a new and different tension. "How much do you know about the keeping and breaking of marriage vows?" he probed carefully.

The little magpie sat up in a quick, fluttering movement. Studiously avoiding his eyes, she stared out at the river, her arms wrapped around her bent knees. Her entire body seemed to tighten, ready to spring skyward like a coil suddenly released from a pocket watch. "Are you talking about the birds and the bees?" she asked warily.

"Yes." Thorne remained perfectly still, certain the slightest movement on his part would send her bounding to her feet and racing toward Barleymow.

She replied in a low, flustered tone. "My mother explained all about that to my sister and me before we left on this trip. But it was scarcely necessary."

"Why was that?"

"I told you," she said, still refusing to look at him. "I was raised on a horse ranch."

Recognizing the touching naiveté in her remark, he tried not to grin at the taut little figure in front of him. "You can relax now, Miss Elkheart," he said. "The quiz is over. I promise I won't ask any more questions of an intimate nature."

"I am thankful for that," Jennifer muttered, and her shoulders slumped in relief. She shook her head, her next comment barely audible. "I will never get over some of the peculiar differences between your people and mine." Then she leaned back on her elbows with a scowl and examined the leafy branches of a tree.

"What do you mean?"

"Lady Idina warned me not to say anything about the facts of life to Avice or any other unmarried lady. She explained that the English do not tell their young girls anything at all about what to expect on their wedding night, right up until the morning of their marriage. I did not realize, till now, it was the same for the unmarried men as well." She heaved a ragged sigh and then went on, still addressing the nearby oak. "Of course, I am willing to answer your questions, Your Grace, but you really should speak to your mother first. She may not want you to know about these things, till the day you are wed."

Jennifer risked a peek at the quiet man. His blank expression told her he was mortified that she knew about his appalling state of ignorance.

"Do not be embarrassed," she told him with ready sympathy. "It is not your fault that the British aristocracy conspires to keep its unmarried men and women in the dark until the day they are packing for their honeymoon."

There was a long, strained pause, and when the Eagle finally gathered the intestinal fortitude to respond, his beautiful baritone came out almost a croak. "Still . . . a fellow can't help but wonder."

"You are absolutely right," she declared, turning to face him. "For once, we are in total agreement. But since it is your people's custom to preserve your innocence, I suggest that you have a heart-to-heart talk with your mother."

He blinked at her, clearly surprised at her plain-speaking. "You're very understanding, Jennie," he said, his blue eyes glowing with warm appreciation. She'd never seen him so . . . appreciative.

She sank back on the blanket with a knowing smile. "My parents warned me, before I left on this trip, that I would encounter some very peculiar customs. *Hesc!* They did not know the half of it!"

Thorne moved to lean over her, one hand positioned beside her head, his fingers toying with her damp braid. "I'm sure this visit has proved to be quite an enlightening experience for you."

Jennie looked up at him, her almond eyes bright with winsome amusement. "It has been very educational," she admitted.

She ran a soft fingertip across his mustache, and he knew, instinctively, she was thinking of their game on the floor of the Nettlefold library and her wager to see his bare chest. He took her finger inside his mouth and stroked it leisurely with his tongue. With a quick, shocked inhalation of air, she retrieved her finger, then cautiously traced his eyebrows with the moist tip. Following the line of his cheekbone with her index finger, she grazed his lower lip with the soft pad of her thumb. The gentle, tentative, thoughtful exploration threatened to drive him over the brink of self-control.

With a jolt of insight, Thorne realized what had gone wrong back there at the bridge—and on the morning in his stable as well. She was like a tiny, wild bird he would have to lure into eating from his hand. She had to come to him—not just of her own accord, but believing it was she who'd made the decision, not him.

There was no need to hurry the wooing. After what he'd heard at Dunleigh Castle, he knew that his own proposed mission to Istanbul would have to be aborted, anyway.

Thorne admitted, at last, what he'd stubbornly refused to recognize. He was falling in love with this impassioned, undisciplined child of nature. She'd make the worst possible duchess, with her tempestuous ways and her unguarded tongue, and he didn't give a good, aristocratic goddamn. For she'd be the most wonderful, glorious, unpredictable wife in all England. And his children—their children—would have the most loving, devoted mother imaginable.

He bent his head, and their cool breaths mingled. "Sweet, sweet, little magpie," he whispered, his heart hammering so fiercely he could barely trust himself to speak. He brushed his lips across hers, and she opened her soft mouth to welcome the invasion of his tongue.

"*Jennie! Thorne!*"

"Damn!" he groaned. He rested his forehead against hers in teeth-grinding, mind-shattering frustration. "I can't believe it."

"Jennie, where are you?" Lady Idina called. The sound of her horse crashing through the stand of oaks, followed by her immediate appearance, shattered the spellbinding moment. "Oh, there you are, dear! I was worried about you!"

Thorne rolled to his feet. "There's no need to shout, Dina," he said equably. "We're fine. Now, go away."

Basil pulled his mount up beside his sister's, a wide, sagacious grin spreading across his genial features as his gaze flickered over them. "We found your boots and jackets up on the bridge," he explained, dismounting. "Miss Elkheart's hat was floating down the Leigh. Dina was certain you'd both leapt to your deaths."

"Why would you think that?" Jennifer asked in amazement as she walked over to Combermere. She took her boots, which he held out, and plopped down on the grass to pull them on. Still grinning, the earl handed Thorne his boots and jacket also.

"What else could we think?" Idina remonstrated as Basil lifted her down from the chestnut mare. "What happened? Did someone fall in?"

"We went swimming," Jennifer explained with perfect composure. "His Grace dared me to go for a swim, and I dared him to dive off the bridge." She looked up and met their incredulous stares. "So we did."

Thorne waved his hand in an all-encompassing gesture. "It's as simple as that. Good-bye."

"Hell," Basil muttered, looking back toward the bridge with longing. "I would've enjoyed diving with you."

"We can do it again," Jennifer promptly offered.

"No, you won't!" Idina cried in alarm. "You get on that horse, Miss Elkheart. You're coming back to the house with me. If you should come to harm on this visit, your grandfather would never forgive me. Nor would I ever forgive myself." She rounded on Thorne. "And you, sir! What were you thinking of, endangering her life like that?"

"Don't blame me!" Thorne disclaimed with a chuckle. "It was Jennie's idea to dive off the bridge. I went along with the outrageous scheme to protect her."

"*Protect me!*" Jennifer sent him a scalding look. "If I did not know better, Your Graciousness, I would think you had been talking to my parents."

The Hunt Ball was the culmination of the Combermere house party. In addition to the guests who'd taken part in the foxhunt, the local gentry arrived to swell the list of lords and ladies in attendance. Lady Idina Nettlefold-Clive was known throughout Warwickshire for her brilliant social gatherings. Everyone arrived in a gay, expectant mood.

Thorne stood beside his mother on the edge of the dance floor, enjoying the spectacle his lighthearted friends provided. Lady Avice's carroty ringlets bounced and jiggled as she galloped around the room in the earl of Combermere's arms. It was good to see Basil enjoying himself after the anguished years of mourning.

Vladimir Gortschakoff's absence came as no surprise. The would-be assassin was probably back in London by now, being thoroughly and scathingly castigated by his superiors for taking unnecessary chances in Warwickshire. Thorne had learned at Dunleigh Castle that the plan for his early demise wasn't supposed to be initiated until after he'd left England on his next assignment. Apparently the Russian count had been in a hurry to get the butchery over and done with, so he could return to Moscow before the coming winter's first blizzard swept down from the Arctic.

Thorne's gaze was diverted as Jennifer waltzed by with Bertie Wheeler. The tall, red-haired viscount held Jennie as though she were made of blown glass, his freckled face screwed into a mask of concentration. You could almost hear him counting out the beats.

In contrast to Lyttleton's measured tread, Jennifer glided across the oak floor with the grace of an angel. Her gold slippers seemed to barely touch the ground. Thorne recalled the first time he'd seen her at St. James's Palace, dancing the quadrille. Her inborn elegance was one of the things that had first attracted him to her. That and her laughing eyes.

"Miss Elkheart makes every partner seem graceful, *n'est-ce pas*?" Lady Charlotte remarked, following her son's gaze to the mismatched couple on the floor.

"She does at that," he agreed.

Thorne was proud of his mother's courageous decision to return to her former social life as though nothing had interrupted it. Since the night of their heartrending confidences, they'd kept an unspoken agreement to let the past bury itself.

"Jennifer entertained me all through supper with her tales of childhood on the Canadian plains," Lady Charlotte continued. "Her escapades as a schoolgirl at the French embassy in the American capital must have driven her teachers close the edge of insanity. It seems only her sister, Juliette, had the power to curb her prodigal ways."

Thorne scowled. Not at the mention of Jennifer's uninhibited playfulness, but at the unfortunate reminder of the seating arrangements at dinner. This time, Lady Idina had placed him at the farthest end of the table from her American guest. Out of pure spite, he suspected, repaying him for the swimming escapade that morning. Unable to catch a word of Jennie's animated conversation, he'd been forced to watch her gossip happily with her neighbors through the entire meal.

Euan Bensen, seated directly on her right, had repeatedly burst into laughter, until Thorne had all but choked on his Pheasant à la Flamande. When Jennifer peeped up at the notorious lady-killer from beneath her lashes and smiled like an impudent pixy, Thorne had seriously considered murder in cold blood.

He'd managed to catch Bensen's eye and, in the space of a second, unleashed all the jealous rage simmering inside him. Taken aback, Bensen lifted his black brows in surprise. He turned his head and looked in curiosity at his lovely dinner companion, who paid no heed to their silent interplay, and then glanced back at Thorne.

This time, Euan didn't smirk in retaliation. Evidently the expression on Thorne's face proved a rather sobering sight for any male, even that muscle-bound rogue. Thorne didn't doubt it. The idea of another man touching Jennie unleashed a howling demon inside him. He'd fought back the urge to pick Bensen up and hurl him bodily from the room.

Lady Charlotte's cheerful commentary intruded on her son's disgruntled reflections. "I knew from the moment I met her, *mon cher*, that I would love to have that charming, spirited girl for a daughter-in-law. It would be like bringing eternal springtime to Eagleston Court."

Thorne smiled at his mother. "You'd be content to see me marry an untitled American girl?" he queried mildly as though the idea had only just occurred to him. "I thought you wanted me to select the daughter of a French aristocrat."

"Not since I met Miss Elkheart," Lady Charlotte confessed. She sighed deeply, shaking her head in resignation. "But it is never to be, *sans doute.*"

"Why such certainty, Mother?" He glanced at the young lady in question, a tender smile curving his lips. "Perhaps I could come to care for the naughty minx."

"Oh, la, la," the dowager duchess of Eagleston exclaimed with a dramatic wave of her fan. "I have no doubt you could fall irretrievably in love with the child. But she would never marry you."

A muscle twitched in Thorne's cheek. This was beginning to sound unpleasantly familiar. He kept his tone blasé, pretending only a lukewarm interest in the subject. "You think so?"

She wasn't fooled by his pose of indifference and patted his sleeve in maternal consolation. "*Vraiment,* I know so. I already proposed the alliance to her and she refused."

Thorne was thunderstruck. "You asked Jennifer to marry me? When?"

"*Voyons!* The very day I met her. But she told me she could never fall in love with an Englishman—"

"Because he couldn't be trusted," Thorne interjected, his words sharp with exasperation.

"Who can't be trusted?" Lady Idina queried. She joined them in the company of Lord Babington, an elderly peer.

"Englishmen, *chérie,*" the dowager duchess clarified with a fond smile. "All of them or none of them, whichever the case may be. I am not sure quite how to phrase it."

"I vow, I can be trusted, Your Grace," the gray-haired gentleman assured Lady Charlotte as he bent over her gloved hand.

"Oh, not you, *m'sieur!* Least of all you," she told the widowed baron with a ripple of laughter. "I was certain you had forgotten your promise to teach me the Military Schottische." With an amused glance at her son, she took Lord Babington's elbow and allowed him to lead her onto the dance floor.

"Who would dare to say all Englishmen can't be trusted?" Idina asked with an annoyed flutter of her black lace fan. But the twinkle in her green eyes gave her away.

"You know very well who said it," he countered wrathfully. "Our incorrigible Yankee magpie."

Thorne was in no mood for jests. The knowledge that Jennie had actually refused to marry him—even if it was his mother's proposal—burned like a short fuse on a large barrel of gunpowder. If anyone else was foolish enough to provoke him this evening, the explosion would be deafening and lethal.

"Why do you keep referring to Jennifer as a Yankee?" Idina prodded. "The truth is, she's a princess. And a very intelligent and charming one, at that."

"A *what?*" he demanded.

Lady Idina smiled serenely at his incredulous expression. She rapped his forearm with her folded fan and leaned closer. "You didn't know? Miss Elkheart's father is a head chief of the entire Cheyenne nation. Strong Elk Heart is one of the four most respected leaders of their people. That makes our darling Jennie an Indian princess."

"Oh, for God's sake, Dina" he growled. "Don't be ridiculous."

"I can't blame you for being annoyed," Idina said with a knowing lift of her brows. Her words dripped with false sympathy. "Finding out that the woman you love is above you in rank must be a trifle humiliating for an illustrious duke like yourself. But Jennifer doesn't hold your lower station against you."

Something in her teasing voice caught Thorne's undivided attention. "What does she hold against me?"

"You mean, outside of the fact that you have no visible skills for earning your own living, no profession or business in which to put your talents to use, no obvious interests other than your travels around the globe collecting useless antiquities in your attempt to relieve your boredom, and no honors, at all, won on the battlefield? Why, nothing, I guess."

"And I suppose she's learned this evening of my father's baser predilections," he said, unable to keep the bitterness from his words. "I'm sure at least one of the chaps hovering around her tonight has wasted no time in filling her in on that score."

Idina's smile disappeared. This time, she spoke with unvarnished sincerity. "As far as I know, Jennifer has heard nothing about your father, Thorne. The other men may be your rivals in courtship, but they are, after all, gentlemen. They would never discuss such a sordid topic in the presence of an innocent young girl."

Thorne's jaw clenched. "You're nothing if not frank, Dina."

"I love you too much, my friend, to be less than honest. Your father was a debauched and perverted lecher. But you're nothing like him. And neither Jennifer nor any other woman could fail to see the integrity and honor that shine in your eyes."

Thorne's gruff words betrayed his aggravation. "What exactly does Miss Elkheart find so lacking in my character?"

Idina grinned mischievously. She cocked her head and gazed at him, as if debating whether or not to answer his question. "Be careful, Your Grace," she goaded. "I watched you at supper this evening and caught unequivocal glimpses of honest emotion. Your facade of amiable negligence is starting to slip. People will get the impression that you actually care about something . . . or someone."

"Dina," he ordered in a quiet tone, "answer my question."

She lifted her brows and smiled complaisantly. "Why, I told you before, Thorne. You're simply not the man she's been dreaming of."

"Are you trying to bait me?" he snapped, his patience finally starting to shred. "Because if you are, you're doing a fine job of it. And should you continue, you do so at your own peril."

Idina chuckled softly at his dire warning. "No, Your Grace. I'm merely attempting to explain things from Jennie's perspective. She honestly believes that she's seen the gentleman she's meant to marry in a vision."

Astounded, he turned his head to look at the dark-haired beauty. She was skipping around the floor to the strains of a lively schottische in the brawny arms of Euan Bensen. Thorne spoke in a strangled voice, scarcely able to conceal his desperation. *"Who is he?"*

Idina opened and closed her exquisite Spanish fan, a frown furrowing her brow as she toyed with it. This time her words rang with genuine concern, both for him and for Jennifer. "She doesn't know."

"You mean she's in love with a bloody phantom?" He stared at Idina in disbelief. "Jennie actually thinks she's going to marry some goddamn mirage she's conjured up from her overactive imagination?"

"Oh, she takes the vision quite seriously," Idina cautioned. "Whatever you do, Thorne, don't start making sarcastic remarks about her spiritual beliefs. Her father and sister also have visions. Like her, they can interpret dreams, their own and others'. It's a gift that apparently runs in the family. If you behave in your usual sardonic manner, you'll alienate her forever."

Thorne's clipped words conveyed his frustration. "I'm not about to go along with this utter rot, if that's what you're suggesting, Dina. Someone has to bring Jennie to her senses."

The dance ended, and Bensen started to lead Jennifer over to them. Lady Idina unfurled her fan and spoke behind the fragile lace in a low, hurried tone. "For once, Thorne, try to put aside your deep-seated distrust in your fellow man, your jaded, world-weary cynicism, and your cold, analytical logic. Try to see life as Jennifer sees it. As a path to follow through one marvelous adventure after another, guided and aided by the Great Powers."

Jennifer and Euan drew near, and Idina reached out to place her white gloved hand on the comely beau's sleeve. "I believe this is our waltz," she told him.

The couple moved onto the dance floor, leaving Jennifer and the duke of Eagleston alone. She gazed at him, warily, from the corner of her eye. He'd glared at her all through supper and hadn't come near her in the ballroom. She didn't know if he regretted their intimate talk that morning or if it was the reckless dive off the bridge that made him look as contentious and challenging as a bull elk in rutting season. She sensed a glittering air of danger about him tonight, hard-edged and brittle. Next thing she knew, he'd be changing forms before her very eyes.

"How wonderful to see Lady Idina dancing," she said in a cautious tone, feeling her way along like a traveler crossing a river bottom of quicksand. "I know she never dances in public."

"Yes," he agreed suavely, "it's nice to see Dina enjoying her own party."

They watched their hostess and her handsome partner move in small, slow circles around the room. Euan kept his arm firmly about Idina's waist, providing the support she needed so she wouldn't stumble and fall.

"What about you, Your Grace?" Jennifer asked, determined to make polite conversation with this brilliant, dangerous, elegant shape-shifter. "Are you enjoying the ball, too?"

"I'm enjoying it now," he said, each soft word as ripe and tempting as a meadow of wild strawberries in the warm summer sun.

She refused to meet his gaze or give him the satisfaction of asking what he meant by the blatantly flirtatious remark. Gazing across the ballroom floor, she tapped her foot to the strains of the waltz and tried in vain to slow the frantic beating of her heart.

Thorne watched the little magpie's preposterous pose of indifference with unconcealed enjoyment. The telltale flush on her cheeks heightened her already vivid coloring. Beneath the ballroom's flickering chandeliers, the reddish highlights in her braided chignon glistened like jewels.

"I was afraid you hadn't remembered," he said laconically.

"Remembered what?"

"That this is my waltz. I was prepared to drag you out

of the arms of your next partner and risk starting a fracas in the middle of Dina's ballroom floor." Without waiting for a reply, Thorne slipped his arm around her waist and whirled her into the stream of dancers.

Her saucy smile tugged at his heart. "You did that the first night we met," she reminded him. "I do not recall that you were very worried about causing a rumpus then."

"Admit it, Jennie," Thorne teased, drawing her slender figure as close as he dared. The delicate scent of wildflowers rose from her hair, and he bent his head, inhaling her incredible sweetness. "You were disappointed to learn there'd be no duel to the death over your hand."

"*Hesc!* I wanted no such thing!" she denied with a burst of laughter.

He smiled down at her in tender amusement, not bothering to dispute the issue. Only a green girl would believe she'd actually seen the man she was going to marry in a dream. Well, if it was romantic melodrama she yearned for, he'd be happy to provide it. He'd play the role of Sir Galahad till she was eating out of his hand like a tame canary. And she'd forget all about her ridiculous belief in visions.

Thorne was waiting for Jennifer when she entered the stable. He stood in the shadows, leaning against a post. The etched-glass lamp she carried encircled her in a rosy glow. She wore a wine velvet opera cloak, the hood drawn up over her hair and tied under her chin with a golden cord.

He had known she'd come to say good night to Barleymow. She'd artlessly confided that she sang the black stallion a Cheyenne lullaby every night before retiring.

It was three o'clock in the morning. The ball was long over. The guests had either departed or gone upstairs to bed, and the servants had, at last, been able to quit for the night as well. The grooms and stableboys were all sound asleep in their quarters over the carriage house. Thorne had made certain of that before he lit the lantern.

"Don't be startled, Jennie," he called softly, as he

stepped out of the darkness. "It's only me, Thorne."

"Eagleston!" She lifted the rose-colored globe higher and gaped at him in surprise. "What are you doing here?"

"I was restless and couldn't sleep," he lied. "So I decided to go for a walk and check on Barleymow."

Thorne couldn't sleep, all right, but his usual remedy was a snifter of brandy and a good Havana, not a stroll to the stables to inspect the cattle.

"Sometimes I am like that after a party," she confided, coming closer. "Grandpapa says I get overexcited. He has the cook make me a cup of hot milk. Would you like me to fix you some? The servants are in bed, but I will be happy to do so."

"No, thank you. I thought I'd take a ride in the moonlight. That usually does the trick."

"You were going for a ride?" Her face lit up in fascination. Just as he'd expected, the outrageous idea captivated her.

"Yes." He paused and then added casually, as if the thought had occurred to him only that moment, "Would you care to come along?"

She walked over to Barleymow's stall and patted his nose. "What do you think, Moxtavevoe?" she asked the stallion. "Would you like to go for a ride under the stars?" The Thoroughbred nickered and nudged her shoulder playfully, as if he understood.

"Well, that settles it, then," Thorne stated as he lifted a halter from its hook. Without waiting for her assent, he quickly bridled the stallion, then turned to Jennifer. "Ready?"

Perplexed, she glanced at the horses in the other stalls. "Which horse will you ride?"

Thorne took the oil lamp from her hand, snuffed out the flame, and set it on a wide board, where it would be safe. "To be honest, Miss Elkheart," he replied, "I'd planned on taking Barleymow." He put out one hand in a conciliatory gesture. "Of course, if you don't want me to take him, I won't. I just thought it would be my way of saying good-bye to the old brute."

"*Hesc*! I did not mean you could not ride him," she cried softly. Her long lashes fluttered in agitation. "Shall I take another horse, then?"

Thorne led the stallion to the stable door with Jennifer right on his heels.

"We can both ride Barleymow," he suggested. "That way, we won't be taking someone else's horse without permission." He sensed her hesitation and added persuasively, "It's considered very poor manners here in Britain to take someone's horse unless you have their prior consent." He hoped she didn't realize that's exactly what he'd just claimed to be doing with Barleymow.

She nodded in understanding. "Yes, I know that. My people learned of the *veho* taboo against taking other people's horses to their grave misfortune." Twisting her cloak's gold cord around her finger, she pursed her lips in deliberation. She obviously knew she shouldn't go galloping over the English countryside in the dead of night with a man.

Just as Thorne had hoped, the unexpected opportunity to take a moonlight ride was simply too appealing. "Very well," she agreed with a plucky smile. "We will both ride Moxtavevoe."

Before she had a chance to rethink her decision, he grasped her by the waist and lifted her onto Barleymow's bare back. "Since you're wearing an evening gown tonight, I think you'd better ride sideways in front of me like a proper English lady."

"But I am not wearing a gown under this cloak," she said on a joyous gurgle of laughter. At the talons of need that raked through his groin, Thorne knew her husky contralto was going to be his undoing yet.

"What's under your cloak?" he grumbled in mock rebuke. "Those scandalous breeches again?"

She shook her head, giggling at his pretense of being shocked. "I am wearing my nightdress, Your Grace. And I do not think *that* is very proper at all."

At her ingenuous words, Thorne's heart crashed into his ribs like a Thoroughbred failing to make a post-and-rail fence. The thought of her silken nakedness covered only by a nightshift was more intoxicating than a whole bottle of brandy.

He was still attired in the formal black trousers and white starched shirt he'd worn to the ball. He hadn't once considered that she might come to the stables after having changed from her fancy satin gown into her nightwear. Had she released her hair from the braided chignon as well?

Desire seeped through every pore in Thorne's body, making it difficult to breathe and even harder to think. Christ, he'd never felt so driven by male sexual instinct— as though nothing, not social rules or the code of gentlemanly conduct, or even practical commonsense, could stand in its way.

Thorne knew he should stop now.

He should abandon his plan to enact the dashing hero taking his lady fair on a romantic—and entirely innocent—ride in the moonlight. But the thought of her slender figure hidden only by the flowing nightgown sent an unbridled primal force reverberating through him. A force so compelling, so pagan and primitive, that all other thoughts, but one, were swept away in its tide.

He wanted to hold Jennie's sweet, nubile body in his arms, the only barrier between them a delicate, feminine nightdress.

Bloody, living hell, how he wanted it.

Thorne looked up at Jennifer, seated on the black stallion's back, and prayed his voice wouldn't betray the effect her guileless remark had on his usual unflappable composure. Somehow, he even managed a grin. "I can see you're also barefoot," he chided gruffly.

She shrugged, unfazed by the shocking impropriety of her toes peeking out from under the velvet cloak. "I did not think the horses would mind."

"I'm sure they don't."

Thorne led the stallion out of the stable and jumped up behind Jennifer. Putting his arms around her diminutive frame, he signaled Barleymow, and they moved off across the thick grass.

Slowly, so as not to waken anyone in the manor.

Chapter 14

Jennifer leaned back against Eagleston's broad, muscled chest and sighed with contentment. Moonlight bathed the landscape in a silvery light. Above them, the night sky glittered with a myriad of stars. Not so many as she might have seen over the Canadian plains on a clear January evening, but stunningly beautiful, nonetheless.

Tonight, the autumn air was cool, yet she felt snug and warm, encircled in the British lord's effortless strength. There was something about him tonight that spoke of a determined resilience, a steely, intrepid tenacity. Gone was the familiar air of a slightly bored, effete aristocrat.

She was reminded of her father and great-grandfather in the way he controlled the high-strung stallion with such fluid ease. His body erect and perfectly balanced, his rein hand low, the other hand pressed firmly against her hip, he rode forward on his thighs and crotch, signaling Moxtavevoe with only the pressure of his legs.

Could it be merely the fact that they were riding bareback that made her think of a Cheyenne warrior? After all, she'd ridden like this many times as a small child, wrapped in a heavy buffalo robe instead of a velvet cape. Her father had often taken her up before him on his painted Appaloosa, keeping her safe from the frigid winter wind in his sheltering arms. Now, looking up at the stars, she could almost imagine she was home again in their peaceful valley.

Eagleston guided Moxtavevoe away from the manor house and into a wooded copse that followed a babbling stream. In the half-light of the round harvest moon, the rushing water sparkled and glistened. Alders grew along its edge, their spreading branches casting deep, impenetrable shadows. Tussocks of rush followed the shoreline, the slender stems providing a haven for families of mallards, now asleep on the muddy bank.

"Where are we going?" she asked.

He bent his head to catch her words, and his lips grazed her cheek. "Anywhere you wish, Mohehya."

"There is a small open-air structure that overlooks the river," she told him. "Lady Idina took me there once to enjoy the view. Do you know the place?"

"Yes," he replied. "It's called Lady Combermere's Folly. Basil's grandmother built the summerhouse on a high knoll to catch the cooling breeze from the water. But that was many years ago. We used to play there as boys, when the building was all but abandoned. I didn't realize it was being used once again."

"Idina had the shelter repainted and refurbished just this past summer. We took a basket lunch there several days ago and spent the entire afternoon. I thought it was especially lovely."

"Then that's where we'll go." He signaled the stallion, and they galloped across a grassy meadow.

Arriving at the folly, Eagleston dismounted, then lifted Jennifer down. While he hobbled Moxtavevoe under a nearby tree, she stepped up into the octangular wooden structure. She pushed her hood down from her head, her long hair still caught beneath the cloak.

Deep, comfortable benches had been built along the open lattice-work walls, and Idina's ivory-and-rose striped cushions were now covered with canvas tarpaulins to protect them from the morning dew. The duke joined her, and they stood beneath the arch of the open doorway, looking up at the sky.

"There's Hercules," he said, pointing out the constellation. He put his hand on her shoulder, turning her slightly. "And Pegasus, over there."

The heavy perfume of night-blooming woodbine drenched the air. The blossom-laden vines clung tenaciously to the white lattice walls and drooped down in spiraling tendrils from the pointed roof. Many of the yellowish-white flowers were spent and faded after the summer's heat, but enough remained to create the illusion of a magical bower.

"This shelter reminds me of my people's cone-shaped lodges," she said in a hushed tone.

Standing behind her, Eagleston put his arms around Jennifer and drew her close. She leaned back against his solid frame in peaceful satisfaction, her face lifted to the stars.

"Tell me about your home in Canada," he encouraged quietly. He kissed her temple, the touch of his lips as gentle and nonthreatening as the brush of a sparrow's wing.

"During the summer months, my family would sometimes camp out in what we called *navenotan*, our tipi. It was made of deer hide adorned with paint and quill work. While our baby brother played under our great-grandmother's watchful eye, Evening Star and I would fish and hunt with our parents along the rushing streams that flowed in the great mountains to the west of our valley."

"Evening Star is your twin's Cheyenne name?"

Jennifer nodded in happy reminiscence. "We would gather wild fruits and vegetables and prepare enough meat to last through the long winter." She glanced over her shoulder at him and smiled playfully. "Did I tell you that my mother is a crack shot with a rifle?"

"No, but I'm not surprised," he retorted with a crooked grin. "Tell me more."

"My great-grandmother, Porcupine Quills, taught us the skills of our ancestors. How to sew and cook and which herbs could be used to make strong medicine. Our great-grandfather, Flying Hawk, told us stories in the evening as we sat around the lodge fire. We learned our people's legends of creation, of how Maxemaheo made the earth and then the people, and of our Cheyenne hero, Sweet Medicine, who warned us of the coming of the white men.''

"And was their coming a bad thing?"

She shrugged philosophically. "Good or bad, it was inevitable. But my people found it hard to comprehend the intruders' strange beliefs. They hanged our warriors for stealing their horses and butchering their cattle, after they had destroyed all the buffalo on which we survived. Yet they believed they had a God-given right to steal our lands. Why, we asked ourselves, should the Creator of All Life look with special favor upon only one race or one nation? Did He not love us all?"

"Understanding the darker motives that drive mankind has stymied the greatest thinkers in history," Eagleston told her. "No one has been able to explain it yet."

"All white men are puzzles," Jennifer conceded. She frowned, looking up a him thoughtfully. "But you are a puzzle within a puzzle, Eagle's Son."

His voice grew wary. "What makes you say that?"

Earlier in the evening, he'd removed his cuff links and rolled his shirtsleeves up to his elbows. He held her now with his arms crossed in front of her, and she ran her palm along his sinewy forearm.

"There is something about you . . . something I cannot quite explain," she said in bemusement. "Not even to myself. It is as though you are two different persons. When I am with you like this, you are not the same man who treats the world and everyone in it with such bored detachment."

"I'm not bored at the moment," he said lightheartedly. "I can't remember when I've felt more alive."

"How about your dive from the bridge this morning?" she inquired. "I think you were pretty wide awake by the time you hit that cold water."

He chuckled at her pert retort. "Swimming in the Leigh doesn't come close to being here with you, Mohehya."

Eagleston waited for her to respond to his teasing, but Jennifer was content to enjoy the tranquil evening. In the silence, the plaintive hoot of an owl carried across the meadow that sloped from the folly down to the river. The rustle of small animals scurrying to safety in the tall grass could be heard faintly, but even in the bright moonlight, it was impossible to make out their shapes.

"Look up there, Jennie," he urged softly.

She looked up just in time to see a falling star trace a path of light across the inky darkness.

"How beautiful!" she whispered. She turned in his arms and raised her face to his. "Thank you for bringing me here, Eagleston. I have not felt so close to my home and my family since we arrived in England. Tonight, they will watch the same stars in the sky overhead and think of their daughters on the other side of the world."

"Call me Thorne," he said, his voice mellow and coaxing. "After jumping off that bridge together, I don't think we need to stand on ceremony."

"All right . . . Thorne," she answered softly.

His gaze lingered on her upturned face. "Sweet little magpie," he murmured. He untied the gold cord that fastened her velvet cape. Bending toward her, he brushed his lips across hers, the tickle of his thick mustache a familiar and pleasant sensation.

Sliding her arms around his neck, Jennifer welcomed the invasion of his tongue. He delved boldly into her mouth, and she greeted him with eager, joyful strokes. Eagleston supported her neck with his hands, making slow, indolent circles around the bumps of her collarbone with his thumbs. Then he bent his head and dipped his warm, moist tongue into the hollow at the base of her throat. The effect was devastating in its erotic tenderness.

"My God, you smell like heaven," he said, his deep baritone hoarse with emotion. He pushed her cloak open, the hint of a smile on his lips. "All evening long, as I watched you dancing with every other man at the ball, I thought I must be gazing on an angel. Now I know that I was."

"*Hesc!*" she protested. "I am no angel." Inexplicably, her voice quavered, and she drew a deep, steadying breath.

In the moonlight flooding through the arched portal, the pristine whiteness of her nightshirt stood out starkly against the deep wine velvet of her cape. Jennifer watched, transfixed, as his hand followed the row of tiny pearl buttons down the tucked front of the long-sleeved garment. Her breath caught in her throat as he lazily traced the embroidered band that ran across the yoke's intricate smocking.

She tore her gaze away from his hand and raised her lashes to meet his heavy-lidded eyes. Their deep blue depths seemed almost black in the shadowy arbor. He cupped her small breast in the palm of his hand, and Jennifer gasped in shock and delight at the incredible feelings that rushed through her. Dazed, she rested her forehead against the front of his starched white shirt, allowing the pleasurable torrent to envelop her.

Eagleston kissed the center part of her hair as he boldly and expertly flicked her tautening nipple through the thin batiste. Her breasts grew heavy, shimmering with an unfamiliar, aching sensation. It took every ounce of her courage to raise her chin and meet his gaze once again. His sharply chiseled features, softened now with tender affection, told her that he'd felt her involuntary response to his touch.

"You make me feel so . . . strange," she confessed. She pushed back slightly, her palms braced on his chest, trying to gather her scattered wits about her.

His sensual mouth curved into a beguiling smile. "A good strange, I hope," he said huskily.

"Very good!" she allowed. Her lower lip quivered unaccountably as she tried to return his smile.

"Let's sit down for a while and enjoy the view from the folly," he suggested, his words low and seductive. She gave her assent with a shy nod of her head.

Eagleston pulled back the canvas covering that protected one of the commodious benches fastened to a vine-covered wall and shoved the tarp aside. Then he lifted the silk-lined cloak from her shoulders. Jennifer could hear his swift intake of air.

Thorne felt as though he'd just been tossed over his

hunter's neck at a bruising jump and had the royal stuffing knocked out of him. He stood in stunned silence, gazing at the breathtaking vision in the center of the gazebo, illuminated like a gilded fresco in a pool of lambent moonlight.

Before coming to the stables to visit Barleymow that evening, Jennifer had unbraided the thick chignon she always wore and brushed her hair out to its full length. Parted in the center, the shiny reddish-brown tresses fell all the way down to her hips in a smooth, lustrous curtain. The dark, straight locks lay against the pure white of her voluminous nightdress in glorious, heart-stopping splendor.

She looked so young, so incredibly vulnerable, standing there in her bare feet and childish smock, he had to swallow a lump in his throat before he could speak. "Idina was right," he said hoarsely. "Your hair is . . . absolutely gorgeous."

Jennifer clasped her hands loosely in front of her, enhancing the portrait of unblemished innocence. She watched him with wide, speculative eyes. "It is just like my sister's," she said, and the confusion in her voice told him that she considered her hair nothing special, at all.

Thorne tossed the cloak across the striped cushions that decorated the summerhouse. Without a word, he reached out and pulled her to him. He buried his hands in the glossy chestnut mass, letting it glide like burnished satin through his fingers. Her delicate floral scent drifted around them, vying with the voluptuous perfume of the honeysuckle.

"I've wanted to see you like this since the day we met," he confessed, his harsh tone betraying his raw emotions.

Amazement rang in her guileless reply. "You mean the same way I wanted to see if your bare chest was covered with hair? Just to satisfy your curiosity?"

Thorne forced a smile, determined to fight back the overpowering carnal desire that was clawing and ripping away at the fabric of his honorable intentions. He had planned a harmless, romantic interlude, nothing more.

"Is that why you asked me to take off my shirt?" he

chided with feigned disappointment. "And all the time I thought you longed to admire my muscles."

Her husky laughter bubbled up. "I was just starting to admire your rugged physique when Lady Idina interrupted us."

"We won't be interrupted now," he assured her.

His gaze never leaving hers, Thorne unbuttoned his shirt. He forced himself to remain calm and still as Jennifer reached out and brushed her fingertips across his skin. He jerked reflexively when she buried her fingertips in his chest hair and lightly caressed his tensed pectorals. With her hands braced on his upper arms, she bent her head and traced the tip of her tongue along the scar that crossed his chest above his left nipple.

His heart thundering, he closed his eyes and prayed for strength. God above, he'd never experienced anything so unbelievably sweet.

Thorne groaned and caught her to him. Sweeping her up in his arms, he carried her to the wide bench and laid her on the outspread cloak. Then he sat down on the edge of the soft cushion beside her. With trembling fingers, he undid her tiny buttons and opened the deep, smocked yoke of her nightgown.

The full October moon bathed her firm, up-tilted globes in its iridescent light. Bracing his arms on either side of her, Thorne bent and touched the tip of one nipple reverently with his tongue, and she whimpered in surprise and delight.

"*Nakoe!*" she gasped as she clutched his arms.

Cupping her breast in his palm, he suckled her, tugging softly on the round coral crest with his lips, teasing it gently until its little bud was taut and puckered, then moved to the other. She murmured to him in Cheyenne, the words so faint and tremulous that he couldn't make out any of the unfamiliar syllables.

Jennifer arched her back, offering herself to the Eagle, as wave after wave of unadulterated pleasure coursed through her. She reached up and tried to push his unbuttoned shirt open wider with awkward, fumbling hands. He stopped for only as long as it took to tear the shirt off and throw it on the floor, then returned to his gentle ministrations. He laved her nipples with his moist tongue till the honey-sweet ache he created inside her spread through her abdomen and thighs. She threaded her fingers through the golden-brown hair at the nape of his neck, and pulled him closer to her breasts in an act of hedonistic abandon.

Thorne slid his hand under the hem of Jennifer's full, gathered nightdress, following the slender curve of her calf and up her smooth thigh. The small dagger was right where he'd expected it. And the chastity cord, as well. This time, he didn't halt in surprise over either. He brought the bottom of her loose-fitting smock up to her hips, exposing her shapely legs. She immediately stiffened and tried to scoot back into the plush pillows.

"Vonahenene," he entreated, "don't pull away from me. I just want to see you, love, the same way you wanted to see me."

She met his gaze and slid the palms of her hands across his shoulders and over his upper arms in a tentative exploration. "But I am not as muscular and strong as you are," she said, her soft mouth curving into a bashful smile. "You may be disappointed."

He leaned forward and nuzzled the delicate curve of her throat. "Only if you have hair on your chest," he teased with a low chuckle.

She giggled in delight. "Not a bit."

"Let me see," he insisted.

He scooped the folds of the voluminous nightgown up in both hands and tugged it over her head. Then he lifted her long chestnut locks and spread them out on the pillow in a gleaming halo. He pulled back to look at her in awe. She was so damn beautiful, his entire body ached with need at the sight of her.

Stricken with embarrassment as his scorching gaze raked over her unclothed form, Jennifer lowered her lids. Her cheeks grew flushed and hot.

"Look at me, Mohehya," he whispered.

She shyly raised her lashes and met his perceptive *veho* gaze.

Never taking his eyes from hers, Thorne covered her small mound with his palm, the fluff of curls surprisingly meager, as though she'd barely reached puberty. Gently, delicately, he spread her silken folds and rubbed the fragile nub with the pad of his thumb. She lifted her hips to meet his touch and released a long, pent-up sigh of pleasure.

"*Nihoatovaz, Vonahenene,*" he said thickly. "I want you, Morning Rose." He kissed her bruised lips with all the passion that enflamed him, his tongue probing and tasting the sugared cavern of her mouth with an endless, unrequited hunger. He could feel her nails digging into his bare shoulders as he tenderly caressed the very core of her femininity. "Tell me you want me, darling."

"I want you, Eagle's Son," she sobbed.

Thorne sat up on the edge of the bench and yanked off his shoes and socks. Then he rose to his feet and shucked his trousers and drawers, as she watched him with wide, wondering eyes.

Jennifer blinked in stupefaction and scooted to a sitting position on the deep cushions. She was acquainted with the basic facts about mating between male and female. For their own protection, her mother had told her and Julie about marital relations before they left on their voyage to England.

But the sight of Eagleston's surprisingly large member thrusting from the dense mass of wiry curls that covered his groin was far more daunting than she'd ever imagined.

"Wait," she cried breathlessly, holding out one hand, palm first. "You cannot do anything while I am still wearing the *nihpihist.* It is forbidden. Only I can take it off."

The Eagle came over to stand next to the bench. He knelt down on the floor beside her, scooped her bare bottom up in his palms, and drew her toward him. She slid across the cloak's golden silk lining like a fawn on a frozen pond, till her legs were dangling over the side of the bench in front of him.

"All right," he agreed softly. "I'll just caress you, while

I wait for you to decide whether you're going to remove it or not. There's nothing wrong with my touching you, is there?"

"N-no," she answered cautiously. "I—I do not think so."

He kissed the valley between her breasts and nudged them with his nose, making the swollen globes sway gently. Then he suckled their achingly vibrant tips. He traced a path down between her rib cage and dipped into her belly button.

With her buttocks still cupped in his palms, he tilted her backward, till she was leaning on her elbows. Jennifer watched him in fascination, wondering what the unpredictable Eagle would do next. He slid his hands down the backs of her thighs and lifted her legs over his broad shoulders.

"What . . . what are you doing?" she gasped.

"Don't be frightened, Mohehya. I'm just going to caress you."

Eagle's Son spread her gently with his fingers, then bent his head and drew the tip of his tongue along the most sensitive female part of her. Jennifer dropped back on the cushions, her head resting on the soft pillow behind her, her arms flung out at her side, as she felt him penetrate her. She bit her lower lip to keep from crying out at the exquisite pressure spiraling upward inside her, the irresistible need for release throbbing incessantly. The blood pounded in her ears like a drum, and she moved her head languorously back and forth in sweet, sexual submission.

"*Nihoatovaz*," she moaned, knowing full well it was what he'd intended to hear all along. "I desire you, Eagle's Son."

Thorne halted and slid his hands lightly over the leather sheath and the narrow cord wrapped around her thighs. "Remove the *nihpihist*, Vonahenene," he whispered.

Trembling convulsively and half-crazed with need, Jennifer reached down and grasped the bone handle of the knife fastened to her leg. She withdrew the weapon from its sheath and held it up between them, its deadly tip pointing toward the Eagle's throat. The razor-sharp steel blade glittered in the moonlight.

The warning she'd given Thorne that day in the stables at Eagleston Court echoed in his mind.

We use the knife to cut off the fingers of any white man foolish enough to violate the nihpihist.

He remained perfectly still, waiting to see what she would do. He could easily disarm her, but he wanted—needed—Jennifer to come to him freely. And he wanted desperately not to break a cultural prohibition that would leave her regretful and unhappy afterward.

With one deft move, she reached down and cut the thin cord that was looped around her waist. Then she cut each piece tied to her slender thighs. She pulled the severed pieces of rope away and dropped them to the floor.

Thorne quickly unfastened the leather sheath from her leg. He pried the handle from her tense fingers, replaced the blade in its intricately tooled holder, and tossed it down beside the rope. Then he moved onto the wide bench and positioned himself between her legs.

"Touch me, Mohehya," he rasped. "Let me feel your cool, dainty fingers caressing my hot flesh."

Her heart racing, Jennifer took his thickened manhood in her hand. The feverish heat of his body seemed to scorch her palm, as she timidly, hesitantly stroked the hard, pulsing length of him. She raised her eyes to meet his gaze, and the look of utter tenderness on his proud, strong features staggered her.

Thorne bent over Jennie and kissed her forehead, her eyelids, her nose, her chin. "Do you know what's going to happen between us, little magpie?" he asked in a suffocated voice.

"Yes. Do you?"

"Yes."

"You had that talk with your mother, then," she commended with a shy, sweet smile of approbation.

At the purity shining in her eyes like a moonbeam from paradise, his own filled with tears. He bent and gently, tenderly kissed her. "Do you still want me?" he murmured against her soft lips.

"Yes," she whispered as she guided him to her.

Thorne eased his turgid shaft into her soft, welcoming warmth and knew that this was meant to be. He could no more have refrained from making love to Jennifer than he could live without breathing. He gathered the gleaming locks of her hair in his hands and braced his forearms on either side of her head. Inch by inch, he buried himself deep within her, until he could feel the tip of his hardened sex pressing against her maidenhead. His entire body shook with the effort to keep himself under control.

"Jennifer," he said hoarsely, "I love you." With a sudden, powerful thrust, he broke through the fragile barrier, smothering her surprised cry of pain with his open mouth. He felt her stiffen and try to push him away. "It's all right, little girl," he crooned. "It's all right. The worst is already over. After this, I'll give you nothing but pleasure."

The moment he felt her relax and open herself up to him, he started to move his hips in steady, even strokes, building the tension to a peak, then allowing it to dissipate, only to rebuild it once again. He braced himself on his hands and lifted his shaft up inside her, giving her every bit of pleasure he could. He knew he shouldn't prolong their first lovemaking. She was too tiny, and he was too big.

Once again, he resumed his rhythmical pumping. "I could make love to you all night long, little doll," he murmured against her sweet lips, "but I want you to be able to walk in the morning. So this time, Mohehya, I'm going to take you all the way there. I'm going to bring those stars down from the sky, just for you."

He felt her respond to his words as well as his body. Her breath came in quick, short pants. She arched upward, tensing, seeking release as her delicate folds convulsed around him. He reached between their bodies and gently flicked her sensitive nub, swollen and erect now from their passion.

"*Namehota,*" she whispered breathlessly. "*Namehota, ze-hemehotaz.*"

Her surrender came on a long, low, sweet cry of joy and wonder, so achingly feminine, so touchingly innocent, Thorne's heart seemed to stall momentarily on its thundering ride to fulfillment.

"Jennie, ah, Jennie," he groaned, as he poured his seed deep within her. He clenched his jaw, the intense pleasure of his climax unequaled by anything he'd ever experienced in his jaded, cynical life.

Thorne moved to his side, taking her with him so he wouldn't crush her with his weight, and cradled her lovingly in his arms. He'd never known such happiness was possible.

Slowly, his heart ceased its tumultuous pounding. His breathing became steady and even, and he was able to speak. He turned his head to nuzzle her cheek and reassure her of his love. "Darling," he said softly, "I will—" She placed her trembling fingers against his mouth, and he gently kissed their soft tips.

Filled with a sense of overpowering wonder, Jennifer met his loving gaze. "Tonight I have flown with the Eagle," she whispered, "past the mountain heights to the clouds above, where we soared free and unfettered on the wild prairie wind."

His gentle laugh was husky with tenderness. "Promise me you'll always recite poetry after we make love, little magpie."

His words brought her back to reality at last.

Jennifer sat up in horror.

"*Ahahe!*" she gasped. "What have I done?"

She'd given herself to the wrong man! She looked wildly about her, searching for her discarded nightdress. Snatching it up, she pulled it over her head.

"Don't worry, sweetheart," he said with frightening complacency. He tried to pull her back into his arms, and she struggled in vain against his far greater strength. "It will be all right," he averred, trying to kiss her again.

Jennifer turned her head away, too distraught to speak. Why had she done such a stupid thing? The Great Powers had tried their best to warn her! Foolish, foolish Cheyenne girl!

Tears of belated remorse coursed down her cheeks. Eagleston framed her face in his hands and brushed the wet drops away with his thumbs. She tried to turn aside, but he forced her to look at him.

"I'll speak to your grandfather tomorrow, Jennie," he promised, his deep voice calm and soothing. "We'll be ma—"

"Don't!" she cried, nearly hysterical. She clutched his wrists in panic. "Please, please, don't say anything about this to Grandpapa!"

Eagleston searched her face, his expression one of profound concern. "I won't tell him about tonight, love. Your grandfather need never know. No one will ever have to know. But I must get his permission for us to be married immediately."

Married!

Jennifer gaped at him in shock. Numbly, she realized that in the *veho* world it would be considered absolutely imperative that they marry at once, now that she was no longer a virgin. Naturally, the British lord would assume that she was frightened by the thought that he might not want to make her his wife, and thereby, save her from social ruin.

She knew that nothing she could say would change his mind. Eagleston believed it was his duty to offer his hand and his protection. His very honor as a gentleman demanded it.

She scrambled off the cushions. "We had better return to the manor," she said, her shaky voice barely audible.

"Yes," he agreed. "We'd better go back now."

Eagleston rose from the bench and put on his clothes. He placed the heavy velvet cloak on her shoulders and tied the golden cord at her throat. Then he picked up the *nihpihist* and the sheathed knife from the floor and handed them to her.

Jennifer took the objects, half-sick with an overwhelming sense of regret. She hugged the symbols of her unthinking capitulation to her breast. It was just as her mother had warned her. As sure as Maheo put the stars in the night sky, reckless little girls pursued a lifetime of repentance.

Why, oh, why had she acted so impulsively after all the guidance the Maiyun had given her? Was it the frivolous *vehoka* blood that ran in her veins? No intelligent Cheyenne maiden would have given herself to the wrong man!

Her eyes brimming with tears, she started blindly toward the steps of the wooden shelter. Eagleston caught her arm and held her in front of him.

"Jennifer, I swear, I'll go to London in the morning and see your grandfather. There's no need to look so heartbroken. We were carried away by our emotions. We're not the first couple to do so, and we won't be the last. But believe me, darling, what happened tonight between us was very rare and very special."

She stared at him in mute trepidation, knowing that she would not be marrying him as he thought. In two days, she would be leaving England with her grandfather for Constantinople, where she would meet the man in her vision. *The man she was meant to love.* This had all been a terrible, terrible mistake, but she could set it right. She knew she could.

"We must go," she announced stubbornly.

"First, tell me what you said in your people's language," he insisted. "You whispered something to me. I want to know what the words meant."

She frowned, trying in her frantic state to recall exactly what she'd said in the throes of passion. Then it came to her.

She'd told him she loved him!

She'd actually called Eagleston *her beloved.*

"I do not remember," she lied.

"You remember," he said tersely. "And I will never forget the words you spoke to me when I was deep inside you. Next time I make love to you, Jennifer, you will say those words again. And you will tell me their meaning."

Taking her elbow, Eagleston guided her down the steps of the folly. He lifted her up on Moxtavevoe and then mounted behind her. When he started to put his arms around her, Jennifer tried to pull away. He didn't say a word. He merely pressed her up against his unyielding strength and held her there, imprisoned between his muscular thighs.

"For an English gentleman," she protested, "you are certainly behaving like a heavy-handed brute."

He gave a soft, derisive snort.

They rode back to Nettlefold Manor in strained silence.

Chapter 15

The last thing Thorne wanted to do was attend the opera at Covent Garden that evening. He hadn't slept in over thirty-eight hours. He'd been thwarted at every turn that day, and he was understandably impatient and irritable.

He guided his mother to a chair in his private box and then helped Lady Idina sit down beside her. He tried in vain to concentrate on the ladies' idle conversation, as he and the earl of Combermere took their places behind them.

The dowager duchess of Eagleston hadn't traveled to London since the death of her husband. Surely her son could set aside his own concerns and enjoy the evening's performance with her, though God knew, the Royal Opera House was not the place he'd have chosen to be at that particular moment. Not when a pair of tear-filled brown eyes continued to haunt him.

Where in the devil was Jennie this evening?

Thorne scowled irascibly. Nothing, absolutely nothing had gone right since he'd arrived at Victoria Station that morning.

"I am told the young singer from Australia has the voice of an angel," Lady Idina said, settling back in her chair and smoothing the folds of her aquamarine moiré gown. "She may one day eclipse the great Adelina Patti."

"Who is this talented soprano?" Lady Charlotte inquired. She waved her old-fashioned Chinese fan briskly in front of her, and the equally outdated ostrich plumes in her hair shivered in the draft. The fun of attending her first stage performance in so many years had the dowager nearly bubbling with excitement. When his mother decided to throw off the shackles of melancholia and rejoin the world, she did it with a vengeance.

Thorne made a mental note to take Lady Charlotte shopping in the coming days and buy her an entire new wardrobe. Now that she'd be going out in society again, she'd want some fashionable clothes.

Maybe the elusive Miss Elkheart would enjoy going with them. Maybe she'd even let him buy her a rope of pearls to replace the chastity rope she'd surrendered so touchingly . . . or a diamond necklace to go with the ring he was going to buy her . . . or some filmy nightwear that her future husband could see right through . . .

Basil leaned forward and patted Lady Charlotte's shoulder affectionately. "Nellie Melba," he said. "She'll be singing the part of Lucia."

Thorne realized he'd been daydreaming like an idiot instead of answering his mother's question. Restless, he thrummed his fingers on his knees and glanced absently around the auditorium.

The opera house had recently been redecorated and restored to all its former glory. The building was filled to capacity. People crowded into the semicircle of booths, the private boxes, the balcony stalls in the third tier, the amphitheater, and the gallery.

In the grand tier, which included the royal box, as well as the duke of Eagleston's private compartment, the cream of London society appeared in their finest raiment. Jewels twinkled beneath the gas lights, tiaras sparkled on elaborate, upswept hairdos, sables and minks were tossed casually over the backs of the velvet upholstered chairs.

Thorne's half-hearted perusal was diverted when the entire audience suddenly rose to its feet. He stood and turned toward the royal box, expecting to see the Prince and Princess of Wales appear.

But it wasn't British royalty who stepped out from behind the plush velvet drapes. To Thorne's amazement, a slim, young woman, with sloe eyes and unbound chestnut hair that fell straight to her hips, walked with imperial grace into the center of the royal box.

Bloody, living hell!

Jennie!

She wore an off-white native dress of simple, uncluttered lines, cinched at the waist with a wide belt. Two long narrow sidebraids, tied with bands of soft white fur, hung down over her breasts. Fastened in her lustrous hair, an ornament of silver, with black and white feathers and dangling beads, caught and reflected the flickering lights from the chandeliers overhead.

"Isn't she marvelous!" Idina exclaimed.

Lady Charlotte's lavender plumes trembled as she nodded. "Oh, la, la! The child is royalty through and through."

"Amen," Basil added.

Jennie, you beauty! Thorne mouthed silently, his heart filled with love and pride.

He slowly became aware that the entire audience was applauding in appreciation of the beautiful girl's unique Canadian heritage and in respect for her father's status as one of the head chiefs of an entire Indian nation. She smiled and waved to her nearly two thousand admirers with all the natural charm and grace of a born princess.

Behind her in the royal box stood Senator Garrett Robinson, with Lord and Lady Salisbury, the British prime minister and his wife. Not until Miss Jennifer Elkheart sat down did the rest of the audience resume their places.

"Why didn't you tell me she'd be here tonight?" Thorne demanded of the two women sitting in front of him.

Lady Idina turned to meet his gaze, her jade-green eyes glinting with mischief. "Because, Your Grace, you never asked. You've hardly said two words since you entered our carriage this evening. I thought you might have something important on your mind, so I didn't want to bother you with idle chit-chat."

"We all came down on the train together, *mon cher*,"

his mother belatedly informed him. "Lady Idina, Lord Combermere, Miss Elkheart, and myself. But the poor child seemed rather distracted. I thought she was looking a little pale. She had a busy schedule already planned this afternoon, so I'm rather certain she never got any rest today, at all."

Thorne glared at them. The devil take it! Were they purposely trying to see how far they could push him before he exploded? Having no idea Jennifer had already returned to London, he'd spent a good part of the afternoon trying in vain to locate Senator Robinson. Why hadn't she left a message for him at her home, telling him of her plans?

"What exactly was Miss Elkheart's schedule?" he asked through clenched teeth.

"Well, first she intended to visit Parliament with her grandfather," Idina said calmly, pretending not to notice the muscle that twitched in his cheek. "And after that, she was invited to high tea at Buckingham Palace. Then she and Senator Robinson were to dine with the prime minister and his wife this evening before coming here."

Thorne directed a scathing look at Combermere. "You, at least, could have told me."

Basil's stunned expression was almost comical. "By Jove!" he protested, "I didn't pay any attention to what the ladies were gossiping about on the train. I took a nap under the morning's newspaper like any sane man would do when surrounded by three chattering females. And since when am I supposed to keep you informed of Miss Elkheart's social calendar?"

At that moment the curtains opened, and all eyes were turned on the stage and the performance of *Lucia di Lammermoor*. All eyes, except the duke of Eagleston's. He stretched out his legs and leaned back in his chair, prepared to spend the evening enjoying the sight of his gorgeous and exasperating future wife.

Tomorrow, he would meet with Senator Robinson and offer his proposal of marriage to Miss Jennifer Rose Elkheart. They'd be wed within a fortnight. If she wasn't pregnant with his child at the moment, she soon would be. He sure as hell had no intention of waiting more than two weeks before making love to her again.

Thorne hadn't slept the night before. After seeing Jennifer safely to her bedroom at Nettlefold Manor, he'd taken Barleymow and galloped back to Eagleston Court. Something she'd told him in the folly had sent him hurrying back to his library and that blasted Russian despatch.

You are a puzzle within a puzzle.

Thorne had spent the early morning hours searching for the answer till he'd found it. A cipher within a cipher! The innocuous text of the letter he'd originally transcribed was merely a ploy to hide the real message.

He'd taken the early train to London with the twin goals of meeting with Lord Doddridge in the morning and Senator Robinson in the afternoon. Neither object had been accomplished. To his chagrin, Thorne had learned that the undersecretary had taken his wife to Brighton for a brief holiday and wouldn't be back at the Foreign Office until the following morning.

And when Thorne called at the Georgian mansion on Park Lane, he'd been told by the butler that the American diplomat wasn't at home, nor would he be home to callers for the rest of the day. The incompetent servant had no idea where Senator Robinson could be found. And, of course, the boob made no mention of Miss Elkheart.

Stymied, Thorne had returned to his town house to find that his mother had arrived unexpectedly, with plans for their attending the opera that evening with the earl of Combermere and his sister.

By the time the lamps were turned up for intermission, Thorne's frustration had dissipated somewhat. He accompanied his mother and two friends to the verandah over the theater's outside portico. At the end of the gallery, Jennifer, Senator Robinson on her left and the Marquess and Marchioness of Salisbury on her right, chatted with the throng of admirers who clustered around them.

The press of people made it nearly impossible for anyone to say more than a few words to the distinguished

American and his granddaughter before having to move on. Lady Charlotte, Lady Idina, and Lord Combermere resigned themselves to waving a friendly hello from across the room, when the crowd parted momentarily.

Nodding briefly to acquaintances, Thorne guided his charges to a safe corner away from the worst of the congestion, then crossed the crimson carpeting to where Jennifer and her grandfather were holding court. He was determined to speak to her.

Once a young lady left the schoolroom and made her debut in Victorian society, she wore her long locks piled high on top of her head, either in a froth of curls or a smooth, elegant chignon. The sight of Miss Elkheart's magnificent unbound tresses was having its all too predictable effect on the normally reserved British peers. Men were stepping on each other's toes to get close to her. Only Thorne's greater physical strength kept him from being squeezed in the crush.

He watched the circus in rueful silence. The effect of the black and white feathers in her flowing chestnut locks was unbelievably exotic. As was the beaded choker necklace that encircled her slender throat. Bloody hell, he couldn't blame the other gentlemen. If Jennifer hadn't worn her hair down last night, he might have been able to remain sane himself.

Jennifer smiled warmly at the people who approached her, greeting everyone with a few gracious words. Just as Thorne attempted to reach out and clasp her hand, she turned away, offering her slender fingers to Lord Sidmouth instead, who promptly drew his chubby wife into the circle that surrounded the two Yanks. Thorne had the uncomfortable feeling she'd avoided him on purpose.

Up close, her costume was strikingly beautiful. The ivory dress was made of butter-soft doeskin. Deep fringes on the sleeves and hem swayed gently with her every move, while tiny silver bells attached to the skirt just above the fringed hem tinkled musically. The intricate beadwork across the bodice and sleeves formed complicated geometric patterns in blue and white. The beaded belt that clasped her tiny waist was similarly adorned, as were the white moccasins and leggings she wore.

"Miss Elkheart," Thorne said quietly, when he was finally able to get close enough. "You look lovely tonight."

She flinched at the sound of his voice. Lifting her obstinate chin, she met his gaze, her dark eyes filled with dismay. If Thorne hadn't known better, he'd have thought she was afraid of him.

"Your Grace is too kind," she replied in a stilted monotone before quickly looking away. As she turned her head, the large silver hoops that hung from her dainty lobes swayed alluringly.

"I attempted to call on your grandfather this afternoon," he chided softly. "Only to find no one at home."

Her gaze flew back to his. She licked her lips, the glimpse of her pink tongue reminding him of her impassioned kisses the night before. "We . . . we had several pressing engagements today."

"So I understand." He bowed with smooth civility. "I will call again tomorrow."

Jennifer put out her hand to forestall him, but she didn't dare tell Eagleston not to come. If he knew of their departure early the next morning, he'd insist on talking to *namsem* this evening. She knew from the granite cast of his jaw that the determined British lord would speak to her grandfather right here in the lobby of the theater, if necessary.

She realized with a start that she was clutching Eagleston's sleeve and staring up at him like some demented wretch. She wanted to memorize every line and angle of his eaglelike features. His strong, prominent nose. His stern, uncompromising mouth. His golden-brown hair and mustache. His blue *veho* eyes.

She wanted to remember the way he looked tonight in the severe formal evening wear. The pain of knowing she would never see him again stabbed through her like a war lance. Why did it hurt so much, when he wasn't the man in her dreams? Her throat constricted, making it impossible to speak. Her vision blurred, and she blinked and looked away.

At the sight of her tears, Thorne stepped closer. "It will

be all right, Jennie," he said, his words audible only to her.

Senator Robinson turned at that moment and offered Thorne his hand. "Ah, Eagleston. How are you? I understand Your Grace was at Lady Nettlefold-Clive's house party. Jennie told me all about it. Said she had a wonderful time. I appreciate everyone's kindness to my granddaughter during our visit to England."

"Thank you, Senator," Thorne replied. He retained the white-haired gentleman's hand in a firm grip. "With your permission, sir, I would—"

"I believe it's time to return to our box," Lord Salisbury interrupted, and Thorne was forced to let go of Robinson's hand or look like a lumbering oaf. Giving Thorne a polite nod of dismissal, the prime minister offered Jennifer his elbow. "We don't want to be late for the next act."

Garrett Robinson immediately turned and placed Lady Salisbury's gloved fingers on his sleeve. "Nice to see you again, Eagleston," he offered with a brief nod and moved off.

"Good-bye, Your Grace," Jennifer said, her words a pathetic croak.

She looked so lost and forlorn, it was all Thorne could do to keep from putting his arms around her and smoothing her troubled brow with kisses. Clearly, she didn't believe that he intended to propose marriage the very next day.

"Until tomorrow, Miss Elkheart," Thorne said softly, trying to tell her with his adoring gaze that there was no need to cry. He would make everything right in the morning. His heart ached for her needless distress, as he watched her walk away on Salisbury's arm with an extraordinary, inborn grace.

She hadn't told him she loved him as he'd held her in his arms last night. But she did, of course. She was simply too young and inexperienced to know it. Even as impulsive and high-spirited as she was, Jennifer would never have given herself to any man if she didn't love him. Thorne was convinced of it. Knowing that, he could be

patient for the few weeks before they could be married.
She'd tell him she loved him on their wedding night.
And the waiting would make it all the sweeter.

"This is excellent cryptanalysis, Your Grace," Lord
Doddridge said, his gaze fastened on the paper spread
on the desktop before him.

Thorne sat sprawled in the armchair in front of the
undersecretary's desk, his jaw propped in his hand. "The
clear text of the original letter was written in a simple
substitution cipher, just as I first suspected," he explained. "But within that text was a much more complicated transposition cipher. It was the very devil to break
because of the dozens of possible combinations of letters."

Lord Russell Doddridge looked up and pursed his
mouth, nearly hidden by his graying brown mustache
and beard. His shrewd eyes narrowed thoughtfully.
"Whatever gave you the idea to look for an inner cipher?"

Thorne smiled with a sense of keen personal satisfaction. "Just something someone said by chance that happened to set me thinking in that direction. Whoever the
cagey Russian cryptographer was, he assumed that if the
letter fell into our hands, we would be satisfied that we'd
obtained the entire message, once we cracked the first
cipher. He probably never dreamed we'd be smart
enough to look beneath it for a second one and find concealed within the routine diplomatic instructions the real
orders the letter conveyed."

"Egad, what luck! And your expert knowledge of the
Russian language has once again proven invaluable."
The undersecretary tapped his thin fingers on the sheet
of paper. "We're going to have to be very careful. We
can't let the czar's Black Chamber suspect that we've broken their double cipher. As long as their secret bureau
believes it has us fooled with its cursed handiwork, we
can predict the Russians' every move in Central Europe
before they make it. Those bloody beggars have had their

sights set on the Mediterranean since the treaty of San Stefano."

"And they're ready to set the entire region aflame in order to get there," Thorne said.

"Damn their miserable hides."

Thorne braced a booted leg on the opposite knee and frowned thoughtfully. The people of Macedonia hadn't known freedom from the yoke of tyranny for over five hundred years. No one could blame them for plotting a revolution.

"When it comes to the Ottoman Empire's oppressed minorities," he said, "the British government has been on the side of the status quo for far too long. We should have offered them our support fifteen years ago. Now it's probably too late."

"As much as I dislike the despotic methods of Sultan Abdul Hamid, Your Grace, I have to agree with Lord Salisbury in this matter." Doddridge tugged dejectedly on one end of his curled mustache. "We have to back the Ottomans, at least ostensibly, in order to block the spread of imperialist Russia throughout the entire region. If we don't, Constantinople may very well fall to the Czar's troops. A damnable choice, but there you have it. Her Majesty stated it quite concisely in her memorandum to the Cabinet. It's a question of British or Russian supremacy in the world."

"Well, I'll be happy to decipher anything that comes in by way of their ambassador's mail pouch," Thorne offered.

"Good, we'll count on it." Doddridge tented his hands beneath his bearded chin, his expression grim. "Naturally, the idea of your going into the province of Thrace to discover if the Macedonian revolutionaries are receiving Russian arms is out of the question. We can't have you wandering around the mountains looking for the leader of the *comitadjis*, now that we know the Ochrana is on to you. From what we've learned in this letter, a member of the Russian secret police is following you right now. If you were lucky enough to make it all the way to Constantinople, you'd never leave that hornets' nest of political intrigue alive. Someone else will have to go to Turkey in your place."

He paused and waited for Thorne to contradict him, but the duke made no such attempt. Doddridge looked down again at the paper and read out loud, "You may give Count Gortschakoff our orders. The moment Eagleston leaves England, he is to kill him."

"Gortschakoff didn't intend to wait for me to leave the country," Thorne commented in a bored tone. "They had to send an agent to Warwickshire to bring him back to London."

Doddridge rapped his knuckles on the desktop, his face flushed with anger. "Damn that cold-blooded Russian bastard! We don't dare have him arrested. As a courier, Gortschakoff's protected by diplomatic immunity. And if we request that the wily count be recalled to his homeland, we'll tip them off to the fact that we've broken their new cipher. Hell!"

Thorne shrugged with resignation. "I knew Gortschakoff followed me to London from Vienna. He'd been tailing me a lot longer than that. His appearance at Lady Nettlefold-Clive's house party in Warwickshire only confirmed that he's a paid assassin. But that's not why I won't be going to Turkey, sir. I told you before that I was through with this cat-and-mouse game. I might not have meant it at the time, but I do now."

Doddridge waited, clearly intrigued. It was apparent he'd expected Thorne to argue about going to Constantinople—under the guise of seeking Roman artifacts—and attempting to contact the leader of the Imro. It was the sort of dangerous assignment that Thorne reveled in, the kind of life-and-death espionage he'd courted since joining the British secret service.

"The truth is, I'm going to be married, sir," Thorne confided happily as he rose to his feet. "And I have no intention of dragging my new bride into danger while I pursue the fleeting thrill of a little blood sport. From now on, you'll see me play the role of the responsible country gentleman. The only excitement I'll be getting in the future will be hunting a fox. The four-legged kind."

"Well, I'll be damned!" Doddridge rose and hurried around the desk. Clapping Thorne soundly on the shoulder, he pumped his hand in astonishment. "Blast it, my boy! This is good news! Jolly good news! Who's the foolish young lady who's actually agreed to give you her hand?"

Thorne laughed, deeply moved by Doddridge's sincere concern. It felt as though he'd just told his father. A father who truly cared about his son and wished him only the best.

"She's the very same young lady you held out as an inducement for me to attend the diplomatic reception at St. James's Palace. None other than Senator Garrett Robinson's granddaughter. Miss Elkheart and I will be married in a fortnight. Sooner, if I have my way."

Doddridge's face fell. He stared at Thorne, a frown creasing his forehead. "Miss Elkheart?" he asked, his tone suddenly serious. "The American heiress?"

"Yes! After my vitriolic criticism of all Yankee females, I'm planning to spend the rest of my life with one. Only Jennifer isn't really a Yank. She's Cheyenne, with some French and Scot thrown in for good measure."

Doddridge edged slowly backward, till he could prop his spare frame on the edge of his desk. He sank down heavily, resting his hands on his thighs. "Have you spoken to Senator Robinson about this?"

Thorne shook his head, supremely confident that the elderly American statesman would offer no objections. After all, the duke of Eagleston was one of the richest peers in the British Empire.

"Not yet," he admitted, grinning broadly. "I'm going to call on the esteemed senator right after I leave here." He pointed to the papers he'd just given the undersecretary. "Only the importance of personally handing you that letter kept me from going there first thing this morning."

"Thorne . . ." Doddridge began. He stopped and cleared his throat with a noisy harumph. "Senator Robinson and his granddaughter will have already left London by now. They were scheduled to catch the train to Dover at dawn."

"Dover?"

"Yes, they're going on to Paris, where they'll board the Orient Express for the last leg of their journey."

Thorne's words exploded in the quiet room like rifle shots. "To where? Munich? Vienna? Budapest?"

Doddridge slowly shook his head, the heartfelt compassion in his eyes unmistakable. "Constantinople, my dear boy. Senator Robinson and Miss Elkheart are on their way to Constantinople."

Chapter 16

The duke of Eagleston was in a cold rage. He banged open the door of his town house, charged down the hallway, and strode into his study, bellowing for his staff as he went. He unlocked his gun case and withdrew a large, double-barreled military pistol. Jerking open a drawer, he found the boxes of cartridges and tossed them onto his desk nearby. If he was going to play a deadly game of cat and mouse across the length of Europe, he intended to be at least as well armed as Vladimir Gortschakoff.

The butler and housekeeper came hurrying in, their astonished faces making it evident he was behaving completely out of character. He'd left his home that morning in the very best of humor. Fairly glowing with happiness, in fact.

But that was before he'd left the Foreign Office and driven to Park Lane, only to find the redbrick mansion across from Hyde Park closed up tighter than a drum, with not even that idiot butler left to answer the door.

Thorne broke open the unloaded weapon and examined it. Then he pointed the pistol toward the clock on the wall and pulled back the trigger, listening to the satisfying click-click of the movable hammer as it struck each barrel in turn. The powerful Lancaster repeater could drop a charging Bengal tiger from a distance of seventy-five feet. Or a man.

"See that this pistol's cleaned and loaded, Hutchinson," he ordered his gray-haired butler. He looked up to find both servants hovering near the doorway in uneasy silence. "I'm leaving on a trip," he snapped. "Have my clothes packed and my coachman ready to take me to the station in less than a quarter hour. And tell Grigsby to get the hell in here. Woodman, too."

At that moment, his valet tiptoed in. "Might—might I ask how long we'll be gone, Your Grace?" the short, slightly-built man stammered. "So I'll—I'll know how much to pack, that is."

"How the bleeding hell do I know, Grigsby?" Thorne roared. "We'll be back when we're back." He tossed the gun on the desk and glowered at the lot of them. "Where the hell is Woodman?"

Mrs. Bainbridge gasped in horror at her employer's profanity and scurried out of the room to give the necessary instructions.

Thorne glanced over at the collection of rifles and carbines that hung on the far wall. Any man wandering around in the mountains looking for Macedonian revolutionaries had better be prepared for trouble. "I'll take my Soper breech action, too. The rifle can be broken down and packed with my things."

"Excuse me, Your Grace," John Woodman said quietly as he entered the room. "I didn't realize you'd returned. I hadn't expected you back till this afternoon."

Thorne glared at his personal secretary. "I wasn't aware I had to make my every movement known to you, Mr. Woodman. Is Lady Charlotte at home?"

The tall, grave young man flushed and threw back his shoulders, unused to such cavalier treatment from an employer known for his suave, forbearing courtesy. "No, Your Grace. Her Ladyship is making some morning calls. She left word for you that she'd be back at teatime. She's expecting you to join her." Woodman picked up a carton from a nearby table and marched stiffly over to Thorne. "This package came while you were out this morning. I thought it might be important."

As Thorne took the box, his heart lurched painfully. An envelope carrying his name had been slipped beneath the string that tied the brown paper parcel. The writing was unfamiliar, though made by a feminine hand. A presentiment of impending doom scraped like a ratchet wheel down his spine. He knew, instinctively, that the precise girlish penmanship belonged to Jennifer Elkheart.

Thorne set the package down on his desk and looked up to find his three retainers standing in a row like wooden toy soldiers. "Well, what the devil are you two waiting for?" he growled. "You have your instructions. Get going!"

Hutchinson leaped forward and grabbed the pistol from the desktop. Grigsby took the rifle from its rack on the wall. Without another word, the meddlesome duo left the room.

Scowling, Thorne turned to Woodman. "Tell Her Grace when she returns that I had to leave on an unforeseen business trip. Lord Combermere will see to all her needs while I'm gone. Right now, I want you to ready my papers on Greek and Roman artifacts, also some banknotes and my letters of introduction in Turkish and French from the Director of the Royal Archeological Society. Oh, and send a message round to Combermere that he'll have to look in on my mother every day or so, till I get back. Lady Nettlefold-Clive will want to know, too."

"Very well, Your Grace."

"After that, you can pack your bags for a trip." Thorne met his secretary's shocked gaze and continued his rapid-fire instructions. "If you leave tomorrow, you can be in New York in eight days, where you will purchase one hundred of the finest quality Thoroughbreds you can find. At least eight of them prime, blooded stallions. In addition, you will acquire three cases of Winchester repeating rifles and fifty boxes of ammunition. I'll give you another eight days for the trip to Alberta."

"Alberta? Canada?"

"Yes. Take the train to the closest stop to a place called Medicine Hat. There you are to discover the exact location of a ranch owned by a Mr. and Mrs. Elkheart." He ignored the look of comprehension on Woodman's thin features. "You will then present them with my credentials and a copy of the marriage agreement we drew up yesterday morning. Is that clear so far?"

"Completely, Your Grace."

I'll expect your telegraph message with the Elkhearts' permission for their daughter to marry the duke of Eagleston to arrive in Constantinople in approximately eighteen days. Twenty at the most." Thorne nodded his dismissal. "Now, get going."

The moment Woodman exited the room, Thorne turned back to the box on the desktop and slipped the envelope from under the twine. Tearing it open, he withdrew the short note and turned the sheet of paper to the light streaming through the window.

His hand trembled slightly as he read.

> *Eagleston,*
>
> *Whenever I recall my visit to England, I will think of you with fond affection. This gift is a memento to remember me by. I hope you will think of me kindly in the years to come.*
>
> *Mohehya*

Thorne broke the cord with a snap and ripped off the paper. Removing the lid from the box, he stared in confusion at the strange object inside. He lifted the curious item for a closer inspection and turned it slowly in his hands. It was a buckskin-covered hoop, webbed with fine string and decorated with the black and white feathers of a magpie, tiny, fragile shells, and long beaded tassels.

A trinket!

A Goddamned Indian trinket!

He'd offered her his title, his fortune, and his adoring self, and she'd left him a bloody, useless trinket. He threw the detestable thing on the desk, resisting the urge to grind it under his heel.

Thorne snatched up the note and read it again, the fury inside him howling like a maniac. Somehow, the words seemed vaguely familiar. He swallowed the bile that rose in his throat, as he realized where he'd seen those words before. By God, he *should* remember them. He'd penned them—or words nauseatingly similar—often enough in his parting letters to his cast-off paramours.

This gift is a memento to remember me by.

A sense of agonizing humiliation swept through him, chasing the rage around in his mind in a tornado of violent emotions. The one person on this entire wretched planet he thought he could trust with his whole heart and soul had flung that trust back in his teeth.

Dammit, she wasn't going to brush him aside like some bad memory! He was going to Constantinople and drop this useless piece of junk in her lap. Then he was going to make Miss Jennifer Elkheart his wife, if he had to drag her to the altar by her long, gorgeous hair, kicking and screaming all the way.

Hell and damnation, he had no other choice.

He *had* seduced her, whether she wanted to admit it or not.

She could very well be carrying his child.

The duke of Eagleston knew how to behave like a gentleman, even if the unbridled and fractious little Yank was no lady.

And he would never make the mistake of trusting anyone again.

The Orient Express left Paris on the sixth of October exactly on schedule at seven o'clock in the morning. As the train chugged slowly out of the Gare de l'Est Station, Jennifer watched the picturesque faubourgs with their gray-tiled mansard roofs slip by.

She had spent one whirlwind day shopping on the Rue Saint-Honoré and sightseeing at the Louvre and the Tuileries. In the evening, she and her grandfather had been the guests of honor at a lavish dinner given by Monsieur Jules Grévy, the French president. Strangely, Count Gortschakoff had also been there. Thankfully, he hadn't approached her.

She'd seen the natty, fastidious nobleman on the station platform earlier that morning and wondered if he were on the train now. She hoped they didn't end up sitting with the Russian count in the dining car. She disliked the man, though he'd never said more than a few words to her. There was an air of death about him. She and her grandfather could always choose to have their meals served in their coach, but that would make the trip seem even longer.

The sumptuous railroad car belonged to Queen Victoria, who'd graciously made it available to Senator Robinson and his granddaughter for their journey across the European continent. Jennifer had learned that it was common for royalty to have their own private coaches waiting on a sidetrack in Paris, instantly ready at their command. She and Grandpapa would return in the same royal coach, when their visit to Constantinople was over.

They were scheduled to meet Julie in England and sail to New York on the twenty-fifth of November. After escorting his niece to London, Dr. Benjamin Robinson would return to Edinburgh to study advanced medical techniques at the university. He planned to sail to the United States in late spring. Jennifer wondered if her uncle had written to Lady Idina again about the possibility of surgery to repair her injured hip. If he had, her friend hadn't mentioned it.

Idina had come to Victoria Station to tell them goodbye. Jennifer had cried as though she'd never see the kindhearted lady again. But Dina had laughed at her tears, saying they would see one another before very long. Spotted Beaver and Black Cloud had been left at Nettlefold Manor, where they'd be safe and well taken care of till her return. It was no wonder their mistress had sobbed brokenheartedly as the train pulled away.

In less than seven days, a distance of over two thousand miles would separate Jennifer from the duke of Eagleston. She took a deep breath and let out a long, ragged sigh. He was nothing more than a beautiful memory now.

"You look a little tired this morning, young lady," Grandpapa said. He patted Jennifer's hand and smiled lovingly. "Too much shopping and sightseeing, I think.

warned you not to buy out the stores on your first visit. We'll be back in Paris soon enough."

She bravely returned his smile, though she wanted to bury her face in her hands and bawl. How had everything gone so wrong? "I am worried about Julie, *namsem*," she confessed. "I have received only one letter from her."

Her grandfather put his arm around Jennifer and drew her close. She rested her head on his shoulder. "Julie's fine," he assured her. "If anything were wrong, we'd have heard from Ben. He's not much of a writer, but he'd let us know if your sister were in trouble."

"But only one letter in over a month!" Jennifer complained. "That is not like Evening Star."

Grandpapa chuckled. "How do you know, sweetie pie? You two girls have never been separated before. Maybe she is no more reliable in her correspondence than her uncle. I've only heard from Ben once, myself."

Jennifer placed her hand over her heart. "There is something wrong, *namsem*. I cannot explain it. I simply feel it here. There have been times when the two of us have spoken to each other without words. Now it is as though there is a tremendous void of silence separating us. As though Julie is purposely withholding her thoughts from me."

Her grandfather touched the tip of Jennifer's nose. "You're being too fanciful," he scolded. "Your sister would never do that to you. Why would she?"

"She would if she were in danger and did not want me to know."

"Nonsense! You're making a mountain out of a molehill. Trust your Uncle Benjamin," Grandpapa said. "He'll take care of Julie."

Jennifer wandered restlessly about the luxurious compartment. Its stylish interior was decorated with typical French elegance. She absently ran her hand across the back of a leather armchair and bent to inhale the perfume of a huge bouquet of yellow roses on a Louis XV table.

"Tell me about the new friends you made in London," Grandpapa encouraged from his place by the window.

"What about that handsome duke who was gazing at you at the opera like a love-struck beau?"

"Eagleston?" she asked in surprise. She peeked at her dignified, silver-haired grandfather from the corner of her eye. She never realized *namsem* was quite so perceptive. "*Hesc!* He is not my beau," she denied. "He is just another English lord. They are all very much alike, you know."

"No, I didn't know. What's wrong with the duke of Eagleston? I thought he was supposed to be a great matrimonial prize."

"I could never marry him!" Jennifer protested. She pretended to admire a tapestry scene on the back of a miniature chaise longue. "And certainly not for some meaningless title!"

"I see."

Jennifer heard the mild skepticism in her grandfather's tone. "Eagleston is no different than any of the other British peers I met," she stated earnestly. "He speaks with a bored drawl half the time. He never seems to exert any effort to earn a living. Aside from traveling around collecting old statues, he spends his life attending soirees and balls. He very likely thinks the choice of flowers for a lady's corsage is the most important decision of the day."

"You don't have to convince me that he's the wrong gentleman," Grandpapa said with an indulgent smile. "I'm not the one who must make that decision."

"The duke is so vain that he left the Life Guards because he didn't like the style of their uniforms," she complained. "He's probably never been married because he doesn't want the responsibility of providing for a family. And he all but admitted he doesn't want children of his own."

"That's quite a list of character defects. What kind of a man are you looking for, puss?"

"I want to marry a warrior like my father."

Garrett Robinson's hazel eyes glinted with laughter. "You want to marry a man who provides for his family through hunting and fishing and breeding horses? Or one who acts as a guide and interpreter for the Northwest Mounted Police in the winter months? That's rather narrowing the field, isn't it?"

She squared her shoulders and clasped her hands in front of her, unable to see the humor in her present predicament. "I want a man who will be willing and able to protect his loved ones, even at the risk of his own life."

"Ah, then he has to be a soldier," Grandpapa stated, confident that he'd solved the riddle at last.

"No," she answered with a loving smile. "He could be a statesman and diplomat, just like you, *namsem*."

"You flatter me, child!"

"I am serious, Grandpapa! I want a life of adventure and excitement. I long to visit faraway places. I only wish I had studied harder, when my tutors tried to teach me world history and geography. But at least, in the schoolroom at the French embassy, I learned the proper etiquette to become an ambassador's wife."

Jennifer knew her grandfather had been sent as a special envoy from the President of the United States to negotiate the touchy subject of reparations for American Armenians, whose families had been killed by the Sultan's troops in a massacre several years before. It was hoped that Senator Robinson could smooth the way for the indemnity claims.

Up to that point Sultan Abdul Hamid had refused to accept any responsibility for the mass slaughter of thousands of innocent men, women, and children in the Turkish provinces, insisting that the carnage had been perpetrated by unidentified wild men. One of the reasons Grandpapa was bringing Jennifer with him was to make his stay in Constantinople appear more like a social visit than an attempt to coerce the sultan into giving in to the Americans' demands.

Jennifer moved to look out at the passing landscape of the Champagne country. She traced an invisible pattern of the evening star on the windowpane. "If anyone should be attracted to Eagleston, it should be Julie. She'd make a perfect duchess. She could converse with him in Latin and Greek over crumpets and tea."

"I don't know. They say opposites attract."

"*Haxc!*" Jennifer exclaimed impatiently. She sank down on the couch beside her grandfather with a scowl. "I cannot imagine anything duller than to sit in a drawing room embroidering serviettes for the rest of my life. I could never be happy married to a duke!"

"Well, if that's how you feel, Jennie, then the duke of Eagleston is certainly the wrong man for you."

Propping her hand in her chin, Jennifer gazed out the window. If that were true, why did it feel as though her heart was breaking? Since leaving London, she'd dreamt of Eagleston every time she'd fallen asleep. Of his lean, scarred, sinewy body bending over her. Of the way he'd made love to her with such passion and tenderness. Each night before going to bed, she prayed that the Great Powers would send her the vision once again, to remind her of the path she was meant to follow, and the man she was meant to love.

Her parents had warned Jennifer about her lack of forethought, of what her mother—in her own special English—would sometimes call "Jennie's ramptious behavior." They lectured her on the need for a measure of sobriety and cautioned her that not everything in life would be exciting or fun. Sometimes they encouraged her to be a little more like her twin in that regard, for Julie was the prudent, contemplative one. Strong Elk called Evening Star his *vehona*, which meant princess, because of her poise and serenity. Julie was quiet, perceptive, and thoughtful.

Jennifer was painfully aware that she was sadly lacking in all those virtues. But surely her one true love would forgive her for what she'd done so heedlessly. A man destined by fate to love her would understand her impulsive nature.

Wouldn't he?

Their first night in Constantinople, Senator Robinson and Miss Elkheart were welcomed with a grand ball given by the British ambassador. They were conveyed in an open Viennese carriage from the magnificent Pera Palace Hotel along the Grande Rue de Pera to the embassy perched on the summit of a steep hill.

Foreigners arriving in the capital of the Ottoman Empire congregated in the suburbs of Pera and Galata, across the Golden Horn from the city of Stamboul. There, ambassadors, ministers, and chargé d'affaires from the various countries of the world lived behind stately wrought-iron gates in fairy-tale palaces. Jennifer learned that while the Europeans called the ancient, walled city and its surrounding environs Constantinople, the Turks themselves referred to their capital as Istanbul.

Statesmen from far-flung countries, along with their wives and grown children, gathered in the British embassy to welcome the American special envoy and his granddaughter. Several representatives of Sultan Abdul Hamid were in attendance, as well. Hassan Pasha, the Minister of Marine, was a favorite of the sultan, and reputedly the richest official in the Ottoman Empire. Which, Jennifer was informed from behind a spread fan, made him very, very rich, indeed.

Tahsen Bey, the sultan's *bash kiatib*, or private secretary, appeared at the ball to extend to the newcomers the compliments of the Commander of the Faithful and God's Vice-Regent on Earth. The slight, thin man was dressed in a long, black, tight-collared stambouline worn over gray trousers.

Speaking perfect French, Tahsen Bey bowed over Jennifer's hand with all the suavity of a Parisian *boulevardier*. "Welcome to Istanbul, Miss Elkheart," he greeted her. He turned slightly, addressing her grandfather. "His Majesty wishes to convey his warm regards and to invite His Excellency and his lovely granddaughter to join him at a state dinner in Dolmabaché Palace tomorrow evening."

"We will be honored to attend," Senator Robinson replied. Jennifer dipped a curtsey, and the charming, soft-spoken man moved on.

Upon Jennifer's arrival that evening, the wives and daughters from the various embassies and legations had proven friendly and outgoing. The women gossiped extravagantly about every man in the room, and Jennifer realized what a small world the realm of diplomacy really was. She would have to curb her impetuous behavior and watch every word she said in public, for there was no doubt it would be repeated over the breakfast tables in the morning.

She stood beside her grandfather, having just returned to him after a waltz with a dashing Italian military attaché. Senator Robinson was deep in conversation with the American minister, Judge Newton Beaufort, a tall, lanky, plainspoken Texan, known to everyone as "Bo." The two men were joined by Beaufort's personal secretary, and the trio stepped discreetly aside to continue their private discussion.

Content simply to observe the wondrous spectacle, Jennifer gazed absently about the room. She recognized the rakish figure of Count Gortschakoff on the far side of the dance floor, conversing with Pasha Izzet Bey. It didn't surprise her that the Russian nobleman was a friend of the head of the sultan's secret police. She'd been told that the cruel, heartless man was the most dreaded official in the Ottoman government. When she'd met him earlier, the pasha's lascivious gaze had swept over her in an openly thorough inspection that had made her skin crawl.

Gortschakoff turned at that moment and caught her watching him. He stroked his neatly trimmed goatee and bowed politely, a faint smile curving his thin lips. She immediately looked away, hoping he wouldn't come over and ask for a dance. Since he had been a fellow guest at Lady Idina's house party, she could hardly refuse.

Close by, two young Frenchwomen, whom she'd met earlier in the reception line, were laughing and chattering like schoolgirls. As she admired the ladies' stylish gowns, she couldn't help but overhear their animated conversation.

"Ah, *la bonne chance*! Look who just walked in!" Mademoiselle Tabeau said excitedly to her friend. "I saw him in Vienna last month, when we were on our way to our post here." The French Ambassador's daughter placed her jeweled fan over her breast as though she were about to swoon. *"Bon Dieu,* I nearly died of longing for just one waltz with him. An older woman told me he was having a torrid affair with an Austrian dancer in the corps de ballet."

Mademoiselle du Lac erupted in a nervous giggle. "Who is he?" she asked. "I do not know the handsome gentleman."

"The duke of Eagleston, *imbécile!*" Michelle Tabeau confided breathlessly. "He's rich, titled, and unmarried."

Jennifer whirled to face the doorway.

Eagleston!

He'd followed her here!

In that first ecstatic instant of recognition, Jennifer's heart seemed to tumble to the floor and roll across the polished boards to his feet. She was filled with a breathless, stupefied joy, scarcely able to comprehend his sudden, incredible appearance. It was as though he'd just stepped out of her dreams.

He looked completely at ease as he threaded his way through the crowd and came to stand beside her.

"Thorne!" she gasped, making no attempt to hide her shock.

A taunting smile skipped across his mouth. He'd grown a beard since she'd last seen him. The golden-brown whiskers were surprisingly thick and luxuriant for only ten days growth. But there was no doubt about it. It was Eagleston.

He lifted her gloved fingers and brought them to his lips. The frosty depths of his *veho* blue eyes were as cold as a Canadian snowstorm. "It's nice to see you again, too, Miss Elkheart," he said in a silken, satirical tone.

With a heart-wrenching pang, she realized he was treating her as if she were nothing more than a chance-met acquaintance. She looked at him in bewilderment, feeling as though he'd stomped on her heart, and stomped again for good measure. She snatched her hand away. "What are you doing here?"

"Didn't I tell you?" he replied glibly. "I had planned to leave for Constantinople the day after I attended the opera with Lady Charlotte. The trip had been scheduled weeks ago. I left at dawn the next morning. I'm hoping to add some pieces to my collection of Roman antiquities displayed in the British Museum." He ignored her shocked reaction to his words and continued, unperturbed. "This city was once an outpost of ancient Rome, long before it fell to Mehmet the Conqueror and became the capital of the Ottoman Empire. It was originally called Byzantium. Did you know that?"

Jennifer paid no attention to the history lesson. Her staccato words were filled with a tortured bafflement. "I thought you were going to . . ." She caught herself in time and clamped her mouth shut. She could have bitten her tongue at her rash words. She'd never admit she was hurt and angry that he hadn't gone to her home in London to ask her grandfather for her hand.

Nehe! What a boldfaced liar! Suppose she'd waited all day long for Eagleston to appear—hat in one hand, flowers in the other, to beg on bended knee for marriage—only to cry her poor heart out when he never arrived. She'd been right all along. Like Wihio, the Cheyenne trickster, the British lord was a cunning, devious shapeshifter. The new beard was proof of his nefarious ways.

The duke tipped his head toward her, waiting for Jennifer to complete her question. "You thought I was going to . . . ?"

". . . to go grouse hunting in Yorkshire," she finished with a weak smile.

The Englishman lifted his brows in feigned amazement. "Now, whatever gave you that idea?" he queried. "I don't remember ever mentioning grouse hunting." The smile became an arrogant smirk as he moved a step closer. "Surely, Miss Elkheart, you don't think I followed you here?"

"Of course not!" she snapped. Mademoiselle Tabeau's words burned through Jennifer's haze of fury and humiliation. "Did you stop and see your Austrian ballet dancer on your way through Vienna?"

This time he really was surprised. "What do you know about ballet dancers?" he growled.

"Enough," she stated calmly, determined not to reveal the empty ache where her heart used to be. He'd purposely let her believe that he knew nothing about sexual relations between a man and a woman. How he must have laughed at her unmitigated naiveté. What else had he lied to her about?

He arched one golden brow sardonically. "Are you jealous?"

"Hardly!"

From the corner of her eye, Jennifer could see the two mademoiselles watching them, their pretty mouths hanging open in delight. The foolish tattletales were clearly listening to every word. She prayed they didn't understand English.

"Let's move away from here," the duke brazenly suggested, "to someplace where we can speak in private."

She waved her fan in a gesture of arch dismissal. "I do not wish to speak to you at all."

Eagleston acted as though he hadn't heard her. "Allow me to escort you to the dessert table, Miss Elkheart," he said as he offered his elbow. His gaze drifted down her rose silk dress and up to the braided crown of her hair with its scattering of rubies. "By the way, you look lovely tonight."

She ignored his arm and started toward the dining room where a buffet had been laid out, letting him follow, if he chose to. Eagleston stayed right at her side.

"I still carry my knife wherever I go," Jennifer warned, keeping her own words low and terse. She surveyed him through narrowed eyes. His only reply was a wolfish grin, telling her he was remembering the last time she'd used her knife—to his immense satisfaction.

They arrived at a table laden with sugared confections, and Eagleston had the effrontery to slip his arm around her waist. Gazing at the sumptuous array, he made a pretense of serious contemplation. "What would you like, Miss Elkheart? Tarts? Bonbons? Ripe blackberries?"

Two could play this game of scarcely veiled insults. "Choose whatever you wish, Your Grrr-aciousness," she purred. "All of a sudden, I am not very hungry. It must be the company I am keeping."

He pointed to one of the cakes. A liveried footman scooped a piece up with a silver server, plopped it on a delicate china plate, and handed it to the duke. "Since you're not all that hungry, we can share," Eagleston told her, waving away the fork the servant held out.

"With you?" Her words dripped with scorn. "I do not think so."

But Jennifer reluctantly allowed the Englishman to sweep her through a set of open double doors, one muscular arm firmly fastened about her waist. She knew there was no point in refusing to go with him. He'd only proceed to make a scene on her very first night in Constantinople. She had no intention of bringing disgrace down on her head, and thus embarrassing her grandfather in front of a roomful of dignitaries.

The moment they were out of sight of the other guests, Eagleston released her. Moving quickly away from him, she walked to the edge of the brick terrace and gazed out at the night. The gardens surrounding the embassy sloped downward to the sea, revealing a panorama of incredible beauty.

In one direction lay the Bosphorus, the narrow straits that divided Europe from Asia. She could see the lights of Uskudar on the opposite shore. In the other direction, the Sea of Marmara led to the Dardanelles and the Aegean Ocean beyond. Ottoman war ships, ocean liners, tramp steamers, ferries, yachts, feluccas, and dhows plied their waters, the golden glow of their lamps bobbing and dipping like fireflies over the waves. Across the Golden Horn rose Stamboul, built on a series of steep hills, its lights twinkling like a thousand brilliant gems.

"Pretty at night, isn't it?" Eagleston said in that familiar, bored drawl, as he came to stand beside her.

His unflagging British insouciance positively set her teeth on edge. Why did he have to come to Constantinople, of all places, to search for his old relics? He was going to ruin her chance to meet the one man she was fated to love. How could she explain that she'd been seduced by another, while that very seducer stood at her elbow, grinning in egotistical triumph?

"The view is breathtaking," she told him tartly. "But I suppose you have been here before."

"Several times," he acknowledged. "No one can do any archeological research in Turkey without the sultan's express permission. That includes the provinces and territories under his dominion. I plan to go into the mountains of Macedonia as soon as I obtain the proper permits."

She lifted one shoulder, letting him know she wasn't interested in his pursuits. The sooner he went traipsing off into the hills, the better.

Eagleston leaned toward her and held a small bite of cake to her mouth. The tangy smell of lemon, mixed with the sweet aroma of butter frosting, tickled her nose. "Have a taste," he urged, the smug amusement in his voice raising her anger to a new and dangerous level. "It looks delicious."

Meeting his satirical gaze, she kept her lips sealed tight.

"Come, come, Miss Elkheart," he goaded. In the glow of the outdoor lanterns, a diabolical light glinted in his clever *veho* eyes. "I allowed you to feed me blackberries. Surely, you won't refuse to let me return the favor."

She opened her mouth for a scathing reply, and he popped the cake inside. The fluffy white icing smeared across her lips. His scorching gaze locked with hers as he wiped her mouth off with his index finger, then slowly and methodically licked away every trace of the icing with the tip of his tongue. Her eyes widened at the daringly suggestive act. Memories of what he'd done to her writhing body with that same moist tongue brought a rush of heat to her cheeks.

"If you recall," he said, his dulcet words deep and coaxing, "you fed me berries to sweeten me up, so you could tell me something of a personal nature. I have an ulterior motive this evening, as well. Only, I want to *ask* you something . . . personal." He turned slightly to set the plate down on the glass top of a garden table, then stepped even closer.

"Very well," she replied coolly. "What would you like to know?"

"What does 'Namehota, zehemehotaz' mean?"

Jennifer clamped her hand over his mouth. "You must not say that!" she cried, her heart pounding. In her agitation, she looked around, afraid someone may have come out on the terrace and overheard him.

Eagleston pried her fingers from his lips. Holding them in his relentless grasp, he pulled her nearer, till the ribbons on the bodice of her evening gown were a mere inch from the ruffles on his shirt. "I don't think anyone else here understands Cheyenne," he drawled. "Unless, perhaps, Senator Robinson is familiar with the language. I could ask him."

She stared into the duke's hooded eyes, aghast at his intentional cruelty. How could he repeat such a tender, intimate phrase after admitting he'd never had any intention of proposing marriage? "Grandpapa knows very few Cheyenne words," she admitted in a shaky voice, "but you must not repeat them again."

"Why not, Jennifer?"

"Because they are not true!"

"You mean you lied when you said them?"

"Yes!"

"Strange," he mused with a cynical smile, "you seemed very sincere at the time."

She wrenched her hand from his grasp and glared at him. He wasn't content to throw her declaration of love back in her face; he had to rub her nose in it. "I think I should return to my grandfather now," she said woodenly. Her lips trembled, but she refused to shed a single tear in front of him.

Thorne made no attempt to hide his icy rage. Not after what she'd done to him. "How like a cowardly colonial to turn tail and run at the least hint of danger," he told her with a caustic sneer. "Just like you ran away from me in London."

"I would rather be a rustic colonial," she shot back, "than an effete, indolent nobleman, whose greatest challenge in life is the discovery of dusty relics that no one else is even interested in."

His derisive rebuke was laced with scorn. "Maybe if you spent a little less time shopping for clothes and a little more time reading a book, you might understand the value of archeology."

"I want my dreamcatcher back!" she declared, sounding like a petulant little girl. Her lower lip jutted out, and she scowled ferociously, as though barely able to keep from crying.

The preposterous demand caught Thorne off guard. He had no idea what she was talking about, but he could see the hurt pooling in her velvety eyes. Bloody hell, must she always converse in riddles?

"Dreamcatcher?" he asked.

"Yes," she said in an agonized whisper. "My father made it for me, and I want it back."

Awareness dawned.

The feathered trinket.

He'd thought it was some meaningless bauble, a frivolous souvenir to remember her by. Apparently she valued the peculiar object very highly. He kept his words calm and dispassionate. "You forgot to tell me what the dreamcatcher was for, Jennifer."

She gaped at him with an expression of complete disbelief. "*Hesc!* To catch bad dreams in its net and let only the good ones through! What else would a dreamcatcher be for?"

"And have you been having bad dreams since you left London?" he asked softly.

She turned away, blinking back tears. "Yes," she reproached, "and they were all about you."

He grinned.

"They were nightmares!" she clarified. "Horrible, terrible, frightening nightmares."

Thorne clucked his tongue sympathetically. "That's too bad, Mohehya. I really wish I could help you, but there's not much I can do about your dreams."

Jennifer whirled to face him, her determined chin tilted

upward, her hands clenched at her side. "You can give me my dreamcatcher back."

"Oh, I can't do that," he protested. "Then I'd be the one stuck with the nightmares. And since the day you gave it to me, I've been having the most wonderful dreams. Shall I tell you about them?"

"No."

Thorne drew Jennie's stiff, unwilling figure into his arms and grazed her smooth cheek with his lips. The sweet perfume of wild flowers, combined with her own delicate scent, brought a rush of vivid sensations to torture him anew.

"I dream that we're back in the summerhouse again," he murmured in her ear. "Holding each other close, just like this. Only, we're naked as before, and you're whispering, '*Namehota, zehemehotaz.*'" He felt her tremble beneath the power of those magical words. "Kiss me, *Vonahenene*," he urged hoarsely.

Jennifer fought the overwhelming emotions that threatened to destroy what few shreds of pride she had left. She'd told him she loved him that night in the arbor and the words had been true. When she was in his arms, nothing else seemed to matter. Not the vision sent by the Maiyun, not Eagleston's meaningless lifestyle, nor his world-weary cynicism.

She had never felt so confused as she did at this moment. Back in England, she'd had no intention of accepting his proposal. Yet now—knowing that he'd made no attempt to ask her grandfather for permission to marry her, that he'd lied that night in the folly when he said he loved her—she felt as if he'd torn her heart into pieces and scattered them to the four winds. One fact remained crystal clear. Instead of calling at their house the day after the opera, he'd left on a trip to Constantinople to gather more artifacts for his personal aggrandizement.

Jennifer steeled herself to meet his treacherous eyes and turned to face him, her lips nearly brushing his mouth. She wasn't some foolish *vehoka* to love a man who didn't love her. "Will you give me back my dreamcatcher?'' she asked, her throat raw and constricted with pain.

"I'll tell you what, little magpie, why don't we share it?" he suggested in a husky whisper. "We can hang it above our bed, and when we fall asleep in each other's arms, we'll both have the same marvelous dream."

At the callous proposal, Jennifer braced her forearms against Eagleston's broad chest and pushed away. If he'd never intended to ask for her hand in marriage, then he could only be suggesting the role of his mistress now. How could he say such a despicable thing?

"*Nehe!*" she hissed in scorn. "I would not share last winter's pemmican with you, white man."

Not waiting to hear his arrogant reply, Jennifer raced across the terrace. She nearly bumped into Count Gortschakoff as she hurried inside.

Chapter 17

The next evening, Jennifer and Senator Robinson were on their way to Dolmabaché Palace in a gilded state coach, escorted by a squadron of the sultan's cavalry riding ahead and behind.

"I'm sorry I had to leave you on your own for so long while I met with Judge Beaufort," Grandpapa said. "Did you enjoy yourself today, poppet?"

"Very much," Jennifer replied. "And I was not alone for a minute. Mrs. Beaufort and I paid calls on the wives of the British, French, and Italian ambassadors this morning. Then we were guests at a luncheon given in my honor at the German embassy, followed by a musicale hosted by Baroness von Stetfeldt that lasted long into the afternoon."

"Not very exciting for you, I'm afraid," her grandfather said with an understanding smile. "Especially when you're so anxious to explore the city. But it's imperative that I discuss my plans for negotiations with the American minister before I approach the sultan."

"I am looking forward to sightseeing," Jennifer admitted, as she gazed out the coach window at the wide boulevard that followed the shore of the Bosphorus. "But I also know that you are counting on me to perform the role of a visiting dignitary. There will be lots of time for me to explore the city later on."

"As the granddaughter of a representative of the United States government, it's important that you attend the functions given by the diplomatic corps," Grandpapa agreed. "The foreign colony in Pera is relatively small. They rely on each other to provide a busy social life. And since everyone speaks French with some degree of proficiency, they manage to converse quite freely with one another."

Jennifer laughed. "They do, indeed! I have never heard so many clacking tongues repeating such unbelievable rumors and scandalous gossip."

Senator Robinson chuckled good-naturedly, then grew serious. "The duke of Eagleston called on me this afternoon, my dear, after I'd returned to the hotel from the American Legation."

"Did he?" Jennifer commented lightly. She held her breath, wondering what had transpired between them, but afraid of what she might learn.

"Yes," her grandfather said. "His Grace asked for your hand in marriage. Quite a formal proposal, I must say, with a written assurance that he would expect no dowry from me or your parents. He is, on the contrary, prepared to give you quite a substantial sum as a wedding gift, over which you may have full control, including the right to leave it to your heirs as you see fit. Along with the bags of gold and a considerable collection of priceless jewelry, he's willing to deed a manor house in Surrey over to you the moment the betrothal papers are signed."

Jennifer's mind whirled. She clasped her hands together to keep them from shaking visibly. Last night on the terrace, she'd assumed Eagleston was suggesting the role of his mistress when he offered to share the dreamcatcher with her in his bed. She'd spent the rest of the evening dancing and flirting with every handsome man in a military uniform. The attachés with the most ribbons on their chest were all awarded a second dance and a coquettish smile.

Eagleston had watched her in moody silence for a short time and then proceeded to waltz with every beautiful young woman there, including the foolish Mademoiselle Tabeau and her equally silly friend. The birdbrained adolescents had practically drooled all over the front of his starched white shirt.

Once again, Jennifer's ridiculous habit of leaping to conclusions had resulted in her own misery. Her heart pounding, she inquired hesitantly, "What did you tell him, *namsem*?"

"The truth, poppet. I explained that the decision of who you would marry was yours alone. But since I could see no legitimate reason to oppose his suit, I intended to exert no influence, one way or the other. I explained that it was my understanding, however, that you wouldn't look with favor on the idea of becoming his duchess. Was that correct?"

"Yes." She released a pent-up breath. "What did he say?"

"Oh, Eagleston was very calm, very cool, as though he'd expected to hear exactly that. But I must tell you, he seems a most determined individual. When he left, he insisted on leaving a copy of the marriage agreement for me to look over at my leisure."

"His Grace is a very stubborn man," she said with a shaky laugh.

"Is there something I should know about you and the duke?" Grandpapa asked quietly.

Jennifer bit her lip, unwilling to lie to her grandfather. She stared down at her clasped hands and prayed for an inspiration. None came. "Why do you ask that, *namsem*?" she hedged.

"Because I had the distinct impression Eagleston was convinced you and he would be married. And rather quickly, at that. The possibility that you'd refuse him didn't seem to enter his mind."

"*Hesc*! I *have* refused him!" she blurted out. "The dratted man has a chronic inability to take no for an answer."

"There was one other thing we discussed," Grandpapa continued soberly. "He insisted on providing you with armed escorts while you're here in Istanbul. They are to accompany you wherever you go."

"How dare he?" she cried, incensed at the rogue's presumptuousness. She clutched the small evening bag laying in her lap and tried to control her spiraling temper. "Of course, you refused him."

Her grandfather shook his head. "He made a very good case, I'm afraid. Naturally, I told the duke that I would bear the expense."

"I should think so!"

"Unfortunately, he didn't. He said he'd already hired the fellows, and if I insisted on paying them a salary, they'd be receiving double wages—but that was up to me."

Jennifer turned her head and stared at her grandfather, unable to believe her ears. "You went along with this preposterous scheme?"

"The duke of Eagleston is a very persuasive man, Jennie." Grandpapa took her hand and patted it consolingly. "His Grace has to travel into Macedonia on a hunt for archaeological treasures, and he's worried something may happen to you while he's gone. Since I'll be tied up in negotiations with the sultan, I think it's in your best interest to have two strong guards at your side whom we can trust. And as long as he's already hired them, why not agree? What would be the point in refusing his offer of assistance?"

Jennifer swallowed back the retort that the duke's hirelings would report back on every gentleman she spoke to, making it even more difficult for her to get to know the one man in Istanbul she'd come here to meet.

Dolmabaché Palace was stupendous. Built along the shoreline at the entrance to the Bosphorus, it was enclosed by high stone walls on the landward side. Jennifer and her grandfather entered through an arched stone portal, its tall double gates of white wrought-iron swung wide by soldiers bearing side arms.

They were ushered into the Ceremonial Hall. Three stories high, with tall bay windows along the walls of the first floor, double windows along the open gallery, and topped with a painted and gilded dome, it was an incredible display of occidental motifs blended with Rococo, Baroque, and Empire ornamentation.

Dignitaries of the Ottoman Empire mingled with diplomats and their wives in the enormous room. Glittering with diamonds, rubies, and emeralds, and decorated with silver and gold, the sultan's admirals, field marshals, pashas, and beys easily outshone the European gentlemen in their severe black evening clothes.

After such a display of magnificence, Jennifer couldn't help but feel a little disappointed in the sultan himself. She'd hoped for a large, robust man dressed in the Oriental grandeur of crimson silk robes trimmed with fur, and a great turban adorned with egret feathers. Instead, Abdul Hamid II was a small, thin, sallow man dressed in a black stambouline and red fez. He had a sharp, hooked nose, sunken eyes, and a straggling black beard shot with gray. A row of soldiers in tall plumed hats guarded his back as he stood at the far end of the room and greeted the guests with dignified formality.

Sultan Abdul Hamid and Lady Idina Nettlefold-Clive had one thing in common. They both ignored protocol and seated people at their table to suit their own wishes. Jennifer was astonished to find herself on the sultan's right and Senator Robinson on his left, while Bo and Dotty Beaufort were sitting in ignominy at the far end of the table, along with the Russian ambassador, Grand Duke Nikolai Streltsky, and Count Vladimir Gortschakoff.

It was no surprise to find the British ambassador, Lord Ellenborough, seated next to her and, therefore, close to the sultan.

Grandpapa had told her that the British government had played the key role in keeping the tottering Ottoman Empire on its feet after the fall of Plevna, when Russian troops had advanced to within six miles of Constantinople in the last Russo-Turkish war. He'd explained that former Prime Minister Disraeli's goal at the Congress of Berlin had been to deny the Czar's hope of gaining access to the Mediterranean by bringing first Bulgaria and then the Balkans into the Russian sphere of influence.

Expecting to see Lady Ellenborough beside her grandfather, Jennifer nearly jumped out of her skin when she looked over to find the duke of Eagleston taking his seat, the Ambassador's wife on his immediate left.

In the throng of people milling about in the huge state reception room, she hadn't once seen the tall, prepossessing Englishman. He must have been skulking in the corridors or hiding outside in the formal gardens. She had no idea the duke was held in such high regard, either by the British ambassador or the sultan. His presence here, however, made it very clear that Eagleston had managed to worm his way into everyone's good graces.

Everyone's except hers.

Her irate thoughts were interrupted by the sultan's cultured French. "I trust that the guardsmen I suggested to the duke of Eagleston will prove satisfactory, Miss Elkheart," Abdul Hamid said. "I know His Grace is extremely concerned for your welfare."

"I am certain they will be quite satisfactory," she replied in a strangled voice. Despite her intention not to glance Eagleston's way again that evening, she couldn't help but look over at the suave, elegant British lord.

Eagleston flashed her a smile of overweening self-assurance. "His Majesty was gracious enough to have his personal secretary, the Bash Kiatib, recommend two reliable escorts for your protection, Miss Elkheart, so you can discover the delights of this magnificent city in perfect safety. We all agree that your well-being is everyone's primary concern during Senator Robinson's visit to Istanbul."

She couldn't believe such outright chicanery.

Such absolute, unmitigated boldness.

Jennifer turned back to the sultan, knowing there was no way she could graciously refuse the guards he'd recommended. To do so would be an unforgivable insult.

Seeing the consternation on her face, Abdul Hamid smiled reassuringly. "If you are worried about the bandits who robbed the train today, Miss Elkheart, let me set your mind at rest. We will find the men responsible soon enough, and they will be severely punished. In the meantime, they would not dare come into the city."

"I—I had not heard about a train robbery," she admitted, glancing at her grandfather in a silent appeal for help.

Garrett Robinson's look of confusion told her that he'd not heard of it, either. "Nor I," he acknowledged. "Where did it happen?"

"The news just reached the city an hour ago," Eagleston explained. "It seems the inbound Orient Express was derailed about sixty miles from Istanbul, where it was boarded and the passengers robbed. A Turkish official on the train had to follow the tracks for five miles to reach the nearest village of Cherkes Baba and give the alarm. By the time help arrived, the robbers were gone."

"Who would do such a thing?" Jennifer asked in horror.

"Macedonian brigands, Miss Elkheart," the sultan said somberly. His dark, haggard features were etched with a doleful frown. "Common thieves, nothing more, after currency, jewelry, watches . . . any gold or silver they can steal. But do not be alarmed. All military and police posts in the area have been alerted. A rescue train has been sent, and the passengers will be brought safely to Istanbul tonight."

"Was anyone hurt?" Senator Robinson inquired. Though he gave no outward sign, Jennifer read the concern in his eyes. The thought that they'd avoided the dangerous mishap by only twenty-four hours was clearly unsettling. By a stroke of good fortune, they had left Vienna a day earlier than originally scheduled.

"Apparently, no one was injured," Lord Ellenborough added. "After the robbers had taken all their money and valuables, the passengers were allowed to reboard their coaches and wait for help to arrive. Luckily, there was no personage of consequence on the train who could have been abducted and held for ransom."

"Enough talk of bandits," Abdul Hamid declared with a desultory wave of his hand. "Let us pursue a conversation more interesting to our young visitor. In point of fact, Miss Elkheart, my aunt has expressed a wish to meet you."

"I would be delighted to call on her, Your Majesty,"

Jennifer said. She set her water goblet down and smiled in sincere anticipation. "Does she live here in the palace?"

"No, the Sultana Pertevalé lives in the Topkapi Seray. But the arrival of a beautiful guest, such as you, has intrigued everyone in Istanbul, including the ladies who dwell in the Grand Seraglio. If it is acceptable, I will send an escort to take you there tomorrow afternoon."

"Yes, please," Jennifer agreed. She looked questioningly at her grandfather, wondering if the invitation included him. Garrett Robinson gave an almost imperceptible shake of his head, and she kept her thoughts to herself.

She glanced at Eagleston, who was watching her with a tantalizing smile. His blue eyes were alight with anticipation, as though he was just waiting to hear her ask if her grandfather was invited to visit the Grand Seraglio, too. He actually seemed to be daring her to do it. She resisted the impulse to cross her eyes and stick her tongue out at him.

"The sultana has heard that you are a native of the New World," Abdul Hamid continued in his mild-mannered way. "She has never met a North American Indian and was fascinated to learn of your exceptional grace and charm, not to mention your lively intelligence. You will forgive her natural curiosity, I hope, if she asks you many questions about your childhood in the wilderness of Canada."

"Of course," Jennifer replied brightly. "It is very kind of the sultana to invite me." She looked over at Eagleston and gave him a smug smile. There, she hadn't handled that badly, at all.

During the sumptuous feast, Jennifer pretended—along with the other guests—not to notice that the Sultan ate only a little rice and a few hard-boiled eggs. Grandpapa had warned her that, although the excellent meal would be prepared by chefs imported from Paris, Abdul Hamid was rumored to be so afraid of poisoning that he would hardly touch his food.

When the meal was over, the sultan invited Senator Robinson and his granddaughter, along with Lord and Lady Ellenborough and the duke of Eagleston, to join him on a tour of the imperial gardens.

The palace was surrounded by an extensive estate. Beds of flowers were laid out in precise geometrical designs, showing the influence of some of the former sultans' European gardeners.

The party was followed closely by uniformed guards, who constantly protected the sultan's rear. As they walked, Abdul Hamid drew Senator Robinson into a private conversation, leaving the British ambassador and his wife to walk in front of them and enjoy the botanical display together. Eagleston and Jennifer were soon well in the lead, although always within view of the sultan, as well as his armed escorts.

The group followed a path leading around the rambling marble edifice to the wide portico that ran the length of the main building on the shoreward side. While the others stood on the steps of the verandah in conversation, Eagleston guided Jennifer down a graveled path toward the Bosphorus.

Along the length of the lawn's edge, five tall gates led to the waterfront by way of a flight of stairs. The white gates were made of intricate cast-iron filigree and linked by a white iron fence. They stopped on a walkway that followed the delicate railing along the entire length of the immense estate on the shore side.

In the combined glow of the gas lanterns and the moonlight, the scene was one of breathtaking splendor. With the addition of Eagleston, broad-shouldered, tawny-haired, and dressed in formal white tie and tails, the overall effect was heart-stoppingly romantic.

Jennifer threw back her shoulders and told herself that under no circumstance would she fall under that rascal's spell a second time. She would prove to him and to herself that she was in complete control of her emotions.

They were well out of hearing range of anyone, including the sentry posted at each of the gates, and she no longer had to keep her comments focused strictly on the loveliness of the gardens.

"It's not going to work, you know," she said pleasantly. "My grandfather would never sign the betrothal contract without my parents' permission." She paused and looked the Eagle straight in the eye. "And no matter what you might tell him about us, he would never force me to marry a man against my wishes."

He stood only a few steps away, loose, relaxed, hands in his trouser pockets. But his velvety voice was filled with seduction. "I told you once that I'd never say anything to Senator Robinson about our lovemaking, Jennie. What happened that night is strictly our own affair. And I have no intention of trying to force you to do anything."

"Then why did you bother to call on Grandpapa this afternoon? Was it merely an exercise in gentlemanly conduct? Or was it a way to salve your conscience?" She looked out over the water and added bitterly, "Rather a tardy effort at proper behavior, whatever the reason."

She could feel Eagleston move closer, till his trouser leg brushed against the full, gathered draperies of her gold satin gown.

"I was furious when I learned that you'd left London without telling me," he said in a conversational tone.

Jennifer kept her gaze fastened on the twinkling lights of the fishing boats out in the straits. "I left you a note."

His deep voice grew a trace more hoarse, betraying the wrath he'd been trying to conceal. "Yes, and a pretty trinket to remember you by. Somehow, Miss Elkheart, the note and the trinket didn't quite make up for the fact that you lied to me."

She spun around to face him. "I never lied to you! I do not tell lies. It was one of my mother's strictest rules."

In the glow of the gas lamp above them, she saw his cynical smile. "Ever hear of the sin of omission? In all the time we spent together at Nettlefold Manor, you failed to mention that you and Senator Robinson were leaving for Constantinople almost immediately after the house party was over. Strange, how that subject never once came up, isn't it?"

"Haxc! What difference would it have made to you? You told me last night you had planned this trip weeks ago."

"I had decided to cancel the trip," he grated, giving up all pretense of his usual, unruffled composure. "I had mistakenly thought our wedding would take place in London. I didn't realize we'd be wed here in Constantinople, instead."

"We are not getting wed anywhere, Your Grace." She turned to go, and he caught her elbow.

"Come sightseeing with me, Jennie," he urged. "I'll show you Istanbul the way no one else can."

"I am visiting the Sultana Pertevalé tomorrow, or have you forgotten?"

"The day after tomorrow, then. I'll send you an outfit to wear. If you go dressed as a young boy, we can move freely about the city."

She took a step back. "You are an incredibly bold man, Your Grace," she chided, pretending to be shocked. But the invitation was immensely tantalizing. He knew it was exactly the kind of outrageous escapade that would appeal to her sense of adventure.

Eagleston put his hand over his heart, as though she'd cut him to the quick. One corner of his mouth curved up in an entrancing half-smile. "I'm only an effete, indolent nobleman, Miss Elkheart," he said, repeating her stinging assessment. "But you'll be perfectly safe with me as your guide. And I promise you, the sightseeing will be exceptional."

"I thought you were going to traipse off into the mountains and look for Roman statuary or pottery or whatever it is you collect."

"Since this afternoon's train robbery, there will be no archeological permits issued by the Turkish officials in the next few days. Not until they've exhausted all their efforts to track down the men responsible and punish them. Every village for a circumference of eighty miles around the site of the wreck will be swarming with police, soldiers, and the sultan's spies. It would be the worst possible time to search for anything in those mountains."

With a show of complete disinterest, Jennifer tightened the back of an emerald drop that dangled from one lobe, then fiddled with the other earring. "My going sightseeing with you is out of the question," she replied in an offhand manner. "It is not proper." She touched the tip of her forefinger to the edge of her mouth in sham deliberation. "Unless, of course, you are going to make up a small party?"

He grinned wickedly. "The smallest possible. A party of two."

"Then the answer is no," she replied. She gazed at him with a thoughtful frown. "Did you, by any chance, tell the sultan that we were engaged to be married?"

Eagleston folded his arms across his chest and smirked in satisfaction. "Not really. When I asked Tahsen Bey if His Majesty would recommend a pair of armed guards to escort the American envoy's lovely granddaughter, both the *bash kiatib* and the sultan assumed that I would never make such a personal request without first getting permission from Senator Robinson. And that permission would most likely be given only if you were my fiancée." His brilliant smile was absolutely disarming. "Another sin of omission, you see, Miss Elkheart. But then, I didn't just claim that I never told a lie."

Jennifer laughed in spite of herself. "What a clever, wicked tongue you have, Your Graciousness," she said softly. "I doubt that I shall ever meet another gentlemen quite so glib."

He clasped her elbow, his muscular body suddenly taut. "Tell me about the man of your dreams, Jennifer."

"What do you know about my dreams?"

"Lady Idina told me that you've seen the man you are meant to marry in a vision. Tell me what he looks like, so I'll know what kind of fellow I'm destined to lose out to."

She heard the underlying skepticism in his voice. He didn't believe a word of it. He was only after more information, so he could use it for his own devious motives. "Whoever he is," she said sharply, "he certainly isn't you! He doesn't act like you, he doesn't dress like you, and he doesn't look like you."

Eagleston slid his hand up her arm to her shoulder. His thumb drew a circle on the bare skin above her tiny puffed sleeve. "Humor me, Jennie," he said. "Describe the man. That way, if I should discover this paragon of masculinity, I'll direct him to you, with my compliments."

At the scarcely veiled sarcasm in his voice, Jennifer realized the face and figure of the man in her vision were already growing hazy. All she could remember clearly was the thick black beard and dusty, hooded cloak.

Since she'd given Eagleston the dreamcatcher, her vision of the mysterious man had not returned. Instead, she dreamt of nothing but Thorne in ever more intense and vivid detail. And in every dream, they were making love.

Jennifer knew it was absolutely imperative that she retrieve the dreamcatcher as quickly as possible. If she didn't get it back, she might never see the vision again. Bit by bit, the memories would fade, eventually to be lost forever. The Maiyun were punishing her for bestowing the dreamcatcher—and herself—on the wrong man.

Filled with a reckless determination, she straightened her spine and clasped her hands in front of her. Her dry throat constricted painfully. "Give me my dreamcatcher, Eagleston, and I will tell you."

Thorne ran his finger along Jennifer's tense jaw and sensed her desperation. "What's the matter, sweetheart?" he taunted softly. "Having trouble remembering your dream man?"

"No," she whispered, and he knew she was lying.

"Are dreams of me getting in the way?" he persisted. His heart tripped against his ribs at the thought. Aware that they were under scrutiny from several directions, he could only bend closer and inhale her intoxicating scent. He touched her lower lip with his forefinger, and she shivered beneath the innocent caress. "Come sightseeing with me, Mohehya," he tempted, "and I'll return your dreamcatcher."

Her husky contralto quavered and broke. "You—you will?"

"Yes."

"You promise?"

"I promise."

She drew in a breath and let it out slowly, thoughtfully, hesitantly. "I am not certain my grandfather will allow it."

"Tell Senator Robinson you're going to explore the sights of Istanbul with your guards to protect you," Thorne suggested in silken persuasion.

"I have never lied to *namsem* before," she said in a scandalized tone.

"Ah, then you have told him about our night in the summerhouse?" At her stricken silence, he chuckled. "Well, well, what do you know. Another deliberate omission. For all the chattering you do, little magpie, you certainly have a way of keeping secrets."

The Topkapi Seray was built on the point of a headland overlooking three waterways, the Sea of Marmara, the Golden Horn, and the Bosphorus. The sultan's squadron of cavalry followed Jennifer's carriage as it entered the walled fortification, known by the Ottomans as the Palace of the Shadow of God.

They drove through a marble gate of staggering proportions, flanked by turrets with conical spires, and entered a vast, grassy courtyard lined with tall cypress trees. The open grounds were surrounded by rows of low buildings, which appeared to be state offices, private quarters for various officials, and military barracks. Here the soldiers dismounted in silence, and she was helped down from the open coach.

Her escort led her beneath the broad eaves of a second, lavishly gilded gate into another wide court of manicured lawns and rose gardens. Domed pavilions, high brick towers, and buildings with columned arcades stood in desolate silence, as though the weight of the years were pressing down on them.

The squadron of soldiers, Jennifer in their midst, followed a narrow path into a garden surrounded by high walls, with a splashing fountain at one end and a lovely reflecting pool at the other. On the far side of the pool stood a blue-tiled kiosk.

One of her ferocious, mustachioed guards knocked at a strong wooden door, banded heavily with iron. It was immediately swung open by a tall, heavyset black man, who welcomed them with a gracious salaam.

"We will wait for you here in this courtyard beside the Blue Pavilion, Miss Elkheart," the Turkish captain told her. "Whenever you are ready to leave, we will escort you safely back to your hotel."

She thanked the officer and entered the Grand Seraglio, her heartbeat fluttering erratically. The ebony-skinned man motioned for her to follow, and they walked down a narrow, high-ceilinged passageway. On either side, small, marble-paved rooms with barred windows rose in double tiers.

Jennifer shuddered. The feeling of entering a prison sent a chill of apprehension down her spine. The twisting, dimly lit corridor led past a maze of stairways, miniature green-tiled apartments, and cloistered gardens so tiny they were scarcely touched by the sun.

Suddenly the hallway opened into a spacious chamber of austere Turkish beauty. It was filled with women—as many as thirty or more—dressed in gauzy silks of every hue. A large, white-haired lady, somewhere in her late seventies, reclined on a low couch beneath a blue stained-glass window. Other females sat on tasseled cushions or small benches scattered around the room. As Jennifer entered and followed her guide to the center of the rug, all the women stood politely.

The Sultana Pertevalé rose from the divan and stepped down from a raised dais to greet her. Taking Jennifer's hand and pressing it warmly, she spoke in heavily-accented French. "You are as lovely as they say, Miss Elkheart. Thank you for coming."

"Thank you for inviting me, Your Highness," Jennifer replied.

"Have you met Alaeddin, the Kislar Aga?" the elderly

woman asked. She motioned to the man towering beside her, and he salaamed again. "Alaeddin is the chief black eunuch of the Grand Seraglio," she informed her guest, and he smiled at Jennifer with inordinate pride.

Realizing that the Kislar Aga must be a highly important personage in their world, Jennifer curtsied and smiled back. "I am pleased to meet you."

"The pleasure is mine, mademoiselle." The bald-headed man spoke in beautiful, lilting French, and she tried not to show her astonishment at the high, squeaking pitch of his voice. He was a huge man tending more to fat than muscle, but still, seemingly quite strong. His loose jowls hung down over the collar of his black stambouline. Like every other Turkish male she'd met, he wore the customary red fez.

Searching for something charming to say to someone of such an important station, Jennifer asked brightly, "Was your father a chief eunuch also, Alaeddin?"

Every woman in the room except the Sultana burst into hysterical giggles. The Kislar Aga grinned widely, his dark eyes glinting with humor. "No, mademoiselle," he replied.

Pertevalé lifted her hand in displeasure, and the women were instantly silent. "Alaeddin was brought here from Africa when he was only a young boy," the sultana explained, smoothing over Jennifer's gaffe. "So his father, alas, was never in Istanbul."

Jennifer had no idea what she'd said to make the other women erupt with such outright hilarity. When the Kislar Aga left the room with a polite *au revoir*, she decided to ignore her obvious mistake and carry on as though nothing had happened.

Looking around, Jennifer felt as though she'd wandered into a fairyland. Above the gleaming flowered tiles on the room's lower walls, mural landscapes of blissful hills and sylvan valleys had been painted in muted tones. There was very little furniture: A few low tables here and there; a three-legged tray holding an unfamiliar game board and playing pieces; and couches with plush cushions along the far wall.

All the women drew closer to Jennifer, obviously curious to inspect her person and dress. It was apparent that Pertevalé was in strict control of their behavior, however, for they shot the sultana hesitant, inquiring glances before approaching.

Jennifer realized that the ladies were of widely varying ages, from their late twenties to as much as seventy or older. Even more surprisingly, almost all of them were fair complexioned with delicate features and bright blue eyes, their lids heavily lined with what looked like charcoal. The younger ones had long, wavy blond hair, casually sprinkled with gems, and smooth cheeks, artfully powdered and rouged.

Some wore small velvet caps, embroidered in gold, perched on their heads at a saucy angle. Beneath tight-fitting bodices, their loose pajamalike bottoms of fine white lawn were banded at the ankles and showed glimpses of their thighs. The older women wore robes or floor-length brocaded dressing coats, with long strands of pearls around their necks and large jewels dangling from their ears. Even they had an extravagant amount of cosmetics on their wrinkled faces.

"Come and sit down," the sultana invited. She led Jennifer to the divan and waited for her to be comfortably seated before sitting down herself. "We are all curious to hear about your homeland, Miss Elkheart. We never leave the palace, but we do hear the gossip of the city through the few visitors who come to call and the eunuchs who guard us. But first, allow me to introduce the ladies. They are most anxious to meet you."

As she gave their names, each woman smiled widely and bowed her head in turn.

"Do you smoke, Miss Elkheart?" Pertevalé inquired. She gestured graciously to a large water pipe that sat on the floor beside the cushioned seat. "We are addicted to smoking *tombeki,* which is tobacco flavored with jasmine. The hookah is one of the few pleasures we can enjoy. That and our Turkish coffee."

Jennifer refused with an apologetic smile. "No, Your Highness, I do not smoke tobacco. Only the men of my people use pipes, which we call *eoxknonoz*. They are used mostly for religious purposes."

Pertevalé accepted her explanation with a nod of serene understanding. "Every culture has its idiosyncrasies, is that not so? Allow us then, to offer you coffee and some *rahat lokum*, which means 'giving rest to the throat.' The Europeans call it Turkish Delight."

Jennifer accepted the tiny cup encrusted with gold and gems and took a sip of the strong brew. Then she politely nibbled on the jellied sweet wrapped in pink paper. Seeing everyone bending forward and waiting for her reaction, she licked her lips and smiled. "It is delicious," she announced, and the women leaned back in satisfaction.

"We hope you are enjoying your stay in our city," the sultana said as she lifted her own cup and took a drink. Jewels of every color winked in the bluish light streaming through the window. Almost every finger on her heavily veined hand was adorned with a large ring.

"Very much," Jennifer stated. "I am learning more about Istanbul every day. That is why I wanted to come to Turkey with my grandfather. I hoped to learn about different people and their customs. May I ask you a question, Your Highness, or is that not allowed?"

The sultana laughed, and her companions joined in, their soprano voices tinkling in the tiled room like tiny, silver bells. "Ask whatever you like, mademoiselle."

"Why do you never leave the palace?"

"We are not allowed to," Pertevalé explained. "All of us here in the Grand Seraglio are the widows of former sultans. That is why they call our home the Palace of Tears. We enter the harem never to leave. When a sultan dies, his wives and concubines live in isolated grandeur. We have beautiful clothes, delicious meals, and fine jewelry. All our needs are cared for by female slaves. But the important word is *isolated*, Miss Elkheart. No male, except the eunuchs who guard us, is ever allowed to look upon our faces or even speak to us."

"Everyone in this room was the wife of a former sultan?" Jennifer stared at a golden-haired woman named Mihri, no more than twenty-eight, possibly younger, and realized that this quiet, graceful person would never know freedom from these gilded apartments. What a stark contrast to Jennifer's childhood on the wind-swept plains of Canada. She thought of her mother and sister imprisoned inside these walls. The concept was staggering.

"There are far more than just us in the palace," Mihri told her with a sad smile. She looked down at her curled-up slippers, spangled with precious gems, and sighed forlornly.

Pertevalé set her coffee cup down on the low table, her painted face etched with care. "My son, Abdul Aziz, had nine hundred concubines when he died ten years ago. Some of them were no more than fourteen or fifteen at the time. These young women are now my responsibility, for I was Sultana Valide, the Queen Mother, until his death. In addition, former wives and slaves of the previous sultans reside here in the seraglio under my supervision. Only the present sultan's wives and his two hundred concubines reside with him at Yildiz Palace."

"I belonged to Sultan Abdul Mejid," a soft-spoken lady in her early fifties told Jennifer. Her blue eyes grew somber. "I was given to him as a gift when I was twelve years old and became his favorite odalisque. He named me Naksh—the Beautiful One. I was only thirty-two when he died."

The chilling realization that this sweet, timid woman had lived for approximately forty years immured in rooms such as these—and might possibly live another forty more—sent a shiver of horror through Jennifer.

"But we want to learn about you, mademoiselle," Mihri said shyly.

"Ask whatever you like," Jennifer replied, relieved to change the topic.

"Start with where you were born, and tell us everything," Naksh suggested.

"First we will have our meal," Pertevalé declared, clapping her beringed hands. "Then Miss Elkheart will tell us all about the New World."

At her signal, a bevy of female servants carried in tray

after golden tray and set them on the low tables. There was a bewildering variety of choices, which everyone cheerfully explained to their overwhelmed guest. Artichoke hearts, fried bits of liver, sheep's brains, anchovies, asparagus, and little hot pastries filled with meat and cheese. The appetizers were followed by roast turkey stuffed with rice, liver, currants, and pine kernels. And finally for dessert, syrup-drenched sweetmeats that melted in Jennifer's mouth.

When everyone was replete, they turned to her with wide, questioning eyes, clearly ready to hear all that she had to say about the marvelous land on the far side of the world.

So Jennifer related the story of her family, telling them of Strong Elk Heart, one of the head chiefs of the Cheyenne nation, and his wife, Little Red Fawn, who had been born in the mountains of Kentucky as Rachel Rose Robinson. She told them of her twin sister, Evening Star, and her young brother, Black Hawk Flying, and their life on a horse ranch set in a beautiful valley within sight of the great Rocky Mountains.

Like pale, delicate orchids, the women listened in rapt fascination, scarcely stirring on their pillows in the hushed, hothouse atmosphere that surrounded and enclosed them every day of their lives. It was an afternoon Jennifer knew she would never forget.

Damian Grueff gave his huge friend a warning tap on the shoulder, and they both stepped back into the lengthening shadows. "There she is," he said softly. "Coming out of the palace now."

They watched the carriage roll toward them with bitter frustration. Miss Jennifer Elkheart was accompanied by a squadron of Sultan Abdul Hamid's personal cavalry.

"Damn," Christo Payeff cursed. "It would have been a whole lot easier if she'd been on that train."

Damian nodded unhappily. Their leader had been so certain he knew the exact day that the American special envoy and his granddaughter would arrive in Istanbul.

"I guess they must have changed their schedule at the last minute," he said.

Soft chuckles rumbled deep in Christo's barrel chest. "I wouldn't have missed that train robbery for anything in the world. Those railroad cars flew off that torn-up track like match boxes. And when Todor went up and down the corridors, trying to calm all the fat old ladies screaming their lungs out, I thought I'd split my gut laughing."

Damian grinned at the memory.

After the derailment, their chieftain, Todor Zadansky, had gone through the coaches, attempting to assure the passengers that no one would be killed. Waving his huge pistol, he'd shouted out in a garbled mixture of Turkish, French, and Greek, for everyone to stay calm. The sight of the weapon in his hand and the enormous dagger stuck in his sash proved to have the opposite effect. More than one hysterical female issued a long, piercing wail and toppled over in a dead faint at the sight of him.

They'd collected moneybags, wallets, jewelry, watches, and every other kind of valuable they could discover. But a thorough search of the entire train had revealed no sign of the American special envoy and his granddaughter.

The disappointment had been galling.

The money they'd hoped to collect in ransom was desperately needed by the International Macedonian Revolutionary Organization. Imro's immediate goal was to supply the masses with arms, smuggled over the frontiers from Bulgaria or bought from Turks willing to make a profit on the illegal trafficking. Their ultimate goal was the liberation of Macedonia from Turkish rule.

Damian and Christo had been sent to the Ottoman capital to see if their prey had slipped past them on a previous train. The two Macedonian Bulgars belonged to a finely spun network of conspiracy built under the very noses of Ottoman police spies and paid informers. Shrouded in secrecy, the Imro's couriers went back and forth with important dispatches. Munitions were brought in and stored at strategic points throughout the provinces. Bombs were distributed to potential assassins. All those activities cost money.

The two *comitadjis* watched dolefully as their target rode by, not four feet away from them. The dark-haired young lady, dressed in elegant European fashion, held a dainty parasol in her gloved hand. There was a dreamy, faraway look in her brown, almond-shaped eyes.

"She's beautiful," Christo said, awestruck. "I didn't think she'd be so little and sweet looking. I've never seen eyes like hers before."

"We aren't going to hurt her," Damian assured his towering companion for the third time. "We'll figure out a way to kidnap Miss Elkheart without having to resort to violence."

The giant beside him heaved a long, lovesick sigh.

Chapter 18

The next morning, Jennifer slipped out of the servant's door of the Pera Palace. Eagleston was waiting for her in the narrow alleyway behind the hotel, holding the reins of two spirited Arabians.

He wore a white shirt with full sleeves tightly banded at the wrists. The soft cotton garment was tucked into the wide waistband of a pair of sturdy black trousers. His gleaming boots, folded over at the tops, reached to the middle of his muscular calves. With his golden beard and thick, wavy hair ruffling in the breeze, he was the picture of dynamic male energy.

Jennifer could feel the stirrings of desire deep within her in an unbidden and unwanted response. She felt as nervous and high-strung as a pronghorn with a pack of wolves on its trail. But she was determined to maintain firm control over her wayward emotions today. She was going sightseeing with this devastatingly handsome male—and nothing more.

Eagleston caught her by the waist and drew her to him. He smiled broadly. There was a suspicious glimmer of laughter in his blue eyes.

"What is it?" she asked in exasperation. "What is wrong with everyone I meet this morning? When I came down for breakfast earlier today, the people acted as if I was wearing my clothes inside out."

He lightly bussed the tip of her nose before lifting her up on one of the caparisoned horses. His hand lingered caressingly on her leg, and he playfully squeezed her knee. "If you went to breakfast dressed in the outfit you're wearing now, I'm not surprised."

She laughed, finding it impossible to hide her excitement. "Of course, I did not!" She glanced down at the lavishly embroidered shirt and loose white trousers of a young male, which Thorne had sent to her hotel room the previous evening. The clothes had been hidden in a large box beneath four dozen long-stemmed red roses.

Earlier, she'd wrapped her long hair securely around her head and hid it beneath the white turban he'd also provided. "I love the boots," she said gleefully. She gazed down at them with pleasure. They were made of soft red leather, so highly polished they glistened in the sunlight.

"I thought you'd like them." Thorne mounted, and they moved along the narrow passageway toward the main thoroughfare that ran past the hotel.

"Who are we supposed to be?" she inquired gaily.

"Traders from Circassia," he said, "come to sell our rugs in the Grand Bazaar. Istanbul straddles Europe and Asia, and as the crossroads of two continents, it's filled with people of every race, color, and description. You're supposed to be my young servant, so don't say anything while we're in hearing distance of anyone."

"Do you speak Turkish?" she asked in amazement.

"Fluently." He grinned at her. "Today, I get to do all the talking, little magpie, unless we're alone. In which case, you may speak, but quietly and subserviently, so as not to draw anyone's attention."

"This is going to be harder than I'd planned," she confessed with a happy laugh.

"Try not to giggle, either," he warned dryly. His gazed lingered on her face, and a smile of tender amusement played about his mouth.

Jennifer realized that the Eagle had caught whatever contagious disease was going around that made everyone smile or chuckle to themselves with some hidden mirth at the very sight of her. She frowned pensively.

They turned onto the crowded Grande Rue de Pera

and headed toward the Galata Bridge, which spanned the Golden Horn. In the raucous noise of the morning traffic, they were free to continue their conversation.

"What is wrong with me today?" she demanded.

"Nothing is wrong with you," he assured her. "You look ravishing in those trousers." But his gaze never left her face, and it seemed impossible for him to stop grinning.

Jennifer reined her horse to a halt in the middle of the stream of traffic. "I am not going any farther without an explanation."

"All right, sweetheart," Thorne said with a nod of concession, and they continued side by side. "As you know, gossip travels fast in Constantinople. One person tells another, a servant repeats it to his master, and pretty soon everyone, who is anyone, knows the secret."

"*Haxc!* I am waiting to hear the secret," she replied impatiently.

Thorne tried not to laugh at Jennie's baleful expression, but the mistake she'd made at the seraglio the previous afternoon had taken the city by storm. Everyone was talking about it. "When you asked the Kislar Aga if his father had also been a chief black eunuch . . . well, people thought it was rather funny."

Jennie wasn't smiling. She stared at Thorne, her magnificent sloe eyes filled with confusion. "I was trying to be polite and . . . and charming," she stated defensively. "How should I have known that his father was never in Istanbul?"

"You couldn't, of course. But that was not what was so funny."

"Go on, tell me," she insisted in a stricken voice. "What was so hilarious?"

He searched for the right words. "You told me once that your father raises horses," he began cautiously. "So I assume you know about breeding a stallion with a mare."

She stared at him as though he were losing his mind.

"Well, then, you probably also know the purpose of gelding a stallion." He paused to let that much sink in.

Her eyes widened in disbelief, and she waited, not saying a word.

"A eunuch is a human male who's been gelded."

She jumped in surprise, unconsciously pulling on the reins, and her mottled gray mare tossed its head in annoyance. "Such barbarity!" she cried. "And the white men dared to call my people savages!"

"Eunuchs have been used since antiquity in this part of the world," he explained. "The Assyrians, the Romans, the Byzantines all practiced castration. The Ottomans merely inherited the custom. At first, the sultans used white eunuchs brought from the Caucasus, but they came to prefer the black eunuchs, such as Alaeddin, from central Africa."

"Why?" she asked, incredulous.

"Sometimes the procedure didn't work. If a black child were born in the seraglio, the sultan could be certain that his harem was being raided by one of the men responsible to guard it."

Her mind whirling at the staggering revelation, Jennifer sat erect in the saddle and stared straight ahead.

As they approached the Galata Bridge, the incredible sight of Istanbul unfolded before them. Scattered across the seven steep hills of the city and crowning their summits, countless palaces, mosques, watchtowers, pavilions, and kiosks pierced the sky. She could see Topkapi Seray high on Seraglio Point, its buttresses, turrets, domes, and semidomes barely visible among the tall cypress trees.

"I saw a painting of this in a museum once," she said in stunned admiration. "I thought it must have been an illusion or some artist's hallucinatory dream."

"Is that why you came here with your grandfather?" Eagleston asked. "Because it looked so beautiful?"

She smiled absently. "One of the reasons."

"The other reason being the man in your vision?"

Jennifer didn't answer. She couldn't tell Thorne that when she'd entered the harem yesterday, she'd felt as though she'd been there before. The sultana's apartments had seemed so poignantly familiar, it had been as though she'd walked straight into her vision. Thorne would only deride her irrefutable sense of déjà vu as some foolish, superstitious belief.

He waited without comment, seeming to take her silence for assent. Then they nudged their mounts forward, clattered over the rickety wooden bridge, and entered the old part of Stamboul.

Eagleston was true to his word. Sightseeing with him was like sightseeing with no one else. His knowledge of history was phenomenal, and Jennifer listened to his vivid descriptions in fascination. She was an eager, inquisitive pupil, asking endless questions, which he never seemed tired of answering.

He took her to the hippodrome and explained that it had been built to resemble the Circus Maximus in Rome and completed in the reign of Constantine.

"You're not able to see the chariots racing around the stadium this morning, are you?" he teased.

She made a face at him. "If I do have the second sight today, I will be sure to keep it a secret from an unbeliever like you."

They visited the Sultanahmet Mosque, known as the Blue Mosque, its six high, slender minarets rising above the great dome, and explored the rose-colored Hagia Sophia, once the greatest cathedral in the Byzantine world. They saw the ancient column brought to Istanbul from the temple of Apollo in Rome and the fire tower of Beyazit. They rode to the aqueduct completed during the reign of the Roman emperor Valens, which was still used to carry water to Topkapi.

Next, Thorne took her to the Archeological Museum, one of the most important of its kind in the world.

"The Ottomans began collecting works of fine art during the reign of Mehmet II," he told her as they stopped before a magnificent statue of a woman carrying a bow and quiver of arrows.

"Who is she?" Jennifer asked with avid curiosity.

"Artemis was the Greek goddess of the hunt, known in early legends as Mistress of Beasts, because of her special love for animals. She was so skilled with the bow, she taught Chiron, the king of the centaurs, how to use them. Her domain was the wild earth, the forests and hills where she hunted." He gave her a wry look. "The legend reminds me of someone I know."

Jennifer laughed at his teasing. "What is a centaur?"

"Another myth of the ancient Greeks," Thorne cheerfully explained. "Half man and half horse. Artemis is depicted with Chiron on some of the specimens in the British Museum that I brought back from Ephesus. I'll show them to you some day."

"Where shall we go now?" she asked gaily as they left the museum.

"Mohehya," he said with a chuckle, "has anyone ever told you you're insatiable?"

"No, but someone once told me I was incorrigible." She gave him a jaunty smile. "Maybe it was you."

They rode through the narrow, cobbled streets of the metropolis, up tiny, isolated byways, down to the busy wharves, and into caravanserai courtyards, where most Europeans would never dare go. As they explored, the wailing chant of the muezzins echoed through the city, calling people to prayer.

They heard a dozen different languages. Istanbul was a polyglot city of self-contained districts centered around mosques, churches, or synagogues. Each community—Muslim, Greek, Armenian, or Jewish—had its own schools, markets, fountains, and public baths. Children played in the steep, winding streets, ignoring the horses and pedestrians that threaded their way through them.

No one questioned the appearance of the yellow-haired Circassian merchant and his adolescent assistant.

"This loose, billowing costume is a perfect disguise," Jennifer stated with satisfaction.

"Yes," Thorne assured her, "you look just like a ten-year-old boy."

She stuck her thumbs in her ears and waggled her fingers at him in reply.

"Watch out," he advised, a smile hovering at the corner of his mouth. "If someone sees you defying your master, I'll be forced to discipline you."

She stood up in her stirrups and looked around in feigned amazement.

"Now, what are you looking for?" he asked.

"The squadron of cavalry that is going to help you do it."

They stopped at a teahouse at midday, its only other customers men playing backgammon in the small, dimly lit room or smoking hookahs outside the open front door. Thorne explained that Moslem women never ate meals in a public place. Their lives revolved solely around their homes.

The two were shown a low table under a trellis in an outside garden, where they'd be able to converse without being overheard.

"I hope you don't mind sitting on pillows?" he inquired.

"I will be quite comfortable here, thank you," she said as she sank onto one of the tasseled cushions. "My people always sat on the floor of their lodges."

Eagleston folded his long legs and dropped down beside her. "Are you hungry?"

"Starving," she admitted, inhaling the wonderful aromas. She eyed the prodigious display of meat, vegetables, fresh fruit, and pastry the waiter set in front of them in wonder. Then watched as Thorne deftly served the *sis-kebabi*, which had been left on a glowing charcoal brazier. The pieces of juicy meat were interspersed with tomatoes, onions, and peppers. Jennifer tried the tender lamb, then nibbled on the delicate asparagus spear.

"It's called *kuskonmaz* by the Turks," he told her, "which means 'birds cannot settle on it.' " Relaxed, his arm resting on his bent knee, he watched her with an odd, shuttered expression, as though gladdened by some inner joyous secret.

She wondered if he was thinking about his proposal and was suddenly reminded of Grandpapa's reference to the duke's bags of gold. "My father's people were nomads," she said, "who owned no more than they could carry packed on their travois. Before the coming of the whites, the Cheyenne moved regularly from what is now the Canadian border to deep in an area of the United States called Texas. So I have never been much given to acquiring material possessions."

Thorne looked at Jennie in delight, knowing she was telling him that she wasn't the least bit impressed with his generous offer of money and jewels.

"I, on the other hand, Jennifer Rose Elkheart," he declared with a satisfied chuckle, "am descended from a long line of acquisitive, materialistic forebears, whose only goal was to amass as much wealth as possible before turning up their toes and leaving their immense fortune to their heirs."

"*Ahahe!*" she replied in a commiserating tone. "Not everyone can be as fortunate as I."

He tipped his head back and laughed out loud. "Sweetheart," he said, "do you always say exactly what's on your mind?"

She gazed at him with wide brown eyes, affecting an injured air. "I thought you were interested in my family."

It was all Thorne could do not to lean over and kiss her full on the mouth. How had he been so lucky to find someone as wonderful as Jennie? Someone ready to throw his fortune back in his face, if she felt she didn't love him. Someone so sweet and innocent, she hadn't the least idea what a eunuch was.

Someone who almost never told a lie.

But Jennifer was lying when she claimed she wasn't in love with him. She'd all but admitted she'd forgotten what the mysterious man of her dreams even looked like. Now she was dreaming of him, instead.

He handed her a pastry rolled in sugar syrup. "We haven't had our dessert yet. Try the *bulbul yuvasi*," he urged.

"Mmm, delicious," she mumbled over the mouthful of honeyed sweet and then swallowed noisily. "What does the name mean?"

"Nightingale's nests." He offered her another kind. "Well, what do you think?"

She nodded, her eyes big with delight as she chewed. "What is the name of that one?"

"A lady's navel," he said with a grin.

She rolled her eyes, pretending to be shocked. She picked up a pastry shaped like a perfect Cupid bow's mouth and put it on his plate. "What is this called?" she asked with a low, throaty gurgle of laughter.

He popped the treat into his mouth and growled in appreciation. "Beauty's lips."

She clapped her hand tightly over her mouth to stifle the laughter.

"Oh, my sweet, little magpie," he said, "I was afraid you'd change your mind about coming today."

When Thorne and Jennifer left the teahouse, they found the road blocked by a stubborn donkey that refused to pull a cart piled high with melons. Instead, they turned down an alley, but the passageway soon became so cramped they could no longer ride abreast. Thorne maneuvered his gelding in front of Jennie's mare to lead the way, his well-honed instinct for survival bringing a prickle of wariness in the close quarters. His apprehension proved well-founded. As they turned a sharp corner, they were suddenly assaulted by four Turks, who ran out of a doorway, reaching for the bridles of their plunging horses.

Thorne kicked the first man, striking him full in the face with his spurred boot, then lashed the other across his head and shoulders with his riding crop. He was vaguely aware that he'd been cut on the hand by the second man's dagger as the fellow tried to slit the saddle girth. The quarters in the passageway were so tight, he was unable to turn his mount around. He glanced back at Jennie, his heart pounding in terror for her, and reached for the derringer in his boot.

The other assailants were grasping at her clothing in an attempt to pull her off the gray horse. Before Thorne could aim and shoot, her knife flashed, and one attacker screamed in pain as she buried the blade to its hilt in his shoulder. She nearly tumbled off the rearing mare, but

omehow managed to keep her seat. The terrified ani-
al's front hoofs struck Jennie's second assailant, and the
an grunted and swore as he crashed to the cobble-
ones.

"Go!" she cried to Thorne. "I'm right behind you."

They galloped through the confined alleyway. When
ey came out onto a nearly deserted street, three armed
ders were waiting. Thorne knew then that it was more
an a chance encounter with thieves bent on robbing a
apless Circassian trader. The ambush had been planned.
ealizing the way to the Galata Bridge and safety was
it off by the mounted trio, he turned his black gelding
oward the western wall of the city.

"This way, Jennie!" he shouted.

They raced their steeds full out, cutting across court-
ards piled high with boxes of oranges, melons, and
ates, past fountains splashing idly in the afternoon sun,
nrough a Muslim cemetery, its carved, linear grave-
tones topped with graceful stone turbans. They charged
nrough an Armenian marketplace filled with sheep. The
nraged screams of the vendors could be heard over the
raying donkeys and barking dogs. The sound of hoof-
eats echoing behind them grew fainter and gradually
ided away.

They stopped, their winded horses snorting and
lowing.

"Jennie, are you all right?" Thorne asked in dread. He
eached over to clasp her upper arm, searching her lovely
ace for some sign of distress.

Her dark eyes sparkled with excitement. "I am fine,"
he announced with a carefree laugh, then looked down
t his hand in surprise. "You are bleeding!"

"It's a scratch."

She jerked her head, signaling her understanding that
he wound would have to be dealt with later. "Which
vay can we go without running into them again?"

"I know a place that's safe," he said, gathering the
eins. "It's only a few miles away."

*   *   *

Eagleston led her through steep, wandering streets bor
dered by cedar and cypress. Charming mansions peeke
through flowering trees, their balconies and latticed win
dows overlooking inner cloisters and gardens. They cam
to a rambling, flat-roofed building that rose up a hillsid
like a series of connected boxes, with arched porticos run
ning along the stark white walls. Deep red roses climbe
up the porch columns.

A servant, dressed in a caftan, opened the door at Eag
leston's preemptory knock. They stepped inside the entr
hall, and at the duke's soft-spoken directions in Turkish
the large, mustachioed man quickly left the room. Inside
the villa was cool and dim.

"Let me see your hand," Jennifer insisted. Thorne hac
wrapped the wound in a piece of cloth he'd pulled from
his saddlebag.

"It's only a small cut," he answered, tension sharpen
ing his words. "It's you I'm worried about, Jennie. I
those filthy bastards hurt you—"

"I am fine," she said, then added in disgust, "but I los
my knife. My father gave it to me on my fourteenth birth
day. Now I will have to admit I lost it when I return
home."

Thorne shook his head in amazement as he pulled Jen
nie to him. He ran his hands over her shoulders and
arms, checked her hands and fingers, then cupped he
face in his palm, searching for any trace of injury. When
he was satisfied she was unharmed, he allowed her to
unwrap the blood-soaked, makeshift bandage.

She took his hand in both of hers and inspected the
oozing cut. "You will not need stitches," she pronounced
with the assurance of a world-renowned surgeon, "bu
you will probably have a small scar."

"It won't be the first," he said with a disinterested
shrug.

Mehmed returned, carrying a brass tray with a basir
of hot water, cloths, soap, scissors, a vial of tincture, and
a roll of gauze. He set it on a low table.

"I can do that for you," she offered. "Binding up battle
wounds is an old Cheyenne skill."

Thorne dismissed his houseman and sat down on a low divan. "I'm at your mercy, little wildcat," he told her with a grin.

Jennie sank down on the floor in front of him and took his lacerated hand without an apparent qualm. He watched her as she worked, her head bent, and warmth stirred deep in his groin. "I suppose, if I'd needed stitches," he said placidly, "you'd have been able to do that, too."

She looked up with a radiant smile. "Certainly, *veho*. When you are raised on a ranch eighty miles from the nearest doctor, you learn how to sew up cuts, set bones, and pull teeth."

"My teeth are fine."

She laughed delightedly. "You forgot your bored drawl, Your Graciousness," she twitted. "After I finish with this, I will inspect your mouth."

"I have a retort for that, but being a gentleman, I won't make it."

"Be careful," she warned, the corners of her lips turning up in an impish smile. "I am the one with the bottle of antiseptic, and you are the one with the open wound."

"Ouch!" he yelped. "You don't have to be so damn generous with that stuff."

"I dabbed on a little extra to disinfect your naughty mind." She glanced up with a sudden frown, and added, "The knife was probably dirty. There is no point in risking an infection."

"You're absolutely right," he gritted, through the pain.

When she was finished, Jennie sank back on her heels and beamed at him, a satisfied expression glowing on her exotic features. She still wore the turban, which sat slightly askew from their frantic ride.

"You were very brave back there, Jennie," he said quietly.

She sat between his outstretched legs, her hands resting lightly on his knees. He didn't stir, didn't move a muscle, afraid she might realize how staggeringly erotic her nearness was.

"It was easy to be brave at a time like that," she said

in a somber tone, her look of gratification fading. "I struck out in self-defense, and when I realized we were safe, I felt the same thrill that comes from diving off a bridge." She lowered her head and studied her tapered fingers. "But I was not brave at all back in England," she continued in a hushed voice. "I should have told you I was leaving for Constantinople. I am sorry. It was cowardly of me to keep it a secret."

He looked down at her curving ebony lashes, his heart weeping for joy at her words. "Why did you, Mohehya?"

"I was afraid."

"Of me?"

She nodded, then lifted her eyes to meet his. "I was afraid that if you begged me to stay, I would not have the courage to leave you."

"Your vision means that much to you?"

She let out a long, ragged sigh. "I am not sure *what* my vision means anymore."

They gazed at each other in silence. Then Thorne lifted his hand to her cheek. "I have an apology of my own to make," he said. "I purposely allowed you to believe I knew nothing of sexual relations between a man and a woman. The truth is, I lost my virginity at fifteen, during my second year at Eaton. A buxom modiste of twenty was very knowledgeable in the arts of seduction—and uninhibitedly aggressive."

"Shame on her!"

He smiled wryly. "I was quite willing, at the time, to further my education."

"Why did you pretend otherwise?"

He smoothed the pad of his thumb across her lips. "No one had ever looked at me with such trustful innocence before," he said, his voice thick with emotion. "When I am with you, Jennie, it's as though I'm seeing everything, doing everything, for the first time. I wanted to experience that first time through you, savoring the rare, exquisite moment. And in a sense, it was the first time for me, as well. For it was the first time I made love to the woman who holds my heart in her hands."

At the quiet tenderness of his words, Jennifer bounded

to her feet. Her thoughts in a jumble, she moved to the center of the spacious room and looked blankly around her, trying to regain control of her turbulent emotions. "Whose home is this?" she asked, her voice a croak.

"Mine." He made no move to follow her, but watched her with a searing gaze.

"Yours? I assumed you were staying at the Pera."

Eagleston smiled at her astonishment. "Since I must come to Constantinople to get the official permits to search for classical antiquities, I find it more convenient to have a home of my own than stay in a crowded hotel."

He rang a small brass bell, and the servant returned bringing another tray, this time with fruit and wine. The retainer listened in silence to his orders, gathered up the medical paraphernalia, salaamed, and retreated.

Eagleston rose and gestured toward an arched, open doorway. "Would you like to see my view of the city?" he inquired pleasantly. "It's quite magnificent."

"Yes." She sighed in relief. He was going to follow her lead and resume their earlier, lighthearted camaraderie. Removing the turban, she released her hairpins, tossed her head and let her braid swing free.

Jennifer followed him onto a wide portico. The sweet perfume of roses swirled around them as she walked to the low, solid railing and gazed out at the Sea of Marmara in the distance. Below them, Constantinople sparkled like a jewel in the afternoon sun. "It is heavenly here," she whispered in awe.

"That's why I named the villa Elysia," he said, coming to stand beside her. "Elysium was the Greeks' mythological paradise, a place of complete bliss where virtuous people went after death."

"Paradise," she repeated, bemused. She looked at the dome of Topkapi, remembering her visit to the seraglio and all she'd learned there. "Beautiful, yet sad and lonely."

He looked at her quizzically, but she didn't try to explain.

"This villa," he said, "and some of the furnishings were once the property of an admiral of the Turkish fleet.

When the sultan he served was deposed, Mustafa Reshid fell out of favor, and his property evolved to the new ruler. I purchased the home and its contents through Abdul Hamid's man of business when it was offered for sale several years ago."

When they returned inside, Eagleston went to the table and started to pour the wine. Jennifer waved her hand in polite refusal. She dropped down on the sofa, tucking her legs beneath her. "I do not drink much liquor."

"I noticed that in London," he said. He set the decanter back on the tray and splashed some brandy into a snifter for himself. "Why is that?"

"My father never allowed spirits of any kind in our home," she explained. "*Nihoe* said that, while alcohol merely destroyed the white man's body and soured his brain, it poisoned the Indian's soul and robbed him of his spiritual dignity."

"Your father is a very wise man," he concurred, coming over to sit beside her. "I shall have to meet him someday. Your mother, too."

She laughed at the thought. "You will have to go to Alberta to do that! My parents do not even visit Kentucky. I cannot imagine them sailing to England."

"Then I guess I'll plan a trip to Canada one of these days."

"I would like to show you our ranch," she said brightly. "And take you into the Canadian Rockies to hunt for grizzlies."

"With a bow and arrow?"

"Not grizzlies," she told him with an impudent grin. "You take the best rifle you own for that, *veho*."

"I can see I have a lot to learn about your customs." Thorne took a sip of brandy and studied her. "You haven't told me about your visit to the seraglio yesterday."

At his comment, her expression grew pensive and thoughtful. "You know a lot about the customs of the Turkish people, do you not?"

"Quite a bit. What would you like to know?"

"Why were the women in the Grand Seraglio fair comlected, when all the Turkish people I have seen on the streets are so dark?"

"The women you met yesterday are not Turkish, Jennie," he told her. "They're Circassians, brought as captives from their homeland on the other side of the Black Sea. Those particular females were likely raised on slave farms. Only the loveliest ever made it into a sultan's harem to have the sublime honor of walking down the Golden Road to his bed. But others like them were sold to wealthy pashas and beys. The Osmanlis have a strong preference for blond hair and blue eyes." He smiled at her open curiosity. "I, on the other hand, happen to prefer brown eyes and long chestnut hair."

She wrinkled her nose impishly. "I always thought golden hair and blue eyes were rather beautiful."

His heart leaped at her artless confession. "I'm very glad to hear that," he replied with a tender smile. "Although no one in her right mind would ever call me beautiful."

Thorne waited, knowing there was more she wanted to say about the doleful, sequestered world she'd discovered in the Palace of Tears.

"When I was in the seraglio, I could not help but compare those poor women's lives with my mother's," she said with a faraway look. "*Nakohe* rides and ropes alongside my father. She chases the wild mustangs on her painted pony and helps gentle the foals in the springtime." Jennie cast him a droll look and added wryly, "My mother spends most of her time in denims and a man's flannel shirt. She only puts on a dress for a special occasion."

He smiled but didn't interrupt her, sensing that her visit to the harem had bothered her deeply.

"My Aunt Lucinda had a canary in her home in Louisville," she went on. "One day, Julie and I set it free. We just opened the wicker cage and watched the yellow bird fly out the window. Luckily for us, it sat in a nearby magnolia and trilled its heart out, until our aunt heard it and coaxed it down. When I think of those sad, lonely creatures hidden behind their gilded walls, I remember

that canary warbling its happy song of freedom." She
sighed and touched the cuff of his sleeve, her head
drooping disconsolately. "What a tragic waste of lives!
Why do they accept it?"

Thorne caught her hand and rubbed his thumb across
her knuckles in understanding. "They have no choice,
sweetheart. The Ottoman Empire is strictly a man's
world. The males, from the oldest to youngest, have a
deep, ingrained sense of superiority, which often reduces
women to the status of mere objects. The Islam religion
teaches that men are the managers over the affairs of
women. If females are rebellious, the Koran tells their
husbands to admonish them. To banish their wives to
their couches and beat them."

Jennifer straightened and threw back her shoulders.
"Nehe!" she declared in disgust, scowling ferociously. "If
any man tried to beat me, I'd cut off his hand with my
knife."

Thorne laughed with joy at her spunk. "I've been duly
warned," he said. "What else do you want to know about
Turkish customs?"

"What is an odalisque?" she blurted out.

He frowned. "Where did you hear that word?"

"At the Grand Seraglio yesterday. A lovely woman
named Naksh told me she had been given to a sultan
when she was only twelve years old, and that she became
his favorite odalisque. I did not want to admit I had no
idea what she was talking about."

His answer was brusque, but honest. "An odalisque is
a female slave in a harem whose sole purpose is to bring
sexual pleasure to her master."

"At *twelve*?" She stared at him in horror.

He nodded, his heart shriveling inside him, his terse
reply low and controlled. "Yes."

"How could a man defile the innocence of a child like
that?" she asked hoarsely. "What kind of savages are
these people?"

As he gazed into her shocked, incredulous eyes,
Thorne knew he would have to tell her the truth—*even
if it meant losing her forever*. The thought that she would

ook at him with revulsion was enough to tear him apart.
The words nearly choked in his throat. "What do you
know about my father?"

She stared at him in bewilderment, unable to follow
the abrupt change in topics. "Nothing. No one in England ever mentioned his name, other than you and your
mother."

"There was a reason for that, Jennie." He paused and
stared down at the brandy swirling in the glass. If he ever
hoped to find the courage to tell her, it had to be now.
"My father was a brilliant man," he began.

"That is not hard to believe," she said lightly. She
touched his sleeve and smiled with encouragement. He
knew she intuitively sensed his dread and was trying to
make it easier. Dear God above, nothing could make it
easier. Not while she watched him with those enormous,
questioning eyes.

He forced himself to go on. "Henry Blakesford's entire
life centered around politics. He garnered political power
the way his forbears amassed wealth. As a child, I rarely
saw him. He spent most of his time in London or at the
country homes of important people. When he did return
to Eagleston Court, he never had a moment to spare for
his son. At a very early age, I sensed his disinterest . . .
his dislike, even."

She made a soft, feminine sound of sympathy. "I am
sorry . . ."

Thorne rose and walked to the open doorway. He
gazed out across the rooftops of the city, unable to meet
her eyes, unwilling to accept her misguided compassion.
"To me, the duke of Eagleston became a faraway figure-
head, an unknown source of authority, an enigma I
couldn't begin to understand. When I attended Eaton, I
learned from my tutors how influential he was in Parliament. Some people even expected him to become prime
minister one day. I heard him speak in the House of
Lords once. He was impressive."

Jennifer sat perfectly still and waited with growing apprehension. Thorne's pain was so raw and fresh, his suffering was almost palpable. Gone was every vestige of

the jaded insouciance, the biting, sardonic wit, the restless boredom. In its place remained a brittle self-loathing.

He turned and looked at her, his features harsh with bitter irony. "As you know, after Oxford, I joined the Life Guards. One night, some cronies and I were roaming the seamier quarters of London, going from one gaming hell to the next . . . drunk . . . obnoxious . . . loudmouthed and carefree as only young soldiers can be. Quite by accident we stumbled into a house of prostitution, where sexual favors can be had for a fee. When we realized the brothel catered to the lowest vices imaginable—the most twisted, perverted appetites of man and demon—we started to smash the place to bits. Our intention, of course, was to bring the night watch."

"Did it work?"

He nodded and came to sit on the divan . . . not too close . . . as though he thought she wouldn't want to be near him after he finished his story. "As we turned the building into a bloody shambles, the customers started streaming downstairs, in all stages of dress, trying to reach the back door before the police arrived at the front. In the middle of the melee, I looked up to the third-floor landing. There was Henry Maxwell Blakesford, my father. He stood in front of an open bedroom door, holding the hand of a little girl. She couldn't have been more than eight."

Jennifer clapped her fingers over her mouth in stunned repugnance.

Thorne's tormented blue eyes never left her face. "The police arrived, and my father was taken into custody. The children were removed from the house and placed in a protected environment." Thorne stopped, took a deep, fortifying gulp of brandy, and set the empty glass on the table. "My father was freed the next day. He had enough influence in government to unlock any jail cell. That afternoon, he came to see me at the Guards. He claimed he'd had no idea what kind of hellish place it was. That he'd only arrived, himself, and was taking the child to a safe abode, when we stormed on the scene. He wept great, heartbroken tears, professing his innocence."

In the paralyzed hush that followed, Thorne covered his face with his hands. "I believed him," he said, his muffled words tortured and anguished. "I believed his expert lies because I wanted to believe them. Because if I hadn't believed them, I would have had to kill my own father to stop him."

Her hands clasped tightly in her lap, Jennifer waited for him to regain enough composure to go on. Her heart ached for the withering humiliation he was putting himself through.

Thorne rested his elbows on his knees, his hands loose, his head bent. "Even Henry Blakesford, however, couldn't face down that kind of scandal. He resigned his Cabinet post and left abruptly for Paris. I learned that the child had been taken into the home of the doctor who'd examined her. He and his wife were childless. I asked to speak to the girl, but her new parents thought it best if I didn't. Naturally, I agreed for her sake. Less than a year later, my father died of a heart attack—in a brothel that catered to his despicable perversions. And the thought that his blood runs in my veins sickens me every day of my life."

Tears streaming down her cheeks, Jennifer rose and went to crouch in front of him. She cupped his bearded face in her trembling hands. The agony in his haunted eyes sliced through her heart. She knew that his support of orphanages in Paris and London were his attempt to make lifelong expiation. "It was not your fault, Eagle's Son," she said, her voice shaking with emotion. "There was no way you could have known that he lied. Who would not have believed his own father?"

"But don't you see?" he said harshly. "I keep asking myself how many more innocent lives he ruined after that day . . . and what I could have done to prevent it."

Rising up on her knees, Jennifer put her arms around Thorne and cradled him to her. "You cannot carry this burden for the rest of your life," she whispered. "You cannot keep blaming yourself for what your father did— or for the fact that you believed him." She smoothed his temple with her fingers and wiped away the scalding tears of remorse. Her throat constricting with sobs, she held him in her cherishing embrace. "I understand what it is like to wonder if you are a part of some unconscious, inherited depravity. I carry white blood in me, yet I know that the *veho* almost annihilated my people. As human beings, we all have something in our heritage that we must learn to accept or we will never know peace."

Gently, tenderly, she framed his face and kissed his forehead . . . his eyelids . . . his cheeks . . . his lips . . .

Thorne's battered heart bathed in Jennie's unqualified forgiveness, as the sunflower bathes in the morning light. He accepted her loving ministrations, allowing her incredible sweetness to flow into his very soul. He realized, at last, what had wrought the miraculous change in his mother. For like her, he now knew, through the insight of Jennie's pure spirit, the healing balm of self-forgiveness.

Thorne held Jennie in his arms as they sat on the divan, the joy of her presence filling the aching emptiness inside him. Talking softly through the quiet afternoon, they reminisced about some of the happy, outrageous things that had happened at Dina's house party. The archery contest. The field hockey game. The foxhunt. The rescue of the puppy and the dive off the bridge. Bit by bit, the dark, turbulent emotions lessened their hold, their power fading in the brilliance of Jennie's sparkling effervescence.

His heart overflowing with love, Thorne looked down at the beautiful girl beside him. He curled a soft strand that had come loose from her braid around his finger, the heavenly feel of it bringing an awakening sexual energy. Her high cheekbones were flushed. Her almond eyes shone with happiness.

"Will your servant come in unexpectedly?" she asked in a throaty voice.

"No," he said. "I told Mehmed I wouldn't need him this afternoon. He's probably down at the wharf, buying some fish for dinner."

"Will he think it scandalous, my being here alone with you?"

Thorne grinned. "He'd better not. Mehmed believes you're a boy."

"I forgot!" she exclaimed. She looked at the turban she'd abandoned and giggled. "I am so used to wearing trousers, I forgot I was in disguise."

He cupped her chin in his palm, bent his head, and kissed her, the taste of brandy mingling on their lips. Her mouth was soft and responsive. The tip of her tongue flicked out to meet his with gratifying enthusiasm. Thorne felt the muscles of his groin clutch and spasm with the pulsating throb of overheated blood.

Jennifer drew back and looked into the Eagle's hooded *veho* eyes. His deep blue gaze smoldered with vibrant, erotic messages. She was suddenly, compellingly aware of her own body. "Would you show me the rest of your home?" she suggested huskily.

"Why don't we start with the bedroom?" He rose to his feet and lifted her up from the sofa.

Jennifer slid her arms around his neck and cradled her face against his throat as he carried her into a large room. An enormous rectangular divan stood against the far wall. Jewels studded the golden canopy that rose to the height of the ceiling above its thick velvet cushions.

She gasped at the sight. "Is it a bed or a couch or a throne?"

"Whatever you want it to be," Thorne replied wryly.

"It looks like it once belonged to a sultan."

"A pasha, actually." He flashed her a boyish smile as he set her on her feet in front of the bed. His gaze brushed over her like a lingering, physical caress.

Thorne fondled her through the loose cotton shirt, and she sighed with bliss at his touch. Tantalizing sensations blossomed and spread within her like the flower-laden vines of the honeysuckle.

Night after night, she'd dreamt of their tryst in the summerhouse, till the yearning was a deep, unrequited ache inside her that refused to be ignored. She longed for him to carry her to the unbelievable heights of pleasure she'd known in his arms.

The hunger in his shuttered gaze sent a thrill down the length of her. She pressed her fingers to the base of his throat and then fumbled with the buttons of his shirt. He quickly removed it, and she greedily smoothed her fingers over his bare skin, burying her nails in the wiry pelt that covered his scarred, muscled chest.

"It has been so long, Eagle's Son," she whispered against his welcoming lips.

"Ah, Jennie, Jennie," he groaned. He wrapped his strong arms around her, clasping her trembling form to his powerful body. "This time I will never let you go."

Chapter 19

Thorne framed Jennifer's face in his hands and kissed her with all the love he felt in his heart. He molded his lips against hers, his tongue tasting deeply of her honeyed nectar. He pressed kisses to her brow, her cheekbones, her fluttering lids, then lightly nipped the delicate curve of her neck. "My sweet little magpie," he murmured, as he dipped his tongue into the hollow at the base of her throat.

"Zehehyaetosznizan," she whispered.

He raised his head to meet her gaze. "Tell me what you said," he insisted, his tone leaving no doubt that this time he would not be denied.

She smiled brightly, her eyes glowing with happiness. "It is your Cheyenne name . . . Eagle's Son."

He gave a low, appreciative whistle. "Such a big name," he declared with a chuckle. But the fact that she called him by a pet name in her own language was flattering beyond all expectations.

Jennie smoothed her palms over his shoulders in frank admiration. "Such a big man," she extolled, giggling infectiously.

Thorne eased her to a sitting position on the edge of the bed, then sank back on his haunches in front of her. Lifting one small foot up on his knee, he pulled off the red leather boot.

Jennifer watched him through lowered lashes. "Are you going to wait on me like a slave?" she teased.

"I am your slave," he told her. He took off the othe
boot, and it joined its partner on the thick rug. Then h
stopped to pulled off his own boots and stockings an
cast them aside. He removed the derringer he'd tucke
in the wide band of his trousers and laid it on the tabl
near the bed.

"Are we expecting a raid by pirates?" she asked wit
a laugh.

"The only pirate you have to worry about is me," h
informed her with a suggestive leer. "And I just happer
to be in the mood for a little pillaging and plundering."

"What about my trousers?" she questioned, bouncin
her little bottom up and down provocatively.

He grinned as he removed her stockings. "We'll get t
your trousers in due time."

A bewitching smile skipped about the corners of he
adorable mouth as she released a long, impatient sigh
"It was easier for you in the summerhouse, when I wa
only wearing my nightgown," she pointed out with sham
sympathy.

"I think I'm man enough to handle it," he said. He
unfastened the empty leather sheath at her waist an
dropped it on the floor, then released the band of th
loose-fitting cotton pants and scooted them beneath he
hips and down her legs. Stockings and trousers wer
added to the pile on the rug.

Gliding his hands up her legs, Thorne rose to his knees
He undid the small buttons on each of her cuffs and th
ones that ran down the front of her embroidered white
shirt, then gently pulled the colorful garment free.

The blood surging through his veins like liquid fire, he
sank back on his buttocks, his hands resting on his knees
and gazed at her. Her curving lashes shyly fanned he
cheeks as Jennie looked down in self-conscious aware
ness of his unabashed perusal.

She sat in front of him, wearing only her ruffled draw
ers and a dainty lace camisole, both spun from cloth a
fragile as a spider's web. The satiny globes of her high
round breasts pushed impudently against the delicate lin
gerie. The soft golden glow of her skin against the pris

ne white garments created a shimmering aura around
er that took his breath away.

"Unbraid your hair, sweetheart," he said hoarsely.
I've dreamed of seeing it falling about your naked body,
ll I was half-crazed with longing."

He heard her sudden intake of air. Beneath his scorch-
ng gaze, her brown eyes grew soft and dewy, as her
ormer playfulness dissolved like snow in the heat of the
un.

She untied the ribbon at the end of the braid and loos-
ned her magnificent hair. With an elegant toss of her
ead, she shook it free, and the dark, reddish-brown
ass cascaded down to her hips, lustrous and shimmer-
ng and glorious to behold. He lifted the straight locks in
is cupped hands, feeling their weight and beauty, as
eir heavy length slid though his fingers like long satin
ibbons.

Thorne placed his hands on her shoulders and slowly
moothed his palms over her bare skin, running the pads
f his fingers along the ridges of her collarbone and down
he firm, up-tilted hillocks that rose above the camisole
o tempt and tease and entice. Their eyes met as he
aught his thumbs beneath the thin lace straps and pulled
hem downward, exposing her perfect breasts to his
iew. Beneath his covetous gaze, her coral crests puck-
red with sexual excitement.

He bracketed her tiny waist with his hands, bent for-
vard, and suckled her, his tongue playing with the taut
ttle buds till he could hear her low, breathless whimpers
f delight. Then he lifted the camisole over her head, and
he lace-trimmed satin sailed through the air to land on
he stack of discarded clothing.

Jennifer bent her head and kissed the scars on his chest,
everently tracing each ridged line with the tip of her
ongue. Thorne's muscles tensed and bunched at the
verwhelming softness of her lips. His mind reeled be-
eath the onslaught of such sweet, unbearable tender-
ess.

She met his gaze as she ran her fingertips over his mus-
ache and beard in mute exploration. Sliding her arms

about his neck, she pressed her naked breasts against his chest and slowly rubbed her nipples back and forth across his wiry mat of hair. Her uninhibited sensuality staggered him.

Never had he felt so needed . . . so wanted.

"Make love to me, Eagle's Son," she said in her deep throaty contralto. "Pillage and plunder and set me burning."

With a muffled laugh that was part groan, he untied the tapes of her drawers and, as they rose to their feet together, the loose garment fell away. She stood before him, as slender and supple as a bow. His hands moved over the delectable curve of her hips and tight little bum as his hardened sex pushed insistently against the coarse material of his trousers.

The pleasure of touching her so intimately . . . the sweet anticipation of what was to come . . . was nearly more than he could bear. His determination to prolong each lingering caress reeled and faltered beneath the rage of lust that burned inside him.

Thorne swept her up in his arms and laid her on the great, canopied divan. "Nihoatovaz, Vonahenene," he said. The Cheyenne words were gruff with a passion he could barely restrain. "God, how I want you."

Hypnotized by the erotic beauty of him, Jennifer watched as Thorne undressed and stood naked before her. Like one of the golden warriors on the ancient ebony vases, the Eagle was lean and angular and breathtakingly graceful. Broad shoulders, upper arms bulging with strength, and a deep, muscular chest created a portrait of unsurpassed masculine beauty.

With open curiosity, her gaze drifted down his narrow waist to his flat belly and jutting hipbones. His powerful thighs were long and corded with muscle. In the curly mat of hair at his groin, his engorged male member stood erect and straining forward, as though trying to reach her.

"You are so beautiful, Eagle's Son," she whispered in awe. She pressed her hand to her breast. "You make my heart ache."

Thorne knelt on the bed and bent over her. He slowly kissed every inch of her unclothed flesh, nipping and sucking and licking. He growled low in his throat as he moved down over her stomach and dipped the tip of his tongue into her belly button.

"Ah, Jennie, you taste so sweet," he crooned.

Jennifer could feel the heat of a blush spread over her at his voluptuous remark. "As good as the ladies' navels?" she asked with a self-conscious little laugh. "Or the beauties' lips?"

He nuzzled her abdomen and growled again. "Mmm, much, much better than those. Like the ambrosia of the gods."

The Eagle spread her legs and caressed her feminine folds, probing her delicate flesh, first with his gentle fingers, and then with the moist warmth of his tongue.

He held her hips securely in his grasp, refusing to let her pull away in embarrassment. She could feel the rough brush of his beard and mustache against the sensitive skin of her inner thighs.

Sensations of exquisite delight coursed through her. She flung her arms out to the side in complete female surrender, allowing him to work his wonderful magic.

"*Nihoatovaz*," she moaned, her head moving back and forth on the pillow, as he slowly and lingeringly made love to her. "Eagle's Son, I want you so much."

She climaxed beneath his caresses, waves of dazzling vibrations surging through her as he continued to sustain and enhance the deep, radiating pleasure.

Then Thorne rose to kneel above her, and Jennifer felt his lean flanks press against the soft insides of her legs. His thickened manhood bumped against her bare skin, the heat of his flesh scalding her.

Taking his rigid erection in her hand, she caressed the throbbing, velvet length of it. She watched his sharp features, half-hidden by the golden beard, grow tense and harsh. His entire body stiffened and shuddered as she gently, lovingly stroked and cupped him. With a groan deep in his chest, he lifted her closer and helped her wrap her legs around his hips.

Driven by some deep, unknowable instinct, like the flight of wild geese across the horizon, Jennifer guided him home.

A feeling of fullness and aching need spread through her abdomen as he inched deeper and deeper inside her snug sheath. She knew so little about the physical joining of male and female, yet she sensed the care and consideration he was giving her in his every touch, his every move.

Bracing his hands on either side of Jennie's head, Thorne held his body still and taut above her. Her full, bee-stung lips were parted, her almond eyes heavy-lidded with a sultry enticement. She stroked her hands across his upper arms and shoulders, then grazed his flat, hardened nipples with her soft fingertips. Her lithe form was flushed with passion. He could feel her delicate tissues fluttering against his hard, hot flesh, as her hips began to move rhythmically, pulling him deeper inside her.

"Take me now," she urged, seeming to sense his intention to establish firm, irrevocable control over her emotions as well as her body.

Thorne refused to be rushed, moving in slow, restrained, unhurried strokes, nudging her, bit by bit, toward the heights he knew she was so desperately seeking. "Tell me the words, Mohehya," he rasped. "Tell me the soft Cheyenne words you know I want to hear."

"*Zehemehotaz,*" she said breathlessly, "*namehota, namehota.*"

Thorne bent over her, his heart thundering wildly in his chest. He kissed her deeply, then resumed his steady, relentless pumping. "Now tell me what they mean, darling."

Her words came at the moment of her fulfillment, as her quivering muscles clenched and tightened around his turgid sex. "My beloved, I love you. I love you."

Joy swelled in his heart as, with a final, powerful thrust, his seed filled her womb, the climax so intense, his entire body jerked and convulsed above her. Then he rolled to his side, taking her with him, still deep inside her. *"Namehota, zehemehotaz,"* he whispered softly in her ear.

They made love twice more that afternoon, then sat on the rose-perfumed portico gazing out across the sea, only to come back to bed and make love once again. They were insatiable, exploring each other's bodies with frank, unreserved delight. Thorne had known that Jennie would be enthusiastic and joyful in her lovemaking, but he'd had no conception of how enchantingly playful she would prove to be.

Propped up against the pillows, they fed each other melon and dates, figs and sweet pastries. Completely naked, they licked the sugary crumbs that fell on each other's chest and stomach and shoulders.

"Am I your favorite little magpie?" she asked him with a tempting smile. She batted her long eyelashes in tantalizing allure as she lazily followed the ridge of a scar with the tip of her finger.

He pulled her close, his hand boldly cupping her breast. *"Mohehya,"* he assured her with a husky growl, "you are my favorite and only little magpie. Don't ever doubt it."

She tipped her head back against his shoulder and looked up at him thoughtfully. "Why did you grow the beard?"

"You don't like it?"

"I like everything about you, Englishman," she said on a gurgle of laughter. "Or have you not noticed? I was just wondering why you decided to grow it."

He kissed the tip of her nose, entranced by her fresh spontaneity. "I'm going to be traveling through the province of Thrace on my search for ruins. I'll need to talk to the villagers about their countryside. As I told you before, love, Turkey is a man's world. Here men are judged by their strength and virility. Being hirsute is considered a necessary requirement." He sent her a teasing look. "You told me yourself, when in Rome, do as the Romans."

Thorne left the bed to retrieve a gift he'd purchased the previous afternoon. He came back to sit on the edge of the plush cushion beside her and placed a gold-handled dagger in its curved, jeweled sheath in her hands.

Jennie stared at the object in wonder. "*Nakoe!* It is exquisite!" she gasped, touching the emeralds, rubies, and diamonds that encrusted it. She lifted her lids, silently asking the reason behind the extraordinary and unusual present.

"Jennie, in a few days I'm going to leave for the mountains," he said. "I'll be gone for perhaps a week." Moved by the obvious disappointment in her eyes, he stroked her cheek with the back of his hand. "I'm sorry, love, but it can't be put off. While I'm gone, I want you to carry this in your handbag whenever you leave the hotel."

She lifted her brows in astonishment at the unexpected request.

Thorne held up his hand to forestall her. "I know you believe you can protect yourself with a small knife worn strapped to your thigh, but I think you should also have a larger weapon you can reach easily and quickly without having to throw your skirt up over your head to get to it."

"Why?" she asked. She pulled the dagger from its sheath and turned it around in the afternoon light that streamed in through the arched doorway. The curved steel blade glinted wickedly.

"I'm not sure how much your grandfather told you about Istanbul," Thorne said, "or even how much he knows, for that matter. This city is a hotbed of international intrigue. Beneath its glittering surface, it seethes with spies and counterspies. Half the population is spying on the other half and reporting to Abdul Hamid's secret police. Graft, corruption, and unspeakable brutality abound. There's a torture chamber on the palace grounds at Yilditz, where the sultan's policemen have carte blanche to extract information from their unfortunate suspects by any means."

Her eyes widened in horror as she replaced the blade in its holder. "A torture chamber? That timid, frightened little man has people tortured? I can scarcely believe it!"

"It's true," he assured her. "All across Abdul Hamid's realm, subjected peoples are yearning for freedom. Revolutionaries in the western provinces are storing up arms and ammunition for the day of open rebellion. And while the Ottoman empire is crumbling, Britain and Russia are snarling at one another like dogs over a bone. Each intends to make certain the other won't take the rich prize of Constantinople."

She looked at him with open skepticism. "But Grandpapa and I have been treated with the utmost cordiality since the day we arrived. Except for the bandits who tried to rob us today, everyone we've met has been kind and considerate. There are thieves in every city—even Calgary and Winnipeg."

Thorne lifted a long chestnut lock that lay on her breast and wrapped it around his fingers, enjoying the marvelous feel of it. He had no intention of explaining that the men who'd attacked them were hired assassins. It would only lead to questions he couldn't answer.

"Sweetheart," he said with a placating smile, "the United States isn't considered a threat by anyone. Your grandfather's country is no more than a frontier outpost to the rest of the civilized world."

"What has all this to do with me?"

"Nothing, I hope. But I want you to realize Istanbul is an extremely dangerous place. Whatever you do, don't think you can go anywhere without the two guards I've hired to defend you. Women in this city are always heavily protected when they venture outside their home. A beautiful young woman like you could be easily kidnapped."

"*Haxc!*" she scoffed. "I would break free and escape."

Thorne shook his head, impatient at her stubborn intransigence. "You'd disappear into some wealthy pasha's seraglio, never to be seen or heard from again. Even the sultan's secret police can't invade the sanctity of a man's harem. There are men in Stamboul who'd think nothing of abducting you and keeping you imprisoned in their home for the rest of your life." He paused in frustration at her pucker of disbelief. Her independent spirit would never accept such a fate. She'd rail against it till it killed her. "That's why I hired Kastriota and Zogu to protect you," he continued sternly. "The fact that they belong to Abdul Hamid's personal bodyguard gives you that much more security."

"But you said the Turks prefer yellow hair and blue eyes. Why would anyone try to abduct me?"

He smiled at her foolish naiveté, his gaze drifting over her exotic features and golden, nubile body. "Believe me, Mohehya, no man in his right mind would choose the pale, washed-out looks of a blonde over your vivid loveliness."

"Flatterer!" she scolded. But she smiled with feminine pleasure at the compliment.

Thorne didn't tell her that the train robbery could very well have been an attempt to seize both her and her grandfather and hold them for ransom. Such an event would have created an international crisis and brought world attention to the goals of the revolutionaries. The Macedonian guerrillas could have demanded an exorbitant amount of money and gotten it. Money they needed for guns. Only the fact that Senator Robinson's stay in Vienna had been unexpectedly shortened by a day may have saved her and her grandfather from being held hostage.

Thorne had been on the train with them, riding in a private coach, and well aware that Count Gortschakoff had followed him from London. He'd stayed constantly on the alert for a possible attempt on his life. But the clever Russian had bided his time, believing, no doubt, that when they reached Constantinople, it'd be far safer to do his deadly work and get away with it. Today, he'd attempted and failed. But he'd try again.

Jennifer looked down at the jeweled dagger in speculation. The idea that someone would actually want to carry her off seemed rather farfetched. Then the depraved eyes of Pasha Izzet Bey came to mind. His licentious gaze had wiped over her like some filthy rag. Maybe Thorne was right. If the chief of the secret police were to snatch her, no one in Istanbul would ever find her.

"Very well," she said, reaching her decision. "I will carry the dagger in my handbag. And I will not go anywhere without my Albanian escorts."

Relieved, Thorne gave her a smile of approval. "Good girl. Now there's one more thing we need to discuss before I take you back to the hotel."

She returned his smile, leaning forward in childlike curiosity. "What is that?"

"Our wedding. I think it should take place as soon as possible." He grinned lecherously. "For your safety and my pleasure."

Jennie's smile slowly faded. She looked at him with huge, solemn eyes. He could read the doubt and hesitation on her expressive features.

Thorne suspected she was once again thinking about the dream man she believed she was fated to marry. The fact that she still clung to the superstitious belief rankled. But this afternoon, she'd told him she loved him, over and over again. It was only a matter of time before she realized the so-called vision was no more than a young girl's romantic fancy . . . an adolescent's natural yearning to discover what was meant to be.

"I—I do not know," she said, looking about the room to avoid his gaze. "It is something I need to think about. We need to think about."

"You realize you could be carrying my child, don't you?" he asked softly.

Her brows snapped together in confusion. "I could not get married without a real Cheyenne courtship. And never without my parents' permission."

He knew she was stalling to avoid making the final commitment that afternoon. "You'll have your Cheyenne courtship," he told her smoothly. "And your parents' permission before we're wed. I don't want any reservations in that pretty little head of yours, after the knot has been tied. I don't want you thinking, two or three years from now, that we aren't truly and legally married in the eyes of your people as well as mine. And I have no intention of ever being 'thrown away.' "

"But how can I have a real courtship here in Istanbul?"

she asked with a shrug of disbelief. "The girl's suitor always sends his gifts to the home of her parents with a trusted friend and then waits patiently for their reply."

Thorne took the dagger and laid it on the bed's soft cushion. He caught her hand in his and squeezed her fingers in a soothing gesture. He wasn't sure how she was going to take the news.

"I sent a hundred Thoroughbreds to your father and mother in Canada before I left London, Jennie," he said. "Eight of them prize-winning stallions with the finest bloodlines. Along with three cases of Winchester repeating rifles and fifty boxes of ammunition. My personal secretary, John Woodman, is accompanying the gifts and will speak to your parents on my behalf. He's carrying a copy of the marriage contract and all the needed credentials to prove my worthiness to your parents' satisfaction. As soon as we have their permission, we'll be married in the British embassy here in Istanbul."

He didn't add that he'd included his list of private commendations for valor in Her Majesty's service as proof of his status as a warrior in his own country. And he'd instructed Woodman to tell Strong Elk Heart that the duke of Eagleston's chest was carved up like a Christmas ham from wounds received in hand-to-hand combat. Thorne hadn't taken any chances when it came to being accepted as the son-in-law of one of the four head chiefs of the Cheyenne nation.

"*Hesc!*" Jennifer said, her mind reeling at his impressive efforts to follow the customs of her people. "All that will take weeks. Grandpapa and I will be on our way back to Paris by the time you could possibly hear from my parents."

Thorne grinned in victory. "Ever heard of the telegraph, Miss Elkheart?"

The next morning, Jennifer visited the Grand Bazaar accompanied by her bodyguards. The uniformed Albanian escorts were a pair of matching giants. Well over six feet in height, they were taller than Eagle's Son, taller even than her father, Strong Elk. With Ismail Kastriota and Kemal Zogu protecting her, a man would have to be either an idiot or a maniac to even think of accosting the American envoy's granddaughter.

The walled and gated marketplace was covered by an immense domed roof. Its colonnaded streets contained thousands of tiny stores, workshops, and stalls. There were even small mosques and bubbling fountains for the weary shopper. The narrow, vaulted passageways wandered through a fantastical display of merchandise, intersected by countless twisting lanes meant to entice the buyer to come and explore.

Hawkers shouted their wares. Others whispered to Jennifer as she went by, intimating their prices were too good to be true. She suspected they were.

Her guards followed behind her, loaded with packages, as she gazed at the wealth of choices before her. Gold necklaces and bracelets studded with jewels, copper ware, carved alabaster, ceramics, thick Turkish carpets, and curved brass lamps straight from the tales of Aladdin. Other shops were piled high with clothing, flowers, fruits, vegetables, and spices. The smell of freshly baked sesame bread, sandalwood, cinnamon, smoked mutton, and tooled leather drifted through the air.

Earlier that morning, she'd planned to go on a carriage excursion through old Stamboul with Mrs. Beaufort, but Dotty had been forced to postpone. Jennifer had decided it was time to explore the famous bazaar and purchase gifts for her family.

But as she wandered through the great marketplace, her thoughts kept drifting back to her overwhelming dilemma.

Was it possible the Maiyun had accidentally misled her?

Or could the Great Powers have sent her someone else's vision by mistake?

Surely Maxemaheo, the All-Father, would know that she could never love a man who considered her nothing more than an object to be used for his own pleasure. A man who might even try to beat her into submission, if she rebelled.

She'd come to Constantinople completely ignorant of its people and customs, following only what she'd seen in her vision. But her visit to the Grand Seraglio—and what she'd learned there—had been appalling and frightening to a young woman who'd known the unbounded freedom of Cheyenne life.

Now more than ever, she wished she had Julie to talk to. Her twin knew the power of dreams. She'd gone to Scotland on a vision quest of her own. What would Evening Star say if Jennifer told her that she'd fallen deeply and irrevocably in love *with the wrong man*?

Naaaa! There was no sense in denying it. She knew that what she felt for Thorne was love. She couldn't imagine ever wanting another man. Even if she risked defying fate by choosing the Englishman, she would never give him up.

The fact that Thorne was a wealthy duke didn't mean her life as a duchess would necessarily be spent embroidering linens. He could teach her about his interests in ancient civilizations. She'd always wanted to travel to different lands. She could go with him hunting for ancient ruins and help him search for shards of pottery and broken statues and whatever else he wanted to find. Even if the polished British lord wasn't the battle-hardened warrior she'd always dreamed of, there was certainly no mistaking his virile strength and unequivocal masculinity.

She smiled to herself, remembering last night. Thorne had attended the reception at the French embassy. They'd danced far more than the two waltzes allowed by social protocol, totally engrossed in each other. No one could have mistaken his proprietary air as he kept her hand securely on his arm, holding her close beside him through the entire evening. To the people who ogled them with overt fascination, it must have seemed a foregone conclusion that she was betrothed to the duke of Eagleston.

Grandpapa had watched Jennifer with fond indulgence as his granddaughter openly leaned against the man she'd once claimed she could never love—and certainly never marry.

It wasn't until she'd crawled into bed, completely exhausted, that she remembered the dreamcatcher. She'd forgotten to ask for it back.

Jennifer's reverie was interrupted by a shopkeeper's melodic call. "Beautiful mademoiselle," he sang out in a garbled mixture of French and English, "come see my wares. Carpets from Kayseri! Spices from the Orient! The riches of Ali Baba are here! Come see how lovely!"

The barrel-shaped man smiled ingratiatingly, revealing a mouthful of gold teeth. Jennifer paused to admire his goods. In the window was a pair of slippers exactly like the ones Mihri had worn, and she thought instantly of Julie. The idea of her cautious, prudent, contemplative sister wearing such sybaritic apparel tickled Jennifer's fancy.

"Do you have other sizes?" she asked the vendor, whose tufts of coarse gray hair stuck out from beneath his red fez like blackberry brambles. "I would need some a little larger than those."

"*Entrez, s'il vous plaît,*" he said with a grand flourish of his arm. "Come inside. I have everything a beautiful lady could want."

She peeked into the store situated on the intersection of two tiny lanes. It was crowded to the ceilings, the aisles so narrow there was scarcely room to move about. Ornate French clocks, Austrian cut crystal, solid silver handbags, and painted Japanese porcelain as fragile as the eggs of a hummingbird vied for the shopper's attention. Magnificent carpets of every color hung on the walls, while rows of glass hookahs stood like sentinels along the floor.

Jennifer motioned for Kemal and Ismail to wait outside by the door and then followed the owner into the shop. She knew her ferocious escorts would lean back against the doorjamb and smoke, watching the people go by with thoughtful, narrowed eyes. She had but to call out, and they'd rush instantly to her aide.

While she wandered through the counters piled high with goods, two men entered through the shop's other door and began to quietly examine a stack of brass trays.

Involved in her purchase, she paid them no attention and scarcely noticed when one of the customers disappeared with the shopkeeper behind a screen of glass beads.

The curly-toed slippers came in countless sizes and different decorations of counterfeit jewels. She bent and held the sole of one against the bottom of her sturdy walking shoe, trying to decide if it would fit. She and Julie wore the same size. Perhaps, she should just try it on.

Suddenly, the second man was at her side. "Have you seen this sublime inlaid box, mademoiselle?" he queried with the engaging smile of an accomplished tradesman. Like so many merchants in Istanbul, he spoke French with a very heavy accent.

Till that moment she hadn't realized that he worked in the shop. He was large and burly, with a head of shiny black hair, a huge, pointed mustache, and friendly black eyes. "No, what is it?" she asked, her natural inquisitiveness aroused.

"It holds an extraordinary perfume found only in the East," he told her. He touched two fingers to his lips and kissed the air. "Like the fragrance of jasmine, only lighter and more delicate. Here, smell its heavenly beauty."

He opened the miniature casket and held it out to her. Jennifer bent forward and took a deep sniff. She pulled back in distaste, shaking her head to clear it. The cloying aroma was sickeningly sweet and made her feel instantly dizzy.

Before she could say a word, he caught her from behind and held a cloth over her nose and mouth, saturated with the same evil-smelling substance. Jennifer was vaguely aware that he lifted her up in his arms like a child, as the whirling, spinning, nauseating black of unconsciousness took hold of her.

Thorne charged into Garrett Robinson's hotel room and shoved the door shut behind him. "I just got your message, Senator. What's happened to Jennie?"

Robinson's face was pale and drawn, his eyes haunted, as he hurried across the rug. His thin fingers trembled when he clasped Thorne's hand. "She's been kidnapped."

Thorne's heart squeezed to a painful halt. God, no! His worst fears had been realized. "How?" he exploded. "How in the hell could it have happened? Where were Kastriota and Zogu?"

Garrett sank down in a desk chair, his shaking hand covering his forehead. "It happened at the Grand Bazaar. They were in front of a shop, waiting for her. Whoever took Jennie must have sneaked her out a side door. The Albanians found her handbag on the floor and the owner unconscious in the back, bound and gagged."

Thorne turned and strode toward the window, raging with impotent fury. "I'll kill them!" he roared. He clenched his hands into fists. "I'll tear those two useless bastards limb from limb for not protecting her."

The senator picked up a crumpled paper from the desktop and held it out. "This note was pinned to the front of the store owner's shirt. She's being held for ransom by some group called Imro. They warned us not to go to the authorities. They want one man to bring the money to a town called Edis Keui this evening. They'll meet him there and escort him to their hideout, where the exchange can take place. They're asking for £5,000 in gold sovereigns. Do you know where Edis Keui is?"

Relief surged through Thorne. Then she hadn't disappeared into some rich pasha's harem. Rescuing her from a band of mercenaries would be child's play compared to searching house to house for her in Istanbul. And the fact that her abductors were after money meant there was a strong chance she wouldn't be harmed.

"It's a small village in Thrace," he said, somewhat calmer, "about eighty miles west of Istanbul on the Tunja River. The area is a stronghold for Macedonian guerrillas trying to overthrow the Ottoman government. Most of the villagers in those mountains have ties either to Greece or Bulgaria. When they're not fighting the sultan's officials, they're quarreling with each other over the eventual ownership of the entire territory."

"I've never heard of them," Garrett confessed.

"Damn!" Thorne cursed softly. "Damn their abomi
nable hides. If they hurt one hair on Jennie's head, I'l
kill every goddamn one of those sons-of-bitches." He
jammed the note into his trouser pocket. "Who knows
about the kidnapping so far?"

Garret moved to his feet and held onto the back of the
chair for support. "I've told no one but you, Your Grace
I honestly didn't know who else to turn to. You're very
knowledgeable about Turkey and its people. You speak
their language. And I know how much you care about
my granddaughter." His silvery brows squeezed together
in pain as he nodded toward an adjoining door. "Kastri
ota and Zogu are in there, waiting for my orders. They
aren't anxious to report the abduction to the police. They
think Abdul Hamid will have their throats slit when he
hears about their bungling."

"If I don't do it first," Thorne said tersely.

"Should we notify the sultan?"

He shook his head. "The Turkish police would only
slow us down. They'd want to send a squadron of sol
diers along, who'd be seen coming for miles in those
mountains. They've had no luck so far finding the ban
dits who held up the train near Cherkes Baba."

"Do you think it's the same men?"

"I'm sure of it."

"Then you think the train robbery was an attempt to
take Jennie and me hostage?"

"Yes."

Understanding dawned in the senator's haggard eyes
"That's why you hired the Albanian guards, isn't it?"

"One of the reasons, yes."

"I'm going to have to tell the American minister," Rob
inson said, wearily scrubbing his face with a heavily
veined hand. "This could evolve into an international cri
sis. If we don't get my granddaughter back at once, Pres
ident Cleveland may very well threaten war. There's a
U. S. cruiser in the Mediterranean right now. Our navy
could sail into the Bosphorus within a week."

Thorne nodded in agreement. "Tell Beaufort to give me
ten days to return with Jennie before notifying anyone in

Washington, including your secretary of state. Also, let
Lord Ellenborough know what's happening. Stay in
touch with him." He held up his hand in warning. "Let's
keep this a tight secret. The fewer people who know Jennie's been kidnapped, the better. We don't want anyone
else muddying the waters. Tell everyone she's sightseeing on the Princes' Islands with Zogu and Kastriota as
her guides."

Robinson picked up a pen and bankbook from his desk
and slipped them in his coat pocket. "I'll go to the Ottoman Bank immediately," he said, "and arrange to get
the money in sovereigns as fast as possible."

"No, I'll take care of the ransom. I've made several
previous trips to Istanbul. I know who to contact. And I
can move much more quickly and quietly than you."
Thorne started for the door.

"Eagleston," Robinson called, his voice thready and
faint. "Can you get her back safely?"

Thorne paused, his hand on the doorknob. He turned
to meet the elderly gentleman's tormented gaze. "I'll
bring her back, Senator. I'll bring Jennie back, if I have
to kill every one of those bloody beggars to do it."

The Orient Express left Istanbul bound for Paris that
evening with Thorne on board. He rode in a private compartment and spent his time cleaning and reloading his
weapons, always keeping one ready beside him. The English sovereigns were stashed in two worn, nondescript
saddlebags on the floor at his feet. He'd had his meal
brought to his compartment. He had no intention of going to the dining car and risking the chance of meeting
someone he knew.

Images of Jennie played through his mind like a beloved melody. He saw her, once again, reclining gracefully on the great canopied bed, feeding him dates,
throwing her head back and laughing with joy. He
squeezed his eyes shut, telling himself she was perfectly
safe.

All the Imro wanted was money.

Hell, they could have all the money they desired.

Just so Jennie wasn't harmed.

He wouldn't kill anyone, if she just wasn't harmed.

As Thorne stood up and stretched, he caught his reflection in the mirror above the wash basin. He'd dyed his hair and beard black before leaving the hotel and changed into a flowing, hooded burnoose that reached to the tops of his boots. With his great beak of a nose, he looked like a Turkish trader, returning to his home in one of the rural provinces from a business trip to the Ottoman capital. Once he reached the Edis Keui station, he'd be riding into the mountains in the company of the revolutionaries. Of course, his final destination remained unknown.

Thorne hoped he'd succeeded in slipping out of Constantinople with no one the wiser. He knew Gortschakof had probably been paying informers to alert him the instant the duke of Eagleston started on his journey into Thrace, ostensibly looking for Roman relics. Whether he'd managed to fool them or not remained to be seen.

The train chugged slowly into the station. It was dark outside, the silhouettes on the platform scarcely recognizable from the curtained window. Thorne shoved his derringer into his boot, then tucked the double-barreled Lancaster revolver beneath the back of his wide leather belt, where it was well hidden by the full, billowing robe. He'd had to leave the Soper rifle behind, knowing the guerrillas would immediately confiscate it. With a little luck, however, he might be able to keep the two guns concealed. At least for a while.

He lifted the heavy, frayed saddlebags over his shoulders, opened the door, and entered the dimly lit passage.

As though listening for him to come out, a man immediately stepped from the open doorway of the compartment at the far end of the coach. He raised a handgun and pointed it directly at Thorne's chest. In that instant the train came to a sudden, jerking halt. Both men were thrown off balance.

Thorne heard the explosion and felt the searing pain in his side as he fell against the paneled wall. The bags of coins dragged him down like anchors, and he crashed to the floor of the railroad car. Stunned, he shook his head, trying to clear it.

"Nice bit of luck, Eagleston," Gortschakoff said with a sneer. "But my second shot will be a little more accurate."

The Russian strolled down the narrow aisle, the hand holding the pistol hanging loosely at his side. "I'm sorry to have to do this," he stated with the cold detachment of a paid assassin. "You've been one of the few real challenges of my career. But my superiors decided you're just too good at your work to let you continue." He slowly raised the weapon.

Thorne fired the derringer, striking the count directly through his left eye.

Three men were waiting as Thorne stepped down from the train at the dilapidated wooden station. They looked right past him, expecting a European in a suit and tie and carrying a large valise. A fourth member of the group held the reins of their mounts, well back on the dirt road that led out of town.

The Bulgers were dressed like rough mountaineers. Thorne had no doubt, however, that they were *comitadjis* of the International Macedonian Revolutionary Organization, whose goal was the overthrow of their Osmanli overlords and the bringing of the northern regions of Macedonia into the Bulgarian sphere. Any possible ties with Russia came through the arms and ammunition smuggled over the border and hidden in their villages for the day of revolution.

Although the British government was determined not to allow the czar to gain a foothold in the area, Thorne, himself, had felt no personal animosity toward the guerrillas. Not until they'd made the fatal mistake of involving Jennie in their schemes.

As the train pulled away, he went directly up to the swarthy trio and spoke quietly in Turkish. "I believe you're looking for me, gentlemen."

The largest, a powerfully built male of enormous

height, stepped forward. "Why would we be expecting you, Turk?" he growled.

"Because I'm bringing you what you've been waiting for."

A second man drew nearer. He scrutinized Thorne for a few seconds, then glanced nervously about. "Let's go," he urged hoarsely.

The third rebel motioned to the fellow holding the restive horses, and they were quickly brought up. Without another word, two of the *comitadjis* took the saddlebags from Thorne and threw them across their animals' flanks.

Ignoring the ache that throbbed in his side, Thorne mounted the extra horse they'd brought along for him. Blood trickled down his rib cage and soaked the side of his shirt. He hadn't had time to check the damage. He just knew it hurt like hell.

The moment he was in the saddle, the guerrillas kicked their fidgety steeds into a gallop. The silent horsemen, Thorne in their midst, raced out of Edis Keui and into the night.

Chapter 20

Jennifer was scarcely able to believe it.

She was being held captive by men in skirts.

Not that there was anything feminine about them. They were all big, brawny fellows with thatches of thick black hair and enormous mustaches or beards. If being hairy was a requirement for manliness in this country, these mountain fighters were as virile as they came. And they fairly bristled with weapons. Each man carried a rifle and had a huge pistol stuck in his scarlet sash. Most had a cartridge belt or two slung across their chests.

But their clothes were outlandish.

They wore elaborately embroidered vests over wide sleeved shirts, white gathered kilts, and leggings. Their square-toed shoes were covered by highly decorated wool gaiters that reached to their knees. Each man wore a soft red cap with a long golden tassel that hung down to his shoulder.

It had been four days since she'd been abducted from the Grand Bazaar. She'd been in their mountain hideout for two of them, biding her time. She had every intention of escaping, but she wanted to be certain her getaway would be successful. It was only a matter of watching and waiting for the right moment to steal a mount and take off.

Her captors hadn't bothered to blindfold her on the journey by horseback from the train station at a town called Edis Keui. They'd assumed that a female would never be able to find her way back alone. She smiled at their *veho* foolishness. She'd been raised on the trackless plains. Her father had taught her how to use landmarks, along with the sun and the stars, to set a course through countryside every bit as wild and rugged as this.

Hearing the sound of hoof beats, Jennifer jumped up from the bed and hurried to the window. In the faint grayish light just before dawn, she could see the tiny village below her. A small group of horsemen rode down the narrow dirt lane that twisted through the houses built of wood and brick on the steep slopes of the valley. The two men who'd kidnapped her were with them, still attired in the coarse shirts and trousers they'd worn in Istanbul. One of the riders, however, was a black-bearded Turk. His hooded mantle flapped out behind him in the early morning breeze.

The thought that he might be a wealthy pasha come to buy her for his harem sent a cold chill slithering down the back of Jennifer's neck. So far, no one had tried to molest her. Todor, their brawny, rough-hewn leader, had assured her that she'd be returned safely to her grandfather as soon as they received the ransom money. But he could have been lying. Maybe these soldiers intended to sell her to the highest bidder.

Jennifer heard the men enter the room beneath her, their voices loud and demanding. She flew to the door and pressed her ear to the wooden panel. It sounded as though they were calling for food and drink. The gnarled, stooped woman who lived there must have awakened and started to feed them, for it gradually grew quiet.

Jennifer sank down on the edge of the lumpy, straw-filled pallet, fighting back an incapacitating panic. She lifted the cushion at the head of the bed, just to reassure herself that the small knife she'd purchased to replace the one she'd lost was still there, ready to be used. Eagleston's jeweled dagger, carried inside her handbag, had been dropped at the time of her abduction. All she could do now was stay calm and wait to see what happened next.

After what seemed forever, she heard footsteps coming

up the creaky stairs. Quickly, she lay down on her side, one hand tucked under the pillow to clutch her weapon. It took all of Jennifer's willpower to remain perfectly still and pretend to be asleep.

The room was dim and shadowy, with only a narrow sliver of early morning light coming in the little window. The latch turned with a noisy click. She cautiously raised her lashes and peeked at the intruder.

It was the Turk.

There was no mistaking the billowing robe or the baggy pants tucked into his high boots. He came slowly and quietly across the room's bare wooden floor to the bed.

She had no intention of becoming an odalisque in his harem—not while there was an ounce of fight left in her. The moment he laid his hand on her shoulder, Jennifer struck out with her blade in a wide slashing movement, aiming for his throat. He captured her hand in an iron grip, twisted the weapon out of her grasp, and flung it on the floor. Before she could let out a piercing scream, he covered her mouth with his hand.

"Shh," he hissed, bending over her.

Jennifer pulled up her knee and struck him square in the groin with her sole of her bare foot. With a muffled groan, he crouched forward in agony, still managing to keep his hand locked securely over her mouth. Wriggling and flopping wildly about, she tried to slide off the bed and make a dive for the knife. He flipped her on her back, placed one knee on the mattress, and leaned over her. She bucked and kicked in sheer terror, as she tried to claw his face with her nails.

"Dammit, Jennie, it's me," the Turk whispered hoarsely.

It took her a moment to realize what he'd said and stop struggling. Her pulse raced frantically as she sought to catch her breath. "Thorne?" she mumbled against his hand. She stared at his black hair and beard in the faint light. *"Thorne?"*

Eagleston took his cupped palm away from her mouth and kissed her hungrily. "Are you all right, Jennie?" he asked, his hands moving over her, gently searching for any sign of injury. "If they hurt you, darling, they'll pay."

"Thorne!" she cried softly, throwing her arms around his neck. "You have come to rescue me!" She covered his hairy face with kisses. The feel of his solid male frame so close to her shaking form brought tears of joy and deliverance. Jennifer clung to him like a lifeline in a stormy sea. Then she slumped back on the cushion and gazed up at his face. "Why didn't you tell me who you were?" she gasped.

"You didn't give me a chance," he informed her as he scooted her over and sat down beside her with a soft grunt of pain. "I'm sorry I frightened you. I thought you were sound asleep and didn't want to startle you awake." He shook his head in reluctant admiration as he pressed one hand to his sore crotch. "Damn. You kick like a bloody mule."

She ran her fingers across his bristly cheek. "Your hair and beard," she muttered in disapproval. "What in the world did you do?"

"I dyed them, love." He smiled at her frown of displeasure. "Don't worry, it's only temporary. A mixture of jelled flaxseed and black tea my valet concocted."

"Why?"

"I'll explain later." He placed his hands on her shoulders. Slowly and carefully, he inspected her again, seeking a telltale sign of injury. His deep voice was gruff with concern. "Did they harm you, Jennie, in any way?"

"No."

He drew her into his embrace, tucking her head beneath his chin and holding her tight. "You're positive? You wouldn't lie to me, would you?"

"No, they did not hurt me," she assured him. "But they made me terribly sick."

Eagleston kissed her temple and cuddled her closer. His words were filled with tender compassion. "They drugged you?"

"I guess so. Whatever they used, it was terrible," she complained, still irate about what had happened to her. "I was violently ill when I woke up on the train. All the rocking and swaying of the railroad car made the nausea worse. I threw up all over Damian," she added with satisfaction. "He was the one who tricked me, so it served him right."

Thorne chuckled, happy to learn that she hadn't lost her irrepressible spunk. "That must have taught him a lesson."

Jennifer pulled back to look into his eyes. "They rolled me up in a carpet and carried me all the way to the train station, right through the crowded streets of Istanbul," she explained. "Of course, I didn't know what was happening at the time. Christo told me later. He said they hoisted the rug up on their shoulders and walked past Ismail and Kemal, as big as life, and the Albanians were none the wiser."

"Christo?"

Jennifer nodded. "The big one. He's been very nice," she admitted, as an afterthought. "He reminds me of Viscount Lyttleton. Lady Idina always called Bertie her gentle giant." Glancing down, she ran her fingers along the braided edge of the dark wool vest she wore. "Christo gave me these clean clothes, since my walking suit was soiled when I was sick. He had the old woman who lives here help me with a bath, of sorts, in a big wine cask. I tried to thank her, but she doesn't speak any French. Only some strange language I did not recognize."

Thorne looked at Jennifer's outfit and smiled. She was wearing a typical Macedonian costume. The white cotton blouse had long, full sleeves, heavily decorated with embroidery along the seams and cuffs. A short vest was similarly adorned with brilliant silk threads. The black pleated skirt reached to the ankles, with a wide sash, a silver buckle, and a cherry-red apron.

Propped up on the headrest, Jennifer held her arms out as though modeling the clothes for him. Her long hair fell in one thick braid over her shoulder. She looked adorable in the colorful peasant garb. Then all at once, she leaned forward and peered at him, noticing for the first time the splotches on the white wool of his burnoose.

"You are bleeding!" she exclaimed, struggling to sit

up. She stared at him, horrified. "*Naaaa!* I cut you! I am sorry!"

He caught her by the elbows and held her still. "You didn't cut me, Jennie. There was an accident on the train."

"An accident! What happened?"

"It was nothing. A man's gun went off by mistake."

"Let me up, so I can see," she insisted.

Thorne sat back, knowing she wouldn't be satisfied until she'd assessed the damage for herself.

She scooted to the side of the bed and rose to her feet. "We need to get these clothes off," she told him insistently, as she tugged on the edge of his cloak.

Thorne helped her lift the loose outer garment off his shoulders. The shirt beneath was stained with dried blood. A cloth provided by one of the rebels served as a makeshift bandage. Damian had helped him tend the wound. The guerrilla fighters had searched Thorne that first night and discovered the pistol. Luckily, they never thought to look in his boot. It was likely they'd never seen a derringer.

Jennifer hurriedly unfastened the buttons down the front of his shirt and tugged it off. She carefully peeled away the crusted material that had stuck to the torn flesh. The wound started bleeding again. "*Ahahe!*" she cried woefully. "You were shot!"

"It's not as bad as it looks," he assured her.

She went to a nearby table and poured a pitcher of water into a washbowl. Grabbing a cloth and a chunk of coarse soap, she came back, set the basin on the floor at his feet, and knelt down in front of him. "Here, she said, "let me examine you." Jennifer tenderly explored the gash in Thorne's side just below the right armpit. "When did this happen?" she asked, gently probing the raw wound.

He clenched his teeth at the sharp jolt of pain. "Four days ago," he answered with a soft grunt as she continued to work on him. It felt as if he'd been mauled by a Bengal tiger. "The men who brought me here kept doubling back, taking unused shepherds' trails to make

:ertain I was good and lost." He looked down at the top of her bent head. "How long have you been here, Jennie?"

"Two days," she answered. "We reached the station at Edis Keui the first afternoon and rode all that night and through the next day. We arrived here late the second evening." She looked up with a frown. "Do you know the name of this place?"

"No," he said, "and we don't want to learn it, either."

Jennifer released a long, thankful sigh. "Fortunately, the bullet just grazed you, though you do have a nice chunk of flesh ripped out of your side." She pressed her slender fingers against his knee. "Thanks to Maheo, you did not bleed to death on the ride here, Eagle's Son. Now, if you can just avoid an infection . . ."

The door swung open. Three of the *comitadjis* stepped into the small room. Todor, their chieftain, was a brawny, middle-aged man with fierce black eyes. He stood with his feet braced apart, his muscular arms folded across his deep chest. Thorne's double-barreled revolver was tucked in the wide sash at his waist.

"I trust you have satisfied your fears about Miss Elkheart's safety," Todor said in his rough, unpolished French. "As I told you on the way here, Eagleston, the young lady has not been harmed."

Jennifer looked up with a scowl. "He is the one who is hurt," she announced crossly. "Could you not see that? We must have some fresh cloth for bandages immediately."

At the sight of Jennifer kneeling at her rescuer's feet, Christo glowered. The enormous man stomped across the bare boards, his fists doubled in rage. Thorne took one look at the expression of pure hatred on the man's coarse features and knew it meant trouble.

Ignoring the fiery pain that lanced through his side, Thorne rose to his feet. "I'm fine," he told the revolutionaries. "We don't need a thing. You have your money. I have the young lady. As soon as it's light out, we'll be on our way."

"I'm afraid not," Todor replied. Offering an apologetic

smile, he lifted his hands in a gesture of resignation. "[I]t seems we have a small problem."

Thorne had a horrible premonition of what was coming.

Damian grinned and pounded his big friend on the back. "Christo's in love."

Thorne didn't have to ask with whom.

Jennie did. "Who are you in love with, Christo?" she questioned in French with an artless smile.

Beneath her brilliant gaze, the giant grew tongue-tied. He hung his head and shuffled his feet like an oversize schoolboy.

"I could be wrong," Thorne stated ironically, "but [I] think the big chap's in love with you, Mohehya."

"*Nehe!*" she cried softly.

"Exactly," he concurred. He looked at the mountain chieftain. "So what happens now?"

"We are civilized men," Todor said. "We will settle this in a civilized fashion."

"I'm all for being civilized," agreed Thorne. "As long as Miss Elkheart is free to leave this village in the morning."

"She stays with me," Christo boomed, suddenly finding his voice. He tapped his chest with his thumbnail. "She will be my wife."

"I cannot be your wife," Jennifer informed the brute kindly. "I am engaged to marry Eagleston."

"Thank you, darling," Thorne told her with a wry grin. "That was probably one thing better left unsaid, but it's too late now."

"Have you heard of the pancratium?" Todor asked.

"Yes," Thorne replied. "It was a sport in the Olympic games. A contest of boxing and wrestling in which no holds were considered illegal."

Damian's teeth flashed white beneath his heavy black mustache. "Not so!" he declared with obvious relish. "No eye gouging or biting is allowed. But other than that . . ." He shrugged expressively, his black eyes glinting with anticipation.

Thorne knew the pancratium had been the ultimate test

of an athlete's strength and courage. It was the toughest
and most grueling sport devised by the ancient Greeks.
Two rivals fought until one of them could no longer defend himself and gave up. Or was killed. The victor was
awarded the highest honors bestowed at Olympia.

"I'm ready whenever you are," Thorne said, meeting
Christo's malevolent stare.

"You cannot fight this man!" Jennifer cried. She
pinched Thorne's bare arm as though trying to make him
wake up and come to his senses. At his resolute silence,
she turned to the three Macedonian rebels. "Can you not
see he has been wounded?" she demanded irately. "He
has lost far too much blood. He is in no condition to do
battle with anyone."

"Can you fight?" Todor asked, his gaze fixed on
Thorne.

"Yes."

Jennifer flew across the room like an avenging fury.
"Eagleston is not a soldier," she told the chieftain, her
husky contralto shaking with anger. "He is an Englishman who spends his time at balls and foxhunts. When
he's traveling, he looks for old ruins and collects ancient
statues. This fight would be grossly unfair!"

Thorne didn't bother to dispute her. The less capable
Christo thought him, the better chance he'd have against
the hulking oaf. The man bested him in height by a good
eight inches and probably outweighed him by ninety
pounds. His longer reach could prove extremely dangerous.

"Nevertheless," Thorne told the rebel leader, "I am
willing to decide this issue by the pancratium."

Todor clapped his hands together to indicate the problem was as good as settled. "As soon as the sun is up,
we'll hold the match. People will want to watch. Now,
it's time for the morning meal."

The moment the rebels left the room, Jennie whirled
on Thorne. "You cannot fight this man," she cried. "It is
madness!"

"I'll make that decision," he said calmly. He tried to

draw her into his arms, but she shoved him away, he
beautiful eyes filled with tears.

"Leave me here, Eagle's Son," she pleaded. "Return t
Istanbul and bring back help."

"No."

She pounded on his chest in frustration, castigatin
him in Cheyenne. When she realized he had no idea wha
she was saying, she switched to English. "You are a stu
pid, pigheaded *veho*!" she shouted, tears of fright and
anger streaking down her cheeks.

Thorne threw his arms around her and held her close
"Jennie, Jennie," he told her softly, "everything will b
all right."

The entire village turned out for the blood sport. Men
women, children, babies in arms. Even the Orthodo
priest was there to cheer Christo on. No one, includin
the three toothless elders, had seen anything like this i
his lifetime. Two strong, well-built men willing to figh
over a lovely young woman in a no-holds-barred contes
that could very possibly end in death.

Thorne stood beside the huge, bull-necked Macedonia
in the middle of the ring of spectators. People sat on th
ground, knelt, or stood, everyone anxious to have a clea
view of the grisly affair.

The original Olympic contestants had fought naked
but Christo and Thorne were given swaths of unbleached
linen for loincloths to protect the virtue of the wome
present. Everyone—male and female alike—was waitin
with bated breath for the sound of bones being crunched
and the sight of blood being spattered. Violence and gor
was what they'd come to see, and that was, undoubtedly
what they'd going to get.

The open wound on Thorne's side was a raw, throb
bing mass of nerve endings. Christo would chop away a
the torn flesh relentlessly, hoping to start the blood flow
ing again. Thorne had refused to let Jennie bandage it. A
strip of cloth wrapped around his torso would only giv
his opposition something to grab hold of.

Thorne studied his powerfully built foe. His only hop

was to use his agility and intelligence to stay out of the big bruiser's reach. If Christo got him in a death lock, there'd be no breaking free.

In the pancratium, the competitors were allowed to punch, kick, break fingers and toes—whatever it took to disable the other man. Seizing an opponent by the throat, hitting him in the groin, trampling on bones, kicking behind the knee, tripping, tearing away an ear was all part of the brutal game. There would be no time limits. They'd fight until one of them was dead, unconscious, or signaled defeat.

He met Christo's infuriated gaze. The man had every intention of killing him. His fellow revolutionaries would consider the Englishman's death one of the hazards of the violent sport. Just an unfortunate accident.

Thorne didn't have the luxury of dispatching his adversary to hell. If the contest ended in Christo's death, the *comitadjis* might very well murder him in revenge for killing one of their best soldiers. But Thorne was convinced that if he succeeded in defeating the Bulgar, he and Jennie would be allowed to go free.

Thorne's clothes were in a pile beside Jennifer, the derringer still safely tucked in one of his boots. If it became apparent that he had no chance to defeat his rival, he'd somehow reach the weapon and shoot the man in cold blood. He'd empty every damn bullet the gun held into the bastard's carcass in order to bring him down. Christo's comrades would kill him, of course, but there'd be no reason Jennie couldn't go free. The ransom had already been paid in full.

"All it takes is a simple tap on your opponent's shoulder to signal defeat," Todor explained to the two contestants. "Or just raise your hand in the air. The winner gets the young lady. I, of course, keep the gold." He looked from Christo to Thorne and back again. "Do you both understand the rules?"

They jerked their heads in agreement.

Jennifer sat beside Damian on the brown autumn grass. She wanted to cover her eyes and not look.

But she couldn't not look.

Ahahe! She knew Thorne didn't have a chance. Worst of all, she had no war paint. If she'd only had some vermilion, she could have protected him with the powerful Cheyenne designs meant to shield a warrior going into battle.

As the two muscular, athletic men circled each other warily, taking their foe's measure, Jennifer bowed her head and silently prayed to Maxemaheo to protect Eagle's Son. To give him the courage of *nanoseham*, the mountain lion, the strength of *voxpazena-nako*, the grizzly bear, and the cunning of *voxcseo*, the fox.

Thorne knew he would have to use the larger man's momentum to his own advantage by directing it, once contact was made. He would have to move first and keep moving. Although the odds favored the taller, heavier contender, the outcome was far from decided. A lean, wiry man could react more quickly than a hulk with bulging muscles. In hand-to-hand fighting, it was possible to maneuver in such a way as to predict what the enemy was thinking and how he was going to react.

With a fluid movement, Thorne feinted a punch to Christo's abdomen with his right fist. The Bulgar assumed he was going to put his entire body behind the blow and lunged forward to meet him, swinging with all his might. Thorne sidestepped with ease, caught the man's leg with his foot, and tripped him. Christo crashed to the ground like a dead weight. Thorne took immediate advantage and kicked him square in the chest as he struggled to rise.

With a roar of outrage at the successful stratagem, the Bulgar rolled to his side, missing the second kick aimed at his lantern jaw. He regained his feet and charged with the grace of a wounded bull elephant. Thorne dodged the man, keeping his weight on the balls of his feet, ready to move in any direction. He'd have to conserve his strength and energy. At all costs, he had to stay on his feet, until he could begin to wear the bloody bastard down.

Dodging Christo's wild punches, he chopped at the rugged face again and again. The Macedonian struck out viciously, maddened by his opponent's technique of feinting, double-feinting, and then delivering a hatchet blow that jarred his head back on his spine. Blood poured from his bulbous nose after one well-aimed hook. His left eyebrow was split, and the lid was starting to puff.

Thorne adjusted to the larger man's pace, anticipating his moves and taking only a few glancing punches. So far, however, he'd only succeeded in enraging the giant.

Keeping his feet wide, his knees slightly bent, his center of gravity low, Thorne played the part of a shadow, dancing back and forth like a will-o'-the-wisp with perfect timing. He had to stay on the offensive and keep Christo off balance.

The strapping Macedonian gave no sign of tiring. And Thorne knew his luck couldn't last forever. One massive blow to the head from that powerful right arm would send him sprawling, unconscious.

Closing in to wrestle, Christo reached out and grabbed hold of Thorne's elbow. In one swift, strong move, he clamped Thorne's hand and wrist beneath his armpit, gripping him like a vise. With a snort of anticipation, Christo dropped to his knee and pulled Thorne over his shoulder. Bringing him downward, the Bulgar rammed his head and neck up under Thorne's right arm and locked him in place. Muscles straining with exertion as he searched for leverage, Christo reached between Thorne's legs with his other hand and grasped his thigh in his strong fingers. Arching his back, the colossus lifted Thorne up in the air and, with a mighty roar, slammed him to the ground.

Thorne had the wind knocked clean out of him. He fought to clear his vision. His collapsed lungs struggled for air. The lacerated flesh over his ribs screamed in agony. Blood oozed steadily down his side. If the match went on for much longer, he'd grow weak from loss of blood.

Bellowing victoriously, Christo aimed a vicious kick at his groin. Thorne spun to his side at the last second and regained his feet.

Christo made a dive for Thorne's leg. Instead of pulling

back, Thorne stepped directly into his opponent's attack. Turning his body slightly, he jolted him hard with his hip and thigh, keeping his own legs spread and firmly on the ground. Stunned by the unexpected offensive move, Christo cursed venomously.

Thorne grabbed the Bulgar by his armpit and hauled the titan upward before he could recover, using his rival's forward momentum to help him. Driving his right arm down between their bodies, Thorne hooked Christo's upper arm with his own to prevent escape. Using the power of his adversary's forward impetus, Thorne twisted and spun him over his hip to the ground.

Christo landed on the back of his neck, his great body slamming to the packed earth with all its force. Thorne knew better than to leap on top of him. The bull elephant was temporarily shaken, but he was still deadly.

Thorne's only hope was to lead Christo into believing that he was about to attempt some clever offensive strategy. The Bulgar would try to avoid the imagined danger and unknowingly assist in the execution of the actual move.

By this time, everyone in the village was on his feet. With Damian beside her—shouting encouragement to Christo—Jennifer watched in stupefaction, unable to believe what was happening. Deep gulps of air seared her dry throat. Her wobbly knees threatened to buckle beneath her. Dumbfounded, she clasped one hand over her thundering heart.

Thorne was using his superior coordination, balance, timing and speed to protect himself from his mighty opponent. For the first time, she was seeing the real man behind the polished, elegant facade. It was as though a veil had been torn from her eyes. She knew with crystal clarity that the scars on his chest were battle wounds. Not the supposed result of some make-believe carriage accident, but injuries earned in close combat.

Eagle's Son was a warrior worthy of the highest Cheyenne accolades. He had counted coup, not once but many times. She pressed her hands to her cheeks and wiped away tears of pride and admiration with shaking fingers.

The formidable antagonists, glistening with blood and sweat, were on their feet now, cautiously circling each other. Christo suddenly reached out with his long arm to snare his foe. Thorne attempted to dodge away, but the Bulgar was surprisingly swift for his size. He caught the Eagle's shoulder in his strong clasp, and they came together with deep, strangled grunts. Facing each other, hands grasping their foe's shoulders and upper arms, heads close, feet braced apart, the adversaries stood joined in a lethal embrace.

Then in a lightning move, Thorne dropped down on one knee. He encircled the back of Christo's massive thighs with his muscular arms and locked his hands. In the same instant, he began arching his sinewy back as he pulled himself closer to Christo's solid body.

Muscles straining and knotted with the Herculean effort, Thorne kept his knee and foot planted firmly beneath him to prevent the Bulgar from driving him backward. The Eagle slammed his head into the hard pit of his opponent's stomach, keeping his foe's weight upward and back, away from his own head and shoulders. Christo's arms flailed in the air, as he sought desperately to regain his balance.

Sobbing in terror, Jennifer clutched her hands to the base of her throat. People around her were shouting and screaming for blood in frenzied excitement. Clearly, they expected one man to die.

Thorne worked his head to one side of Christo's body and drove his shoulder into the man's midsection, while at the same time pulling his opponent's legs tighter against him, keeping him continually off balance. Using every bit of the strength he had left, he drove his large foe in a staggering, backward circle, till the Goliath toppled over like a tree.

The Macedonian twisted back, trying to support his weight with his hands. In that instant, Thorne released his hold and sprang up. Putting all the force of his body behind the blow, he kicked out, striking his adversary in the exposed trachea with the hard edge of his bare foot.

Christo fell flat on his back, stunned and unable to

breathe, his arms flung to the sides. Thorne stomped with all his might on the man's outspread hand and heard the gratifying sound of bones snapping beneath the impact. The titan groaned and cursed in pain. He struggled to a kneeling position, bringing his crushed fingers to his chest to protect them.

Dropping to one knee behind him, Thorne caught Christo's other wrist in a relentless grip and twisted his arm behind his back in a savage hammerlock. Without a twinge of regret, he neatly and mercilessly snapped the bone. The entire setup and takedown had lasted less than two minutes.

Thorne staggered to his feet. He stood over his disabled foe, his breath coming in great, heaving gasps. He waited to see if Christo would try to continue the match with five crushed fingers and a broken arm.

With an ear-splitting roar of fury, Christo clambered to his feet. He lurched around to stand in front of Thorne. His face was a mass of welts, one eye swollen shut. His great body was streaked with blood and sweat. His right arm hung useless at his side. Then slowly, deliberately, the Bulgar grinned and raised his smashed hand in defeat.

The sound of the villagers' cheers echoed through the mountain valley. Suddenly people were surging forward across the hard-packed ground, clapping both competitors on the shoulder and shouting hurrahs.

Exhausted and aching in every muscle of his bruised, battered body, Thorne turned to find Jennie. She was walking slowly toward him as though in a trance. Tears streamed down her cheeks.

"Eagle's Son," she said simply, "I love you."

He managed a crooked smile as he pulled her into the curve of his arm. She pressed her slender hand against his grimy, blood-spattered chest and lifted her beautiful face to his. What he saw in her misty gaze made his heart trip and stumble. There was no mistaking how she felt.

Absolute adoration shone in her eyes.

*   *   *

They reached Constantinople four days later. The train chugged into the station below Seraglio Point just before sunset. Dusty and rumpled, Jennifer and Thorne were dressed in the same clothes they'd worn when they left the mountain hideout. They had been so weary by the time they'd finally climbed aboard the rail coach, they'd fallen sound asleep in each other's arms.

After an enormous feast and wild celebration, the guerrillas had guided them to Edis Keui, taking them by a circuitous route to be sure their captives would never be able to lead the Turkish officials back to their village. Thorne cautioned Jennifer not to tell the *comitadjis* she could easily find her way to the train station without their help.

Before they left the stronghold, Thorne conversed at length with Todor and learned that the rebels were being supplied Russian arms. He'd seen the boxes of rifles and cases of ammunition that had been smuggled into their stronghold.

On the train, Thorne had told Jennifer that he was a secret agent for the British government. He'd been sent to Turkey to find out about Imro, and its connections with the czar and the Russian secret police. The cultured, urbane English lord used the ploy of searching for ancient treasures to hide his real purpose for traveling in foreign countries. By that time, nothing about Thorne would have surprised her.

Ready now to leave the coach, Jennifer looked down at her brightly embroidered vest and skirt. She smoothed the wrinkled red apron fondly. "Do you think Grandpapa will recognize me?" she asked with a smile.

Eagleston chuckled. "Easier than he'll recognize me."

She cocked her head and studied his black hair and beard. Dressed in the flowing cloak of a Turkish merchant from the provinces, he would certainly fool her grandfather.

Thorne had telegraphed the British embassy from Edis Keui, and they were expected. As he and Jennifer stepped down from the railroad car, she spotted her grandfather and waved happily. Grandpapa was standing beside

Judge Beaufort and Lord Ellenborough, who'd also come to meet them.

Before they could reach the waiting trio of Europeans, Jennifer and Thorne were halted by Pasha Izzet Bey and a troop of Turkish soldiers. "I regret to inform you, sir," the chief of the sultan's secret police announced coldly, "that you are under arrest for the murder of Count Vladimir Gortschakoff."

Jennifer clutched Thorne's arm. "What is he saying?" she asked in confusion. "What is he talking about?"

Eagleston clasped her hand, attempting to calm her. "It's all right, sweetheart," he said, his tone cool and unruffled. "Go stand beside your grandfather. Do it now, Jennie."

Lord Ellenborough rushed forward. "This is totally unacceptable," he protested angrily. "This man is a British citizen. You can't arrest him."

Grandpapa put his arm around Jennifer's shoulders and cautiously drew her away from the troopers, who stood with their rifles at the ready. Izzet Bey's gaze flickered over her like the forked tongue of a rattler. She shuddered at the unqualified evil in his black eyes.

The pasha smiled patronizingly at the British diplomat. "We have witnesses who swear they saw the duke of Eagleston leave the train on which the Russian's body was found. He will be taken to Yildiz, where we can question him. If he is innocent of the crime, he will, of course, be immediately set free with our profuse apologies."

Thorne knew the death of Gortschakoff was only a pretext for Izzet Bey to interrogate him. The real reason was the Macedonian revolutionaries. Somehow, the sultan's spies had discovered that Jennie had been kidnapped. The pasha would try to extract all the information possible about the *comitadjis* and their mountain stronghold. Under the expert skill of his notorious sadists, few men could not be broken.

Todor and his compatriots had made no secret of Imro's plans for revolution. They'd talked openly of their goal: Macedonia for the Macedonians. All over the mountainous countryside, rifles and cartridges were being smuggled in coffins, beneath sacks of rice, and in carts filled with turnips, right past the noses of the Ottoman police. Quantities of food and medical supplies were being secretly stored in their homes and monasteries.

All that information would be in his report to Lord Doddridge when he returned to London. But Thorne had no intention of giving away the location of the rebels to the sultan's perfidious chief of police. Izzet Bey would promptly dispatch Turkish troopers, known for their cruelty and bestiality, to massacre every man, woman, and child in the village. The mountain hideout would be soaked in blood.

At a signal from Izzet Bey, the troopers surrounded Thorne, and he was marched to the pasha's waiting carriage.

"No, no!" Jennifer cried hysterically. "They cannot take him to Yildiz." She clung to her grandfather. "They will torture him there! They want to find out about the men who kidnapped me."

"We'll get him released," Grandpapa assured her. "We'll take you to the hotel first, where you'll be safe. Then Lord Ellenborough and Judge Beaufort will go with me to see Abdul Hamid."

But Jennifer was certain the sultan would never release Thorne until his secret police learned everything they could about the revolutionaries who were trying to throw off their Turkish shackles.

Wait!" she said, grasping at her only chance to help Thorne. "I know who might be willing to aide us. The Sultana Pertevalé is Abdul Hamid's aunt. She could speak to him on Thorne's behalf. Please, Grandpapa, before you go to Yildiz, take me to the Grand Seraglio. I will meet with her and beg her assistance, while you talk to the sultan."

Her grandfather frowned in deliberation. "I'm not so sure . . ." he began.

"Hell, Senator, it's worth a try," Bo Beaufort said in his Texas drawl. "These Turkish officials can stall you with more damn red tape and flowery phrases than a politician who's just been elected for a second term. We're goin' to need all the help we can get."

Robinson looked at Lord Ellenborough questioningly. "Let her try," the British ambassador encouraged. "It won't do any harm, and it just may bloody well do some good."

Trembling with fear that her request might be refused, Jennifer entered the Palace of Tears for the second time. The tiny rooms along the narrow passageways were dim and silent. An eerie sensation of waking slumberous ghosts oppressed her as she followed behind Alaeddin.

The sultana received her immediately. "Mademoiselle," she said in surprise, "what brings you here so suddenly?" The thoughtful blue eyes studied her for a moment, taking in the provincial costume. "I can see that you are upset."

"I—I have come to beg a favor, Your Highness," Jennifer said. She clasped her hands in front of her to still their trembling. "The man I am to marry has been arrested by Pasha Izzet Bey. They have taken the duke of Eagleston to Yildiz Palace, where they will question him. Please, can you do anything to save him?"

Pertevalé motioned for Jennifer to sit down on the divan beside her. She listened quietly as her distraught guest told her what had happened. Then the elderly woman called for a servant, who left the room with her instructions. In a few minutes, the Kislar Aga appeared with a paper and pen.

"I will write to my nephew," the sultana offered with kindness. "I am certain that when Abdul Hamid receives my request, he will release your young man." She quickly wrote a few lines, folded the note, and handed it to Alaeddin. The eunuch salaamed and left the room.

"How can you be so sure that the sultan will honor your wish?" Jennifer questioned, torn between hope and despair.

The white-haired lady smiled enigmatically. "My nephew is greatly in my debt," she explained. "When my son, Abdul Aziz, was deposed by a powerful man named

Midhat Pasha, he was imprisoned here in the Topkapi Palace. Abdul Hamid was declared the new ruler. My son died five days later. At the time, it was said that he had committed suicide by slashing his wrists with a scissors. Nineteen doctors testified to the fact."

"I am sorry, Your Highness," Jennifer said in bewilderment. "I did not know that."

The sultana looked down at the numerous rings on her plump fingers. "Two years later, when Abdul Hamid had the reins of power securely in his hands, he decided that Midhat Pasha was too dangerous to be allowed to live. My nephew came to visit me here in the seraglio. He asked me to retract my story that I had given Aziz the scissors he'd used that terrible night. The sultan wanted me to swear that Midhat had hired a palace gardener to stab my son to death."

Jennifer was unable to contain her curiosity. "Did he?"

Rather than answer the question, the sultana rose and walked to a game board on a low table. She bent and moved the ivory pieces idly about. "Midhat Pasha was lured back to Istanbul from a self-imposed exile in Switzerland," she said.

The sultana's voice was so low, Jennifer could barely hear her. She leaned forward on the couch in rapt fascination, straining to catch every word.

"He walked straight into a trap," Pertavelé continued softly. "Izzet Bey arrested Midhat Pasha and charged him with regicide. At the trial, the gardener swore that Midhat had hired him to kill my son. The conspirators were both sentenced to death."

Jennifer waited in horrified silence, not knowing what to say.

Sultana Pertevalé came back and sat down on the silk cushion next to her. "The gardener was never executed," she said calmly, and Jennifer read in the Sultana's shrewd eyes what she would never say aloud. The man had been bribed by Abdul Hamid. "The gardener lives quite comfortably on a pension granted by the sultan," Pertevalé continued. "Midhat Pasha was banished to a province in Arabia securely under my nephew's control. Two years later, he was strangled. His embalmed head was sent to Yildiz, to be personally delivered to Abdul Hamid."

"*Nehe!*" Jennifer exclaimed in disgust.

"And so, Miss Elkheart," the sultana said with a sad smile, "I am certain that Abdul Hamid will honor my wish. No one, least of all my nephew, would like to have this unfortunate incident resurrected. In treacherous times like these, some things are better left buried and forgotten."

"I understand, Your Highness" Jennifer replied. She met the sultana's gaze with complete sincerity. "I will never mention what you have just told me to anyone."

Pertavelé rose to stand beside the couch. "And now, mademoiselle, it is time for me to retire for the night. Since no man is allowed inside the seraglio, I will have you wait for your fiancé just outside the harem gate in the Blue Pavilion. You will be perfectly safe there. The Kislar Aga will look after you until your loved one comes."

The sultana started to leave the room, then turned back. "I, too, once loved a handsome young man," she said. Her thin lips curved into a smile of fond reminiscence. "I bore him six children. May your marriage be equally blessed by Allah."

Exquisite blue tiles covered the walls and the octagon floor of the open pavilion. A portico supported by blue marble pillars surrounded it on all sides. Along the seaward wall, a series of graceful arches framed the darkened outlines of minarets against the star-studded sky. A fountain splashed in the courtyard, the only sound in the hushed evening.

Jennifer sat on a cushioned bench beneath an ornate gold canopy, quivering with fright. She clung to the slender hope that the sultana had been correct in assuming Abdul Hamid would grant his aunt's request. Could the villainous despot truly be afraid of having Midhat Pasha's mock trial and eventual strangulation talked about once again? Jennifer recalled the sultan's furtive ways, his paranoia about being poisoned, his terror of assassinaion. His deeply ingrained cowardice might overrule his political judgment.

The possibility that Thorne was being tortured at that very moment sent a stab of pure anguish through Jennifer. He'd told her that suspects were taken to Yildiz for that very purpose. She quaked at the thought of his helplessness in the hands of Abdul Hamid's secret police. Gruesome images of Thorne being cruelly mistreated haunted her, and she fought down the bile that rose in her throat.

Jennifer covered her face with her hands, trying to ward off her terrible imaginings. Surely, Grandpapa would succeed in gaining an audience with the Sultan before Izzet Bey could begin his ghastly work. She moved to her feet, unable to sit still any longer. Striding restlessly back and forth across the tiled pavilion, she gazed numbly at her surroundings.

She moved to stand beside a glowing brazier which the Kislar Aga had lit to keep away the night chill. The tall black eunuch had brought a tray of fruit, along with a jewel-encrusted gold tea set, and left them for her on the low table beside the divan. With a deep salaam, Alaeddin had told her she had but to knock on the door that led to the harem, and he would instantly appear. Heartsick with dread, she hadn't touched any of the food or drink.

Pictures of Thorne being purposely burned or cut or broken or mutilated kept flitting through her terrified mind. If he were not freed, if he did not return to her alive, she could never go on living.

Sinking to her knees beside the couch, Jennifer pressed her hands to her chest and bent her head. Her unadulterated terror seemed to suffocate her. Tears streamed down her cheeks to plop on the blue velvet cushion.

"Maxemaheo," she whispered, "Creator of Life, please save my courageous warrior. And if you cannot rescue him from the clutches of his enemies, take him swiftly to that place of bliss in the world above the clouds."

Through her tears, Jennifer looked up at the stained-glass windows of the female slaves' apartments. They

glowed with a soft light, their exotic floral motifs hiding
the treasured odalisques of past sultans, slowly withering
with age, from the view of lesser mortals.

Deep, racking sobs shook her. Crouched over the
bench, she rested her head on her folded arms and wept
for the tragic widows immured within those walls.

She wept for herself.

For if Thorne were killed, she would never again know
happiness. Like those pathetic, hopeless women, she
would live a half-life, existing only in the past, dreaming
of what once was and could never be again.

With the resolution of a Cheyenne warrior-woman,
Jennifer summoned all her inner strength. She wiped her
wet cheeks with her palms, knowing she must be brave.
She must not give up hope. Even now, she could be
carrying Thorne's child.

The hushed sound of a footfall brought her to her feet.
Her heart aching with fear, her limbs trembling, she hurried across the tiled floor to the portico's edge, knowing
that it could very well be her grandfather, come to tell
her they'd failed.

On the far side of the courtyard, a man stood in the
shadow of an arched doorway, partially illuminated by
a shaft of moonlight. He wore a long, flowing Turkish
cloak, dusty and travel worn. Most of his face remained
in shadow. She couldn't see his eyes. But the heavy black
beard and mustache were unmistakable.

Her vision . . . the vision that had haunted her dreams
for so long . . . had come to life.

She raised trembling fingers to her lips, the tears once
again flowing freely.

Thorne was here.

He was alive!

The man she loved more than life itself.

The man she would love for all time, though the stars
faded from the sky and the moon gave up its light.

The courageous warrior whom the Great Powers had
shown to her in a vision.

The battle-scarred warrior she was meant by fate to
love.

Sobbing with joy, she raced toward him. "*Zehemeho-az*," she cried. "Thou, my beloved one."

Thorne opened his arms and drew her into his sheltering embrace. "*Namehota, Vonahenene*," he said, his deep voice hoarse with emotion. "I love you, Morning Rose."

Jennifer lifted her face for his kiss, and the familiar tickle of his beard and mustache against her skin seemed like very heaven.

Epilogue

November 1886
Grosvenor Square, London

"Tell us about the wedding, Your Grace," Lady Idina urged. Her green eyes twinkled with happiness for the bridal couple as she accepted the glass of champagne from the butler.

"Yes, *chérie*," seconded Lady Charlotte from her place on the sofa next to her. "Tell us all about it."

Jennie sat perched on the arm of an upholstered chair beside her grandfather, her black-and-white spaniel lolling at her feet. From across the room, she met her husband's eyes and smiled enchantingly. "The wedding was perfect," she declared without a moment's hesitation. "Is that not so, Eagle's Son?"

Thorne stood in front of the fireplace in their town house's formal white-and-gold salon, surrounded by all the people he loved. "The wedding was perfect," he agreed. "The bride was beautiful—"

"And the groom was handsome," his wife interrupted with a happy gurgle of laughter.

"Well, what did you wear?" Dina insisted in exasperation. "Tell us everything, down to the smallest detail."

Seated in the comfortable armchair, Garrett Robinson looked up at his granddaughter, his hazel eyes aglow with fond affection. "Vonahenene chose what every young Cheyenne girl dreams of wearing on her wedding ay," he told them. He paused to take a glass of champagne from Hutchinson's tray and continued in a stentorian voice, as though reading out loud from the society column in the London *Gazette*. "The blushing bride wore an ivory doeskin dress trimmed with long fringe, blue and white beads, tufts of white fur, and tinkling silver bells."

"*Vraiment?*" Lady Charlotte interjected eagerly. "And how did she wear her hair?"

"I was just coming to that." Garrett reached up and tweaked his granddaughter's earlobe. "Not in the tidy chignon she's wearing now," he said with a chuckle. Jennie's lovely hair fell straight down her back, her two sidebraids fastened with white fur. Over one ear, she wore an ornament of silver with the black and white feathers of the magpie."

"Did you walk your granddaughter down the aisle, Senator Robinson?" asked Lord Combermere from his spot beside Thorne.

"Not exactly," the white-haired gentleman replied. He patted the puppy's head and smiled enigmatically

"*Non?*" Lady Charlotte expostulated, fluttering her lace fan in wonder.

"No," her son said with a wry grin. "To everyone's immeasurable delight, Jennie was carried into the ballroom of the British embassy on a thick Turkish rug held by Judge Bo Beaufort, Lord Ellenborough, and her two Albanian bodyguards in full dress uniform, plumes and all."

Lady Idina nearly spilled her champagne down the front of her pink silk morning dress in her surprise. She peered at the bride in fascination. "You were carried in on a rug?"

Jennie nodded complacently. "Dotty Beaufort and I searched every shop in the Grand Bazaar, but there was not a single buffalo robe to be found. Not in the entire city of Istanbul. So we settled on the next best thing. A blue-and-white silk carpet from Kayseri, fringed with tassels. Thorne and I brought it back with us for the nursery at Eagleston Court."

"Then what happened?" Basil asked, as he accepted his glass of champagne from the gray-haired servant.

Jennie beamed. "Then *namsem*—my grandfather—lifted me down from the rug and presented me to Eagle Son as his bride."

Lady Charlotte turned her head to look at Thorne. "And what were you wearing, *mon cher*?"

Thorne grinned. "Actually the groom's apparel was a bone of contention before the ceremony," he admitted. "My bride-to-be wanted me to appear before the entire diplomatic corps of Constantinople attired in only my trousers and shoes. She was adamant that I be married shirtless. I, however, insisted on white tie and tails."

Everyone stared at Jennie in patent astonishment.

At their dumbfounded expressions, she folded her arms and lifted her stubborn chin. It was obvious she still wasn't happy about her husband's final decision on that issue. "I wanted people at the wedding to see the mark of valor on my groom's chest," she stated in an aggrieved tone. "*Hesc!* I was marrying a warrior who had counted coup on the battlefield. I thought every guest present should know that my husband would be able to protect his wife and future children from his enemies."

"An estimable desire," Lady Idina agreed at once. "I can't imagine why he refused."

Jennifer met her husband's doting gaze. "I am certain he had his reasons," she said with a sly smile.

Just the two of them knew he was an agent for the British secret service, but they'd told their friends about Jennie's abduction. Basil and Idina knew that Thorne had disguised himself as a Turk and had been shot as he traveled into Thrace to meet the Macedonian revolutionaries. Proudly, Jennifer had told the story of the pancratium match and Thorne's victory over the ferocious guerrilla.

"And who performed the ceremony, *chérie*?" questioned Lady Charlotte fondly.

"An English holy man," Jennifer answered. "Thorne felt that, since my father was not there to marry us, we should accept Lord Ellenborough's suggestion on the matter."

"Holy man?" Combermere turned to his friend beside n, seeking a somewhat clearer explanation.

"Reverend Parmer ministers to the needs of the Ancan faithful there in Galata," the duke told his captited audience. "The kind gentlemen was willing to fill for Strong Elk Heart in his absence. We did, however, ad a telegram from Jennie's father giving us his bless-g."

"Well, you were right, dearest," Lady Idina said with olissful sigh. "The wedding was absolutely perfect."

Jennifer looked around the room at her loved ones. Vhat about you?" she asked. "What has happened here hile we have been gone?"

Lord Basil met his sister's gaze, his eyes warm with otherly regard. "Dina and I are going to Edinburgh," told them with obvious satisfaction. "She's agreed to : Dr. Robinson examine her. If it appears that the surry he's proposed will be a success, she'll be operated a at the medical university there."

"*Nakoe!*" Jennifer exclaimed, jumping up from the arm her grandfather's chair. Spotted Beaver scrambled to s feet, his tail wagging eagerly. "I know that if anyone n help you, my uncle can." She hurried over to the sofa id embraced her friend. "And we can all go on the train gether," she added. She moved to stand beside her hus-ind in front of the marble mantelpiece. Slipping her arm ound his waist, she leaned her head on his shoulder. Thorne and I are leaving in two days with Grandpapa join Julie and Uncle Benjamin."

"You've heard from your sister, then?" Idina asked ith obvious relief.

Jennifer frowned. "Only a telegram of congratulations our marriage," she admitted. "But we will soon be in dinburgh, and Evening Star can tell us in person what ie has learned on her vision quest in Scotland."

"Now that everyone has their glass of champagne," horne announced, "I'd like to propose a toast."

The assembly of family and friends rose to their feet, ces glowing with happiness.

Thorne gazed with tender devotion at the sloe-eyed

beauty cradled in the crook of his arm. His voice w
filled with joy, a joy he'd never dreamed possible, as I
raised his glass in a salute of unparalleled pride and lov
"I proudly present to all of you, the new duchess of Ea
leston."

"To the duchess of Eagleston," Lord Combermere sai

"Here, here!" everyone cried, and Spot joined in tl
toast, excitedly barking his congratulations.

Bursting with happiness, Jennifer met her husband
deep blue eyes. She lifted her glass to him in return.

"To Eagle's Son," she said simply, "my courageo
veho warrior."